Richard Haley was born in West Yorkshire, and He began his working life in the trade, then undertook administration and personnel work for an international company producing man-made fibres, which gave him plenty of opportunity for travel.

Now retired, he lives with his wife in his native town, Bradford, which inspires the background to this series. His first John Goss novel was *Thoroughfare of Stones* (also published by Headline) and he is currently writing a third.

Also by Richard Haley

Thoroughfare of Stones

When Beggars Die

Richard Haley

HEADLINE

First published in 1996
by HEADLINE BOOK PUBLISHING

First published in paperback in 1996
by HEADLINE BOOK PUBLISHING

10 9 8 7 6 5 4 3 2 1

ISBN 0 7472 5074 X

Printed and bound in Great Britain by
Cox & Wyman Ltd, Reading, Berks

HEADLINE BOOK PUBLISHING
A division of Hodder Headline PLC
338 Euston Road
London NW1 3BH

For David and Anne Sykes,
in memory of all those jolly dinners at the Napoleon

'When beggars die, there are no comets seen . . .'
(Julius Caesar, Act 2, Scene 2)

One

Bruce Fenlon was waiting for me in the George that evening.

'Must be a week,' he said, as Kev, unasked, placed a gin and tonic on the bar in front of me.

'I've been keeping an eye on a bloke. Most of the action took place between him leaving the office and getting home.'

'Leg-over?'

'But complicated. It's a family business and the man I'm watching is having an affair with the owner's wife, as well as ripping him off. I feel certain you can imagine what worries the owner most.'

'If he's Yorkshire born and bred, it's got to be the money.'

'Quite so. As he said, it took him twenty years to build up the business but he can find another wife in a couple of weeks.'

'His heart's obviously in the right place.'

Grinning, he ordered himself another beer. It was late August and the evening sun slanted across dust-motes through the lancet windows of Beckford's oldest pub.

'Before I forget,' he said, 'I've given your name to a man called Marcus Snee. He works for Zephyr Insurance. Do you know him?'

'Only *of* him. It wasn't encouraging . . .'

'He's a smallish chap with serious hang-ups about being

1

small. He's Claims director for Zephyr. They say he's pro-grammed not to pay out until punters threaten GBH. He's never off the phone to our traffic people, checking on acci-dent reports, double-checking on accident reports, never taking piss off for an answer.'

'Is that normal?'

'Only with Marcus. The rest tend to accept what they're told. Life's too short and the punters pick up the tab in the end anyway.'

'Where do I come in?'

Sunlight caught his glass, giving a rich tint to the beer left in it. He held it up. 'Takes me right back to Tenerife. We used to go in a little bar every evening before dinner, the whole room full of sun, views over the sea. God, I wish I were back . . .'

I waited, patiently smiling. He liked holidays. It was one of the reasons he'd not rise much higher in the Force, good though he was. I signalled for another gin.

'Marcus Snee . . .' I prompted.

'Right. About a month ago a man called Simon Marsh is driving towards Harrogate on a quiet road after dark. The road bends sharply at one point and he drives straight through a side rail, crashes into a valley and kills himself. The PM finds he's mixed sedatives with alcohol and probably nodded off at the wheel. The inquest rubber-stamps that. Misadventure.'

'So?'

'Big insurance pay-out. I'm talking big big . . .'

'So why don't they pay out?'

'There are more companies than Zephyr involved and as I understand it the others aren't quibbling. But Marcus wants an investigation on the Zephyr claim before he'll authorise payment of their share.'

2

I glanced at him, over a glass half-way to my lips.

'Am I missing something here? A guy tops himself in a road accident and the police conduct a routine investigation?'

He nodded, beginning to smile.

'And someone routinely identifies the body, there's a routine PM and a routine inquest?'

The smile widened.

'The body *was* released, I take it? There *is* a Death Certificate?'

'Right in every particular.'

'And this Marcus character wants a *PI* to investigate a month later? Is he the full shilling? Does he think Marsh was got at? Suicide?'

'You'll have to talk to your man about that.' He held his glass up to the sunlight again, his mind still mainly in Tenerife. 'There's loads of money involved, that's the turn-on for Marcus. Just ride along with it, the company's going to pay out in the end but not till he's gone through the motions. It'll be easy money, John, take it and run . . .'

I didn't particularly like easy money. It could be deeply boring. On the other hand I couldn't afford to turn down work.

'I still don't understand. I don't come cheap. Is Zephyr really going to let him pay good money to look into a case the police have put the lid on?'

'They let Marcus do as he likes, because he never gives in, no matter whose nose he gets up, until he's satisfied *himself* he's got a bona fide claim. And often enough – enough to cover the sort of fees he pays people like you – he does save the company money.' He had the smile then of a man enjoying a private joke. 'I'm sure he'll tell you all about it when you see him.'

'I can't wait . . .'

Zephyr Insurance owned an entire modern high-rise block in the city centre, not far from the town hall. The company had actually been founded in Beckford, in the great textile days of the early part of the century, and they'd concentrated on cornering the lucrative marine-insurance market that went with the shipping into the area of the thousands of bales of wool from every part of the globe. They had diversified rapidly into all classes of insurance and had expanded into every major city, but Beckford had always retained the head office. They were regarded as being hard-nosed but squeaky clean.

There was a separate floor of Zephyr House for each class of business, with the Claims department sharing part of the Household floor. I pressed the lift's touch-sensitive key, trying to decide if people connected to the insurance business were, as a breed, the least attractive business people I ever dealt with. They seemed to haunt my office. Had I got contents insurance, health insurance, accident insurance, a pension plan, employer's liability, public liability, professional indemnity – the list seemed to grow year on year. The life insurers were the jolliest and seemed the most generous, offering drinks *and* lunch, their eyes glittering with bonhomie, desperation and greed. They got a hefty commission from your first year's premium, but could then feed on you no longer, the white, smiling teeth could only snap once before the eyes glazed with indifference.

'John Goss,' I told the pretty auburn-haired girl in reception. 'To see Mr Snee.'

'Just a moment, Mr Goss,' she said, with a wide professional smile, her fingers already keying a number. 'Mr Snee, Mr Goss is waiting in reception . . . No, I'm afraid there's no one free at the moment . . . Yes, they're all speaking . . . Yes, *all* of them . . . Me! Mr Snee, I'm queuing *six calls* . . .'

She put the handset down sharply, switched back on the glowing smile. 'Mr Snee will be with you in a moment, Mr Goss, if you'd care to take a seat. Would you like a coffee?'

'Have I time, if he's only going to be a moment?'

'If you haven't, just leave it,' she said with polite neutrality, already pouring from a flask into a flowered cup.

But there was plenty of time to finish it, as she'd obviously known, five minutes to be precise. The delay was to show me what a big man little Mr Snee was. He'd wanted me to be taken to his office, but this was the Nineties and there was no staff to spare for looking after visitors any more – you did it yourself unless you were top cat. And Marcus Snee wasn't.

Someone suddenly erupted into the reception area as if released through a trapdoor on a pantomime stage. He darted towards me with all the bustle of a man squeezing me into an important and demanding schedule. As I got to my feet, his face visibly tightened at the six or seven inches I had on him. He handed me his fingers to shake briefly, said hello to my tie.

'This way, Goss,' he muttered and began to lope rapidly down a vast open-plan office, where banks of VDUs flashed and bleeped, rapping out queries as we passed along the central gangway.

'That return ready yet, James – I promised to fax it at three . . .'

'I'm still waiting for the Anderson cheque, Martin – the client's lawyer must have it in time to bank it . . .'

'Make a note to see me at four, Joan, I need to review the Ellis file . . .'

I could tell it was done to impress, and they answered with

the cold politeness of people working for a prat in a tight job market. He seemed indifferent to their barely concealed hostility, possibly even getting off on it – some people did.

Things were better in his impressively spacious office – for him at least. He went behind a large desk and scrambled nimbly on to a large chair, raised to its full height. I, meanwhile, crouched on the lowest chair I'd ever seen, so that I now looked up at him.

He was stocky and pink-faced, with oiled black hair parted down the middle, and wore the standard insurance man's pin-striped suit and striped tie. But the suit was lightweight and new-looking, the tie silk and the shirt handmade. There were touches of gold everywhere – links, watch, ring. He might have been small but by God he was natty.

I said: 'How can I help you, Mr Snee?'

'Did DS Fenlon give you any details?'

'One or two. A claim from a widowed Mrs Marsh . . .'

'I asked Fenlon for the best private man he knew, Goss. I have a good rapport with the police. I'm a phone man. I like to bypass the forms and the niceties – speak to the boys in blue direct. They help me a lot because I cut the crap. It's the way to get things done – we understand one another. Ask anyone at York Road if they know Marcus Snee – I shouldn't think there's anyone who doesn't.'

I waited attentively. I was used to waiting and listening. He could ego-trip for an hour – it would all find its way on to the bill.

He had a single file on his gleaming mahogany desk. He tapped it. 'Mrs Marsh's husband died in a car crash. We seem to be committed to writing her a cheque for half a million.'

'Life insurance?'

'*Term assurance.* You'll probably not know the difference.'

It was becoming difficult to keep my face free of the hos-

6

tility of the people out on the floor.

'As I understand it, with my limited layman's knowledge,' I said mildly, 'life insurance provides a guaranteed pay-out, either on death or at the end of a fixed term, whichever comes first. Doesn't term assurance simply provide a payment on death within a stipulated period, say twenty years? If you don't die you don't collect. Which makes it cheaper.'

'A *lot* cheaper. Cheap as chips. We're talking, what, off the top of my head, about one-eighty a month for ten grand's worth, over twenty years. Long odds, you see, against a man in good health dying before he's fifty these days. People take out term assurance to cover the mortgage if they should die young, give their spouses tiding-over money. Simon Marsh had term assurance. He didn't pay us much but we'll be paying his widow a fortune.'

'Perhaps he couldn't *afford* life insurance,' I said feelingly, having recently forced myself to take out an expensive life policy which would mature at an age I could barely contemplate, let alone believe I'd ever achieve.

'Everyone in his position has life insurance. Self-employed, making decent money . . .'

'Everyone?'

'I'm sure you have.'

The shrewd, big-headed little prick had me there.

'A bit of both,' I admitted.

'There you are then.'

'Perhaps he had a life policy with another company.'

'He did.' He gave me a faint, superior smile. 'But it wasn't anything to write home about. I told you I was a phone man – I've done a bit of ringing around. He *did* have a life policy, but he also had more term assurance *plus* accident insurance. Now why so much term assurance?'

'Was there anything to stop him?'

'He could have as much as he could afford. But it looks iffy. His widow stands to cop more than a million, with half a million coming from Zephyr. Don't *you* think it looks iffy?'

'Have the other companies paid out?'

'They're on the verge of it. If they want an easy life that's up to them.'

'Perhaps he was just anxious to make sure his wife was well provided for in the event of his death. If he needed to drive a lot. What sort of money was he making?'

He didn't like this question. He shrugged. He fiddled with a gold-topped fountain-pen. 'A lot, I suppose,' he said finally and with reluctance. 'He was a computer expert – designed and installed systems for small to medium-sized firms.'

'Well, if he made, say, fifty to a hundred thousand a year, a million's only equal to about ten or fifteen years' earnings. If his wife was used to the life-style that goes with good money . . .'

I wondered if Snee's colleagues had already taken the same line; I could see I was telling him something he didn't wish to hear.

'But all that term assurance,' he said, a defensive note creeping into his voice. 'If he'd rolled up the premiums he was paying for term assurance he could have had a decent life policy.'

Which presumably would have provided a fraction of the death cover. We both knew it, and it would only annoy him further for me to point it out.

'I don't know anything so far about the inquest,' I said. 'Did anyone pin down why he was mixing alcohol with sedatives?'

'He was having business problems. The recession. He was going through a bad patch.'

'Do you . . . think his death might have been suicide?'

He sighed. 'It wouldn't have made any difference. The policy would only have been invalidated if the insured had committed suicide within the first year of taking it out, the principle being that no one takes out insurance and waits a year to top himself. He, or she, wants to get it done with. At the end of a year they'll almost certainly have got over being suicidal. These policies of Marsh's had all been running more than a year.'

I kept my expression carefully neutral. If I went on raising any more reasons why Mrs Marsh should be paid out promptly, on watertight policies and following her husband's death in a car crash, which may possibly have been suicide, but it didn't matter anyway, I'd be talking myself out of a job.

I think he too felt I wasn't somehow entering whole-heartedly into the spirit of the thing.

'Well, don't *you* think it iffy?' he demanded petulantly. 'All that term assurance . . .'

I did in fact think it was odd. But I thought a lot of human behaviour odd. I knew a man who had his entire savings invested in Premium Bonds, who'd won about a thousand pounds in five years, but it was his money and he was making the choices.

'What would you like me to do, Mr Snee?'

'That's up to you,' he said, as if it were obvious, the faint petulance shading into faint belligerence. 'Look around at the scene of the accident, check with the people who serviced his car, keep tabs on Laura Marsh.'

I stopped myself from pointing out what he'd certainly know, that routine checks would have been made by engineers, working for both police and insurers, on brakes and steering and tread-depth. I wondered what he thought my keeping an eye on Laura Marsh would prove. That she might be having an affair? That she and her lover might somehow be responsible for Marsh's death? It all seemed too ridiculous for words. I felt that Snee wanted this farce of an investigation mainly because his colleagues thought he should simply nod the claim through for payment. Marcus against the board. Why not let myself be guided by Fenlon, who had the inside track on Snee, take the money, and make the right noises? The trouble was, it depressed me. I was after all a professional and took pride in giving good value. I was still tempted to turn it down, even though I had my business to think of and my goodwill. Insurance work could be a useful earner and Snee, whatever I might think of him, seemed to generate a lot of it.

'Do you think Mrs Marsh might have tampered with the car in some way?' I said, trying not to sound like a character in *The Mouse Trap*.

'He had those sedatives in his system, didn't he? What if she slipped those to him?'

I studied his pink face, assuming he was joking, and ready to break into the smile I supposed he'd expect. But he wasn't joking. 'Mrs Marsh, did you slip barbiturates into your husband's Scotch?' 'I can't lie to you, Mr Goss, yes it was me. It's a fair cop. How did you guess?'

'I'll . . . check around,' I said. There seemed nothing else to say.

'Good. I'll leave it to you.'

'How much time do you want me to spend on the case . . . as a rough guide?'

'Say four or five hours a week. I have a good idea how you people operate,' he said knowingly. 'You do half a dozen things at the same time, unless you get a special fee to work on a single case. Just fit this in with the wines and spirits at whatever your going rate is.'

'Isn't it . . . rather urgent? If the lady's waiting for a payout . . .'

'She'll just have to go on waiting till we've completed our investigation, won't she. I'll tell her lawyer I have my man looking into it and I'll be paying when your enquiries are complete and satisfactory. Those are our rights when this kind of money's involved.'

I wondered if this was another aspect of the realpolitik – the longer I poked around the longer Laura Marsh's half-million stayed on the money market, or wherever Zephyr kept the more liquid of their funds, steadily clocking up size-able interest.

'You ... needn't be too worried about not letting Mrs Marsh *see* you're keeping an eye on her, by the way. You have my full authority to be a bit up-front.' He smiled unpleasantly, the first smile of the interview. 'People with something on their minds often give themselves away when they know they're under surveillance. We once had a claim from a *titled* VIP, Goss, for an extremely valuable painting. We're talking serious money here, not half a million. The claim looked Persil clean. Skilled art thieves had neutralised all the alarm systems put in at our request, and carried the painting through a mile of woodland to their getaway vehicle. The police had given it a lot of attention, told us everything pointed to professionals.

'I was the only one to find it iffy, Goss. Know why? Every-thing handled by knight of the realm's agent. I went up there myself, titled gent too upset to discuss it, speak to the agent. Couldn't fault the agent's story, couldn't fault the agent – a decent, honest, country type whose father had been agent before him.

'But why wouldn't Sir Michael – that's not his real name, I mustn't divulge that – why wouldn't he speak to me himself? Well, it might have been that he was genuinely too busy, or that he couldn't face the questions. I played a hunch, Goss, because my nose told me there was something just that little bit, just that tiny bit, how shall I put it . . .'

'Iffy?'

'*Exactly!*' He gave me the encouraging glance of a teacher reaching the first glimmer of intelligence in a backward child. 'It seemed iffy. I put an investigator on to it, told him to do what I'm telling you to do with Mrs Marsh – keep an eye on Sir Michael. Shadow him. Let him see your car. Use the same restaurants, go to the same functions, the same livestock sales and so forth. If Sir Michael wanted to know what the hell was going on, we were trying to find out if there was anyone he came into contact with who might have the sort of background that would bear scrutiny.'

He sat back. His pink face had become even pinker, his mouth hung open a little and there was the slightest sheen of moisture along his forehead. From where I sat, watching him from between my knees, it was like looking at one of Bacon's screaming popes.

'But Sir Michael never did dare to ask what we were up to, Goss, because after a few days her ladyship came to see me. She told me what had happened. The surveillance had driven Sir Michael to the verge of a nervous breakdown. You see, he'd *sold* the picture, shipped it very quietly to the States, where the buyer was sworn to secrecy. Sir Michael had done the business with his son and had the innocent agent fronting. We didn't have to pay out fifty pence, and the investigator's fee was well worth it.'

He threw himself back, this time almost disappearing from view. His chair was of the all-singing, all-dancing variety that wheeled and swivelled and reclined until it was almost flat. Suddenly his face was back above mine, like a film close-up, his eyes gleaming, his chest heaving, with the reliving of what I sensed must have been his finest hour.

'Not a penny piece, Goss!' he cried. 'So no one questions

me any more about whether or not I hire investigators.'

I nodded admiringly, certain that someone had. Pointed out the bloody silliness of investigating anything as open-and-shut as the Simon Marsh case. Office politics, an urge to keep the half-million in the coffers as long as possible – there seemed no other reason for me to be there.

'What happened to Sir Michael?' I said, as if I didn't know.

'We . . . decided not to proceed. Certain very powerful men contacted me and explained what a sick, worried man he was – taxes, crippling overheads, the usual carry-on. They told me the publicity would almost certainly kill him. I was invited to dinner at the Hall. I could see for myself the appalling strain he'd been under. These were *very* important men, Goss, they told me what a valuable part he'd played in politics – behind the scenes, of course. The party, and the country, owed him a debt you couldn't begin to put a price on. As you can imagine, we'd no desire to drag his name through the mud for a single aberration. We agreed that if he paid our out-of-pocket expenses we'd take it no further . . .'

He spoke almost reverently. I could see him in a dinner-jacket that looked too new, wide-eyed and perspiring among the decanters and the candelabra, while the big people of the Ridings ate him with the rest of their supper. It also occurred to me that it would in any case be in Zephyr's best interests to keep the thing quiet – the publicity could easily tempt other unscrupulous Zephyr punters, with stronger nerves than Sir Michael's, to take a crack at the big one.

'So don't be afraid of being seen by Laura Marsh, Goss, if you feel she might possibly have something to hide.'

It wasn't easy accepting such a dubious commission from a man I'd taken such an instant, non-reversible dislike to, but I knew that if I didn't there were plenty out there who would.

'Very well, Mr Snee,' I said politely, taking out my notebook. 'If I could have some details I'll make a start on Thursday, if that's convenient.'

'Quite convenient,' he said casually. 'You can leave it until Monday if you're stretched. But keep me informed, would you. I like a report by phone each Friday between ten and eleven, no later, no sooner, followed by a brief typed report to reach me over the weekend. Send your account with each report and I'll ensure it's paid within three days.'

'Well, thank you, Mr Snee,' I said, a warmer note creeping into my voice, even as I realised that he paid the hired help on the nail so that he could twitch their strings with a surer touch.

He rapped out all the details I needed rapidly and concisely, slipping massive horn-rims over his rather blobby nose as he studied the file on his desk.

'Well, goodbye, Goss,' he said, closing the file with a snap. 'You'll not mind seeing yourself out. I'm sure a skilled investigator like you can find your way out of our general office.'

This appealed keenly to his sense of humour and he began to laugh with a peculiarly cawing sound, throwing himself backwards yet again on his private merry-go-round. I arranged a warm smile on my face and left with a sigh of relief. As I passed the reception desk I flicked my head upwards at the pretty girl. She couldn't stop the conspiratorial grin briefly slipping past the neutral mask.

Two

'Wow!' Norma said. '*Imagine* having the sort of husband who insured himself for over a million. Imagine having a husband at *all*, come to that. I suppose if anything happened to Ronnie that object he took up with would claim it. Having said that, the way *he* smokes and drinks, I doubt he could get himself insured for more than fifty quid . . .'

'Are we discussing this case or your bloody ex-husband?'

'Believe me, if Ronnie had found anyone daft enough to insure him for a million I'd still be glad he pissed off. Yes – the Simon Marsh case . . .'

'Well, the only remotely dodgy aspect Marcus Snee can dream up is all the relatively cheap insurance Marsh took out. But he was never off the road . . .'

'And he could always cancel it, couldn't he. Perhaps term assurance was a stop-gap until he could sort out a pension package.'

'That's a bloody good point. He was a busy self-made man, perhaps he simply hadn't had time to get himself properly sorted out and he took this cover to be on the safe side. *I* think he was being considerate. Go on, let's have the female reaction . . .'

'We are talking a fair amount of middle-class wealth, aren't we.' She glanced at the summary she'd typed up from my

15

notes. 'His own business, a house on Tanglewood, a BMW. They were probably living at the rate of fifty K a year at least.'

'Exactly my point. If she's used to living well, a million seems in proportion.'

'See what you make of Laura Marsh,' she said. 'If she seems quiet and respectable, as opposed to loud and brassy and already throwing wild parties with unsuitable men like Ronnie, there seems no point in taking it too seriously. But knowing you, you almost certainly will . . .'

'Are you Alan?' I said to his back.

'Won't be ready till four,' he said, '*whatever* they said in reception. *And* it'll have to be booked back in – I'll have to have the engine out to fix those leaks . . .'

'I'm sorry to hear it, but it's not my car.'

He straightened up from the car's entrails, a tall, wiry man with fair hair in a pony-tail.

'I'm John Goss,' I told him. 'I'm a private investigator.' I showed him my identification wallet. 'I'm working for Zephyr Insurance in connection with the death of Mr Simon Marsh in a car accident.'

'They've already been, mate. There was an engineer round inside twenty-four hours.'

'I know that, Alan, this is pure routine. There's an insurance claim on his life, and before the insurers will pay out they want an independent report. You'll already have been asked this, but was there anything mechanically wrong with the car you knew about? You know, like this one you're doing now, where the fault can't be handled in a routine service and it has to be rebooked?'

He rubbed a hand across his forehead, leaving a faint smear of oil, shook his head. 'Believe me, mate, if there *had* been something starting to go wrong he'd not have used it in case he got stranded, he'd have hired. To tell you the truth, he couldn't leave his bloody cars alone. He was always booking them in for service ahead of time, and they hardly ever needed much doing. He was a car freak, see. He'd touch up the paintwork himself, change the oil, fit new fan-belts, lamp bulbs, hose the engine.' He gave me a twisted grin. 'You know what they say about car mechanics – when you bring it in for service we just open the bonnet and wave an oily rag at it. Well, with his motors that's usually all we *needed* to do.'

I grinned. 'Even though you'd say you'd done it all anyway . . .'

'Listen, mate, see that?' He pointed to a printed sheet stuck to the car's windscreen. Someone in a nearby bay began stripping paint from a damaged car with power tools and he had to shout. 'It covers everything in a service, and we have to tick every box to say we've done it and sign it, right. The customer gets a copy, the boss gets a copy. Because if the Bill come round here, saying we haven't tightened up wheel nuts and fixed the brakes, and some bugger's totalled hisself, we might as well close down.'

A day later I went to have a look at the Marsh house. Tanglewood Lane was about four miles from the city, on the side of town that edged on to open country. At its far end there were two reservoirs, at different levels, the upper feeding the lower down narrow, stepped gulleys. They were more like natural lakes, with earth tracks along many of the perimeter stretches, and the hills surrounding them were covered in dense forest trees. It was an attractive address.

The houses on Tanglewood were large, solid and expensive, and the Marsh house was no exception. It stood in a lengthy garden which sloped down gently from the left side of the road, so that the two-storey house itself was in a hollow with, beyond it, the same sorts of trees that surrounded the reservoirs. In a road of intensely private houses it seemed somehow the most enclosed.

I parked about a hundred yards from the house, then walked as far as the woodland view and back, glancing at the house each time I passed it. The front garden was terraced, with well-tended strips of lawn on each level and beds filled with seasonal flowers. The house itself looked equally carefully maintained.

The second time I passed it, a woman stood just outside the front door, watering geraniums in an urn-shaped planter. She was of medium height, with dark, straight hair falling loosely to rather broad shoulders and a very pale skin, one of the palest I'd seen. She wore a black turtle-neck sweater and black pants.

She looked up as I passed, and every professional instinct prompted me not to meet her eyes, but to pass on casually, a stroller back from the beauty spot, as if I were engaged on normal surveillance. But this wasn't normal surveillance, where in most cases the mark never saw me at all, this was a Snee special. He wanted me to be seen. He'd not been able to get Sir Michael out of his head, had wanted to live the old glory days, make a mountain out of what I was certain wasn't even a molehill.

And so I let my eyes meet hers for several seconds. She returned my look incuriously, absently, almost forlornly. It was exactly the sort of look I might have expected from a woman striving to recover from a partner's untimely death. And people were my business.

I got back in my car, shook my head with a wry smile. A man so meticulous about the state of his car that he'd not drive a yard in it if the slightest fault had been detected, and a decent-looking woman who clearly grieved and quietly tried to fill her life with small activities to keep the loneliness at bay. I didn't think she gave a toss about the cool million they'd have to pay her. It would only buy things.

I started the car and drove along to the road that would take me to the city. I was wasting my time, but if Snee wanted to pay me to waste it that was his business. I'd leave the case now for another day – I was only supposed to be giving it a few hours a week. But as I drove on to my next assignment I thought again about Marsh's obsessive attention to the details of his cars. I supposed I wasn't much different myself, forever checking tyre pressures and dipsticks and battery levels. I was in and out of my car twelve hours a day most days; it had to be totally reliable. And if you were a detail freak in one area it tended to spill over into another, so that you began to run your life by the Greenwich time signals.

It seemed the only real oddity about the case was that Marsh didn't appear the type who'd mix alcohol with sedatives and then drive a car. If he'd been half toying with suicide why not just take the pills and booze and *sit* in the car? If he'd taken so much life cover on board he must have been a responsible type, and would such a person have driven with impaired senses in case he injured someone else? But he'd had money worries, he was in a state of mental upheaval and probably not himself. And when people were not themselves, as I'd found out many times through my job, it was usually impossible to know how they'd react. Anything went.

He had the sort of brown ruddiness that went with lengthy exposure to wind and sun. He was fiftyish, sturdy, blue-eyed and had brown hair going grey. He wore moleskin trousers and a battered green jacket in a houndstooth check. The farmhouse had been considerably extended, the newer stone and tiling, though an excellent match, not quite seamless with the old. He led me from the yard directly into a large square room fitted out very efficiently as an office. A middle-aged woman worked at a word-processor near a lattice window.

'It's good of you to spare me the time, Mr Watkins.'

'Call me Jess.'

'And I'm John.'

'What can I do for you, John?'

'I believe you were the last business contact to see him . . .'

He sighed. 'What a mess it's left us in. What a mess, eh, Kate – when *will* we have a straight edge?'

The woman smiled shyly, but went on softly pounding her keyboard.

'But the real tragedy is Simon, of course. A brilliant man.'

'Could I ask what he was doing for you?'

He took off his jacket and flung it on to a chair, where it fell to the floor. An elderly collie crept from beneath a table and sniffed at it. 'We run a co-op. We were six farms scraping along and so we joined up and made a reasonable living.'

I nodded. I suspected reasonable meant excellent, but you'd never find a Yorkshire farmer admitting to making more than would cover the groceries.

'For my sins,' he said heavily, 'I was talked into taking on the administration. The rest pretended they only understood farming.'

He gazed with what seemed wistfulness across the yard to the distant, sheep-dotted slopes as if he wished he too could enjoy the luxury of simply farming.

'John, can you *believe* the detail involved in running six farms to their maximum capacity? There's all the things we buy in bulk – fertilisers, feedstuffs, spares – and then there's the milk quotas, flock and herd details, wages, all the CAP paperwork. We were trying to cope with a couple of PCs. I told my partners we either invested in a dedicated system or *they* could do the bloody books and I'd go back to driving a tractor.

'I'd . . . heard about Simon. He'd designed similar packages in the area. I sent for him. I didn't really know what I wanted, to be honest . . . something that would do everything. He was there before I'd half finished. He knew exactly what I needed and he'd draw . . . what do you call them . . . little flow-charts showing how it would all hang together. Brilliant! The day he died was his second visit and we were going to firm up the contract.' He shook his head sadly. 'Back to the drawing-board now, but this new man . . . he's not in the same class.'

'How did he seem . . . that afternoon?'

'Edgy. Definitely edgy. He'd left his car at the Wheatsheaf along the road there and walked the rest of the way. Said he needed to clear his head. He didn't look at all well. Pale. Shaky. I thought he was going down with something. When I shook his hand it felt like a face-flannel. I asked him was he not well, but he said he'd be all right. Anyway, when he got his papers out he was a different man, doing his little drawings and so forth. It was as if he couldn't wait to lose himself in his work. It wasn't as if he was selling himself, it was as if talking about something he seemed to enjoy so much sort of took his mind off other things. But they say he had business worries.' He shrugged. 'Don't we all. The recession . . .'

'The recession.' I nodded. 'Was he here late?'

'Lateish. Say seven. We were just about on top. I'd given him a firm go-ahead to make a start on the software and order the printers and screens.'

'Did he want a down-payment?'

'That's an odd thing. The *first* time I saw him, the week before, he told me all the preliminary advice came free, but if I decided to go ahead he'd need a down-payment of ten thousand. I was more or less in a position to find that kind of money . . .' He glanced at me warily. 'I'd just had the milk cheque so we had a little bit of cash flow . . . But he said not to bother, he'd pick up the cheque next time he saw me. It seemed odd, but I didn't argue. Who would?'

'Who would indeed. So he left you about seven and went to pick up his motor at the Wheatsheaf?'

'They say he was quite a regular down there with doing so much work in the area. He'd have a couple most nights on his way home.'

'Well, thanks a lot, Jess, you've been a great help.'

'And you're from the insurance, you say . . .'

'Indirectly. I'm an independent investigator putting together a report in respect of a life insurance pay-out.'

'What's there to report *on*?' he said, furrowing heavy brows. 'He drove through a fence and killed himself, God rest his soul.'

'Oh.' I shrugged. 'I suppose the Zephyr want to be scrupulously fair to their other clients and say they investigated the claim thoroughly.'

'Go on,' he said. 'While they're investigating they're not paying, are they. Searching for loopholes – I know them buggers. Well, I hope they don't lead that poor wife of his too much of a dance with all the other worries she'll have on her plate.'

I wanted to agree, to tell him his Yorkshire savvy was spot on, that I was working very slowly for a tight-fisted bastard who'd try to find a loophole if his own mother put in a claim for a stolen suitcase. I smiled non-committally, client loyalty stretched to breaking point.

It was quiet at the Wheatsheaf. I was beyond Skipton and well into Dales country, and the pub probably made its money with the lunch-time tourist trade for bar snacks. At six there was just a handful of locals.

I ordered a gin and tonic from a small, pretty barmaid, who gave me a mechanical smile. As she handed me my change and turned away, I said: 'Excuse me, miss, but can you remember if a man called Simon Marsh used to come in here early doors up to about a month ago? About five-ten, slim, fair hair . . .'

She suddenly flushed, but before she could speak a man who was fiddling with a pump mechanism and looked to be the landlord said sharply: 'Who wants to know?'

He straightened up. He was burly, balding and had a face with the sort of lumps and deformations that indicated either an earlier career in the ring or involvement in a great many bar-room brawls. I'd met his type before, and I sensed that if I didn't admit to some kind of authorisation he'd tell me nothing, from simple bloody-mindedness.

'I'm working for an insurance company,' I said. 'Mr Marsh died in a car crash last month and there's a claim involved. We'd just like a few details of his movements leading up to his death . . .'

'The police done all that, didn't they?'

'Oh, yes, the police have closed their file. This is separate. For claims above a certain amount the actuaries need a routine report,' I said glibly. 'I understand he was in here the night he died . . .'

He watched me closely for some time in silence, giving an impression of a mind struggling across terrain deeply littered with the remains of many brain cells. 'He might have been,' he admitted reluctantly.

'Did he come in much?'

'Happen two or three times a week.'

'Did he drink much?'

'Couple of vodkas.'

'Vodka?'

'Never nothing else.'

'Was he drinking vodka on that last night?'

'Oh, don't ask me,' he said, his slender reserve of patience almost exhausted. 'I can't remember every toothful of short we serve. Madge might know. Yes, Charlie . . .'

He moved away, leaving the still slightly flushed Madge looking at me uneasily.

'Can you remember, Madge,' I said, 'whether he was drinking vodka that night?'

'No,' she said at last, in a low voice. 'He just had a couple of spring waters – he said he had a lot of work when he got home.'

Madge had remembered very well. But then, good bar staff often developed a memory for the details of customers' drinks.

I nodded. 'He was with Mr Watkins earlier, at Ermistead Farm. Jess Watkins said Mr Marsh left his motor in your car-park. Is that right?'

'He . . . may have done. I wouldn't know . . .'

It seemed odd that her memory could be so precise about some details, so vague about others.

'If he didn't leave it at the farm he couldn't really leave it anywhere else, could he?' I said, with a friendly smile. 'The roads are so narrow around here, not many lay-bys . . .'

She shrugged. Suddenly she began to wash glasses in a sink below the bar, displaying a cleavage that passed, sharply defined, between small, firm breasts that had the faintest bloom of talcum. She had long, auburn hair, pale-green eyes, a small, full mouth. She'd applied a great deal of make-up with the expertise of a woman who devoted a lot of time to it, like an assistant on a cosmetics counter. I wondered if the blusher concealed a genuine deepening of colour.

'Madge,' I said softly, 'were you having an affair with Simon Marsh?'

There was no ambiguity about the flush this time. It suffused her cheeks, lapped over on to her throat and the visible part of her chest.

'I don't know what you're talking about!' she said furiously, but in a voice that was little more than a hiss, and too low for the others to hear. 'Who the hell do you think you are, barging in here . . .'

An elderly farm worker had walked in; she almost scuttled towards him in relief. 'Yes, Alf, usual?'

After that, she'd not return to where I stood. The landlord crouched over the bar, locked in muttered conversation with two cronies. It looked as if I'd had what information I was going to have.

I went back to my Mondeo. So that was why he called in at the Wheatsheaf so often, because he and Madge had become an item. I wondered what difference it made to the case, if any, apart from being another possible aspect of his mental turmoil.

Had Marsh taken the affair more seriously than Madge? She'd flushed to the nipples, but I'd seen nothing in her expression you could define as sadness, and I'd been watching her face very carefully. I could guess at the scenario – husband a modest earner, perhaps kids, Madge working nights for a few pounds to help out. Along came Marsh with his nice car and his nice middle-class manners – perhaps she'd hoped an affair might lead somewhere more permanent. But Marsh was dead now, and she didn't want to know about it, and above all she didn't want her husband to know about it, because she was going to have to go back to making do with him.

* * *

I looked over into the valley. The fencing was a simple structure, basically metal stanchions carrying metal poling, and all painted white. It wasn't much of an obstacle against anyone leaving the road, but there was a grass verge between the road and it, and the road was little used anyway – if Harrogate was the hub of a wheel this road right-angled between two of its spokes. Cars passed me at the rate of one every two or three minutes.

I began to walk along the verge, away from the black-chevron warning sign at the bend where Marsh's car had become airborne. The road rose sharply and straight for a good half-mile above it, but the chevrons must have been glowing like landing-lights in the full beams of a car in country darkness. He had to have nodded off. A long day with Jess Watkins, money worries, perhaps some kind of a hassle with Madge, sedatives, two or three whiskies.

I wondered why he'd drunk Scotch and not vodka. If I'd been half toying with suicide would I have stuck with my normal gin? Would I have given a fiddler's? Wouldn't I simply have drunk what happened to be in the hip-flask of the glove compartment, which was what Marsh had done?

I examined the verge as I trudged up the road in the hot early-September light. It was pure instinct, there seemed no real point in doing anything but walk through this case. 'Isn't it perfectly obvious what I'm about, Watson?' I muttered, with a rueful smile. 'Do you need an explanation for *everything*?'

A minute or two later, I added: 'And if it really is so obvious, Watson, I wish you'd be good enough to tell me what the hell I'm supposed to be about.'

I shook my head and walked on until I reached the top of the steep stretch. I stood looking down to the distant chevron sign where the road swung out of view. On the right was woodland, lapping down to the roadside, on the left the valley the car had crashed into with, beyond it, a pattern of farmland fields, glowing in the mellow light. The scene of the accident was yielding nothing very much, but it was nice to be wandering about in shirt-sleeves in the heat and the clear air, the brain in neutral.

I gave one final glance across the overgrown verge. Sunlight gleamed dully off two small rusty metal clamps attached by red elasticated fabric.

'My God, Watson, what have we *here*?' I picked up the object. 'Inevitably you will not have the smallest idea and I shall have to tell you. This, Watson, is what is commonly known as a sock-suspender. I know this because my father had a pair, which he wore, so he told me, in the Fifties, before the invention of what he called, with no little relief, the "grip-top sock".'

I tossed it aside and walked back to the bend. I ducked beneath the repaired railing and began to pick my way down into the valley over scree-like ground, interspersed with rocks and tussocky grass. A rough, narrow path ran along the valley floor, which I assumed was kept defined by ramblers, but the land itself seemed otherwise of little practical use.

I glanced back up to the road. Some of the rocks were heavily scored, in a pattern that marked the car's progress down the valley wall, and there was an area of fading disturbance where it had come to rest. But there was no evidence of scorched earth or grass, so the car couldn't have exploded – you couldn't mistake the mess left by a car that had. I wondered how rare it was for a car to have fallen so far without the tank rupturing, a fuel line severing, a spark from crumpling metal lighting the blue touch-paper. Perhaps he was travelling with an almost empty tank. Drivers seemed to fall into two groups: those who travelled with the tank somewhere between the red zone and half full, and those who never allowed the needle to drop too far below the half-way mark, and tended to think in terms of topping up when it fell below three-quarters. I was in the latter group, and I also carried two sealed containers in the boot holding spare gallons. Marsh had also seemed to be into that kind of detail, and I'd have thought that his car, like mine, would have been a floating petrol bomb.

It all seemed to come back to the mental state he'd been in. Why, for example, wasn't he returning to Beckford on the more direct route via the Skipton bypass, why had he been detouring in the direction of Harrogate? And where had he been between leaving the Wheatsheaf at, say, eight and landing at the bottom of this valley, having taken sedatives and drunk whisky, but not in sufficient quantity for the Coroner's Court to bring in a verdict of suicide?

I doubted if I'd ever be able to find out where he'd gone after leaving the Wheatsheaf. Madge wasn't going to tell me, assuming she knew, because she now had too much to lose. The sooner Marsh was forgotten the better. In any case I didn't believe she'd know. Marsh had been badly stressed, every aspect of his life seemingly in crisis. I thought he'd simply driven around the area, distraught, trying to calm himself with pills and booze, for hour after hour, until oblivion had beckoned and perhaps not been too energetically fought off. And if he *had* driven for several hours, using the lower gears a lot on narrow winding roads, it might have explained why his tank was so low, assuming it had been. For once in his life perhaps he'd not given a toss about stopping for a fill-up.

'There you go,' I said, slipping a pound coin in his grubby hand.

'Thanks, boss. I'll be able to buy a bit of supper now.'

'I know what you'll buy,' I said, sighing, 'and it'll be anything but food.'

He grinned on yellow and decaying teeth. He wore a T-shirt, a corduroy jacket, jeans and trainers. The clothes were dusty and crumpled, but they seemed in marginally better condition than those of the others.

'I haven't seen you for a while. Where've you been?'

He shrugged. ''Ere and there . . .'

I doubted he could remember. I supposed one city garden looked much like another.

'Where's your pal?'

'Pal?' He glanced vaguely around at the handful of vagrants sitting in the late sun on the nearby benches.

'That bloke you used to sit with mid-summer . . .'

He thought about this at length, forehead corrugated in concentration – it could have been a decade ago.

'You always used to sit together. He wore a donkey-jacket, fortyish . . .'

'Oh, '*im*!' he said, as if his life was as crowded with faces as an MP's. 'Oh, 'e got a job, diden 'e. 'E got work, 'e did. Scaffolding. 'E were a scaffolder by trade, see, and 'e got work scaffolding somewhere.'

Nearby heads began to swing round tortoise-like, faint surprise replacing apathy in grimy faces as the vagrants struggled to cope with the bizarre concept of one of their number choosing to return voluntarily to that alien, barely remembered world of overalls and P45s.

'I'm pleased to hear it,' I said, half glad, half sorry. I wasn't too surprised. He'd appeared somehow new to living rough and in reasonable physical shape. All he'd seemed to need was the chance. I could remember the longing, the near-desperation in his eyes. And then, while I was still thinking about it, they'd both gone walkabout, as their kind did.

''E'll be round won day,' he said. 'I'll tell 'im you asked after 'im.'

'Can't he get you a job?' I said.

A look of profound unease crossed his stubbled face. 'I never asked 'im, did I. What wiv moving round a fair amount. I never know where I'll be, know what I mean . . .'

'You must ask him,' I said firmly, 'next time you see him. You're not getting any younger and you can't go on living like this for ever.'

He found this puzzling. He glanced towards the others, all now once more gazing vacantly over the garden. They were all older than him and *they* were still living like this.

'Will you do that,' I said, 'ask him to try and get you work too?'

He looked unhappily from the others to me, to the pound coin in his hand, as though wondering if he were to give it back to me I might go away. 'You from Reverend 'Opper?'

'No, I'm nothing to do with Reverend Hopper. Has *he* been trying to get you work?'

'Like I say, boss, it's difficult wiv me moving around, see . . .'

'It's time you settled down then,' I said. 'If your friend could find you a job you could get yourself a room to rent and stop living like this. Now when he comes back you must ask him.'

'Right you are, boss.'

The capitulation was as suspect as it was sudden. If he appeared to agree to this absurd request I might leave him alone. I glanced at my watch. Well, I would leave him alone now, but I'd be back.

I passed on to my office. It was in one of the older city-centre areas, in a refurbished building that overlooked one of the last cobbled streets in town. Parking was unrestricted, but after eight-thirty in the morning you could forget it. I was always able to beat the deadline, but from ten onwards I was in and out of the office all day, and I hired a space on a permanent contract fairly cheaply in a multi-storey. Going to and from this car-park meant that I had to walk through a network of subways that led into and out of the circular garden beneath a roundabout where vagrants tended to hang out, despite efforts by the council to keep them moving. For the past two or three months I'd given the two redeemable-looking tramps small hand-outs and wondered what I could do to get them back into the normal world.

Because of the guilt.

Three

During my third spell of surveillance at Tanglewood Lane she drove out from her house in a blue Peugeot. I went after her to the junction and then, separated by two or three cars, followed her on the ring road to a branch of Sainsbury's. I had to keep reminding myself that total anonymity was *not* what it was about, that it didn't matter if she caught a glimpse of me, if not several. It was irritating, like trying to write with the wrong hand, but I forced myself to drift along behind her among the scattering of pensioners and young mothers.

She bought bread, soup, coffee, several microwave 'meals for one', cheese and fruit. Then she went to the wine section and bought a litre of vodka. No potatoes or green vegetables, no meat, no wine.

I wondered if that was the pattern of her days – coffee at breakfast-time, soup or cheese at lunch-time if she could be bothered, a carton you slammed in the micro for four minutes at night. She seemed to drift along the aisles on auto-pilot, smiling absently when she and an old lady had a small collision. At the check-out she paid by card, then trundled the trolley out to her car, where she transferred the items to a travel bag. Our eyes met twice, once in the wine section and once in the car-park. Her glance each time was brief, her eyes incurious with what I was certain was the preoccupation of endless pain.

I tailed her car back around the outskirts until I saw it turn off along Tanglewood, then I drove on to other work.

I returned the following afternoon. At about half-past two I saw her leave the house and make slowly towards the reservoirs. She still wore the black pants and turtle-neck sweater, but there was a cool wind and she also wore a blueish-grey parka. Her dark hair, previously arranged in a loose style, was now drawn into a neatly coiled bun at the back and anchored by an ornate enamelled slide. I wondered if that was how she got through some of the time, perfecting the look of her hair in a classic style which no one could now admire, no one that mattered, just an investigator and a handful of people walking dogs.

There was a point at the far end of the first sheet of water where the man-made paths and stone buttressing gave way to a stretch of natural terrain that sloped directly into the reservoir. Mallard, moorhen and geese gathered here in the hope of being fed scraps by the regular passers-by. Mrs Marsh halted, took bread from one of her coat pockets and began tossing pieces carefully in every direction, to give all the birds a chance. She started to make a clucking sound and a pure-white goose separated itself from the rest and approached almost to her feet.

'Hello, Binkie,' she said, in a small, clear voice. 'How are you today?' She gave the goose its own special ration. It picked at the scraps almost indifferently, seeming only to want her close presence. She gave it a wistful smile, as if it were the only living creature she could turn to for solace. There was always a handful of people at the feeding spot and I stood among them, neither obtrusive nor particularly anonymous. She suddenly turned from the goose and walked in my direction. 'Why are you following me?' she said coldly, her grey eyes resting levelly on mine.

I gave an inward sigh. I'd never thought this a good idea. The knight of the realm had shat himself; she simply thought I was a sicko. I shrugged, tried to smile disarmingly. 'What makes you think I'm following you?'

'I've seen you twice outside my house, once at the supermarket and now here.'

I could only admire the acuteness of her memory. I'd thought it would take several more days before she really began to suspect, she had seemed so preoccupied on the two or three times our eyes had met as to be scarcely registering me.

'It must be coincidence,' I said, trying not to let my voice sound as lame as the words.

'I don't believe in coincidence,' she said, her small voice clipped and incisive. 'I think you're something to do with Zephyr Insurance. My solicitor told me they were being difficult. They're still "investigating" a claim against my late husband's life insurance, he tells me, and then I keep seeing you.'

The goose she called Binkie had followed her and stood at her feet, making soft, throaty noises as if comforting her. She glanced down at it, her eyes briefly clouded and vacant, as if caught by an almost physical wave of pain. 'I could have done without this right now,' she said in a low voice.

I turned away and gazed bleakly over the rippling water. It didn't pay to be thin-skinned in a profession where so many of the jobs I handled were to do with people who stole and cheated and lied, but I would never be case-hardened. I could have throttled Marcus Snee. People were my business, and they rarely came more transparently sound than Laura Marsh. I'd never wanted to let myself be seen, knowing exactly how intrusive such overt tactics were going to appear to someone totally blameless. And now I'd found out exactly *how* intrusive, with a woman who carried a pain around with her that seemed so palpable it was like mist clinging to her obsessively groomed hair.

'I'll . . . not deny it, Mrs Marsh,' I said finally. 'And I'm sorry to add to your difficulties at a time like this. I'm a private investigator, hired by Zephyr to do exactly what your solicitor told you – look into the claim. I'm simply doing a job. If it's any consolation, I didn't want the job and I'm convinced in my own mind that everything is as it should be.'

I'd take myself off the case in the morning. It would mean burning my boats with Zephyr but the monumental plus would be not having to deal with Snee again.

She scattered the remaining scraps of bread. Binkie stood motionless at her feet, staring up at her. 'I've known him at least a year,' she said. 'He used to have a partner but the ranger thinks a fox got it. I don't know why he took to me. We're not even sure he *is* a he. They're funny, aren't they . . .'

'I think he must be a he,' I said, 'seeing as you're putting him off his food.'

She smiled faintly, her gaze briefly meeting mine before sliding away to the distant tree-line. She began to walk then, back towards the entrance, past water that glittered in the slanting September light, against which floating ducks seemed like shadows. I watched her go. She turned round and said: 'You might as well walk with me now I've blown your cover. Is that the correct terminology or is it just something they say on television? It wasn't, frankly, very difficult to blow.'

I fell in step with her. 'It wasn't meant to be. It was supposed to be up-front. It was designed to make you uneasy in case there was anything, anything at all, about the claim that could be challenged. Believe me, had I done it my way you'd never have known I was there.'

'But what am I supposed to have *done*, Mr . . .?'

'Goss. John Goss. Look . . . Mrs Marsh . . . Zephyr owe you an awful lot of money and they have a Claims director who hates paying out. Don't worry about it and try not to take it personally, if that's possible. They *will* pay out, take my word, they're just being . . . thorough. And I'm afraid they're within their rights.'

'But what could I have *done*?' she said again, her voice high and plaintive against a thin, gusting wind. 'Everything's been dealt with by the police. I'm not even badgering them for the money. I'd just like to get it settled so I can sell up and get away to . . .'

Her words trailed off. Away to some home town, I wondered, back to the reassuring scenes of her youth and childhood?

I turned to her. 'What *could* you have done?' I said, because I was certainly not going to tell a grieving widow what Snee was day-dreaming she might have done: somehow tinkered with her husband's drink so she could pick up a million and fly off to Spain with the man who helped improve your backhand at the tennis club. 'All I can really tell you is that I was engaged to investigate the circumstances of your husband's death and examine your life-style in a rather crude and obvious way. Well, I've done exactly that and I can honestly say it's been as upsetting for me as I can see it is for you.'

We stood looking at each other, in the courtyard of the ranger's house. Then she smiled wryly.

'It's a dodge, isn't it? So they can hang on to their money as long as possible . . .'

'It would be . . . unethical for me to comment,' I said, also smiling.

We walked on, the short remaining distance to her intensely private-looking house.

'I'll say goodbye,' I said. 'And apologise once again for all this . . . nonsense.'

'Would you like a cup of coffee?'

'Well . . . thank you . . .'

She led me down an expensively paved drive that curved round to run along the front of the house. She unlocked the panelled front door, releasing the thin whine an intruder alarm makes in the thirty seconds before alarm-bells automatically ring. She went quickly across the hall and into the kitchen; the whine ceased. The houses on Tanglewood were more vulnerable than most, backing as they did on to woodland.

The hall was large and rather dark. It was hung with several landscapes painted in strange, startling colours, full of leafless twisted trees and brooding fells and heavy menacing skies. There was a half-moon table with cut flowers in a vase and several unopened letters, which all looked to be bills, on a brass plate.

'In here, Mr Goss . . .'

'John, please.'

'Very well. And I'm Laura, as I don't need to tell you.'

'You're the only Laura I've known.'

'It was my mother's name and *her* mother's . . .'

She took me into a large room at the rear of the house that overlooked a narrow back garden and the dense forest trees that seemed to spill from the woodland area.

'Do you mind instant?'

'It's what runs in my veins instead of blood.'

'It's rather a faff with the cafetière. We always use it in the evening but . . .' She broke off and went away. Like so many recently bereaved people she could not break the habit of talking about her partner in the present tense.

I glanced around the room. It had the same dark tones as

the hall, with furniture that looked to be genuinely antique. The fireplace, though containing the inevitable pretend-coal, had a dark-oak surround, and there were shelves on each side, full of leather-bound books. Large, heavy easy chairs were upholstered in dark-gold material, there was a dark-green carpet and dark-green wallpaper that had a slight sheen. The television was concealed in a bow-fronted cabinet and a partly open door beneath the bookshelves indicated a concealed music system. There were more landscapes on the walls, with their striking colours and odd perspectives, all of country that seemed to have a brooding aspect, as if soon to be engulfed by torrential rain, to have its deformed trees damaged even further by forked lightning, or torn out at the roots by a howling gale.

A framed photograph stood on a side-table of a man I took to be Simon Marsh, as the likeness matched the rough description I'd got together myself – slim, fair-haired, regular features. What my description hadn't included had been an open smile of great charm.

I wondered how many hours and days she'd spent in this room since he'd died, staring at that photograph with the empty, clouded gaze I'd glimpsed by the reservoir.

She came back with the coffee, in delicate pale-blue cups and saucers, on a wooden tray.

'Do sit down . . . John . . .'

We faced each other from two of the large, heavy chairs, the cups on a sofa table between us.

I said: 'I'm sure you'll treat everything I've said this afternoon in the strictest confidence, Mrs . . . Laura. It's all been highly irregular to say the least.'

'Shades of the detectives in Waugh's *A Handful of Dust*. Life does rather seem to be imitating art. I'm sure Zephyr would regard it as treating with the enemy.'

'I've . . . decided to pull out. This isn't my kind of work. I'm used to dealing with people who really are cheating in some way, not . . . people like you. I'll tell them I can find nothing remotely untoward in your claim.'

She sipped some of the coffee. 'How long would the investigation have lasted?'

I shrugged. 'Three . . . perhaps four weeks. I've only been giving it a few hours a week. They weren't regarding it as a top priority, which probably says everything.'

'Why not carry on? Why should you lose money if Zephyr are silly enough to go on paying you for pretending to keep an eye on me?'

I glanced at her, faintly surprised. 'I find it very upsetting. I can see perfectly well how your husband's death has affected you. I thought you'd be glad to see the back of me.'

'If you pull out they'll only engage someone else. I think I prefer being investigated by someone I've got to know.'

The combination of astuteness and implied approval was as delicate as the china of the cups we drank from.

'Well . . . if you're sure you're happy about it . . .'

'Quite sure.'

'Insurance work can be very useful, and my PA is anxious for me to capitalise on the Zephyr connection.'

'Then that's settled.'

She smiled her first full smile. The skin wrinkled around her eyes a little, giving a powerful impression of a sympathetic nature. Her eyes held the attention in other ways; grey beneath slightly hooded lids, they gave her a faintly sleepy look that seemed both sexy and vulnerable. She'd taken off her parka, and the black turtle-neck defined rather wide shoulders and the sort of shallow breasts that retain their shape well. I'd have liked to have seen her across the lamps and flowers of a table in a good restaurant.

We sat for about half a minute in the almost total silence of her drawing-room. There was a wall clock with a pendulum, but it was an antique reproduction with a battery drive, and that too was silent.

'Are you married, John?'

I shook my head. 'I think I'm the sort of man more suited to relationships. Private investigation doesn't really go with a wife and children and *Wildlife on One.*'

'Relationships . . .' She gave her faint smile. 'My poor dear mother never really grasped what the word meant in its pejorative sense.'

'Your parents were Beckford people?'

'Leicester. That's where Simon lived before he began to do so much work in the Ridings. We migrated north; we've been here just over two years. I'll probably go back . . . when the dust settles.'

'That's where most of your friends are, I suppose . . .'

Her unfocused gaze slid past my face to the shadowy back garden. 'We never had many friends. Simon's work was rather like yours – open-ended, hard on married life. He was on the road so much, or designing systems, or catching up on technical advances, or rushing off to a system breakdown. I tended to make my own life. Fortunately I like books and music and . . . feeding ducks . . .' she said, with a slightly throaty chuckle.

She had the sort of clear, almost alabaster skin that it was impossible to imagine coated with sun-tan, and it seemed to emphasise her ease with the cloistered life she appeared to live. She gave an impression of wide hats and dark glasses and sitting on the shady side, of taking almost a keener pleasure in the winter months, when weak and dusty suns balanced briefly on dark horizons.

'Can . . . your husband's business be carried on?'

'Oh, no. Simon was a near-genius. He got a double first in Maths. I got a second in English Lit. I simply did his office work – letters, invoices, credit control, hiring temporary computer people. The business died with him.'

She smiled an inward smile. 'I'd rather like to write a novel. I've done occasional journalism for regional magazines, but there was so little time for a book. I doubt there'll be any money in it, but it would make a pleasant change from software and hardware and CPUs.'

And money would be no problem, once the last insurer coughed up. It seemed an ideal way of life for the sort of woman she seemed to be, a reader and a thinker, at ease with the solitary hours I imagined writers would have to put in. I could see her writing with elegance and skill, drawing on her wide reading for the apt quotation, thinking up the telling metaphors on her daily walks, perhaps even making a success of it, because it wouldn't matter a toss if she was successful or not.

'Perhaps you ought to try your hand at one of those dark Gothic novels,' I said. 'I have a feeling there's a gap in the market that's never really been filled since Daphne du Maurier died.'

'How odd you should say that,' she said, with a sharpness that took me by surprise, her eyes suddenly intent. 'Why did you, do you suppose?'

I shrugged, slightly uneasy. 'No reason. I've always had a soft spot for *Rebecca*, perhaps that's it. My mother reads it about once a year.'

It wasn't quite true. I think the suggestion had been instinctive. There were those disturbing canvasses on the walls, the heavy furniture, the shadowy room, this sad, attractive woman living a solitary life near woodland and water, her husband's death being looked into by an investigator, even though there was no mystery to unravel – perhaps I'd imagined she'd be drawn to the kind of fiction that contained similar elements.

She gave me one of her fleeting half-smiles. 'I think you're being rather ambitious for me, John.'

'Well, if you ever want to know any of the oddities of behaviour of people under stress I could give you quite a few,' I said, smiling and getting up. 'I must go, Laura. Thanks for the coffee. I very much hope you can begin to sort your life out soon . . . you've had a bad time . . .'

There was a sudden moist gleam in her eyes and then she led me into the hall.

'I enjoyed our little chat,' she said in a voice that sounded both wistful and sincere. 'It makes such a change from talking to Binkie, good friend though he, or she, is.'

'If you like,' I said, 'I'll give you a ring when I intend to keep you under observation. Not a word to Zephyr . . .'

'It shall be our dark secret.'

She stood looking at me with the door half open, smiling faintly, but with eyes that seemed heavy again. She must have been very much in love with him. Meanwhile he'd been humping Madge the barmaid, and before her how many others on his nights away, while this attractive and intelligent woman, who now endlessly grieved, dealt with his paper work and waited patiently for the time-bites he could spare her? One of the two worst aspects of private investigation was the false fronts you were forever stripping from what seemed ideal marriages. The other was to turn up ugly facts about someone that a partner hadn't discovered in all the years they'd been together.

We watched each other for a moment. I wanted to touch her hair or stroke her arm, in a gesture that owed nothing to sex and everything to sympathy. Our right hands seemed to move of their own volition towards each other, as if we were relations or close friends parting.

And then we let them fall, and I walked out into the long shadows of the declining September light.

Four

'Jason's Well,' Kev said. 'That's where they hang out. Loafing around, dressed in rags, drinking cheap wine. I don't know what women must think, having to pass that lot, and it's the only way across Southgate Road if you don't want to get yourself killed.'

'They won't go in hostels,' Tom said. 'They'd sooner take their chances sleeping rough.'

'They want quietly putting down,' Kev said. 'I know it sounds callous but they're no good to themselves and they're no good to society.'

Fenlon turned to me with a smile. 'I think he's got it all sorted now. We tell Brussels to get stuffed, flog rapists, hang murderers, sterilise single mothers and give the winos an armful of arsenic.'

He drank some beer, glanced back at me. 'You've got your po-faced look on . . .'

I sighed, shrugged. 'Oh, I don't mind his blather most of the time, but when he goes on about the vagrants it touches a raw nerve.'

'I don't get it,' he said. 'We're talking human garbage here, John, and the police and the council waste hours trying to get them off the streets. It does no good, frankly, to slip them pound coins and fags like you keep doing.'

'They're human beings. They're hungry and not very well and they've lost hope.'

'Oh, come on, we've both been around, we know some problems just don't have answers. They won't go in hostels and they either can't or won't work. They've always been there and suddenly you've got this hang-up . . .'

I ordered the second round of our evening two-drink ration, sipped a little of my gin.

'Last spring,' I told him, 'a woman asked me to trace her husband, who'd taken off without a word. She didn't want him back, she was living with another man, but she'd help him with money if he needed it. Conscience. But she kept on stressing that she'd not live with him again.

'I . . . tracked him down to a derelict warehouse in Huddersfield. Living rough. He told me that when they got married they swore they'd never leave each other, however tough things got. Well, he'd meant it, she hadn't. She'd left him and he'd nothing else to live for that mattered.

'I've never been able to get his face out of my mind. I tried to talk him into making a new start, gave him a fiver . . . I knew he'd spend it on booze. He wouldn't listen and I hadn't much time – I had another job waiting. Next morning I rearranged everything so I could give him a couple of hours. He was a good, decent bloke and he needed help. I went back to Huddersfield first thing – the police were just cutting his body down from the beam he'd hanged himself on.'

Fenlon drank lengthily, lit a cigarette, looked at me, shrugged. 'Well, it's a tragedy, I agree, but why blame yourself? The wife's to blame, if anyone, except these days nobody seems to be to blame for anything . . .'

'I feel if I'd stayed with him that afternoon I could have talked him into making a new start. As it was, I'd told him his wife had sent me to look for him but she'd not have him back.

Good news, bad news and then I left him brooding . . .'

'Yes, but . . .'

'Yes, I *know*. No one's to blame. Only for once in my life I got involved with a down-and-out. He wasn't a statistic or a bundle of rags in a doorway, he was a man I'd learned a lot about and could relate to. And that's why I've been trying to help a couple of tramps in the subway. Well, one got lucky and found work and I'm trying to talk the other into reclaiming himself. Call it misplaced guilt, call it obsessive behaviour, you're almost certainly right on both counts.'

'You get too involved, John,' he said mildly. 'It's the same with everything you do. I know it's one of the reasons you get so much work, but you can't go on for ever taking it all on board and delivering twenty ounces to the pound.'

We'd been close friends since childhood and knew each other very well, perhaps too well. I knew he was a good policeman who'd got as far as he was going, and he knew that if I'd been able to go into the Force the same personality traits he frequently advised me against would have driven me so far beyond him as to be out of sight.

'Just to change the subject,' he said, 'how did you get on with short-arse Snee?'

'Bruce, Bruce!' I glanced round in mock wariness. 'You do mean vertically challenged, of course . . .'

'No,' he said, grinning. 'I definitely mean dwarf.'

'He was debatably the most objectionable man I've ever met.'

'I knew he would be,' he said cheerfully.

'The case is a total no-no, as you can imagine. How could it be anything else? His only angle is to keep his hands on the money as long as possible.'

'That's Marcus . . .'

I told him the story so far – the car mechanic, the farmer,

the mistress, the valley, the widow. He was the only man I ever discussed current cases with; his discretion was total.

'Can't think why you even bothered going through the motions,' he said, 'you could have gone up to Ben Rhydding and read a novel for all it meant to Snee.'

'I can't do that. He's paying me for an investigation and so that's what I have to provide, even though I know it's a waste of time.'

'I'd have walked through it,' he said superfluously.

'About the only thing I turned up that was even half interesting was that his car didn't burst into flames when it hit the ground. I wonder how often they do explode when they fall a long way . . .?'

He shrugged, his mouth turning down at the corners. 'It's not something that happens all that often, outside the films. Most accidents are routine prang-ups, hitting another vehicle, going off a bend and hitting a wall or a tree, that kind of thing. I could speak to one of the engineers, I suppose . . .'

'Don't bother. It's not really important. I'm getting a profile of sorts on Simon Marsh and he just seemed the type who'd keep plenty of juice in the tank, which I'd have thought would make the car more likely to explode. Don't they try to give excess fuel the heave-ho if a commercial jet has to make a forced landing?'

Fenlon's brow furrowed. 'But he'd been on pills and booze, hadn't he?'

'I thought of that. If you're as stressed out as he was, do you give a sod about the needle touching red?'

'Well, I wouldn't, but you might . . .'

'That's the point, you see. Do you carry on all your usual habits instinctively whatever state you're in?'

'I suppose you'll only know that if you ever do go over the top.'

'My conclusion . . .'

'And he was nannying too, was he. I daresay that was part of the problem. Well, it would be with me – you can imagine the flak I'd be getting from Enid.'

'Little Madge. A looker, but couldn't care a sod about the accident.'

'Which means she probably just saw him as an escape route.'

I nodded. 'If you live in a tied cottage with a pig-man or whatever, Simon Marsh, with his looks and his job and his fancy car, must have seemed like someone to go nap on. Benidorm, Karaoke nights, her very own Fiat Uno – she must have thought there was everything to play for.'

'And when he buys it it's more of a bloody nuisance than a tragedy.'

'And you hang on to the man you've got, even if he does play darts and spit in the fire.'

'You don't think the widow suspected?'

I shook my head. 'She had no real reason to. He was always on the road, working long days, nights in hotels. No, from where I was sitting she looked to be in a great deal of straightforward pain. She could handle it – in control, friendly, outgoing, jokey even – but it just seemed to make you sense it more strongly than if she'd broken down. And all for a guy who was probably giving one to most of the bar-maids in North Yorkshire.'

'She seems to have made an impression on you.'

'I liked her a lot. Intelligent, plenty of common sense, couldn't care less about being investigated.'

'Better you, I suppose, than having a serial rapist following her about.'

'Thank you.'

'Attractive?'

'Not conventionally. Nice skin, eyes you can't stop looking at.'

'You'll never have a better chance, Goss. Someone you can get on with who'll soon be worth a million . . .'

I smiled, shook my head. 'I don't think she'll think in terms of another man. I could be wrong. I think it was all for Marsh and she'll just live now with what they had. And she'll certainly not *need* a man around – not with *that* loot.'

'Snee . . .'

'It's John Goss, Mr Snee, reporting in on the Marsh case.'

'Yes, yes, go ahead . . .'

I telescoped my activities of the past week as tightly as possible, but every few seconds he would break in – 'Yes, yes, yes . . . go on . . .'

'That's about it,' I said calmly, trying to rid my tone of brusqueness, because irritating people seemed to be one of the ways he got his kicks. 'And Mrs Marsh is aware now, by the way, that I'm keeping her under observation.'

The first note of genuine interest showed through his barely concealed indifference. 'Ah . . . good. How's she reacting?'

The words: 'Like a very sad woman who's lost a husband she was deeply in love with in a tragic accident,' trembled on my lips for a second. I said: 'Exactly as I'd expect a woman to react who seems to have nothing to hide. She lives very quietly, has few if any visitors, and when she leaves the house seems to go either shopping or walking round the Tanglewood reservoirs.'

'Stay with it, Goss,' he said curtly. 'We didn't crack Sir Michael overnight. Stay with it.'

'What sort of time-scale?'

'Let's say another three or four weeks. If there is anything to hide, it'll come out. If not, it's given us a bit of breathing space to get that inordinate amount of money together.' Fenlon was right – the genuine investigative work I'd put in meant so little to him I could have spent the time at the cinema. 'Ring me next week, Goss, eh. Keep in touch, there's a good chap.'

It was a month of mixed, almost spring-like weather, with endless permutations of sunlight, wind, rain and bruised-looking cloud. But there were calm days too, the sorts of days more in season with the merging of summer into autumn, days which began with clear white mists which were slowly burnt off by an enlarged sun. On days like this I would arrange my schedule to give me a time slot to drive to the enclosed house near the reservoirs in the early afternoon.

On seeing my car near the gate she would walk along the paved drive in her parka and dark pants, smiling her faint, sad smile, her hair sometimes taken back, sometimes loose to her shoulders, and we would set off to the woodland, where the sheets of water stretched glassily to distant banks, whose outlines were still faded by traces of mist.

She would always have scraps for the ducks, always spare a minute for the besotted Binkie, who would stand alone, when we moved on, and could still be seen, when we were a hundred yards away, in the same spot, seeming to follow our progress wistfully.

Sometimes we walked as far as the upper reservoir. There were wide, shallow steps leading from one level to the next, and she seemed drawn to the roaring water that cascaded past us down the gulley, and the way she looked, standing against that greenish flow and boiling white spray, gazing gravely on with an almost child-like absorption, was an image that frequently stayed with me as I went on to other work.

'I'm to keep you under observation for another three or four weeks.'

'How nice . . .'

'By the end of October you should have your cheque. There'll be no reason for them to withhold payment any longer. If there was any justice they'd pay you interest to cover the delay. You might mention that to your solicitor, he might be able to screw something out of them.'

She shook her head. 'I'll wait patiently till they decide to pay and I'll take what I'm given. I'm not indifferent to the money, but I'd not realised how well Simon was covered – I'd been thinking in terms of having to look for a job, and sooner rather than later. It all comes as a tremendous relief. It gives me the luxury of choice.'

'They'll take advantage of your easy-going attitude, you know . . .'

We walked for some time in silence.

'I shall miss our walks,' she said.

'Me too.'

'You've been such a help.'

'I know I shouldn't say this, but I feel you need more help than the Zephyr. They've been very narrow-gutted about all this, as we say in Yorkshire.'

'The house goes on the market next week, but they've told me not to hold my breath. It's going to be a long time before the house market really picks up. I'd have a better chance if it were a semi in a popular area, but detached houses a long way from schools and bus stops are tending to stick. Not that it matters very much now, but it would have done – the equity was our only real asset.'

I glanced at her.

'Simon was struggling. He was doing really well in the mid to late Eighties, but with the recession so many of the sorts of

52

firms he dealt with were either going to the wall or not in the market for new systems. We were just about covering our expenses in the end. I was trying to persuade him to give up the business and go back to working as an executive.'

'I shouldn't have thought he'd have any difficulty finding a job, a clever man like him.'

'It's a very youth-orientated field and he was in his late thirties. The burn-out rate's quite frightful. And of course the struggle to keep up to date with the endless advances in technology. There's all this talk of networking now, main-frames are *passé*. He couldn't decide which way to go and it all added to the strain on him, poor man. I tried to talk him through his problems, but he did rather tend to bottle things up.'

It seemed doubly tragic that he'd not been able to sort himself out, with such an intelligent and sympathetic partner behind him. I wondered if Madge the barmaid had meant more to him than I'd imagined, had been a bigger part of his problem than his business worries, an aspect it wasn't possi-ble to talk to Laura about. Not then anyway, not until he'd perhaps made the decision to leave Laura for Madge. And that in itself must have been an impossibly difficult decision to make.

'Are you staying until the house is sold?' I said hopefully.

'No. Too many memories. It'll be a relief now, frankly, to make a new start in different surroundings.'

For about a fortnight we met two or three times a week and took the same walk. Then one day she said: 'I think you ought to know I've decided to go up to the moors tomorrow. It's a decent forecast and I have an overwhelming urge for wide skies and open country.' She smiled. 'You can continue your investigations up there if you like, of course, but if you can't spare the time, Bolton Abbey's where I'll be.'

'I really feel I need to make certain you really *are* going to Bolton Abbey,' I said gravely. 'You might be just saying that.'

'I suppose you've got a point. I shouldn't think the Zephyr would like me left to my own devices up there; their worst fears might be realised, whatever *they* are.'

'It was very good of you to let me know. This unexplained gap in your movements could have looked very awkward for me had it come to light.'

And so I followed her Peugeot out to Bolton Abbey, where we parked, and then walked up through Westy Bank Wood to the moorland plateau. It was a day of changing skies, with cloud-shadow moving rapidly across springy turf.

Once on the moor we scarcely exchanged a word for fifteen minutes. She looked about her, grey eyes gleaming in the angled sunlight, at the sweep of the land and the shaded hollows and the river's distant glint, with the same intense absorption with which she'd gazed at crashing water in the reservoir gulley. Her dark hair was loose today, sometimes flying back from her face, sometimes forward to conceal it. She seemed to revel in it, tossing her head with a faint smile, as if the wind were an element like water and the excess could be shaken off.

'I've always wanted to live near open country,' she said, 'and close to water. Where the wind blows through trees and makes the windows rattle and the doors creak, and when it snows you're isolated for days at a time . . .'

I thought of those striking paintings on her walls, of terrain not unlike that we walked on, with their tortured-looking trees and menacing fells and lowering clouds that seemed to threaten forked lightning and ceaseless rain.

'Did you spend your childhood in the country?'

'It all goes back there, doesn't it,' she said, her voice small but clear against the buffeting wind. 'To childhood. Every-thing we are, everything we become, all our ambitions, dreams, desires – everything built on the foundations some-one else prepares for us . . .'

I shivered slightly. I thought how carefully my parents had prepared my own ground. It wasn't their fault that the final structure hadn't come up to their expectations. Nor mine.

'That's very true,' I said.

'We lived about ten miles outside Leicester in an isolated house near a river. There were woods and open fields . . . it was wonderful.'

'What was your father's line?'

'Oh, dear.' She walked for several paces in silence. 'I've always had difficulty with this one. To be honest, I don't really know, even now. He was self-employed but he was in touch a lot with certain government departments. I think he was a sort of agent, who helped to arrange introductions for the sale of equipment abroad and work out rather compli-cated deals. He was in the Middle and Far East a lot. A sort of fixer, I suppose, for use of a better word. It probably sounds rather sinister, and if you think it might have something to do with the arms trade I must admit the thought has often crossed my own mind. He'd never discuss it; he always told me to tell people he was in import-export and leave it at that. I think that's why he wanted to live in such an isolated spot. Mother and I were delighted. It's not that he didn't get on with people, it was just that it would have been difficult to live the life he did among neighbours. He was away such a lot.'

'Did your mother work?'

'She was an artist – she had quite a good local reputation.'

'Those pictures at your house – her work?'

'Do you like them?'

'They're . . . unusual.'

She gave me a fleeting smile. It was no answer and we both knew it. They were riveting, they couldn't be ignored, but for me they were unsettling and abstruse – the visual equivalent of those pieces of Third Programme music for drum, xylophone and cello: challenging, perhaps the art of the future, but not something I wanted to relax with a gin over at the end of a long day. I wondered if the landscape buyers of the Leicester area had shown the same lack of taste and foresight, and this was why her reputation was only local and 'quite good'.

'What name did she paint under?'

'Lilian Rushworth. People find them difficult,' she said, reading my thoughts with total accuracy. 'My husband does . . . did.'

He continued to live in the present tense for her after all these weeks, as if her mind still hadn't coped with the concept of his total absence.

'Is she still alive?'

'She died ten years ago next month.'

Her voice had suddenly trembled, tears glittered along her lashes. I touched her arm gently. She'd been so controlled, so calm about her husband's death, despite the underlying impression of intense grief, but cried now for her mother. I felt I could understand – her husband's death had been so recent she had instinctively focused all her energy to deal with the blow, as if antibodies had gathered to fight an infection. But it seemed to have left her vulnerable to an older infection, from a wound not yet fully healed, the death of a beloved parent.

We walked on in silence. Finally she said in her normal voice, 'I'm afraid I was emotional. I didn't mean to embarrass you. I suppose it suddenly hit me, the two people . . .' Her voice disappeared into the wind.

'I understand, Laura, really. My father died prematurely. It was like losing my best friend.'

We walked on again, and then she said, brightly: 'Well, at least *my* father's still alive, even though his habit of secrecy lives on. I see him regularly, but it's difficult to talk about a shared past when we scarcely had one. Poor old thing, I think he's sorry now he spent so much time away from home. Age must be odd, if you did things wrong, living with the regrets day after day.'

'Still living in the house near the river?'

She shook her head. 'Too big for a man on his own. He's taken a much smaller house nearer town.'

'It must have been rather a lonely childhood. Any brothers or sisters?'

'I think when I was born Mother decided children weren't a very good idea. Too much of a distraction from her painting.'

She was now back in control and, as with many of the things she said, her small, cool tone seemed to give no indication of her true thoughts. To me, it seemed a strange rather impersonal upbringing; her father's obsessive desire for privacy from other adults must have meant Laura's enforced privacy from other children. Coming and going as he did, and mainly going, he must have seemed a remote and shadowy figure. While her mother immersed herself in painting those esoteric landscapes, a way of life that could be viewed either as an artistic temperament allowing nothing to come before the fulfilment of artistic achievement or, in a woman with a house to run and a child to care for, a massive self-indulgence.

'I read,' she said almost dreamily. 'I can't remember ever *not* being able to read. I would lose myself in a book. Literally – I was sitting with my back to an open fire one day and I'd not realised how hot it was becoming until I smelt burning. It was my cardy, starting to singe . . .'

I suppose we all use our own childhoods as a yardstick to measure others by. How bizarre hers seemed in comparison to my own – some gaunt, isolated house, perhaps without central heating, with lofty rooms inadequately warmed by coal and logs, a woman compulsively painting in a sky-lit attic, a ghost for a father, and little Laura burning her clothes as she became lost in *Black Beauty* and *Oliver Twist* and *The Arabian Nights*, and having perhaps a closer relationship with the cleaning woman than she did with her own mother.

Yet she talked about it with such intense affection, in a voice filled for the first time with what seemed to be unreserved emotion and warmth. It was as if, unable to discuss the recent past easily because of the pain involved, she found a displaced solace in the intact and complete happiness of her childhood years.

She said: 'I dare say it was very different from yours.'

'Different planets,' I said. 'My childhood seems to have been all pantomimes and parties and beaches, and kicking a ball about with Dad.'

'Rather like Simon's. Rather like most children's, I suppose. He used to say it should have made me shy and odd, unable to form proper relationships. Farouche was one of his favourite words – "you should have come out of it farouche." The funny thing was, though I had hardly any friends my own age, I met an awful lot of people.

'Mother would drop me off at the local school and then begin her own work – she always said it was only amateurs who waited for inspiration, true artists simply forced it out. She would work all day virtually non-stop. She'd finish about four and devote the rest of the day to me. We'd walk, ride bikes – I learnt more from her than I did at school, she knew so much about trees and plants and wild life . . . She always had her evening meal with me, then she'd help me with my work, watch some children's programme. It made up for the time she'd shut herself away and be furious if she was disturbed. Really. She had a marvellous personality . . .'

She glanced at me; I smiled politely – I think she sensed I felt that between my childhood and hers there was still no contest. She said: 'About two evenings a week she would fill her house with people. Other artists, writers, actors – anyone with artistic leanings. They were mainly amateurs, of course, but there were a few professionals and semi-professionals. You only got through the door if you had a genuine love for books or painting or the stage, and she couldn't be fooled – poseurs never came twice.

'People queued to get in. I suppose it was the modern equivalent of a salon in eighteenth-century France. It was her only real extravagance – she was indifferent to formal holidays and clothes and motors; her car must have been fifteen years old. She'd get a caterer to bring buffet food, and there was always plenty of wine.

'Mother was the real draw. She had such energy, such a love of life and artistic endeavour. She'd make the artists bring their pictures and the writers their work in progress, and she'd get them all talking about style and content and technique. She'd make the writers do a reading and the actors do a turn. They *all* had to sing some kind of song for their supper. They loved it, being bossed and bullied – she could bring so much out of them. Some of them are household names now – Bernard Stocks, Colin Windle, Amanda Shoe-smith; they all had some rough corners smoothed off by Lilian Rushworth.

'I was supposed to be too young to be involved, but she'd either forget she'd seen me creeping about or turn a blind eye. Of course, as I got older I was allowed to be there officially. First it was to serve the wine and the sausage rolls, and then I was pressed into giving some kind of order to the readings and the singing and acting – you know, linking and introducing the different performances, a sort of MC, I suppose; left to themselves it could all get very chaotic.

'You couldn't go to Mother's salons and simply *exist*, you had to do something . . . but I'm sure it stopped me from turning out farouche.'

It was a Laura I'd not seen. Her lower lip had trembled slightly with the frisson that sometimes comes with the recall of distant memories. She was on this great, wind-swept moor, but she could have been anywhere, her mind was totally immersed in that milieu where people sang and did bits of Beckett and read fragments of novels and mulled over the influence of Munch. And I felt pleased that the discussion had helped her to escape from her unhappiness, however briefly, into times that had given her such intense pleasure. I couldn't have begun to guess at the animation she kept battened down beneath that controlled manner.

'I see what you mean,' I said, 'about not being lonely. It must have been an unusual time.'

'I didn't want to go to college,' she said. 'I felt I'd miss it all too much. But she made me, of course . . .'

It was difficult to grasp the point she was making, and we now had to pick our way down from the moor to the road that led to Barden Towers, in single file because of the narrowing of the track; and for the next ten minutes we were unable to talk. When we reached the road the animation had died and her face had taken on the faintly guarded expression I knew so well.

'I looked out of my bedroom window on Monday evening,' she said, once we were walking side by side again. 'The light was fading, but I thought I recognised your car go by.'

I wondered if I caught a slight accusation in her tone. Her eyes rested steadily on mine. I gave her a faintly sheepish smile and shrugged. 'The situation, Laura, is that I'm supposed to keep you under observation. Now we both know it's a nonsense, but I have to produce a weekly formal report to Zephyr showing that I've kept watch on you at different times of day and evening, not just when you're walking or going to the supermarket.'

'Oh . . .'

I seemed to sense the slightest implication that I mistrusted her – if we were friends now and agreed that the investigation was a sham, why didn't I tell her about *all* the times I watched her movements?

'There didn't seem an awful lot of point in telling you when I simply rolled up and went through the motions,' I said truthfully.

She too shrugged. 'It just seems such a waste of your time, John, why not simply pretend you're keeping an eye on me?'

It was exactly what Fenlon had said, and the answer seemed to get more pompous with repetition.

'I . . . really can't do that,' I said. 'It's probably difficult to understand, but I feel I must actually do what I log down for Norma to type up. I like to think I've built up a reputation for integrity, professionalism – if I were ever caught out *not* doing exactly what I'm charging for you can imagine the dent my reputation would take with the people who use me all the time, mainly solicitors. John Goss is taking the money and skimping the work. I know it seems absurd, in this very absurd situation, but does it make any kind of sense?'

Her vestigial smile flickered. 'You're a very honourable young man, aren't you?'

'My father was a police detective,' I said, 'with firm ideas on right and wrong.'

'No shades of grey?'

'He only considered shades of grey when he was buying a suit.'

She smiled again briefly, then turned to look at the rising sweep of moorland we'd just picked our way down from. Two things seemed to relieve her endless sadness – memories of childhood and outdoor life. She gazed up to where the purple horizon met the incandescent edges of heavy, sailing cloud. It was almost as if the terrain absorbed her into itself. She seemed like the sort of bird that could be tamed to live in captivity, but only found itself when soaring and planing freely in its natural habitat.

We began to walk again. 'And yet,' she said, as if the previous discussion had never been interrupted, 'we're spending time together, the watched and the watcher. How would that look on your record if it were to come to light?'

The smile was rather sly this time, as if she'd edged me into the cul-de-sac of a moral maze.

'My brief was to be conspicuous. It was explained to me very carefully how agitated a claimant with something to hide could become under scrutiny. I simply did as I was told, and the fact that we've made contact hasn't stopped me meeting the terms of reference. It could even be seen as a better chance for me to monitor your movements more effectively.'

Her grey eyes met mine almost broodingly, with a glance difficult to interpret. I'd had endless practice in reading people, but I'd known few who gave less away. And yet some kind of wrong note had been struck and seemed to vibrate with a harshness only she could detect, as if she were the sort of skilled conductor able to pick up the incorrect bowing of a single stringed instrument beneath the wind and brass.

I was puzzled. We'd talked it all through before – she'd even asked me to stay with the case when I'd said I was going to take myself off it. But now she seemed put out. Was it because of the couple of hours obbo I'd not bothered telling her about? Was it because she'd let herself be lulled into regarding me as a friend and confidant, and then suddenly remembered I was only doing a paid job of work? I didn't know, but I felt impelled to make some kind of amends.

'Look,' I said, 'in two or three weeks my last pointless report on Laura Marsh will be with Zephyr and you'll be paid. When we reach that stage I'd like to ask you out to dinner for making the job so pleasant and easy.'

We looked at each other. I was glad to see one of her rare full smiles. 'Thank you, John,' she said simply, 'I'd like that very much.'

The awkward moment passed, my obscure gaffe apparently forgotten, and we walked on down a road so free of traffic at this time of year that it might have been the private road of one of the estates that owned so much of the surrounding land.

'Barden Towers,' I said, as we approached the monument.

'Fifteenth century,' she said. 'Built as a gamekeeper's lodge and converted into a residence for Lord Henry Clifford, known to the locals as the Shepherd Lord because he liked open country and solitude.'

It was one of the first indications I was to have of the formidable amount of precise detail she carried around in her memory, available at a second's notice. I wondered if she had an affinity with solitude lovers, living and dead. Perhaps it was one of the reasons we ourselves had become friends – though I knew many people and could project an impression of gregariousness, I lived much of my life alone.

'I never knew that,' I said, 'and I've been coming here since I was eight.'

We walked along the side of the Wharfe then, the final

stage in the circle that would return us to our cars.

'What about John Goss?' she said. 'You know such a lot about me and I know nothing about you.'

'Nothing to tell. Single, thirtyish, self-employed, long working days that usually include weekends. The end.'

'I'm not sure I'd want to go to dinner with someone who sounds so uninteresting. I really do feel you ought to add a little detail to something you couldn't even call a sketch.'

'Be warned, you'll die of boredom . . .'

'Let's begin with where you live,' she said firmly.

I wasn't playing hard to get, but I knew from long experience how incredibly mundane people found private investigation to be, once they were past their preconceived ideas. Women friends, scenes from novels and old films lingering in their minds, had often been curious about the work I did, a curiosity rapidly satisfied when I began to explain the unglamorous slogging routine, the endless waiting in cars, the dogged tracking of missing persons, the bread-and-butter errand-running for solicitors. But in her small, cool voice, as we walked past a river swollen with the recent rains, she wouldn't let me off the hook, and seemed genuinely absorbed in the minutiae of my daily round.

'But how can you *prove* someone's living beyond his income? Perhaps his partner has a big salary, perhaps he was left money or won a Premium Bond . . .'

I smiled. 'That's exactly what they always say. "I had a thousand on Dreamboat at a hundred to one . . ." and so on. So you very politely ask for details of the bookie, the race, the day of the race. If it's Premium Bonds you ask to see the bond; Pools money, evidence of Littlewoods' cheque in their paying-in book; inherited money, the executor's advice. They can hardly ever provide proof, and they usually throw in the towel.'

The detail seemed to fascinate her, or perhaps it was a way of providing herself with further distraction from her sadness. The questions seemed almost relentless. PIs are not police-men and we tend to cut corners. She seemed able to sense that I used a number of questionable techniques in my search for information, with an intuition rather puzzling in a woman who would appear to have led a fairly sheltered life, and in the end I became as absorbed in answering her questions as she was in asking them, searching for forms of words that would make my admittedly dubious methods sound like means that justified admissible ends, not always successfully. She was like an astute prosecuting counsel who disarmed by friendliness, and I began to realise what an incredibly analyti-cal mind lay behind those grave eyes, to go with the data-bank memory.

We were silenced then, as we passed that narrow, rocky stretch of the river called the Strid, where the water foamed and roared, as if a wired cork had been released on some massive surge of carbonated wine. I suppose it was flattering to find someone taking such a close interest in me, but as we passed on to where our cars were parked, I realised what an unprecedented amount of information I'd let go about my life and work. It made me suddenly uneasy in a way difficult to define. I was a private sort of man, nursing my own hang-ups as discreetly as possible, tending to talk in little depth to the women I had occasional relationships with, as they were not normally affairs calling for much emotional expenditure. It could have been that I'd lost the confiding habit. Or was surprised that anyone could find my humdrum life so deeply interesting. I didn't know. But I wasn't certain I'd enjoyed having my life broken down into its component parts, held to the light and scrutinised so scientifically.

We stood finally in the car-park. She gazed back wistfully

to the country behind us, that we'd spent most of the morning encircling, as if she wished she were back on the high, wind-scoured moor, as if she could have begun the walk all over again. I wondered if the Shepherd Lord had managed to marry someone as in tune with fields and rivers and wood-land as she seemed to be.

I glanced at my watch. 'Fancy a pub lunch?'

'I can't remember the last time I went in a pub . . .'

Her old man had made up for it, I thought, as her car followed mine down to Skipton, the husband she never seemed to stop pining for, he'd known his way around pubs very well.

It was an hour of simple pleasure. We found a pub on the high street where a fire of genuine logs blazed in a great stone fireplace. She took off her parka, to reveal the rather broad shoulders and the firm, shallow breasts, and we sat side by side on a leather banquette in the sort of contrasting light that went with old buildings and narrow windows, a very deep shade sliced by hard sunlight in which dust-motes glist-ened through drifting pipe smoke.

We both had a gin and tonic, and then I ordered simple plates of steak-and-kidney pie and a small carafe of the house red. She ate sparingly and I thought of those little microwave meals she would toss indifferently into her supermarket trol-ley. Perhaps she'd lost her appetite when she'd lost Simon.

'I was quite hungry,' she said finally, but leaving a good third of the food on her plate. 'It must have been the moor-land air.'

'Or just getting away from . . . things in general . . .'

She put a cool, dry hand briefly over mine. 'I had a lovely hike. It seems ages since I became rather frightened by this man I kept seeing who seemed to follow me around. And now you're like an old friend.'

'I'd like you to think of me as a friend, and that you can call on me. Any time . . .'

She smiled one of her rare, open smiles. 'You ought to be careful, young man, about offering help. I'm going to need all sorts of help when everything's settled.'

'Just lift the phone . . .'

I wanted to help her, to look after her even, until she was through this difficult time. She seemed so very vulnerable, despite her obvious intelligence. Fenlon had kidded me about the million plus she'd collect, but her money meant nothing to me, and I knew she sensed that, would have known if it had, she had that kind of perception.

'There'll be a lot to do when Zephyr can bring themselves to open their wallet,' I said, 'especially if you're moving out of the area. It's a lot for a woman on her own to cope with.'

It depressed me slightly then, to think of her leaving so soon, trying to flee the memories and hoping distance would provide the psychological break that would let her start rebuilding her life.

'Very well,' she said, still smiling, 'we'll face my moving problems together, shall we . . .'

I poured the last of the wine.

That night, as I sat over a brandy after a very long day spent catching up with the work I'd put on hold to wander over moorland, those rather odd words of hers came back to my mind: 'I didn't want to go to college. I felt I'd miss it all too much. But she made me, of course . . .'

It seemed odd she should appear almost to regret having had to go to university, even now. Yet she'd met Simon Marsh at university, the man she'd fallen in love with, the man whose death had turned her into the walking wounded. I wondered if it was an instinctive defence mechanism. Had –

she been allowed to stay at home she'd almost certainly have married one of those aspiring young writers or artists who'd flocked to her mother's house. She'd never have met Simon, never have fallen so deeply in love as to be so totally devastated by his death. Had she stayed at home she might have missed out on the highs, but she'd not have had to pick her way along this canyon-sized low.

I believed I had the answer to Simon's death now, was certain of it in fact, not that I was ever going to know if I was right. It made no difference to anything, it was completely academic, but I like to think things through to their logical conclusion.

It was the way I was.

Five

'Right,' Fenlon said, 'Simon Marsh at the bottom of a valley in his motor. I was actually speaking to one of the uniforms who was first on the scene this morning . . .'

'There was really no need to bother . . .'

'No bother. I had to speak to them about one of our bad lots we think's pushing in the Harrogate area, and I asked him about the Marsh accident on the off-chance. Well, then, I was told that the engineer who checked the car out, what was left of it, had tried to cover everything he could get at. Partly to ensure the vehicle hadn't been tampered with, partly to ensure everything possible's on file for the various interested parties, including insurers. And the examination *did* cover the state of the petrol tank. Your surmise was spot on, the tank was so low it was almost empty. You were also right in your assumption that a car without much petrol is a lot less likely to go up like a hydrogen bomb.'

I nodded, pleased to have my deduction confirmed, not that it made the slightest difference.

'What happens', I said, 'when your car runs completely dry and you're bowling along?'

'Never happened to me, but I suppose the engine starts misfiring, and if you ignore that it just dies on you.'

'And you'd know to pull in?'

'If you were right in the head. If you don't pull in you're going to have to push it in. I mean the petrol gauge has *got* to be the thing you look at if it starts peffing and coughing. Where's this taking us?'

'Nowhere in particular. I think Marsh couldn't give a sod about his petrol tank. And I think he deliberately drove his car into the valley. But I don't think he wanted it to look like suicide, as he may not have known that the policy would pay out anyway, so he just took enough pills and booze to make people think he was trying to relieve stress, and then nodded off at the wheel.'

He watched me quizzically.

'He had a lot of problems,' I said. 'Laura told me they were just about covering their living expenses. So what do you do when there's not enough money coming in?'

He shrugged. 'Cut back on non-essentials – dinners, holidays, clothes . . .'

'Exactly. And one of the significant outgoings Marsh must have had was the money he was paying for term assurance. He could have cancelled that overnight, there was no endowment involved, but he didn't, he kept it going.'

'So that she'd be provided for?' he said. He looked sceptical. 'Not too many people commit suicide over business worries, you know, aside from Lloyd's names who lost every farthing . . .'

'I think his business worries were a big part of it, but I'm certain the main problem was Madge. I suspect he was crazy about her and knew he could barely support one home, let alone two. But I think the biggest problem of all was that he couldn't bring himself to hurt a woman he'd been with so long and who cared about him so much. I think he knew what it would do to Laura if he left her. I have the evidence, believe me, I've *seen* what it's done to her, him getting killed.'

He considered this, drinking the last of his beer. 'I dare say you're right. You usually are, you're a good people watcher.' He glanced at his watch. 'I'll have to cut it short this evening. Compulsory overtime . . .'

As we left the George, he said: 'Zephyr still retaining you?'

'The longer I investigate the longer the half-million stays in the sock.'

'What a doddle . . .'

'Most relaxing. We went for a walk on the moors together the other day. It seemed simpler than walking a quarter of a mile behind her with a false nose and a gamekeeper's hat.'

'Cosy . . .'

'Speak plainly, do *you* think it's unethical, me palling up with someone I'm supposed to be investigating?'

He glanced at me. 'Why do you ask?'

'Oh . . . it was just something she said.'

'It's only as unethical as Marcus sending you on a bogus assignment so he can hang on to the dibs a bit longer. Do you think there's the remotest chance she has anything to hide?'

'Not the remotest.'

'There you are then. You worry too much.'

'I just seem to be getting rather involved, that's all. I've promised to help her sort out her affairs when she finally gets the Zephyr cheque. She's a clever woman in some ways, but she can be vague about money and I'd not like to see her get ripped off. They say when someone dies or you get divorced the one person you need to talk things through with isn't around any more.'

'You know, Goss,' he said, grinning, 'the only thing I find suspicious about you hanging around Laura is this sudden nobility you've developed.'

'It'll probably make *her* suspicious too, when she stops to think, all this loot she's picking up and all this help she's

71

being offered by a man who can just about see clear to the end of the month.'

'I can see dangers ahead. You a toy boy who's lost the will to work, and then finding yourself given the welly and ending up with this appetising lot . . .'

We'd emerged from a subway; the circular garden stood before us, where the vagrants were gathered, silently drinking cheap wine and smoking fragments of cigarettes. I gave the one I'd got to know slightly a pound coin. He tended to sit a little apart from the rest, as if not quite ready yet to identify with their state of ragged griminess, which was several degrees worse than his own.

'Thanks, boss . . .'

'You are a dick,' Fenlon muttered. 'You do realise the more hand-outs you give them the more we'll get. They're like pigeons . . .'

Ignoring him, I said: 'Has your pal been back yet?'

'Pal?' The vagrant glanced round at the other benches and I realised we'd have to go through the same rigmarole as before. He couldn't remember the conversation and his friend seemed to have disappeared into the dense alcoholic mist that swirled around his memory.

'The man who used to wear the donkey jacket and the red jumper,' I said patiently. 'You used to sit with him . . .'

'You mean Suss?'

'Was that his name?'

''E's gorn, 'as Suss. 'E got a job scaffolding . . .'

'I *know* that. Has he been back? He said he'd come and see you.'

'Nah, 'e's not been back. 'E *said* 'e would, but 'e never. Not yet . . .'

He stared past us with unfocused gaze, looking slightly aggrieved. I wondered if it was because of Suss's broken

72

promise. It could as easily have been the state of his feet or alcohol punching holes in the lining of his stomach.

'Well, when he does come back you must ask him to help you find work. That's what friends are for . . .'

He looked back at me, his mind seeming to grapple with a concept as abtruse to him as the Theory of Relativity.

'John . . .' Fenlon growled irritably, 'I've got a desk this high . . .'

'Just give me half a minute, Bruce,' I said in a low voice. 'You can see he's in reasonable shape beneath the stubble and the bloodshot. He just needs a break . . .'

'Oh, *Gawd* . . .'

I had to admit the man did nothing to help his own case, gave no indication of pining for the sort of break I had in mind, as the one called Suss had done. I wondered if Suss was leaping among the poles and planks now with his old agility, perhaps even confident enough to be wolf-whistling pretty girls again, and wanting no reminders of his life's lowest ebb.

'Look,' I said, scribbling my name and office number in large letters on a page of my diary, which I ripped out and gave to the man. 'If you do see Suss ask him to ring this number. Will you do that for me? Just ask him to ring the number . . .'

He looked from the paper to me uneasily, as if beginning to sense I might be a Greek who bore a gift in one hand and a length of lead piping in the other.

'Don't know if I can do that, boss. I move around a lot, don't you see . . .'

'Thank God for that,' Fenlon murmured.

'What does '*e* want?' The man glanced from me to Fenlon with a look of hostility. It had taken me most of the summer to gain even this fragile rapport with him, and now I was springing a stranger on him, yet another suit, and one who not only hadn't put his hand in his pocket but had a hard look that struck a distinct warning bell.

'Just a friend of mine,' I said soothingly. 'Now promise me you'll ask Suss to ring that number.'

'If you say so, boss, but like I say I move about . . .' He stuffed the paper indifferently in his pocket. He'd find it two days later, spend perhaps five seconds wondering why it was there, and then use it to light his dog-end with. He hadn't asked why I wanted Suss to ring me, as if sensing he wouldn't want to know the answer. Suss had displayed initiative, and I'd thought I could talk to him, perhaps persuade him to try to get some kind of labouring work for the man he'd befriended when they'd both been living on plonk and crusts. I knew the man himself would do nothing, would very soon be sunk into the same irretrievable state as the men around him.

I had so little time to spare, but I was beginning to realise that the only way I'd sort him out in the end, if at all, would be to devote at least half a day to the problem.

'*John!*'

'Right, Bruce, let's go. Just indulge my guilt complex. I know it'll all probably end in tears.'

He gave me a faintly sheepish look. He was a good-hearted man beneath the patina of cynicism all plain-clothes policemen, who saw little of life but its downside, tended to develop. Arranging his face into a smile with an effort he said to the man: 'Have you tried the Job Centre? They might be able to find you something. That's probably where your friend found his job.'

'They 'adn't got nothing in my line, boss.'

'And what line's that?'

''Eart surgery . . .'

He broke into wheezing almost soundless laughter, in

which some of the men on nearby benches joined, more it seemed to be companionable than because they still retained any emotion that could be defined as a sense of humour.

'They wasn't wanting no 'eart surgeons that day, boss,' he said, before going into further paroxysms of near-silent laughter.

'You'd have made a good straight man, Bruce,' I said, grinning myself as we crossed to the opposite subway, leaving them all shaking and wheezing like the puppet audience of *The Muppet Show*, life imitating art only too closely.

'*What* a wrench it must have been to tear himself away from such jolly times with the Jason's Well fun crowd,' he said sourly, 'your scaffolding friend.'

'And finally a Mrs Marsh rang just after lunch. I said you'd ring back, but she said she'd be in town this afternoon and asked if she could call in. I told her you were aiming to be back for five; she said she'd come about quarter past and it wouldn't take more than a couple of minutes.'

'Oh . . . right . . .' I glanced at my watch; the last half-hour before Norma left was usually a busy one.

'Could that possibly be the Mrs Marsh you've been checking up on for the Zephyr?'

'The . . . same . . .'

'I dare say I'm being incredibly naïve but aren't people you're investigating not supposed to know about it?' she said ominously.

'Do I have to explain *everything*, Watson, when there is so much to be done. I must be in Surrey by nightfall. The scoundrel with the withered arm, he may already know the whereabouts of the palimpsest . . .'

'Stop pratting about, John. How come you've made contact with her?'

'I didn't. She made contact with *me* . . .'

I knew she'd not let me off the hook. In the time left before Laura arrived I explained the situation to her. I'd been hoping I could get through the case without her grasping the truth. Despite Fenlon's relaxed attitude to my getting to know Laura, I think I'd always been aware of what Norma's reaction was going to be. I'd inherited her from the man who'd taught me the business and sold me the agency, and he'd been a man who'd lived by rigid codes of conduct.

'I can't believe I'm hearing this,' she said. 'It's just not professional, John, you know it's not. Your job was simply to look on. And when she approached you, you should have put her off, whether she knew you were keeping an eye on her or not.'

'Oh, come on, Norma, the whole thing's a piece of non-sense,' I said, meeting her eyes with difficulty.

'That's not for you to decide. You were given a brief by Zephyr and you should have stuck to it.'

'If you want the truth, I very nearly packed it in. With a woman like Laura Marsh I found the whole thing so *bloody* distasteful . . .'

'Then all *I* can say is you've still got a long way to go. You've been trying to break in with the insurers for fully three years, and the first real chance you get you want to throw away.'

'All right, all *right*,' I said irritably, 'I nearly blew it. I couldn't help feeling sorry for the poor bitch, that's all . . .'

We looked at each other. I couldn't remember the last time we'd been so close to such a full-scale fur-and-feathers row, and we both hated any kind of break in the harmony we'd built up to run what was a very tight ship.

'Oh, John . . . this is a *case*, an assignment. You say Marcus Snee is simply trying to slow down the pay-out and I'm sure you're right. But you should simply be going through the motions. If there's nothing dodgy about her life-style she hasn't got a thing to worry about. And *she* should have known better than to let this friendship develop . . . I can't get it together, I really can't . . .'

'You'd have to meet her to understand. She has no relations up here, no real friends. She's just a woman very much on her own, trying to cope with sudden death . . .' I broke off. 'Well, look, she'll be here any time, I'll introduce you . . .'

She arrived at five-fifteen, almost to the minute, wearing city clothes for the first time – a pale-green jacket over a white blouse, and a grey pleated skirt.

'Hello, John,' she said, with a faint smile. 'I'll not take up much of your time, I know how busy you are . . .'

'Never too busy to see you.'

'What a nice set-up you've got. And the building has such charm – I suppose it goes back to the time of the German merchants in the nineteenth century . . .'

'I was lucky. When I bought the agency the deal included a twenty-five-year lease. Space is like gold around here – we've still got street parking, you see, and the sort of rents that go with the *vieux carré*. This is what we rather grandly call the general office, where I usually work with Norma unless I'm seeing a client, though I'm not much in the office, as you can imagine . . .'

I led her through the main office to my own, where Norma was pretending to examine a file from one of my cabinets.

'Ah, Norma, this is Mrs Laura Marsh . . .'

'How do you do, Mrs Marsh.'

'Laura, please . . .' Laura said. 'I suppose John has told you abut the rather odd circumstances of our becoming acquainted.'

It was almost as if she sensed the heated discussion that

had just taken place, could pick up from the atmosphere the vibrations of Norma's strong feelings.

'I'm afraid Norma doesn't altogether approve of the acquaintance,' I said, striving for a light-hearted note and not quite making it, 'but I felt sure she'd understand the situation if she were to meet you.'

'I had my own doubts, John, as you know. I believe I did say that Zephyr might think you were treating with the enemy,' Laura said, her glance sliding from my eyes to Norma's.

'I'm sorry about your husband's death, Mrs Marsh,' Norma said. 'It must be a very difficult time for you. But Mr Goss's client *is* the Zephyr and I felt it was unethical that you should have made contact during the case itself. When it's over that would be a different matter, of course.'

Laura's eyes moved back to mine; I gave her a sheepish smile. This was not the way I'd wanted the meeting to go. I'd simply wanted Norma to *see* her and spend a couple of minutes or so in casual chat. But she was older than both of us and it was as if we were getting a talking-to by a senior member of the family, though she spoke in a pleasant manner that tempered the words a little. She was a Yorkshire woman, she'd always tended to speak plainly.

'I'm sure you're right,' Laura said, her eyes still on mine. 'It was my fault. I think it was because John was my first real contact with the outside world for rather a long time and I took advantage of his sympathetic nature.' There seemed a sudden forlorn quality to her usual sadness.

'I suppose it's how it *looks*, Mrs Marsh,' Norma replied, in a gentler tone. 'We're only human, and I know Mr Goss has reservations about the case, but there is a great deal of money involved and he *was* engaged to check you out . . .'

'Oh, he's done that,' Laura said ruefully, '*very* thoroughly, even though we *have* got to know each other.'

'I'm sure he has, but what if he *had* found anything untoward? Or if anything had come out later? I'm sure you can see the effect it could have on his reputation if the friendship were to come to light.'

The two women exchanged lengthy glances. It was as if some sort of perception seemed to pass between them that was off my wavelength; perhaps you had to be another woman to intercept it.

'I'm sure you're right,' Laura said once more, in a low, almost dispirited voice, and I wished I'd not involved Norma now, that I'd trusted my own feelings, because it seemed that all Laura had had recently was my friendship, and she was being told that even that should be withdrawn.

A phone began to ring in the main office. 'I'll get it,' Norma said, and with a polite, neutral smile for Laura, left us.

'Saved by the bell.' I gave her a wry smile. 'I'm sorry about that. Don't take any of it personally. She's been with the agency since day one and she's very protective about its reputation. To a fault, as you can see.'

'I understand, John, really I do. It was just that . . .'

She didn't finish the sentence, but she didn't need to – the last four words summed up how we both felt.

'Sit down,' I said, 'and we'll have a proper chat.'

'No,' she shook her head firmly. 'I know how it is around offices when it gets past five. I just came in to ask you something, but I hardly think I can now. I think it might be best if I just went.'

'Look,' I said, 'Norma is as critical to the agency as I am myself; you wouldn't believe the expertise and the contacts she's got stored in that greying head of hers. But I've been here since I was twenty and she tends to forget that I'm a mature man now and can sometimes make my own decisions, even if I don't always go by the book. Just go ahead and ask me what you were going to ask me.'

'I was . . . going to invite you to the house tonight. For a drink . . .'

'Well, I'd like that very much.'

'But . . .'

'No buts. Let's just keep it between the two of us.'

'All right.' She smiled a little more cheerfully. 'About half-seven?'

'I'll look forward to it . . .'

When I returned from seeing her out, Norma was feeding mail through the franking machine.

'Don't you think you were just a little bit hard on her?'

She glanced up pensively. 'To be honest, I hadn't intended to spell it out like that. But she brought it up herself – the way you got to know each other – almost as if she *wanted* a reaction.'

'Well, she certainly got one . . .'

'What had she come in for, by the way?'

I thought fast. 'Oh, she just wanted the name of a reliable estate agent for when she comes to sell up.'

She turned off the machine, put the elasticated bundle of mail in her shopping bag. 'I still can't really get it together . . . why she wanted to get to know you . . .'

'Isn't it obvious?'

'Not to me. It's all very tragic, but she must have *some* family she can turn to for comfort, she must have neighbours. Why let it all out on a man she hardly knows who's supposed to be making sure everything's straight up for the insurers?'

'What family she has got is down in Leicester and if you've ever been on Tanglewood Lane you must know it's not the kind of place where people start to get pally in much less than five years. I just happened to be convenient, even though I shouldn't have been.'

'You don't think she's coming on a bit strong – as the grieving widow . . .?'

'No. I'm certain she *is* grieving.'

'She's not a young woman, John. And she's obviously middle class. I'd have thought she'd be the type to keep it under wraps in public and let her hair down in private.'

'She tries very hard to do exactly that. There are just times when she can't keep it up.' I smiled. 'They haven't all got your crablike shell, you know. What *have* you got against her, apart from her daring to get friendly with me when she should have known better?'

She took her jacket from the coat stand, glanced through the window to check that her car wasn't blocked, looked back at me. 'I don't know, John,' she said simply. 'I wish I did. It's just that when I look at Laura Marsh I seem to see a kind of wariness . . .'

I stood at the window for a couple of minutes, watching her manoeuvre her Astra past the closely parked cars, smiled again. I wasn't really surprised that Laura seemed wary on meeting the woman who organised so much of my life; I was certain that what she'd sensed in Norma was a kind of possessiveness. There was nothing that would have pleased Norma more than to see me settle down with a suitable woman, and yet I think any woman I'd introduced her to would have provoked the same guarded reaction and felt the same wariness – it took me back to my youth and the way my mother had been when I'd taken the latest girlfriend home for Sunday tea. There'd been wariness and critical inspection there too, behind the polite words.

It was just Norma in mother-hen mode.

* * *

I wondered if the friendship had moved into a new phase. I'd had coffee with her and I'd taken her for a pub lunch. But drinks at the house was different. Perhaps she was now taking me up on my offer to help her with her affairs. I wondered if I could hope that it might be the start of something that would eventually lead somewhere beyond friendship. We could still keep in touch, even when she moved away – I was nothing to do with her tragic past. I supposed I was day-dreaming, but I was hooked now, hooked on her grey eyes and her long, dark hair and the pale glow of her marble skin and her cool, small voice. And her impression of almost unfathomable depths, the impression that what you saw was the smallest part of what you got. I thought again of those powerful canvasses of her mother's and felt that getting to know a woman like Laura Marsh would be like entering terrain that bore no resemblance to any I'd ever seen, full of opaque pools, and trees that threw disproportionate shadows, and hills that glowed more violet than blue. She was the first woman I'd ever known whose mind attracted me as much as her body.

But when I got to the house near the water, a car stood outside the gates, a grey Escort. I drew in behind it, spirits sinking. Did this mean she had visitors? Friends, relations? It could be a stroller's car, of course, except that strollers tended to park near the entrance to the woodland and rarely, if ever, walked round the reservoirs at dusk, not in the Nineties they didn't.

I went slowly down the curving paved drive and rang the front doorbell. A moment later she answered it, wearing a black dress that emphasised the almost startling whiteness of her skin.

'John! Do come in. My brother-in-law's here too. I'd like you to meet him.'

I was shown once more into that large, sombrely furnished room. It was rather dimly lit, the leather-bound books and the cabinets and the heavy fabrics seeming almost to soak up the glow from the scattering of table lamps, themselves shielded by thick silk shades.

A heavy man of medium height stood on the hearthrug, with dark-brown hair and a beard, and wearing horn-rimmed glasses. He was casually dressed in an off-white Aran sweater, which made him look even bulkier, brown corduroy trousers and brown suede shoes. He bore a faint resemblance to Simon Marsh, as his brother had appeared on the photograph I'd seen on my first visit, but I doubted I'd have known they were related had I not been told.

'This is Simon's brother, John – David . . .'

'How do you do.'

We shook hands. Heavy though he was, there seemed a nerviness about him, a slight uneasiness in his faint smile. I'd formed the impression that Simon had been a man who lived on his nerves – perhaps it was a family trait.

'Sit down, John . . . what would you like to drink?' She gave me a sidelong smile. 'I *can* offer other things than vodka, by the way.'

I returned the smile. Vodka was the only drink I ever saw her buying at Sainsbury's. Marsh intercepted the smile and looked slightly puzzled.

'G and T, please.'

She went off. We watched each other warily across the dark Indian hearthrug like two male dogs of the same species. I was bitterly disappointed that it wasn't going to be just me and her. Perhaps he picked up the signals – I seemed to sense a similar hostility from him. My spirits ebbed lower. I'd looked forward so keenly to being alone with her in the lamplight, having a couple of drinks and listening to that

small voice laying out the fascinating contents of that brim-
ming mind. Perhaps I could have begun to suggest ways I
could be of help to her, few people knew as much about
reliable professionals as I did. But perhaps she'd just been
tactfully kind in the pub, because this competent-looking
brother-in-law was bound to be the man she'd really turn to,
he was family, after all.

'I . . . suppose Laura's told you of the rather strange circumstances of our getting to know each other?'

'Yes,' he said, almost curtly. 'You're working for Zephyr,
aren't you?'

'Not . . . actually *for* them. Acting on their behalf.'

'This is a bloody bad business!' he suddenly cried. 'Making
the poor kid feel like a criminal. The other insurers have paid
up, why are you lot shuffling your feet? She just wants to get
on with her life and she can't sort out a bloody thing till
Zephyr come across.'

He clearly operated on a half-inch fuse. He jumped to his
feet and began pacing about agitatedly, his heavy body loom-
ing over me almost menacingly. It threw me. Not a lot, though:
I was used to people flying off the handle in my business.
But they were hardly ever people I was supposed to be having
a quiet drink with. For a couple of seconds I felt the impotent
anger of a messenger being thrashed in the palace yard. And
then I took a breath and told myself he was simply taking his
role of guardian very seriously and happened to be the sort of
man who felt the quickest way to get results was to kick arses.

'I must stress I'm an entirely independent agent, David,' I
said mildly. 'I personally have no control over Zephyr's payment policy. My brief is simply to investigate the details of
the claim.'

'When the police have wrapped it up? When there's been a
PM and an inquest and the poor devil's been laid to rest? It's
a disgrace, a bloody *disgrace*.'

He was almost shaking with anger now. I watched him striding up and down, my spirits touching the point where there was nowhere left for the mercury to go. I thought wistfully of how it might have been, just me and her, perhaps a little delicate music, perhaps even my hand hovering comfortingly over hers.

'It's a big pay-out,' I said evenly, 'and the company's within its rights to investigate a claim, even when there seems little to investigate. I dare say it will all turn out to be rather a formality.'

He glanced down at me, the light winking feebly off his heavy glasses. I was picking my words with care. I could tacitly admit to Laura that the company's sole objective was to slow down payment as long as possible – I daren't give any hint of that to him. That would be like putting a fresh clip in a pistol. He'd be down at Zephyr tomorrow, banging on Snee's desk and quoting John Goss as saying it was simply a stalling operation.

She came in then, to my relief, with prepared drinks on a silver tray, together with the bottles themselves and the makings. She put it down on a sideboard at the back of the room and brought the drinks to the sofa table. She'd not asked Marsh what he wanted, so they were obviously on a level of closeness where she didn't need to. It would have increased my depression had I not reached apathy. It rather looked as if he visited quite often and I must have missed him on my irregular periods of observation.

She'd taken in the atmosphere and his agitated state at a glance, and she sat down with a questioning look at him. He also reluctantly sat down.

'I've been having a go at John,' he admitted heavily, 'about these bloody insurers.'

'But, David . . . he's nothing to *do* with it.'

'That's his story too.'

'Oh, *really* . . .'

'Well, he could *tell* them, for Christ's sake. He could tell them everything's perfectly all right and they must pay up,' he said, the hand that held his drink trembling slightly.

'But he *can't* do that. That's nothing to do with him. Oh, can't you see, they want to hang on to the money as long as possible, some insurers are *like* that . . .'

She'd said it, not me. I'd carefully arranged my face into a non-committal look. For a second, the suspicion crossed my mind that they might be playing nice policeman, nasty police-man and, though speaking very different lines, delivering the same message – would I please get Zephyr to pull their finger out.

I dismissed the thought as unworthy. Only a few days ago she'd told me she'd wait patiently for the settlement and take what was on the table. Coming to terms with her grief was her main preoccupation, everything else at this stage was marginal.

No, it was all down to Marsh. I wondered why he was pushing so hard. It was probably genuine compassion. I reluctantly accepted that his motives were sincere despite the unpleasant way he put them across. Perhaps he was short on time. Perhaps he lived in the Midlands, as Laura and Simon had done, and was here on a flying visit.

Laura smiled at me, raising her eyebrows a fraction, as if to say I shouldn't take it too seriously, this was the way he was. The black dress looked as if it was an expensive favourite, and was exactly right for her. It had what I believe is called a cross-over bodice, tightly fitted, which defined her shallow breasts perfectly, and was pleated in the skirt. The extreme delicate whiteness of her skin was an endless fascination against the darkness of dress and hair. It was as if I could fully appreciate the way she looked for the first time – Marsh's brusqueness had been a major distraction. I wondered if she wore the dress because of her widowed state or because for once she wanted to abandon the pants and turtle-neck and show herself at her best before two male guests.

I sensed Marsh's eyes also on me, and I caught their brooding glint in the room's shadows, but his expression was difficult to analyse. Was it contempt or irritation that I dared to look at her with what had clearly been admiration, or was it something darker? Possessiveness? Jealousy even?

If he'd been friendly and outgoing, I'd not have thought what I did then, but I couldn't stop myself wondering if he had no intention of letting anyone 'take care of' Laura except himself. By October she'd be sitting on a million, and a million pounds needed skilled handling. I knew from the considerable experience I'd had working for solicitors how rapidly well-meaning friends and relations could reduce a sizeable inheritance to petty cash. I wondered what Marsh's own circumstances were, whether he might have his eyes on some of the money for a little pet scheme of his own.

The eyes still rested on mine, seemingly as inimical as before. I had to accept then that he might have similar suspicions about me. Like many people, he probably equated private investigators with seediness and cash payments in brown envelopes, and before him was an investigator who'd have a very good idea of the size of Laura's claim and who seemed to be giving her the warm glances of a man keen to get his feet under the table.

We were probably both misjudging each other.

'Do you live locally, David?' I said, in what I hoped was the open, friendly manner of a man only there for the gin.

The words gave him a start, as if he'd been as preoccupied as me. He glanced at Laura and was about to speak, when she said: 'I rather wish he did at a time like this. He just calls in when he's in the area . . .'

'From . . . Leicester?'

He nodded abruptly, but Laura added: 'We came north, David stayed put. We missed him such a lot. The brothers were very close.' She gave him an affectionate smile, but his expression only softened marginally.

I said: 'It often pays to move on. I should think most of the boys I was at school with have left the area. A lot of it depends on how you make your living. With some occupations you've almost *got* to move. With others, like mine, you can more or less make the same living in any large city. Perhaps that's the sort of job David's got?'

It was a trick people like me tended to use all the time, concealing the need to know inside a soufflé of polite, inconsequential chit-chat. I sensed that a more overt approach would make him even less communicative than he already was. And I'd decided I needed to know as much about Marsh as possible, even though I accepted that his abrasive manner was affecting my judgement. I was after all in the business of checking people out, and perhaps the most useful service I could provide for Laura, in this sham of an investigation, was to make sure she was placing her trust in the right man. It seemed ignoble, but between Marsh and myself I could only be absolutely certain that one of us had no unhealthy interest in her expectations.

His glinting horn-rims had moved from me to Laura, as if he half expected her to speak for him again, but she merely smiled faintly and remained silent. It might even have been an uneasy silence, but I could see no reason for it.

'I'm . . . involved with a company that prepares other firms' payrolls,' he said at last.

'Ah, yes, I've heard of them,' I said breezily. 'Because they do nothing else they can make worthwhile economies of scale, and it saves small- to medium-sized firms the expense of a payroll clerk.'

'That's . . . about it,' he said reluctantly. 'I follow up enquiries and try to sell the package.'

'Anywhere in the country?'

'Anywhere . . .'

'You must be in orbit. Does your wife not mind you being away so much? I daresay she's used to it . . .'

Again a glance passed between them. 'I'm . . . not married . . . now . . .'

It did nothing for my depression. It had to mean I was out of the picture, assuming I'd ever been in it. Not only was he divorced or separated, he was clearly on close terms with his brother's widow, who would shortly combine attraction with wealth.

'You'll have another drink, John?' She crossed the hearth and picked up my glass. I wondered if I detected the faintest hint of reproach in her manner, whether her acute perception had enabled her to sense in seconds the fishing trip I was engaged in, and found it intrusive.

Perhaps I should let it go. Had he been charming and white-haired and wearing a suit, I knew perfectly well I'd have had every confidence in him; yet those things wouldn't have guaranteed his suitability for looking after her money. Perhaps David Marsh was simply a rather introverted man who found it difficult to judge the delicate line between assertiveness and aggression. And maybe he simply cared for her like a brother.

She put down my glass, her eyes resting gravely on mine. I felt she'd been anxious to make this a pleasant evening – it was probably the first time since the funeral she'd entertained even as modestly as this. She'd taken care with her appearance, kept an eye on the drinks, been determinedly cheerful. And yet her underlying sadness had seemed marginally deeper than ever tonight. She'd looked towards Marsh so often; I wondered if the resemblance to Simon, slight as it was, was a constant reminder of life before the crash, of a time perhaps when the three of them had sat in this room as we sat now, talking and drinking.

'What you need, Laura,' I said, on a genuine impulse, 'when your affairs are finally in order, is a decent holiday. Somewhere like Madeira perhaps, where they have a good year-round climate . . .'

I wondered if I detected relief at my apparent switch away from any further probing of Marsh's background; she seemed almost to pounce on my words. 'Madeira sounds a lovely idea. It can often be seventy Fahrenheit even in December. If I went in January, the African daisies would just be out. Can you believe, the island's only thirty-five miles by thirteen, and yet there are still people in the outlying villages who've never seen Funchal. It's the mountainous terrain, I suppose . . .'

I'd seen the sadness lift before in the exercise of that formidable memory, and an hour drifted past as we talked about old holidays, though in fact she did most of the talking. I wasn't really into holidays and Marsh just seemed relieved to have the attention taken from himself. Or perhaps, like me, he was genuinely pleased to hear the animation in her small voice as she talked of vacations that all seemed to have had one common factor – remoteness. It was an absorbing catalogue of isolated cottages on windswept headlands, or at the foot of cloud-hung fells, or near dense forest, always it seemed rented out of season, when other people could be counted on one hand and the weather relied on to be at its most elemental.

'Poor Simon,' she said, laughing, 'we stayed in a cottage beyond Derwentwater at the top of a track where you really needed four-wheel drive and a *lot* of clearance. He took it too quickly coming down one day and there was the most frightful grinding noise and something dreadful happened to the gear box . . .'

'Half-shaft,' Marsh said.

His correction, possibly involuntary, caused them both to become silent. She looked at him, her face turned from mine. He held her glance briefly, one side of his mouth twitching slightly.

'Oh, of *course*!' she said. 'You were with us that time, weren't you. Simon was *so* upset, his beautiful BMW. It took ages to get it towed away and repaired . . .'

It was as I'd thought earlier. They'd spent a lot of time together, the three of them, even sharing holidays. It seemed to leave me nowhere in the looking-after-Laura stakes.

'But what about you, John? You can't go from one year to another without a break.'

'Oh . . .' I shrugged. 'Now and then I have a couple of days in London. I work a lot with an agent there who helps with traces. As you probably know, a lot of mis-pers – missing persons – are teenagers, and most of them seem to end up wandering around Piccadilly Circus sooner or later. I spend a couple of hours with him, have a browse in Foyle's and then go to the theatre in the evening.'

'A theatre buff!' she said. 'What did you see last?'

For the next half-hour the talk was all on plays, about which, inevitably, her knowledge was encyclopaedic. She seemed to have a critic's perception for trends and content, could name the leading actors in every major play for what seemed like the last quarter of a century. Marsh took no part in any of this, had barely spoken, in fact, since he'd corrected her single memory lapse about the damage the uneven track had caused his brother's car.

The evening then seemed to draw to its natural close. My glass was empty and a further drink wasn't offered. I acted on the polite middle-class hint and got up.

'I'd better be going,' I said. 'Heavy day tomorrow . . .'

They also got up. He said a rather awkward 'Goodbye', didn't offer to shake hands again, left Laura to see me to the door. We looked at each other in the hall.

'It was so good of you to come,' she said. 'It made such a change, having a little company.'

Her grey eyes still shone; I knew she wasn't simply being polite. She touched me briefly on the arm and held the door open, as I set off along the curving driveway. I turned at the gate and raised my hand, giving myself one last glimpse of the way her marble skin looked against the dress in the light spilling from the hall. It was strange how the animation had seemed only to increase the air of vulnerability. It must have been the memories.

I passed Marsh's Escort. I decided I'd been hard on him. The trouble with being an investigator was that you could never stop investigating – it became second nature to scrutinise mannerisms, to study aspects of behaviour, to listen carefully to words and the spaces in between. The simple explanation, after lengthy exposure to born and fluent liars, was the one I'd become almost pathologically incapable of accepting.

Yet despite giving him the benefit of the doubt, there were things about Marsh I couldn't stop myself uneasily trying to rationalise. I listened to the couple of messages on my answerphone, studied the faxes on my home machine and went through the papers Norma had put in my document case. I had one last gin and put on the late film.

Wasn't an Escort rather a modest car for a man who spent so much time on motorways? He looked fortyish – wouldn't that mean he would be a senior executive by now? If he had to pound motorways at that age, which in itself seemed unusual, wouldn't his status entitle him to something grander?

And why had the Escort been bought locally? Surely his company would have a deal with some Leicester firm for discounted vehicles.

The name on the laminated strip, sealed to the rear window of his car, was of one of Beckford's main dealers.

Six

Something happened then that drove the Laura Marsh case completely out of my mind, together with everything else I was working on.

It was the night after I'd had drinks at Laura's house. I was sitting at home, writing up notes for a report, when the phone rang. I picked it up and spoke my name, but the caller, who must have hit a wrong key, simply put down the phone without comment. It meant nothing then, it happened anyway several times a year, but I remembered it later.

That was about nine p.m. At around ten-thirty the phone rang again. 'Mr Goss? This is Valerie Collins, Norma's next-door neighbour. I'm afraid she's been hurt . . . someone broke into the house. We've had the police . . . they arranged to send her to Casualty. She wanted me to let you know . . .'

'I'll go right away, Valerie. How badly hurt?'

'She . . . she got a nasty bang on the head. She's very dazed, but she's conscious . . .'

'I'll be there in ten minutes.'

I drove anxiously through the quiet streets, hoping to God she was going to be all right. Blows to the head could be dangerous things, with lengthy after-effects. We went back a long way, she and I. In my life of brief relationships, Norma and Fenlon were the only two people I could always depend on. They were like family.

95

There was little or no parking in the Infirmary grounds these days, extensive as they were – visitors parking in staff spaces, outside loading bays, or even in areas marked AMBULANCES ONLY, had killed it for the rest of us. I left the car in a distant side-street and ran the rest of the way.

It was as busy as ever in Casualty, but not as busy as it would be when the pubs emptied, and even then only a pale imitation of the Grand Guignol it would be at the weekend, when the blade artists began to loosen up over their ten or twelve pints after a hard week's pimping and pushing.

I gave mine and Norma's names at the desk, and was asked to wait in a room almost the length of a tennis court, which had once been a quarter the size. It was a growth industry, Cas.

'Mr Goss?'

A thin woman, youngish, with large eyes and rather frizzy brownish hair, stood before me. 'I'm Mrs Collins . . . Valerie. Norma described you . . .'

'How is she, Valerie?'

'I don't know. They took her off somewhere and asked me to wait.'

'How did it happen . . . do you know?'

'I . . . saw her come back home about ten. It's her Centre night. I wanted to ask her if she'd baby-sit Friday . . . I gave her a couple of minutes to get in. When I went round the door was ajar and . . . and I heard her cry out. God, it gave me a shock. I pushed the door a bit – I should have gone back for Laurie, but you don't think, do you – and I just saw someone rushing off towards the back door, and . . . and Norma holding her head . . .'

'Was she bleeding?'

'No, it just started swelling . . . terribly. About there . . .' She pointed to the left side of her own forehead.

'All right, Valerie, you've done a great job and I'm very grateful.' I patted her arm. 'Can you remember *anything* about the guy who did the runner?'

She shook her head. 'There was only a landing light on – it's the one Norma leaves on to make it look as if there's someone in. He had dark clothes, wore a balaclava . . . that's really all I saw . . .'

'Tall? Short?'

'Sort of average, but I couldn't be certain . . .'

We sat down, among women who stared into space, hands held to faces, and men who talked in worried murmurs. About five minutes later a middle-aged nurse called Valerie's name and then mine. We raised our hands and she came across to us.

'For Mrs Norma Hanson? Are you relatives?'

'This lady's her neighbour, I'm her boss . . .'

'The doctor's checked her out. She'll probably be all right. She'll just have a bad headache for a day or two. Have you cars? Can one of you take her home?'

'No problem . . .'

'There's a policeman waiting to speak to her and then she can go.'

'Has he gone in yet, the bobby?'

'No. He's the one standing at the desk.'

'I'll catch you later, Valerie,' I said, and went over to the policeman, a young uniformed constable.

'I believe you want to speak to Mrs Norma Hanson . . .'

'That's right. You know her?'

'She works for me. I'm John Goss.'

'Not the PI, by any chance?'

I nodded. I was well known in police circles, even among the uniforms, if only for the publicity that had surrounded the Rainger case. 'Do you mind if I sit in? I'll be interested in seeing the bastard who hit her nailed myself, as you can imagine. I'd like to hear it while it's fresh.'

'I've no objection . . .'

The nurse took us along a corridor, bustling with medical staff, and into a small ward of curtained cubicles. She pulled one of the curtains aside. Norman lay on top of the bed in her blouse and skirt, on a strip of paper that looked as if it had been torn from a gigantic kitchen roll. She was very pale, the large swelling on her temple now turned the usual browny-purple colour and glistening with the medication it had been treated with.

'Oh, John,' she said faintly, 'am I glad to see you . . .'

I squeezed her hand. 'They say you're going to be all right . . .'

'I'm PC Walker, Mrs Hanson,' the young policeman told her. 'Are you up to telling us what happened?'

'I'll try . . .'

She began, in low exhausted tones, to confirm the details I'd had from Valerie Collins. She'd been at the Community Centre, returned home to find the door locked as she'd left it. But once inside she'd heard someone moving about, who'd then attacked her.

'You didn't try to stop him,' I said, 'get in his way?'

'Oh, John, for God's *sake*,' she said in the slow faint voice that was in such startling contrast to the brisk one I'd always been used to, 'the business we're in, I *know* what to do. I got to one side, out of his way, told him just to get out . . .'

'But he struck you just the same?' PC Walker said.

'I was . . . already ducking away when he hit me. That's why he didn't get me full on. He meant to.'

'You think so?'

'I'm positive. He had his arm raised to have another go when Val pushed the door open . . . I think she saved my life.'

Her eyes, suddenly widened by the memory of fear, stared past us unfocused. 'He seemed half crackers . . . I think he'd have gone on hitting me until . . . I think he'd have killed me, or as good as . . .'

A little dramatic embroidery could have been forgiven in anyone who'd just come through such an ordeal, but Norma had a strong, literal mind and had always, in my experience, been able to describe things exactly as they were.

'What made you think that, Mrs Hanson?' The worthy constable worked steadily through his questions, as he'd been trained to do.

'I just *knew*. Why hit me when he didn't have to? I was certainly no threat. Normally they can't wait to get away . . . you know, don't you, John. He was just in a mood to give someone a battering . . . I could *sense* it.'

As long as it was a middle-aged woman living alone, without even a dog to defend her. I clenched my fists in impotent anger. The western world seemed to get sicker by the minute.

'Could you describe him?'

She shook her head. 'Dark clothes. Balaclava. Stocky . . .'

'Height?'

She shook her head again. 'It was all too fast. I was already crouching down. Middle is as near as I can go . . .'

'And when the neighbour came – a Mrs Valerie Collins,' he said, glancing at his notes. 'What happened then?'

'He was going to hit me again, as I said. He just ran off through the back door. And before you ask, nobody made any attempt to see which way he went.'

'Any idea of the weapon, Norma? Any idea at all?'

'It could have been a torch. One of those big, heavy car torches.'

'Perhaps with a rubberised case,' I said, 'which would go with a bruise like that and no broken skin.'

PC Walker put away his notebook. 'Well, we'll do what we can, Mrs Hanson.' He didn't even attempt to inject any optimism into his tone, not with the number of break-ins that took place in this town every night, even though this had been a little more than a routine break-in. 'Do you think you could make a list of the stolen items as soon as possible. If you don't feel well enough to drop it in at the nearest station we'll arrange to pick it up. You'll need a police reference for an insurance claim.'

'He didn't seem to be *holding* anything,' Norma said, even more slowly, as if his words had just prompted this realisation. 'Apart from the torch, or whatever it was . . .'

'Pillowcase at the back door probably,' I said, 'full of whatever he'd decided to take. You might have caught him having a last scout round . . .'

The policeman went, the nurse returned. She told Norma to take it easy for twenty-four hours, to return immediately if the pain increased or she had any memory loss or visual disturbances. I helped her into her coat and then, while she sat with Valerie, I went and brought my car to the passenger pick-up point outside the Casualty entrance.

'You've done a great job,' I told Valerie again. 'You almost certainly saved her from some very disabling injuries.'

'Shall I come and sit with her for an hour? It's no trouble . . .'

'No, you've done enough. I'll look after her now.'

'I daren't think what might have happened if you'd not called when you did, Val.' I could feel Norma's arm trembling through the thin raincoat. 'I'd not have been coming out of Casualty tonight, I'm certain of *that* . . .'

I drove her back to her house, a modest semi in Westbury, the house she'd bought with her ex-husband when they'd first married. Valerie had locked it up when they'd taken Norma to the Infirmary and I now had the keys. The front door was secured with an elderly Yale lock.

I took her inside and sat her in the living-room, then lit the gas-fire on a single radiant and put the kettle on for some tea. From the kitchen I could see into the dining-room, where each drawer in the sideboard had been emptied on to the floor and the contents of the cupboards simply scooped out. The front room seemed more or less untouched, but the bedrooms would look as bad as the dining-room. There was no more depressing sight to come home to, as I knew from bitter experience, especially if mindless vandalism had been added to the disorder of routine burglary.

'I'll be all right now, John. You get off home. I'll give Val a call if I need anything. It must be past midnight . . .'

'No chance, I'm staying the night. I've got my emergency bag in the car.'

'Oh God, I can't do with a man wandering round the house, I might wake up and think Ronnie had come back – it'd be worse than getting hit over the head.'

She was making a brave stab at the Norma I knew and traded insults with, but she looked very relieved all the same. I gave her a cup of tea. 'Look, Norma,' I said gently, 'you've got locks on your doors I could open with a cigarette packet, let alone a credit card. And no intruder alarm. You're not just a soft target, the word that springs to mind is gooey.'

'Oh . . .' she shrugged wearily. 'It's a quiet neighbourhood. There's always someone around – Val on one side, a retired couple on the other . . . there's hardly ever any trouble.'

'People always say that till they get their houses done over. I used to say it myself. Well, in the morning it's going to be the deadlocks, front and back, window-locks and an alarm.'

'Here, hold on, young Goss, these things cost money, and with the lousy pay I have to scrape by on . . .'

'I'll cover it,' I said firmly.

'And take it out of my salary, I suppose . . .'

'A pound a month wouldn't be worth the administration . . .'

'Bonus, then. When it gets to Christmas I suppose I'll have to whistle for it . . .'

'Look, woman, you're going to be sod-all good to the agency if you keep getting clonked on the head – it's known as protecting my assets, assuming you could be considered an asset.'

'I *knew* that was the real reason – not me and the pain but who'll do your bloody typing . . .'

She knew it wasn't true, knew I didn't want her ever to have to go through an experience as frightening as this again, but it was heartening to hear her clawing her way back to her usual withering form, even if her exhaustion meant she couldn't deliver the lines with the old assurance.

She went to bed then and I sat for an hour watching the late programmes in an effort to relax my mind so that I could sleep. But I still didn't sleep, not for a long time, because I couldn't stop going over the events of the night and wondering if the attack on Norma really had been the random incident it had seemed.

'How do you feel?'

'As if I'd been hit on the head with a large, heavy torch. Coffee?'

Few people could make coffee with quite her flair, the aroma had drifted upstairs as I'd been shaving.

'There's juice if you want it. Cornflakes. After that you're on your own. Who was it said getting shot of a husband means never having to do another fry-up.'

'Coffee'll do fine. My appetite doesn't kick in before lunchtime.'

102

I sat down at a tiny kitchen table. Apart from the front room this was the only room that had been left relatively untouched, the intruder assuming presumably there'd be nothing in the cutlery drawers worth up-ending them for, though I knew that burglars often checked fridges for food and wine, so they could prepare themselves a nourishing meal when they got back home.

I crossed to the fridge-freezer. 'Does everything seem in place in here?'

'Yes. I've checked both parts. In fact I had a quick shufti round the rest of the house and I can't really see that *any-thing's* missing. I had about forty pounds in an old biscuit tin and it looks as if it wasn't even opened. My jewellery box is intact as well. Not that what's inside would bring more than a hundred pounds – Ronnie was never one for letting his imagination run riot. I used to leave the paper open on the page about Richard Burton giving Liz Taylor a diamond as big as her head, but the penny never seemed to drop.'

I was pleased to see she was rapidly recovering her form, her voice almost as strong as it was in the office. She'd always been, in her own words, a tough old sod.

'The video's still in place,' I said, a detail I'd noticed last night.

'*And* the portable telly and the CD player . . .'

We moved round the house then, doing a detailed check. Norma felt dizzy if she bent over, and so I packed her pos-sessions as neatly as possible back into the drawers and cup-boards, apart from those in her bedroom, which she modestly insisted on 'seeing to' herself later.

'Well,' she said at last, 'I'll do another check when my head stops being whoozy, but as far as I can see *nothing's* gone.'

We looked at each other. 'I can't get this together,' I said. 'Why turn the place over and not even open the biscuit tin? Have you got *anything* he might possibly think he could turn into cash? Share certificates, a large-value Premium Bond, a building society passbook . . .?'

'I should be so lucky. But I do keep what papers I have got in a big envelope under the mattress in my bedroom. It's still there.'

I thought about this over another cup of coffee, then I began to arrange for the replacement of the locks and the wiring in of an alarm. PIs usually have strong links with firms which install security equipment, to whom they often bring considerable business, and I was able to persuade the one I dealt with most to give the work priority.

'It should be in by mid-afternoon,' I told her, 'and I'll not be going till it's up and running.'

'That's all I need — you under my feet *and* the biggest headache I've had since Ronnie won seventy-eight pounds fifty on the pools.'

'I knew you'd be pleased.'

And I knew she *was* pleased, despite the strong independent spirit she'd developed since Ronnie had left her, that she was just glad there was a man around the place until she'd begun to come to terms with the most frightening experience of her life, even though in a week or two she'd be saying it didn't begin to compare with the possibility that she might come home one night and find Ronnie sitting on the doorstep with his wordly goods in three Morrisons' carrier bags.

I spent the next half-hour on the phone advising the solicitors I did routine work for I'd not be available this morning and rearranging any appointments I had in my diary. I made Norma sit quietly with her morning paper, but I could sense her eyes resting anxiously on me as I rejigged the day's work, as if she were to blame for our time being a write-off.

Two men from the security firm arrived at ten-thirty, Bruce Fenlon called at eleven.

'Norma, love, how are you? I picked up the details this morning . . .'

'I'll live, Bruce,' she said, her old persona almost completely intact now.

'By sheer good luck,' I said angrily. 'Christ, Bruce, is battering people you happen to be robbing standard practice these days?'

'Not that I seem to have been actually robbed,' Norma added.

'He wasn't *tall*, this guy, Norma?' Fenlon said.

'She shook her head. 'Middling, but I can't be sure. But not tall.'

'And it was definitely a balaclava? Not a baseball cap, back to front?'

'Definitely a balaclava . . . that's the one thing I'm sure of. So's Valerie . . . that's the woman next door who came in in the nick of time, thank God.'

'The artist with the baseball cap works the Beech Hill area. He specialises in beating up very frail old women who keep eight pounds in a vase on the mantelpiece. It had his stamp. God, don't say we've got another one . . .'

He flushed, and I sensed the anger that even hardened policemen couldn't contain when faced with violence against the vulnerably innocent – the elderly and the very young.

'But you say nothing's been stolen?'

'Nothing obvious,' Norma said, 'and believe me, anything that isn't obvious isn't worth taking.'

Fenlon looked at me. 'What's the point – they don't break in just to knock someone about; that's an optional extra.'

'I've given it a lot of thought,' I said slowly, 'and I'm just beginning to wonder if someone's bearing a grudge. I've helped to get quite a few bad lots the sack, and I've given evidence in court several times. I've been told "You're dead"

more than once. I've even seen it mouthed from the dock.
They tend to watch a lot of television.'

Fenlon shrugged. 'We get all that round the clock, John. It
never comes to anything – they've got short memories. Most
of them drink and shoot up so much their brains are fried
anyway. We had a guy last week who couldn't remember
which girlfriend he was supposed to be living with, and I'm
not joking.'

'I accept that, but in any case they don't really want to try
anything on with the police, not once they're back in the
streets. But I'm a private man and I haven't got your kind of
protection . . .'

'Am I missing something here,' Norma said. 'I thought it
was me who got a headful of long-life batteries.'

'That's the point, Norma, if anything happened to you the
agency would go into a nosedive. We made a joke of it last
night, but it made me think all the same . . .'

'Oh, come on, John, you're the brains in the business.
You'd be able to find someone else and train them up. You'd
have a thin time for a few months and then . . .'

'What if putting you out of action was the first step? What
if we had a right vicious little toerag here who decided to do
it the slow way – first injuring you, then perhaps screwing up
my reputation in some way, then finally going for
me.'

'You can't really believe that, John,' Fenlon said, with a
reassuring glance at Norma. 'The sort of garbage we deal
with just don't think that way, it needs brain cells. It's a lot
more likely the guy hadn't even started picking out the things
he wanted to take . . .'

'He'd already gone through the house . . .'

'They sometimes do just that. See exactly what there is and
then decide what's worth taking.'

'Nothing in my case, by the look of it,' Norma said. 'I think I'll cancel my contents insurance.'

But her face had taken on the pallor it had had last night at the idea there might be someone out there intent on damaging both of us.

'I'm sorry, Norma,' I said, putting a hand on her shoulder, 'I really didn't mean to upset you. I think Bruce is probably right. I'm just spelling out the possibilities because I want you to go very, very carefully for the next few weeks. Make sure the deadlocks are always fastened and keep the alarm on even when you're in the house – you'll soon learn how not to trigger it off by mistake. Always tell Val your movements and if you want me around, any time at all, just pick up the phone . . .'

'Don't you think I see more than enough of you at the office?'

I didn't spell out any other possibilities. I really didn't want to scare her, though I did want her to take her own safety very seriously. But I was still wondering if there might be one further possibility for the attack, though it seemed if anything even less credible than the one I'd just outlined.

And it wouldn't have occurred to me, had I not had a phone call in which someone had simply put down the phone without speaking. Which could have meant that someone had hit a wrong key. Or that someone had wanted to get an exact fix on where I was last night.

Seven

'A favour, Bruce. I need an address.' I gave him the number of Marsh's Escort.

'You'll be in the George this evening? I'll have it then.'

Really professional PI work is virtually impossible without reliable contacts in the police force, which is why so many ex-policemen become investigators. I wasn't an ex-policeman, but to men like Fenlon and a few others I had credentials almost as good.

That evening, when he'd taken his first mouthful of beer and inhaled deeply from his first cigarette, he said: 'That number you gave me, it's a bit odd. Unless there's some change in the pipeline at the DVLA, it's registered to Blair Motors themselves.'

I thought about this. 'I suppose it *could* mean they'd used it as a demonstrator model for a few months and then sold it cheaply to the guy, and the paperwork's still in the system.'

'Could be a hire-car, of course. Don't Blair's have a hire department?'

'Nice one, Bruce! I'd not thought of that. That's *got* to be the answer . . .'

He smiled. 'And that solves all your problems?'

'I have an uneasy feeling the problems are just beginning.'

'Who drives it, anyway?'

'David Marsh. Brother of the late Simon Marsh. I met him a couple of nights ago at Laura's, she'd invited me round for drinks. He's a stroppy bastard. I was hardly through the door before he starts giving me a bollocking about Zephyr being slow to divi up.'

'What business is it of his?'

'That's what I can't help asking myself. To be fair, he's probably doing his best to sort things out for her, but the king-size attitude problem doesn't help. Anyway, I noticed his car had a Blair Motors' tag on it, and it seemed odd because he reckons he lives and works out of Leicester. But if he's *renting* it seems odder still.'

He was smiling again. 'If it's not broke trust Goss to try and fix it. This case has just been too bloody tame for you, hasn't it, an affront to your professional pride. Look, man, PIs *pray* for work from Snee – it's invariably a piece of piss, and he pays on the knocker. How about the *obvious* explanation, for Christ's sake: the guy's own car goes on the blink while he's in the area and so they lend him a motor while they're fixing his. It happens all the time.'

I gave him a faintly sheepish grin. 'You're almost certainly right. But we are talking a million sovs here, and suddenly the brother-in-law crawls out of the woodwork, is either separated or divorced and seems a bloody sight more anxious about the insurers paying up than she does.'

'I'd probably be making the same sort of noises for *my* sister-in-law,' he said reflectively. 'And so would you, if you had one.'

I knew I was being more than marginally paranoid about Marsh, which was why my instincts had been to bounce my suspicions off Fenlon's robust sense.

'He could be weaselling his way into diverting some of the money in his own direction,' I said hopefully.

110

'I should think there's a strong possibility,' he said. 'Nobody knows better than you what people can be like when they hear the rustle of serious folding. But she's not a kid and she should be able to see it coming.'

'That's part of the trouble. She's still in shock and it puts her at risk. On top of that, she's a bit above money – I mean, she's never going to be the kind of millionaire who has the FT Index pinned up on the lavatory door. She's pleased about the loot, and the freedom it'll give her, and she's clever, but it's blue-stocking clever . . . you know? I think she might be too trusting, and if Marsh starts feeding her a line about this fantastic off-shore investment that'll yield twenty-five per cent nett . . . well, do I need to spell it out?'

'Look, John, if the guy gets her to invest the lot in a hole in the ground there's absolutely nothing you can do about it. And if she happened to be funny-looking and read Mills and Boon and bred budgies as a hobby, you'd not be able to wait to send the last report in.'

He was right on every count, and I bought my round and we began to talk of other things.

'Blair Motors – how may I help you?'

'Hire department, please.'

'Putting you through . . .'

'Hello – Rentals . . .'

'Perhaps you can help me,' I said. 'My name's Marsh. I have one of your cars on hire and I'm not quite sure when it's due back. Would you check for me, please.'

I gave her the model and the number, heard the muffled clicking of VDU keys. 'There must be some mistake,' the woman at the other end said finally. 'The vehicle's on long-term rental, with seven days' notice required to cancel. And I have the hiree as *Mrs* Marsh.'

'Oh, of course,' I said, thinking quickly. 'She's not at home at the moment and I'm just sorting things out. We're moving away from the area in a few weeks – that's why she put off buying a new car.'

'I see,' she said, with polite indifference. 'Well, we'll need seven days' clear notice to cease the agreement, Mr Marsh, and each week's rental to be paid in advance, of course, as arranged.'

'Of course,' I said. 'Thanks for your help. Just one other thing – how long have we had it now?'

'Since – the twenty-eighth August . . .'

I put my car phone on its stand and sat staring through the window. It seemed I couldn't let go. I knew Fenlon was right – it was *her* money, *her* brother-in-law and *her* life; yet I'd not been able to stop myself checking out that motor. It was the way I was. But by the time I'd lost the struggle against leaving well alone, I was totally sincere in hoping I'd be told what I was almost certain I was going to be told – that Marsh had hired the car for a couple of days while his own was off the road. With my better feelings more or less to the front, I *wanted* him to be a caring brother-in-law, whose abrupt manner concealed an urge to do his best for the wife of the brother he'd been so close to. I wanted Laura taken care of, even though I still felt I'd be the best person to do the care-taking. The fact that I fancied her was neither here nor there, because it meant exactly that – that I fancied her and not her money.

I think it was the first time in the Laura Marsh case that I seemed to detect a true warning note – a sound as sinister as a soft regular drumbeat. Was David Marsh not just wifeless but also jobless? Unable even to afford his own car, was he cadging the use of one from Laura? And if so, what else was he hoping to cadge? There was suddenly a faint desperation in the way I sought to put some other, more innocent construction on it.

Without success.

'Hello, Mr Snee. John Goss reporting in . . .'

'Good man. Nothing new, I take it?'

'No change. She goes for walks, goes shopping, gardens. She had one visitor, who turned out to be her brother-in-law.'

'Yes, yes . . .' he said indifferently, not even wanting to know how I knew it was her brother-in-law, though I'd have had an answer in place had he asked. 'Now this is the form, Goss; keep your surveillance going for another fortnight and then I'll write towards the end of October to say I can approve her claim for payment within a month. Once she knows it's on the way another month won't seem too long to wait, it never does. In fact I dare say I could stretch it to six weeks . . .'

'My PA will put the formal report in the post today,' I told him. 'Thanks again for the assignment. If I can be of any help in the future . . .'

'I'll certainly bear you in mind, Goss. You work very efficiently. I've always got time for a good man.'

I put the phone down on the objectionable little sod, then rang Laura. 'It should all be over in about a fortnight, Laura, my investigation, but that must be strictly *entre nous*, of course . . .'

'Oh dear,' she said, in her small voice. 'I *shall* miss you being around. It was such a comfort to know there was a strong man keeping an eye on me, even if it *was* for that nasty old insurance company.'

'I'll . . . miss our walks.'

What I meant was that I'd miss her, miss the way she looked in the parka against glittering water, her hair sometimes loose, sometimes taken back, miss the fleeting smiles and the grave, intelligent eyes.

'You'll keep in touch?'

'Of course . . .'

'It's been a great help to be able to talk things over with someone . . . outside the family . . .'

The hesitation was slight, but it was there. And 'the family' had to be Marsh. Her mother was dead, she wasn't close to her father, she was an only child. I wondered if Marsh was getting oppressive, was trying to organise her as forcefully as he'd tried to organise me.

'As I said, any time you want to talk things over . . .'

'Thank you, John.'

'I was wondering, now that the end's in sight, if I could ask you out for that dinner we talked about up on the moors.'

'Name any evening,' she said, and I could sense her smiling, 'and I'm sure to be free . . .'

The vagrants did rather well the following Friday as I made my way past the circular garden to the multi-storey car park. My old friend had been missing for a few days, but was now back, like a wild duck instinctively homing in on the lake that had been its breeding ground. The days were cooler now and he wore an ancient raincoat of a cut and material I associated dimly with the coats my father had worn in my Seventies boyhood.

'Thanks, boss,' he said, as I handed him a pound coin. I was aware of the handful of other vagrants looking on enviously, as they always did. Normally, I ignored it, because I couldn't afford to hand money to them all on an almost daily basis, and it was this man I was hoping to reclaim, a goal that seemed increasingly unlikely of achievement. But tonight my pocket jingled with pound coins to use as minor tips at the restaurant; I found myself handing out the money to them. Maybe I wanted them to have some kind of a buzz of their own. I was taking Laura to dinner, and they were never going to know what it was like to stand beneath a shower and put on fresh clothes and call for an attractive woman.

'You won the Pools, boss?'

'I haven't seen you for a day or two. Where've you been?'

'I move around a fair amount.'

I detected a faint note of pride in an initiative that still kept him wandering around the city's districts on obscure errands, perhaps to lay his head in a derelict building with a different view, to warm his hands at a better blaze, to hang about the back doors of restaurants that provided more exotic scraps. The other vagrants simply sat, rarely moving anywhere, except to the benefits office. They were like trees already dead, but which in spring continued to put out a few withered leaves.

'Have you seen your pal yet?'

'Pal?'

I looked at him with a sigh. Norma's word-processor had an in-built memory, which would retain everything she'd typed until it was powered down at the end of the day, and it seemed this man's memory was cleared with the same total despatch the moment he settled down to sleep. I wondered what I should do about him. He was still in good shape, as good shape as the man in Huddersfield who'd hanged himself. Hurrying along one of the city streets a couple of days ago, I'd seen men dismantling scaffolding from buildings that had been sand-blasted, and I'd decided to return, during the next gap in my schedule, to see if any of them knew the whereabouts of the man called Suss, but when I finally got back, the planks, the rods and the men were all gone.

I did a lot of work for the electrical-goods and flat-pack

warehouses, where bent employees were forever chancing their arm about removing complete stereo systems on the drip. I knew just about every warehouse manager in town. I wondered if I could get one of them to find labouring work for a strong-looking man, if I could get him cleaned up and found accommodation. I wondered if I was in danger of doing the man more harm than good; he always seemed content enough, as content anyhow as the average domestic animal.

But if he could have held a coherent thought down, could still project his mind forward, surely he'd not want to end up like the rest whom, in any case, he instinctively kept a slight distance from. Grime and stubble had aged him, but it was simply like make-up, the Huddersfield man had looked old too, but I'd known him to be barely forty. How long would this man have before pneumonia carried him off? Five years? Ten? Against the thirty or forty he could expect if he were on a proper diet, living clean and warm, doing work that would give him back his self-respect, perhaps to the point where he could return to the people he'd broken from – wife, mother, brother . . .

I determined to make a start. I'd get in touch with the caring agencies, ring my contacts in the warehouse business, take advice.

'See you soon,' I said.

'Take care, boss . . .'

'Come in, John . . .'

She wore a dark-green dress this time, of fine jersey wool, with a rounded neckline and long sleeves. She'd drawn her hair back, and when she turned to take me in I saw it had been arranged into one of those complex and attractive braids I often saw young television actresses wearing. The time and care she'd taken with her appearance was like a delicate compliment.

We stood smiling at each other among the heavy pieces of hall furniture and the strange paintings with their twisted trees and dramatic skies.

'I thought you'd like a drink before we went.'

'That would be nice.'

She led me into the large, silent drawing-room, with its books and its dark surfaces and its dimly glowing table lamps.

'G and T?' she said, but she knew my preference and had the Gordon's and the Schweppes ready and waiting. 'May I ask where I'm being taken?'

'The Ash Tree. Not far from Harrogate. Do you know it?'

She shook her head. 'I don't know any of the restaurants up here,' she said simply. 'We never went out.'

They'd been here two years; it was a long time not to have had a night out; she'd spent such a lot of time alone. Yet she never seemed lonely. Sad, unhappy, but not somehow lonely. It was probably her inner resources.

'Has . . . David gone back to Leicester now?'

'I suppose so. I never really know where he is, he moves around such a lot.' She sipped her vodka. 'He'll suddenly show up, out of the blue. That's how it happened the night you met him. I didn't think you'd mind him being here.'

'Quite the reverse,' I said, wondering if my insincerity sounded as obvious to her as it did to me. But I couldn't bring myself to believe he'd shown up on the spur of the moment. I knew about the hired Escort now, and I was as certain the meeting had somehow been contrived as I was that the hire of the Escort was being paid for by Laura.

I said, 'David must have been a great help when Simon had his accident . . .'

'I couldn't have coped without him.' Her eyes became

sombre. 'They were so close. There was hardly two years between them.'

'Did David never think of moving up here too? If he's always on the road I don't suppose it would matter too much where he lived.'

She shrugged. 'Oh, I think he considered it at one time, but . . . with most of his friends and family down there . . .'

'Oh, I *see*. He's got children. I believe he mentioned he was divorced, but I don't think he said anything about a family.'

'He's . . . separated,' she said, with something of the reluctance of Marsh himself when I'd asked casual-seeming questions about his private life. 'He may divorce eventually. There . . . aren't any children. By family I mean his parents – they're still alive . . . Can I freshen your drink?'

She gave me a warm smile, reached attentively for the bottle. Unencoded, those final words meant she didn't want to answer any more questions about Marsh. She sensed that my politeness concealed a genuine curiosity, because women were rarely fooled by what seemed to be small talk.

'I really think we should be going,' I said. 'There's a drive of half an hour or so . . .'

We went back to the hall and, as she moved about switching on certain lamps to make the house appear occupied when we'd gone, I wondered why they were both so cagey about discussing his background. It wasn't as if she was secretive by nature, she'd told me plenty about her own – the shadowy father, the arty mother, the smouldering cardy, the parties.

But Marsh seemed to be off limits.

She draped a dark cashmere shawl over her shoulders, which she'd decided would be all the protection she'd need for the short time we'd be out in the cool September air. Her lips were touched with an almost brownish lipstick, her

eyelids tinted faintly in green. The understatement was perfect for her smooth marble-white skin. She released the thin
whine of the intruder alarm and stood for a moment, smiling
her faint smile, gravely and openly basking in my unconcealed admiration.

I'd forgotten to turn off my car radio; it was playing on a
low volume on the Classic FM station. I made to silence it,
but she said: 'I really don't mind. It's Sibelius, isn't it – *The
Swan of Tuonela*.'

And so I let that sad elegiac music play on as I drove out
along silent country roads towards Harrogate.'

'This is very kind of you, John,' she said once, 'I've been
looking forward to it all day . . .'

She laid her cool hand over mine where it rested on the
wheel, then abruptly withdrew it, as if she'd touched a car
door handle that had built up static. She'd held my hand or
arm before, once or twice, but those had been simple friendly
gestures. I glanced at her, but she was gazing now at the
dense woodland that spooled rapidly past her window, flaring
briefly into light and colour in the sweep of the car's
headlamps.

I wondered if she too shared something of my ambivalence, and found coping with it almost as hard. I was certain
she knew I fancied her, fancied her mind, it sometimes
seemed, almost as much as her body. At the same time, no
one I'd ever known had brought out such an overwhelming
urge in me to comfort and protect. My mind seemed to slip
uneasily from one mode to the other – the sad woman's self-
appointed protector looking on with distaste at the eager
male who wanted to take her clothes off.

Could she be sharing something of the same confusion?
Grieving for the man she'd loved, but craving physical presence – kisses, stroked hair, a hand fondling a breast? He'd

been dead some time now, and how much longer had it been, if he'd been having an affair with Madge, since he'd actually made love to Laura?

But the guilt we shared, if that's what it was, seemed to evaporate in the cheerful atmosphere of the restaurant bar, among the sounds of laughter and rattling ice and soft piano music, to become suspended by our mutual urge to spend a couple of hours having an uncomplicated good time.

'Have you decided where you'd like to live yet?' I said.

She shook her head. 'I can't even decide whether to go north or south.'

'The north isn't as crowded,' I said. 'And it's cheaper. I know the Dales quite well. Would you like to look round the area some Sunday? I'm sure we could find something suitably remote for you to consider.'

'Are you sure it wouldn't be any trouble?'

'I'd enjoy it. I've got a certain amount of weekend work for the next fortnight, but after that, if we could find a nice day . . .'

'A nice Keatsy sort of day . . .'

'That's right – one of those really close bosom-friends of the maturing sun . . .'

The Ash Tree was well known for its eclectic cuisine – I'd brought her in the hope that some dish or other would tempt her into eating a substantial meal – I knew from her supermarket trips how effectively her grief had killed her appetite.

But she continued to eat sparingly, and I wondered if food was of little interest to her, possibly due to a metabolism that required only small amounts. She had a sliver of melon and then a small piece of ungarnished veal with an equally small portion of broccoli. She wanted nothing else then except coffee. She drank normally though, and her memory for wine was as formidable as it was for random detail. I had ordered simply by number, and the bottle came shrouded in a napkin and the label shown only to me, but one sniff and one sip and she was able to pin down the Bordeaux to its château and almost to its year.

She seemed to make up for her relative indifference to food by the intense pleasure she took in the restaurant's ambience. Her real hunger appeared to be for swagged velvet and fresh flowers and candles, for the discreet popping of corks, the jingle of cutlery and the hum of conversation. The way she seemed almost to devour the atmosphere of people enjoying life made me ask: 'Do you *really* want to live in total isolation?'

She smiled, nodded. 'I shall have to buy a very big freezer, of course, and I'd want access to the usual services. But I do need space and silence.'

'*Need* as opposed to like?'

'Need,' she said firmly. 'I have to be able to think very hard without distraction.'

'For that novel?'

'You see, I want to write the sort of book that when the tide comes in and sweeps all the others away will still be left, like those limpets that seem to become part of a rock. And that sort of book will need a lot of me and I will need a lot of privacy.'

There was a decisiveness in her voice I'd not heard before. I was seeing a Laura of sudden focus instead of the sad and drifting Laura I'd thought I was beginning to know. I wondered why she demanded such perfect conditions to write this book that wouldn't be washed away by the ebb tide. Other women seemed able to juggle their writing careers around the demands of children, husbands and part-time jobs.

Perhaps she'd made the demands of Simon's career an excuse for attempting little beyond the pieces she did for regional magazines. And perhaps his death, yielding, as it had done, sufficient money to give her complete independence, had brought guilt into the equation, the urge to channel her creative impulse, to give it her very best shot, to produce something worthy of the small fortune his far-sightedness had provided. Perhaps it was to be Simon's memorial.

'I wish you every success,' I said. 'Let's see if we can't find the sort of house that's guaranteed to be totally cut off from Christmas to Easter.'

'Not so cut off that friends hesitate to call . . .'

Our eyes met across candle flame, and I wondered if I would be regarded as one of the friends who could be relied on not to hesitate to call; if I might one day be invited for the weekend. I could see it, that rambling, converted farmhouse with rooms at slightly differing levels, and views over misty water to blue-tinted hills. I could see her late at night wearing a long white cotton night-dress, her hair in a single plait, carrying a candle in a pottery holder; before the protector gave a snarl of disgust, and I was back in the mode of caring guardian who took genuine pleasure in helping a decent woman who'd had a bad time to enjoy life a little.

I was still in caring mode as we began the drive back. David Marsh had been at the back of my mind most of the evening. He'd been running around for some considerable time now in a car hired in Laura's name, and the more I reluctantly mulled it over the more it seemed that the hire car could be the thin end of some sinister wedge. I was certain he'd know the exact number of the final insurance pay-out, after the closeness the three had always shared.

I'd wanted to give her some kind of warning, but not during dinner. Now seemed the right time, as I drove along silent roads, and we were relaxed and at ease with each other. The Classic FM station was playing an obscure, to me, piece by Boëllmann, that she could inevitably name, tell me the suite it was from and the year it had been composed. I suspected the organ was one of her favourite instruments – it seemed to go with her urge for isolation and reflection and subdued backgrounds. When the piece ended I said: 'I want to raise a delicate matter, Laura, and you may think it's none of my business, and if you do just say so.'

We glanced at each other in the faint backwash of light from the car's headlamps.

'Go ahead, John,' she said quietly.

'To be blunt, you're going to be a wealthy woman. And when you become wealthy you often find people trying to take advantage of you. I'm simply asking you to be careful. You're very intelligent, but your life's been turned upside down, and when you're in that state it's often difficult to tell that people have ulterior motives, however kind they seem to be.'

She was silent for the time it took the car to cover a quarter of a mile. 'I . . . hadn't really thought about it, to be honest. I know it's an awful lot, but . . . but it means so little by the side of losing Simon. It's kind of you to think of it, but I hardly know anyone in this area, and when I move I shan't know a soul. They'll not have a clue about the money.'

'You'd be amazed how quickly they can find out. A man once hired me to check on his daughter's new boyfriend. This man was wealthy, but there was no indication his daughter would ever be given much beyond a private education and a comfortable life-style while she lived at home. But at twenty-one the girl came into a considerable inheritance from a great-aunt, which no one outside the family should have known about. But the new boyfriend had got it together. He himself was well-connected, well-spoken, drove a Porsche, had a good job . . . and was so deeply in debt that marrying money was his only real option.'

'What happened?'

I smiled wryly, hoping she wasn't getting so absorbed in the detail she was missing the point.

'Oh, she married him. She told the father to get lost. It lasted eighteen months, by which time a good third of the inheritance had gone in settling his gambling debts. She'd have settled them till she was penniless, except that she found out he was also spending a good deal of her money on a mistress.'

'How did she find out about the mistress?'

It was a good question, the sort I doubted if anyone but she would have thought to ask. 'Because her father hired me again. *He* was suspicious, not the daughter. He was right, of course. The mistress pre-dated the marriage. Anyway, the rich girl divorced the husband, but she never spoke to her father again for interfering. She also came to my office and told me I had the mentality of a sewer rat.'

'Poor John – shoot the messenger . . . and the real sewer rat was the husband . . .'

'He just happened to be a sewer rat she couldn't stop being in love with.'

We fell silent again, as the open country roads gave way to ribbon development, and then we were driving down into the dark mass and the flickering necklaces of street-lamps of the city sprawl.

I said: 'All I'm trying to say is don't be too trusting, not even with the people who . . . might seem close to you.'

'Not even you?' she said at last, her voice so low as to be almost inaudible.

'Only trust me,' I said, 'until I ask you if you could lend me a couple of thousand till the end of the quarter.'

I swung on to the ring road and we didn't speak again until we were outside her house. I wondered if her silence meant I'd got through to her. I'd gone as far as I decently could. She seemed to be including me in the people close to her, but I'd made it crystal clear I had no interest in her money. It only really left David Marsh.

How much did it cost to rent a modest motor – twelve, fifteen sovs a day? Say a hundred a week. About five hundred already. Had she not had money in the pipeline she couldn't have paid for it, because Simon's business had already been rocky. And if Marsh was paying for it why was it in her name? But he'd not be paying for it.

'You're welcome to come in,' she said. 'Coffee . . . a nightcap . . .'

'I'd . . . better not,' I said. 'Heavy day tomorrow. Thanks all the same.'

It wasn't true. I didn't have heavy days. I ran on nervous energy and I rarely needed more than six hours sleep. I didn't go in because when I went in with a woman it had usually been tacitly established that I'd be staying the night. I knew with her this was out of the question, and I wasn't keen to tantalise myself by what I'd be missing if I simply sat with her for half an hour, looking at her sleek hair in the lamplight and listening to her soft voice. Her desirability had steadily increased from the moment she'd opened the door to me in the jersey-wool dress.

'Thank you,' she almost whispered. 'Thank you so much for the pleasure of your company . . .'

She looked straight ahead, her profile as sharp and linear as the image on a cameo brooch against the yellow light of street-lamps. I had never seen her more troubled, she seemed unhappy almost to the point of desperation as she gazed down the silent road.

I touched her arm. 'Laura . . .'

She turned back to me, forced a thin, painful smile. 'It was a lovely evening.'

'I hate to see you so upset. Is it . . .?'

She nodded. 'The usual. I'm sorry. It's not fair on you . . .'

She suddenly leaned over and kissed me on the cheek, rapidly but almost passionately. 'Good night, John. Ring me, won't you, soon . . .'

We both got out and I went with her as far as the ornamental iron gate, then watched her walk down the paved drive, the clipping of her heels the only real sound in the midnight silence; watched her pass along the front of the house, with its pattern of lights that were meant to simulate occupation.

Except that there was one light too many. I felt the short hairs prickling on my neck.

'Laura!' I hissed.

I ran down the drive on the soles of my feet. She stood at the front door, latchkey about to be inserted. She stared back at me, eyes wide with shock. 'There's a light in the study,' I said, in a low voice. 'It wasn't on when we left . . .'

There was consternation in her eyes now and the hand that held the key was shaking. But then she said: 'Yes, it *was* John. It's one of the ones I leave on!'

Fear had given her voice a sudden high-pitched edge.

'No, it *wasn't*, Laura. Believe me . . .'

'I'm *sure* I switched it on!'

I put a finger to my lips; she was speaking too loudly. There was no question of my being wrong, I had the trained investigator's memory, endlessly honed by the detailed scrutiny I gave to so many buildings after nightfall. I could no sooner stop it spilling over into private life than I could stop my hair growing. She'd only *thought* she'd done it.

I said: 'I'll go first . . .'

126

'John, I'm *positive*!' She seemed unable to contain the almost hysterical shrillness.

But she let me take the keys from her. I opened the door slowly; the alarm immediately began to sound its preliminary warning tone. I glanced at her, puzzled. If anyone *had* broken in, the alarm, after about thirty seconds, would have activated the deafening inside hooter and the clanging outside bell, unless it could have been turned off at the control box. The only key holders to the box would, in theory, be Laura and probably a trusted neighbour. But if someone had broken in and managed to neutralise the box there should now have been no sound at all.

I said: 'Where do you turn it off?'

'The kitchen – just inside the pantry door. Turn it to the vertical . . .'

I moved cautiously through, located the box, turned off the warning tone with the second key on her ring. I came back, shaking my head. 'Strange. Everything seems in order.' I thought for a few seconds. 'I don't suppose you've got one of those mechanisms in the study that turns the lights on and off in a random sequence, to give an impression of people moving about?'

Her body sagged against the drawing-room door.

'Of *course*!' she said, her voice almost gasping in relief. 'It must have been in the off mode when I switched it on. Oh, *John*, don't give me *shocks* like that . . .'

'I'm sorry, Laura, really . . . But a woman on her own, in a quiet road . . .'

I pushed doors open as I spoke, glancing into the drawing-room and the dining-room and the study itself, which contained a solid mahogany desk and chair, a fax, an answerphone and a personal computer and printer.

'Shall I glance round upstairs? Just to be on the safe side.'

'No!' she said, the shrill note suddenly back in her voice. Then she closed her eyes, put a hand to her forehead and said in a more normal tone: 'Please don't go to any more trouble, John, everything's obviously in order. Thanks for being so vigilant . . .'

But for a moment her face darkened with an emotion difficult to be sure about, though it looked suspiciously like anger. Perhaps she was just very tired, the exhaustion that lingered after the pain of a bereavement, intensified by the unusual stimulation of a night out.

I didn't persist. I would have done, but when I'd glanced around the study I'd looked up at the ceiling fitting. It was an ordinary light bulb set in a wide, rather shallow shade, designed to spread as much light as possible over the work area. The type of mechanism that would have lit the bulb in a random manner would have been a timing device that is inserted into the cable's socket between the socket and the bulb. There was no timer there, the bulb's bayonet fitting was engaged directly with the socket. Nor was there any device wired into the light switch itself, nor into any of the wall sockets.

There was someone in this house.

That person was obviously upstairs, and almost certainly in the loft. The study light had been off when we left, was on when we returned. It could only have been turned on by human hand. Whoever was upstairs had either been in the house all night, or, if he, or she, had come in during our absence, must have had a key to turn off the intruder alarm, then reset it for Laura's return.

'Good-night, Laura,' I said quietly, touching her briefly on the arm. 'If you ever need me for anything, anything at all, just give me a ring.' I handed her a card. 'Car phone, office phone, house phone. I'll nearly always be available on one of those three. Don't forget . . . any time . . . day or night . . .'

'Good-night, John,' she almost whispered. 'I'm sure I'll be all right now.'

I wondered if she sensed I'd picked up on the third presence. My hands seemed to tingle with the urge to put my arms round her, tell her I could sort it out, whatever it was, all she needed to do was confide in me.

I opened the door. Our eyes met briefly. Her lower lip was trembling. Perhaps I should have gone ahead and put my arms round her.

I got in my car, in half a mind to sit in guard on the house, all night if necessary. But I didn't honestly believe she was in any danger. Not physical, at least. Mental, almost certainly. I'd be no wiser about Laura Marsh if I stayed here till daybreak.

I started the car, drove off slowly. I'd learn nothing by standing guard, but there was one useful check I could make before going home. Tanglewood Lane ran past Laura's house from the distant main road to the reservoirs – the only car on it at this time of night was mine. All the houses in this affluent area had sufficient garage and parking space to keep family cars on their own premises. In Laura's case, there was a single garage at the end of the paved drive that curved down from the gate and ran along the front of the house, and at the side of the garage a substantial carport. Laura's car would be in the garage; the carport was deserted. I didn't believe whoever was in the house had come on foot, it wasn't a convenient house for pedestrians, as Laura had pointed out.

From Tanglewood Lane, three small cul-de-sac drives ran off to the right, as you approached from the main road, two of them curving so that their ends were out of sight. Slowly, I drove along each of them, and in the last, one of the two that curved, I found the car I was looking for, at the extreme end,

parked out of reach of lamplight, beneath the overhanging
trees of a nearby garden. It was, as I'd known it would be, the
hired Escort of David Marsh.

Eight

I slept badly that night, unable to get her trembling lips and her heavy eyes out of my mind. She was older than me, yet she always seemed younger, as vulnerable people so often did, younger and more naïve, trying to handle loss and grief and all the administrative details of a new life at the same time as she tried to cope with . . . what?

I knew now she was sending out near-frantic signals, felt certain it was one of the reasons she'd instinctively sought my friendship. Marsh had some kind of hold over her. He had keys to her house, could come and go as he pleased, drove a car rented in her name, had kicked my backside to hurry the Zephyr payment along.

What could that hold be? In my lengthy experience of what went on underneath large flat stones, I'd found it tended to involve one of three types of leverage, occasionally a combination of two. It could be the sort of sexual domination the gambler had held over the wealthy young woman, it could be some form of blackmail, or it could be conscience.

It took me some time to get my mind round the first, but I had to accept the closeness the Marsh brothers and Laura had always shared. They'd even gone on holiday together. Painful as it was even to consider it, I wondered if, on one of those holidays, when Simon had been temporarily absent,

David had contrived to seduce her, had become so attractive to her, such an addiction, that she'd been unable to kick the habit. I could accept that it had left her love for Simon unaffected, that love itself might have had nothing to do with it. These things happened all the time, real life was normally a lot messier than television.

I thought about blackmail. I'd have preferred it to be blackmail – it was something I felt able to accept and handle; I'd seen quite a few blackmailers down the road. But it seemed a non-starter. I'd have thought the only blackmail he could have attempted would have been to threaten to expose their affair to Simon, when Simon was alive, but when Simon was alive there'd have been no money for him to blackmail Laura about.

Conscience? Had David Marsh once lent his brother money, perhaps start-up money for the business, a substantial sum maybe, when David himself was doing well? And perhaps he was doing well no longer, had become a victim of the endless redundancies, and was calling in his marker, perhaps not just wanting his loan back but more besides, to set up his own business, on the principle that *he'd* not demurred when *they'd* needed the ante.

That could be a flyer. It went with the hire-car and the apparent lack of a firm base. It wasn't as easy to sort out as blackmail, but I liked it a whole lot better than the Svengali scenario, which usually wasn't possible to sort out at all and tended to end up with words like sewer rat flying around.

I wondered what he'd consider a reasonable loan to be in the Nineties – a hundred thousand, two, a quarter of a million?

There was one other aspect to the business of Marsh having access to Laura's house. I still had the break-in at Norma's very much to the front of my mind. I couldn't forget the phone call at my own house, when the caller's phone had been silently replaced. What if someone *had* been checking to make sure I was in? Could it possibly have been David Marsh? If I was in my own house I couldn't be out checking on anyone's movements, especially Laura's, during which time I might by chance have spotted Marsh or his car, and wondered what he was up to. But if I was at home he'd have a clear field.

To do what? Stage a phoney burglary at Norma's as a cover to disable her so badly she'd be unable to return to work for months, if ever? Which would mean I'd have to work day and night to keep my agency on an even keel. Which would mean my attention would be distracted not only from Laura but from a brother-in-law who might just be wanting to extract a slice of her fortune for himself.

I wondered if any of that could be possible. It was the man's vaguely menacing attitude I couldn't forget. He'd tried to browbeat me within the first five minutes, had probably only laid off because he'd detected a note of warning in my polite disclaimers, could see I wasn't the type it was wise to push too far. But was he trying to bully *her* and finding it a much easier proposition, because she'd had her defences breached by the confusion of grief, by having no one in her corner, by having that sort of blue-stocking vagueness about money itself? And he needed me out of the way. In case I warned her about him. Or – more likely from where he was sitting – in case I fancied a slice of the Zephyr action for myself.

I finally abandoned sleep at six, showered, dressed, drank instant. If only she'd confide in me. She'd been very near the limit of her self-control. She'd known he was there, that he'd be wanting answers, wouldn't let it drop till he got them. I was certain that was how it would be.

I wondered why she felt she couldn't talk to me about it. She trusted me, knew I couldn't give a toss about her money. Was it because she felt it was all too personal, too family, too much to do with the special relationship the three of them had had? Or was it because the problem had seemed so intractable, whether she confided in me or not, that there seemed no point in talking about it? That was probably nearer the truth.

I knew I had to get her to trust me. What she desperately needed was the impartial advice that only I could provide. I'd been sorting out men like Marsh most of my working life.

It was a relief to get to the office, sip some of Norma's decent coffee, and give my mind a brief respite from the complexities of the Laura Marsh case.

'You all right, Norma? I wish you'd taken some time off . . .'

'For the hundredth time, I'm as right as rain. If I had more time off I'd have a right old tangle to clear up here and that would be worse than the headache.'

'No increase in pain, nothing funny with your eyes . . . how many fingers am I holding up?'

'Eleven. Satisfied?' she snapped, her exasperation tempered by an affection you had to have known her a long time to be able to detect.

'You'd pretend you were all right if you couldn't see across the room or remember what day it was, wouldn't you, you old fool. Look, when I'm out I want you to spend a bit of time reviewing the cases I've had over the past year that led to sackings or court appearances, and give me a list of names. Right?'

'Don't you think I've got enough on with this lot?'

'Norma, it's *important*. You get the names, I'll check where

134

the sods are now. If we can eliminate them I'll be able to accept that Bruce was probably right – the guy hadn't decided which gear he was going to take when you surprised him.'

Or that there was an outside chance David Marsh was in the frame.

She turned to the post with alacrity – it was obvious she was over the shock of the attack. The window and door locks, combined with the intruder alarm, had given her confidence, as I'd known they would, and she was now keen to put the affair behind her, though I could trust her to be vigilant, if not perhaps as vigilant as I was going to be on her behalf.

We normally spent an hour going through the mail and setting up my appointments for the day. My schedule would then be written into the desk diary with a photocopy I could take with me. I'd leave the office about ten, rarely to return before late afternoon.

'You've scribbled a word that looks like "vag" on today's page,' she said. 'I do hope it's not as personal as it sounds . . .'

It had all been sucked into a black hole, the handing round of pound coins to the tramps, the guilt aroused, when I'd been full of the euphoria of taking Laura out, by seeing them with their half-empty bottles of cider and wine, eating scraps of food from old supermarket carriers, the resolve I'd made to do something, *anything*, for the one who looked in reasonable shape.

'It's short for vagrant,' I said. 'There's a chap in the subway who looks a cut above the rest. I wondered if I could get him a labouring job at one of the warehouses. Look, Norma, do me a favour, would you, and ring Shelter or whoever and ask what the form is for getting him lodgings and rehab.'

'Oh, John, I know you had a dreadful experience in Huddersfield, but it's given you such a hang-up . . .'

'Agreed. It's quite irrational. I just can't shake the feeling that if I'd stayed with the guy I could have talked him out of it. One more hour and he'd still be alive. I feel the only way I can make up for it is to try and get someone off the street in his place.'

'Oh, love . . .' she said, in a gentler tone. 'You shouldn't take these things so much to heart. I'm not being callous, but they do tend to choose the life. It's very sad, but they just seem so completely inadequate. You could pull out all the stops for this man and a week later he'll have gone walkabout again.'

'I'm sure you're right. Bruce says exactly the same. But this one might just be worth the effort. If he was cleaned up and decently turned out, I'm sure Barry Nolan at Bowling Suites would give him a chance, he's a good boy scout for all the hard-man image. Will you do that, ring Shelter or Catholic Housing or the Samaritans . . .?'

'Just call me Mother Teresa . . .'

'I've always felt that inside you there was a human being struggling to get out . . .'

'Just don't run away with the idea, my lad, that there'll ever be a room at *my* house for this new pal of yours,' she said darkly.

'Look, Norma, the poor bugger's still got *some* standards left. I think he'd sooner go on living in the subway.'

'Cheeky sod!'

It proved to be an unusually absorbing day, and when it was over I realised I'd not thought about Laura once, following a night when I'd thought of little else. And I was glad of it, because I knew, as I sat waiting for Fenlon in a snatched half-hour at the George, that I was becoming obsessive about her. I had an obsessive nature and I carried it around like a two-edged sword – it was sometimes my greatest asset, sometimes, when it flew back on me, an almost disabling character fault. Trying to rehabilitate a vagrant was just one small part of it.

I wondered if I'd got the Laura situation completely wrong. Had I read far too much into Marsh making himself comfortable at the house on Tanglewood, could I perhaps even be casting Marsh as Norma's attacker simply because, if I were honest, I resented him being around Laura?

So I bounced it off Fenlon again, though this time it was in a mood of resignation. But if I was resigned I was also more relaxed, as if released from a duty that had become onerous to the point of colouring every aspect of my day.

'It was the car that bugged me. It all really started with that. It's hired in her name, you see, on an indefinite rental, but he's the one who's swanning around in it. She's got her own.'

He shrugged. 'So . . .?'

'So why's she paying for it?'

'Perhaps she isn't. Perhaps it was just convenient for her to hire in her name and pick it up for him.'

'Why didn't he hire in Leicester then? That's where he's supposed to hang out.'

'Look, John, you've established that he's separated. That probably means that if he's got problems his wife doesn't want to know. So he turns to his sister-in-law. Let's say he *has* been made redundant; well, a lot of men don't like to talk about it because it's a blow to their pride. And it's probably his own situation that makes him so abrupt. So Laura bank-rolls him till he gets going again. Five hundred quid, even a grand, isn't going to make much of a dent in the million, is it; Christ, the *interest* on a million must be two big ones a week, give or take. And he *was* her husband's brother and they did get on.'

'But why's he hiding himself in her house?' I said dolefully.

It was a bad half-hour for self-inflicted wounds.

He signalled Kev for another round and lit a second cigarette. 'You don't really need my input to that, do you?'

My shoulders sagged. 'He's giving her one . . .'

'I'd have put it more delicately to spare your feelings. But
no one knows more about extra-marital ferret than you do.'

I picked up my chinking gin glass. 'It's the option I
wouldn't accept and I think I knew it was the real one almost
from meeting the guy. So I gradually turn him into a nasty
piece of work who's bullying her for a share of the loot. And
really, he's done nothing to deserve it except drive a car she's
rented, stay at her place now and then, and . . . well, sleep
with her, I suppose.'

'Tough luck,' he said. 'She sounds a nice lady.'

'I suppose what threw me was her reaction to Simon's
death. Believe me, she's hurting. If I'd seen signs of massive
relief because of being free to marry David . . . but it's not
like that. She can't hack it, and nothing that's going on
between her and David makes any difference to that.'

'Complicated,' he agreed, 'but nothing surprises you in our
game. God, some of the relationships on Dresden *Place*!'

'I know – life writes lousy scripts . . .'

'Look, I've not met her so I've no axe to grind. But just
think, if it's not twisting the knife too much, she may have
been putting it out for David for years, and suddenly her old
man totals himself. Well, it's not going to look very nice to
anyone if she's still putting it out while the body's going cold,
let alone to a decent type like John Goss, who's been such a
big help and obviously fancies you.'

I nodded. 'And I suppose we have to take into account that
Simon was having it off with barmaids. It could have been an
open marriage.'

'It all seems to fit. The hire-car stuffed up a side-street, her

138

going over the top because you've got eyes in your arse and he's cocked up the lighting plan. And what you also have to remember is that Simon died mixing drinks with barbiturates. Now from what you say, what drove him to it was almost certainly worry about his business and this barmaid he was shafting, but it could have been construed as depression because his wife was being unfaithful. It wouldn't make any difference to the insurance money, but perhaps Laura thought it might and didn't want you passing it back to Zephyr so Snee could pretend it was another can of worms he'd have to look into.'

'You'd have to meet her,' I said, 'to understand how difficult it is for me to accept all this. Even though I think you're probably right. Oddly enough, Norma has her own suspicions about her – she met her the other afternoon. I just wonder if she's picking up the vibes on Laura's double life, if that's what it is, playing it straight as the grieving widow with me, but quietly having it off with Marsh. You know how women seem to be able to pick up on these things.'

He nodded slowly. 'Thing is, for all this carry-on with David Marsh, Simon was probably the best friend she'd got, even if he did share it out. They'd been together what, ten, fifteen years. He'd made bloody certain she could be unhappy in comfort, you can't knock him for that.' He glanced at his watch. 'Well, I must go, old son. Better luck next time, eh, though I've got to admit it's not going to be too easy finding another good-looking widow who's just copped for a million, even a jammy bugger like you.'

He winked, grinned, strode off through the early-doors crowd. He knew I was depressed, but I was also John Goss, a free agent; there'd be other women I could chat up, sleep with, wine and dine. It was a life-style he very much envied, and when it went wrong he couldn't always conceal a secret satisfaction, because even your best friends can't stop themselves getting off on the times you blow it, as La Rochefoucauld once pointed out, though I dare say his words have lost something in my translation.

But Fenlon's was the voice of reason. It all depended on how you saw the situation, and I'd seen it by vision clouded by my growing affection for her, as if it were one of those computer-designed pictures in which others could see the shapes of animals and trees, but I could see only the superficial images, because I'd not allow myself to adopt the simple techniques for looking beyond them.

It was my old problem – getting too involved. I could remember an English master, red in the face, shouting did I want to produce and direct the blessed play as well as take a leading role. Nothing had changed in sixteen years, only now it was Laura's set-up I wanted to control, a complex way of life that probably went back years, no doubt made complete sense to the people caught up in it, and which could quite easily be damaged by my ill-advised tampering.

'Yes, yes, yes,' I murmured wearily, as I trudged back to my car.

That's when I began to draw away from Laura. I was keeping an eye on some warehouse bandits, a job that took care of my evenings, and I crammed my days like a suitcase with every assignment that came along, even those I tended to be choosy about. I regularly worked a ten-hour day; for the next week or so I pushed it to thirteen or fourteen, so that life was reduced to bed and work, with no further sleep lost about the woman on Tanglewood Lane.

I still saw her regularly, as the Zephyr job hadn't quite ended, but I made no attempt at contact. I followed her to the supermarket, was there when she set off for her walks, occasionally watched the house in the evening – all the usual things I could log down on my worksheet with a clear conscience, absurd as Fenlon and Laura, and probably even Snee himself, seemed to find it. But then, I was the kind of man who could see nothing particularly odd about Erich von Stroheim, when playing a role that required him to carry a camera round his neck, insisting on the camera being loaded with film.

I never saw Marsh's Escort again and I certainly didn't go looking for it. It could only delay the painful business of pushing the Laura situation into an attic compartment of my brain that I then hoped to seal. Her eyes met mine, of course, several times. And twice she began to make towards my car, before halting and turning back to what she was doing, put off by my polite, detached smile, by the fact that I made no attempt to get out of the car to go and meet her.

Then, one day, as she set off for the reservoirs, she gave me a polite smile and a wave as formal as the Queen's from the back of a Rolls. I looked on bleakly as she walked away, knowing it meant that she too had accepted that it was best if we simply acknowledged each other but didn't speak or touch, like people on either side of a glass wall.

I watched her progress along Tanglewood, in the blueish-grey parka and black pants, her hair loose today, and then, when she'd disappeared through the entrance to the reservoirs, I left my car and walked slowly after her, more to stretch my legs than to keep her in sight.

Beyond the entrance stood the lodge, in its open-ended courtyard, of the council employee who guarded the area, cleared leaves and cut back undergrowth. You crossed the courtyard to reach the reservoir path.

She was standing in the middle of it. 'John . . .?'

That was all she said, just one word, in a low, hurt voice. It was like a single chord of music, a sudden smell or taste, that instantly returned the memory to some missed and favoured time, and I was back in the recent past, when we'd walked and talked together, and I'd gone back with her to drink coffee in her roomy kitchen, with its hanging copper pans and its earthenware bread bowl, and the type of solid-fuel stove that literary critics now needed only to name to define with precision a certain genre of women's fiction.

'Hello, Laura,' I said, with mock breeziness. 'I'm afraid I've been terribly busy. I'm sorry I haven't had time for a word . . .'

Her grey eyes slid from mine with what I could tell was reproach, despite the control she normally had over her features. It was as if she'd actually spoken the words: 'You too . . .' I was suddenly irritated, because I'd begun to feel almost noble about keeping my distance, about not being an added complication to the already complex situation I now accepted she was in with Marsh.

She walked slowly away, towards a reservoir that this afternoon seemed as big as a Cumbrian lake, the illusion of size enhanced by the October mist that cut off its far end.

I slowly followed her. I knew I'd been over-zealous in distancing myself, had been too abrupt, hadn't given her the slightest chance to come to terms with the fact that I'd made the decision to phase myself out. But I'd known my limitations: that I couldn't do it the gradual way, not with someone who attracted me as much as she did; known it would have to be all or nothing.

She looked so very young from behind, with her loose hair and her track shoes and her old clothes, she looked as untried, as much on the brink of life, as she must have looked in her college days. I'd been very hard on her. All I'd been able to see had been my own side of the equation, my attraction to her, my preoccupation with walking away, so I could get back to the protective routines and the unbroken sleep. But that meant she got nothing. And all she'd ever wanted had been simple friendship, which was all she herself had ever offered. The idea of physical attraction had been all my own and she had never, at any stage, encouraged me to think it went both ways. I knew she'd *realised* I was attracted, but had seemed to accept it as a compliment, which was what sensible women did, at the same time as they gracefully refused to encourage it.

And from where she stood it perhaps seemed I'd withdrawn the things that only I could give her: sympathy, understanding, advice. I accepted it was barely possible for me to be completely fair to David Marsh, but even pushing myself to the point of positive discrimination, he still came across as a brusque and self-absorbed man. Perhaps it was simply not in his nature to provide the kind of support she needed at a time like this, whatever other emotional needs he'd been able to satisfy.

I suddenly found myself walking rapidly, until I overtook her slow, drifting footsteps. I couldn't stop myself putting a hand on her shoulder.

'Oh, John,' she said in a low voice, turning to me on the almost deserted pathway. 'Please walk with me. Please come back for a coffee. Have I upset you in some way? I'd begun to rely on you for so much, you can't begin to know . . .'

I walked round the reservoir with her, waited while she spoke to the adoring Binkie, went back with her to the large, secluded house and drank coffee. We never stopped talking, we were like close friends who'd been living in separate countries for six months. And that evening, despite the self-imposed work-load, I found the time to take her out to dinner again. I didn't look to see what pattern of lights she'd left on and so I didn't know, or care, if the pattern was intact when we returned.

I said once: 'I . . . really am sorry if I seemed to neglect you. I've had such a full schedule. I keep asking Norma to take pity on me . . .'

'I understand, John . . .'

And perhaps she had understood my true motives for that period of aloofness, that I realised she grieved for one man, lived with another, yet needed me too; and perhaps she even understood the problems I'd had coming to terms with the situation.

I said: 'I knew you would.'

It marked the end of the distancing operation.

Nine

'John – you're off the case!'

'How can you possibly know? I only knew myself yesterday.'

'They wrote! I've had a letter from that dreadful man you told me about – Mr Snee. He says his examination of my claim is complete now and the accounts department will be forwarding a cheque towards the end of November . . .'

'Which you *should* have had in the middle of August.'

'Oh, it's not going to make much difference, now I know it's on the way.'

'That's what men like Snee count on. Anyway, I don't suppose I should knock the guy – I've had several weeks of very easy money out of it, and . . . I got to meet you . . .'

'You've been a tower, John – we mustn't drift apart now it's all sorted out.'

'I'll be there for you, Laura,' I said firmly, 'as long as you need me.'

'I'm going to give you a surprise.'

'What sort of surprise?' I said, pleasurably certain it would be another dinner at a good restaurant, for which this time she'd pick up the tab.

'If I told you it wouldn't be a surprise. Can you spare a weekend?'

A *weekend*. I could scarcely believe it. A whole night under the same roof. Where? That trip to the Dales to look for a house for her? Some theme weekend, where an expert would talk on art or literature? Dinner, B and B in some ancient inn with a view of Holy Island? Nightcaps in either her room or mine . . .

The elation ebbed even as it began to flow. It would *have* to be the three of us, just like the old days when it had been the two brothers and her. It was out of the question he'd let her go off alone with me. He *had* to be seeing me as the con-artist I'd once tried to convince myself he was.

'I do hope that silence means you're looking through your diary . . .'

'Correct. I was trying to decide how to rearrange my work. This coming weekend would really be as good as any . . .'

'Excellent. I'll pick you up in my car at ten on Saturday morning . . . yes?'

'Would you prefer to use my car? It's bigger, and if there'll be three of us . . .'

There was a short silence. '*Three* of us . . .?'

'I . . . thought . . . David would probably be coming too.'

'What made you think that, John?' she said, a cool note entering her small voice.

'Oh, I simply thought . . . if it's a celebration because we're separating Zephyr from their money . . . David would be involved. He was as anxious as me to see you sorted out.'

'Well, I'm sure he'd think it a lovely idea, but this is my special thank you to you, and so it'll just be the two of us. He'll understand . . .'

The warmth was back in her voice again.

'Right!' I said. 'I'll leave my car where it lies and be ready with my toothbrush at ten on the dot. And . . . thank you, Laura, thank you very much. I'm looking forward . . .'

'I *do* hope you'll enjoy it. I've given it such a lot of thought . . .'

I was sure she had, too, because that was the way she was. I could imagine her working out the details as she sat in her shady drawing-room, listening to some slow, throbbing piece of organ music – I wondered why I could never imagine her watching television. I was very touched. It seemed an excessive display of gratitude for what had cost me so little – simply being available, the proverbial shoulder to help her through a bad time. She'd already given me so much by the pleasure I got from simply being with her, the way she looked in her elegant dresses, the ability she had to make me feel a little sharper, a little wittier than I really was. The phrase 'feel-good factor' could have been minted to describe the effect on me of Laura Marsh.

She'd caught me on the car phone. It was late and I'd been keeping watch on the ringleader of the warehouse bandits. I'd seen an estate car turn in the man's drive, one I knew belonged to a local fence, had seen through field-glasses two large, square cardboard boxes, of the kind televisions come packed in, being hurriedly passed out through the kitchen door and in through the estate's tailgate. The next time the man from the warehouse eased a piece of merchandise past electronic devices that had gone curiously silent, it would be his last. He himself would name his accomplices. He'd not face the humpy alone – honour among thieves was an entirely literary concept that had as much credibility in the dark side of the city that I knew as burglars who wore striped jerseys and black masks.

I drove home. I had never heard her so animated and I realised just how much the delay in the Zephyr payment had added to her difficulties. Until it came through she couldn't plan properly, or make firm decisions about a new life, couldn't get away from Tanglewood Lane. She couldn't escape the atmosphere of Simon alive and the pain that had followed Simon dead.

And now she was free to live anywhere she liked, to concentrate on her novel, to make a serious attempt to come to terms with his death and build a life that would be all her own, free of ghosts.

I put an M and S meal for one in the micro, poured myself a gin. Where did David Marsh fit in now? If he and Laura *were* an item, surely they'd now be in a position to set up together. So how could he go along with Laura taking a young, healthy man like me away for the weekend, whose private fortune, if it were laid end to end in pound coins, would reach about as far as the garden gate?

The micro began to bleep. I took out the container, scooped the food on to a plate, began abstractedly to eat, so little aware of taste and texture that it could have been either caviare or porridge. I wondered if I could begin to take a guardedly optimistic view once more, whether Fenlon and I, for all our hard sense and realism, had both been wrong. Perhaps it had simply been conscience after all. She'd wanted to do anything she could for her husband's brother because of the old – innocent? – closeness, was merely providing him with wheels, shelter and a backhander until he'd managed to sort himself out.

And hadn't wanted me to know he was staying at Tanglewood *precisely* because she didn't want me to come to the conclusion she was having an affair with him.

It seemed optimism was definitely in order. The weekend away together put a completely new spin on it. Had to. I began to smile. My taste-buds came back to life.

'Christ!' I said. '*Not spaghetti sodding bolognese!* How many times have I told Norma how much I hate and detest the bloody stuff!'

* * *

'Those names you gave me, Norma, the possible grudge bearers. I've checked out two of them – the one called Mills is out of the area altogether and the one called Ebden is genuinely trying to go straight – he's working up a carpet-cleaning business. That leaves four to go . . .'

She shrugged. It was behind her now. I suspected she didn't really want reminding about it. I'd made her house as secure as any house could be, and she was being carefully monitored by both sets of neighbours. There'd been no follow-up of any kind, possibly because she was in fact so well protected. Or because it had been a completely random incident.

Her attitude was catching. It was tempting to put the attack out of my own mind. She'd turned up six names of men who'd got the sack or a short stretch through my detection and I'd make a thorough check on each one of them, but I was beginning to accept that I might have read too much into it. There was an awful lot of it about; it seemed you only had to pick up a local paper to see the dreadfully bruised face of some poor old pensioner injured during a break-in. Perhaps Norma's assailant *hadn't* had time to pack up his pillowcase, perhaps it had been frustration that had made him lash out at her, in the same way that young burglars – and they were mainly young – would deliberately trash your house if they could find nothing to their liking.

And as for David Marsh being a possible assailant, I was beginning to accept that I'd had very personal reasons for wanting to believe him the kind of man who'd do anything as complicated as disabling Norma in order to keep me out of his way. He really had little to fear from me; he and Laura were related, they went back, he was with her a lot of the time. If part of her money was what he was after he was always going to have first call.

I still mistrusted him, probably always would, but not now quite to the point of thinking him capable of battering a middle-aged woman with a car torch, especially now that it seemed possible he wasn't Laura's lover after all.

Norma said: 'I rang Shelter . . . about your down-and-out friend.'

I felt a twinge of guilt – once more my preoccupation with Laura had put my conscience on hold.

'And . . .?'

'They can find him dormitory accommodation – no problem – and sort out food and clothing, but they do point out that so many people fall through the net because they simply can't face any kind of institutionalisation.'

'I can see that. But what about finding him a room of his own?'

'They can probably do that as well, and they can give you all the advice you need for getting him back in the system. But they say the onus would have to be on you – you'd have to guarantee the rent and settle him in and find him work. They weren't enthusiastic.' A note of quiet triumph had crept into her voice. 'They say when people start amateur do-gooding, however worthy their intentions, it's usually Shelter left picking up the pieces.'

'I'll speak to him. If he's absolutely against it I'll let it ride.'

'Oh, John . . .' She shook her head.

'If you say it once more, you're fired . . .'

'What – about you always getting in it up to your eyes?'

'You needn't work out the day. I'll be able to find some bright kid at a third the price.'

'On the other hand,' she said, as she placidly went on opening mail, 'the fact that you *do* get in it up to your eyes brings in the business. I think they feel they get the best of the bargain.'

'Right,' I said, 'now we've sorted that out to your satisfaction, perhaps we can look at the diary. I don't want anything that involves Saturday work because I'm going away for the weekend.'

'Going away!' she cried. 'Going *away*! You don't *go* away for weekends. You haven't been away for a weekend since you followed that poor gorgeous Mr Rainger to Esk Head.'

'All right, leave it out . . .'

She began to giggle. 'You must be the only man in England who goes on murder mystery weekends where they have real murders.'

'I'm warning you, woman, you're treading on eggshells.'

'Who's the lucky lady?'

'I said nothing about a lady . . .'

'Well, if it was just you, you wouldn't go at all. Your only real friends are bobbies, who are all either working or under the thumb. It can't be one of them, so it must be a woman.'

'Are you expecting some sort of response?'

'I just hope the poor creature doesn't think that prising you away from your work means anything. Admittedly she comes with good form if she can interest you for longer than a couple of dinners at the Ash Tree.'

'I always knew it was a grave mistake letting you anywhere near my private diary.'

'You forgot to put the initials in, by the way.'

'I didn't need to – I knew who I was going with.'

Her face became suddenly impassive. After a silence, she said quietly: 'It's Mrs Marsh, John, isn't it.'

It wasn't a question. It caught me off guard and I couldn't react quickly enough with some jokey denial. 'Look, Norma,' I said finally, 'I really think my private life . . .'

'Sorry I spoke,' she cut me off. 'You're quite right, what you do when you leave here is none of my business.'

'I really can't see what you've got against her.'

'In that case, let's talk about something else. Like your appointments, for instance.'

'The case is over. Zephyr wrote to say they're paying the claim. It's what they should have done in the *first* bloody place. She's paying for this weekend as a thank you . . .' She went on studying mail as if I'd not spoken. 'Oh, come on, Norma, this is the second time we've ended up arguing about Laura Marsh . . .'

'Excuse *me*, *I'm* not arguing . . .'

'But you're giving me the silent treatment and I know what *that* means.'

She finally looked across at me. 'You know my feelings about her, John. I still think it was a big mistake to get involved.'

'But the case is *over* . . .'

'Not officially. If you'd met up with her six months later and taken her out then that would have been a different matter. In fact I'd probably have been all for it.'

I could believe it. She'd always wanted to see me settled. Had the timing been right the John and Laura story could have had a lot going for it, even though she'd have preferred me to find someone nearer my own age.

'I'm sorry, John, I can't get rid of the feeling she *wanted* to get to know you and there's something she's not letting on about.'

I sighed. She was right, of course. Laura *had* concealed the truth about her background; that, for whatever reason, David Marsh was living part of the time at her house. But I was certain that was *all* she was concealing, just as I was sure she'd turned to me because she needed simple friendship.

'Oh, Norma . . . it's all so open and shut. The entire case. We've checked everything out, me *and* the police. And the Zephyr have had their tongue in cheek from day one. They must have saved something like seven or eight grand in interest by not paying out when the claim first went in. That's how business is these days, you know that as well as I do. I just see a very unhappy woman who wants a little company.'

'Well . . . *you* might . . .' she said, looking past me with unfocused eyes.

'And what's that supposed to mean?'

'You're a young man, John. A very clever young man, but this attractive older woman comes into your life and you can't be blamed for getting off on the big, sad eyes routine, no man could.'

'Oh, come on, she *is* attractive, I'm not denying it, but I just like her as a person. She's fun to be with, interesting, witty . . .'

'That might all be part of it.'

'Part of *what*, for God's sake?'

'I don't know. I wish I did. But it wouldn't be the first time you've been taken in. Remember Fernande Dumont and her talent for deception . . .?'

'But I always knew *she* pretended to be things she wasn't. That wasn't why the case went belly up . . .'

'But the deception helped, didn't it . . .?'

'The Rainger case was a can of worms, from beginning to end. Everything about Laura and the Zephyr claim checks out and always has done.'

'Except Laura herself. Who could possibly be an older and more skilful version of Fernande.'

'If you knew her as well as I've got to know her I'm certain you'd change your mind.'

'Perhaps you're right,' she said, with a sudden smile. 'And if you know her long enough I'm sure you'll find out which of us is wrong. Have a nice weekend.'

I think she meant it too, that she wished she *could* have

seen Laura in a different light, for my sake, because she could sense the effect Laura had had on me. And I wished I could tell her she was right, about Laura having something to hide, but I'd not got the Laura–David relationship together yet, and I didn't want to talk to Norma about it until I had. It would simply be another ball she could run with and I couldn't do with any more wrangling, it got me starting my day in the wrong mood.

Because whatever *was* going on between Laura and Marsh, if anything, I knew it made no difference to the sort of woman Laura was. But I knew Norma still wasn't happy about the weekend, and it gave me a lingering feeling of uneasiness.

It was the best surprise I'd ever had. She'd booked seats for *City of Angels* at the Prince of Wales in London, that complex and ingenious show which appears to be about a private investigator, but which you gradually realise is a story within a story, the investigator and his activities being the continually shifting creation of a writer who is being pressed for changes by a film producer. From opening scenes that seem totally confusing and chaotic, it is as if box after glittering box is sprung, until the true contents are at last displayed. I sat totally absorbed, spellbound by the clarity and brilliance of the concept.

I'd been so lost in the show that it was only when we went to claim the interval drinks I'd ordered in advance that I realised that this couldn't be her type of theatre. It didn't match the picture I now had of her, sitting in her dim rooms that throbbed with dark, powerful music as she pondered the themes of that dark, powerful novel that I already felt certain would outsell du Maurier. A bright, modern show like *City of Angels*, ingenious as it was, would not be her choice, she'd be drawn to straight plays, narrow in appeal, the more tortuous and convoluted the better.

She said: 'Do you like it?'

'Tremendously.'

'I thought it seemed appropriate. A PI seeing a show about a PI.'

'I'd not have minded what we'd gone to see, Laura. Why didn't you choose something more to your own taste?'

'I didn't know you were an expert on my taste,' she said, with her faint smile.

But she didn't deny it. It was all for me, this weekend, this night out, and no woman I'd known had gone to such thoughtful lengths to ensure I had a good time.

She'd arrived at my old semi on Bentham Terrace sharp at ten, then driven me to the multi-storey car-park at the side of the Beckford Crest Hotel. From there we'd walked along the connecting subway to the railway station. From Beckford we'd gone to Leeds and at Leeds she'd led me to a platform I knew only too well.

'It's got to be either London or some point in between.'

'You'll just have to wait and see, won't you . . .'

But it was London. We sat opposite each other in first-class seats and she refused even to let me go to the buffet car, but insisted on going herself. She returned with coffee and sandwiches in one little carrier bag, and a half-litre of dry white wine in another.

She was happier today than I'd ever seen her, though happiness was altogether too positive a word. She smiled a lot and talked cheerfully, her grey eyes flickering between racing, misty fields and my face, but the sense of her unshakeable sadness was still there, as if a lake's surface was rippling over depths that remained motionless and unchanged.

We drank the chilled wine and ate the sandwiches, as an intermittent band of sunlight fell across her sleek, dark hair and brought out the muted colours of the diamond-patterned grey turtle-neck sweater she wore for the journey. We talked about John Goss. It was the morning on the moors all over again – her interest in my life and cases seemed inexhaustible. It was peculiarly flattering to a man who woke up most mornings feeling there were only two jobs down from a PI – window-cleaning and the buses. But she listened with such concentration, asked such intelligent questions, that I would begin to believe, as so often with her, that I might not be quite such a boring bastard after all. It was one of her best qualities – and she had many – that sympathetic spotlight she could turn on you.

'I'm doing *all* the talking again,' I protested.

'But it's all so intriguing, the way you can winkle so much out about people. It must be so very strange, when you start to learn things about someone whom the people they've been with for years don't know . . .'

I glanced at her with a faint, wry smile. Because she herself was probably one of that sad band. I knew about Simon's other life in North Yorkshire. I didn't think she did.

'We're going to talk about *you* now,' I said firmly. 'Tell me about your college days. You were studying English Literature, I believe . . .'

'English Lit with a French subsid. It was all wall-to-wall books, just as it had been at home. Simon was doing Maths, of course. It . . . seems an unlikely friendship, I suppose – he was orientated towards figures and those hideously complicated formulae that always reach an exact conclusion, and me – I was into people and the inconclusive lives they lived. After I graduated I spent a year at a French school as an assistant, to improve my accent. When I came back Simon had disappeared into the commercial world and I lost touch with him.

'But we met again at a reunion dinner dance. We'd neither of us found anyone we particularly fancied. So we got married.' She smiled her faint smile again. 'That's absolutely *all* there is to know about me.'

I said: 'I suspect there's only about one tenth of Laura Marsh visible above the water-line.'

The smile faded; she looked sharply away at the speeding landscape and I felt I'd said something that had jarred her comparative happiness, reminded her perhaps of the sort of problems presented by David Marsh, when all I'd meant to imply was what I sensed to be the depth and richness of her mind.

'Did you ever go out to work?'

She nodded. 'I taught. The plan was that I'd write in the holidays. I suppose I imagined that would eventually be my life – the writing. Mother had always been so keen, of course, she felt I had talent. Simon . . . was working for an international company that specialised in computer networks for firms with branches. He was one of the first to define the gap in the market – the small operations that needed the sort of inexpensive dedicated systems the big companies didn't want to know about. He set up on his own. Perhaps with hindsight it would have been better if he'd stayed put.'

She spoke in her usual controlled tone, but I wondered if I detected the slightest note of resentment, bitterness even.

I said: 'But he'd not have been as happy . . . staying put . . .'

'He wanted the challenge of designing complete systems, being in control.'

'So you stopped teaching . . .'

'I was sucked in, John. He had to have administrative back-up and the idea was I'd do it for a year or two, then go back to teaching. But he was one of the first in the field and he began to do rather well, and I was now so involved it had become virtually impossible to phase me out. And then the next recession came along and he began to do rather badly, and then . . . well . . .'

He'd mixed pills with alcohol and crashed into a valley.

She took the top from her plastic cup with sharp, untypical movements and sipped the black coffee. 'Mother thought I was quite mad. She had rather a lofty attitude to commerce – the arts always took total priority with her. *She* thought I should leave Simon to his own devices and concentrate on my own ambitions. But it's never so easy. I suppose,' she said slowly, 'you could say Simon realised his ambitions at the expense of mine.'

I was certain of the bitterness this time, understated yet intense, like the notes in certain organ pieces that are so low you seem to sense rather than actually hear them. And now she'd have the time and money to write the masterpiece she was convinced, in her own quiet, steely way, she was capable of. I wondered how often she must have reflected on the bitter irony of it, that the chance for the right conditions, to achieve the goal she'd craved for so long, had only come about through the death of the man she'd loved, even though his ambitions had swamped her own.

At King's Cross, we'd taken a cab to the Berkshire Hotel, just off Oxford Street, and she'd thrust a five-pound note at the driver before I could get my wallet out. The hotel wasn't wildly expensive, but it wasn't cheap, and I still thought this treat too lavish for what help I was supposed to have given her. She'd taken adjoining rooms on the fifth floor, because of her usual urge for silence, and certainly at this height the noise of traffic and the cries of street vendors were barely whispers. My room was large and airy with highly polished furniture and a marble-tiled bathroom. It was all rather grander than the hotels I normally used on my working trips.

'I don't know what to say . . . you really shouldn't have gone to all this expense for me . . .'

'I'm involved as well, you know – I can't tell you how glad I am to get away from Tanglewood Lane for a couple of days.' She stood looking down from the window in my room. 'Do you remember telling me I should take a holiday when the claim was settled? Well, I decided I didn't want to spare the time. I want to look for my new home now, get on with my work. But I did need a break. A weekend in London with you seemed a perfect compromise. Does that make you feel better about the expense – to know you're an essential element in my therapy?'

I smiled. 'That puts it in quite a new light.'

She turned from the window; her eyes rested gravely on mine. 'I'll soon be rather rich, John. I know you have a good idea of the full amount. I'm so glad it means so little to you that you're even concerned about the cost of this weekend.' She smiled faintly. 'Is that your instinctive Yorkshire thrift? Have you read Maugham? He once said that money was like a sixth sense that enables you to make the most of the other five. That's all it will mean to me. You and I, I think we're both rather indifferent to fancy life-styles . . .'

She turned back to the window, so that her profile was sharply outlined against the light – the slightly aquiline nose, the down-turned crescent of a mouth, the hair drawn back into its discreetly ornamented slide. I wondered what, if anything, might be encoded in her words – that it was such a profound relief to get away from David Marsh, to whom perhaps money *did* represent a fancy life-style, and the bite I couldn't stop myself thinking he was putting on her?

'Do be careful, Laura.' The words came of their own volition. 'I've seen money envy destroy lives. Look, I know two or three men I'd trust with my shirt. Any one of them could advise you on the best way to invest your money so you'll have an income you don't need to worry about. That's what you'd like, isn't it, a monthly cheque, so you can concentrate on your work?'

'That would be ideal.'

'Give me the go-ahead and I can get one of these people to come and see you next week. Any time to suit you.'

She glanced over her shoulder at me, the old troubled look back in place. 'I'll . . . think it over carefully. I'll . . . let you know next week. It's so good of you to take all this trouble.'

There could only be one reason why she needed to think it over. David Marsh. Because David Marsh had probably tried to convince her he knew so much about investment that *he* could do the financial advising.

'All right,' I said lightly. 'I suppose there's no real rush till the Zephyr cheque comes through, but you won't want it sitting around in a building society for very long at eight per cent gross.'

'I shan't. I promise . . .'

She moved briskly away from the window then. 'This is *supposed* to be a treat, and here we are getting heavy about something that bores us both rigid. I'd like to go to Foyle's. What about you – you can do anything you like, of course . . .'

'I think I'll come too.'

We decided to walk, to stretch our legs, she in a stone-coloured raincoat in a trench style with epaulettes, her eyes taking in the crowded scene with the almost bird-like intensity she'd given equally to sweeping moorland. Despite her warmth and her trusting manner, she had a kind of detachment, a single-minded concentration, that I felt I'd recognised in one or two of the people I'd worked for – the solicitor determined to head the biggest commercial practice in town, the entrepreneur driven to becoming a household name, the restaurateur who spent eight hours in one of his restaurants and eight in another, six days a week.

At Foyle's we separated, me to browse through the new biographies, she to search out some specific reference book about the Twenties; perhaps that was the period in which her novel was to be set. An hour or so later, I went in search of her, through the maze of rooms, and eventually came upon her looking at a pyramid of books of one of the latest bestsellers. But there was no envy in her glance, she seemed to look on with a sort of calm objectivity, and I realised she was now in a position to put critical success above financial, which was probably in any case the ranking she'd prefer.

Later, I showered and then joined her in her room for a drink from the refrigerated cabinet. Then we went to the restaurant for an early dinner, with which she'd ordered champagne. From reception we were led to a private-hire-car, waiting to take us to the theatre – everything meticulously planned by Laura in advance.

After the heat of the theatre, it was so refreshing to be out in the cool autumn air that we decided to walk again. It had rained earlier and the wet streets reflected the lights of cars and the coloured fluorescent signs of theatres and restaurants.

'Let's walk up through Soho,' she said. 'I believe it's taken on a new lease of life recently, leaving Covent Garden nowhere.'

So we made for Shaftesbury Avenue and plunged into that densely built wedge-shaped district at the heart of the West End. Her facts were right as usual. The sleaze of the strip clubs and the porn shops and the furtively sidling tourists seemed to be being pushed aside by a new young crowd who had rediscovered the area and were making it their own. The streets were awash with the light that volleyed from the open doors of crowded pubs. People stood out on the pavement with their glasses, talking in big, cheerful groups that spilled on to the road. Others even sat in chairs in the street, despite the earlier showers.

'Do you . . . want a drink?'

'I think I'd rather wait till we're back at the hotel.'

I'd put the question tentatively because, though I'd once taken her to a pub in Skipton, I couldn't easily associate her with the noise and laughter and the easy camaraderie of the Saturday night bar parlour. She seemed to walk through the streets as if on a sort of field trip, in which she could study the behaviour at first hand of some obscure and esoteric tribe she'd read about in a travel book. Her sharp, impassive gaze seemed to miss nothing as she looked from side to side – a bearded man who played an accordion, two girls who danced at a street corner, screaming with laughter, a crowd of students who sang a folk song, a tall, thin man with staring eyes and a wide black hat who held a peculiarly riveting surreal conversation with himself.

'Beckett-like, would you say?' she murmured, with her faint smile.

'Perhaps a touch of Pinter there too . . .'

'I suspect he's never seen either, so he must be a true original.'

We walked into the comparative silence of Soho Square and along its west side. A voice from the recessed doorway of a faceless shop whispered hoarsely: 'Got any change, guv?'

He sat in frayed clothing on what looked to be an old sack. I automatically felt in my pocket and handed him perhaps one pound fifty in tens and twenties. It was difficult to tell where the rags he sat on ended and those he wore began.

'Thanks, guv . . .'

There'd been a pound coin among the change; I fished it

out and gave him that too. He accepted it with a weary nod, but no further word. He looked emaciated and ill. I wondered how he would survive the overnight frosts of late autumn, even in central London, where the heat of the buildings produced a temperature several degrees above normal.

'You all right?' I said uneasily. 'Do you need help? You don't look well . . .'

'I'm okay, guv,' he whispered. 'Thanks for the change. I'm just resting me legs tempory. It's just tempory, see. G'night . . .'

Already the note of suspicion was in his voice that I recognised from the vagrant in the Beckford subway. Help could only mean officialdom and dormitories and loss of freedom, and it seemed too high a price to pay for food and warmth and medical help.

I went on. Laura hadn't broken her pace by a step, seemed in fact to be walking so rapidly as to be almost out of sight in the gloom, though I could still hear the faint clipping of her heels. It took me some time to catch her up.

'I'm . . . sorry about that,' I said, when I reached her side, where her sharp pace still didn't alter. 'I have a bit of a hang-up about vagrants. They seem to sense I'm a soft touch . . .'

'I don't think giving them money does them much good,' she said, cutting me off almost brusquely.

'That's . . . what my police friends tell me. They say the state would look after them, but they seem to want their independence, if you can call it that . . .'

'They'd be better off dead. If we keep giving them money they'll just go on living that dreadful quarter-life a little bit longer. They're no good to themselves, they're no good to the community; it would be a mercy to gather them up and give them a nice warm drink that would put them to sleep, like sick animals that can't be cured.'

'I . . . suppose that's one way of looking at it. It just seems extreme. The problem is, they're not all completely beyond the pale. Often all they need is a chance . . .'

'If there were anything in them they'd never have got into that state, John. And once they're in it the most compassionate thing we can do is to release them from a dreadful existence.'

'Well,' I said, with a faint wryness, 'you seem to have very strong views on the subject . . .'

'I believe if we go along here we'll not be too far from the hotel . . .'

That seemed to signal the end of any further discussion about vagrants. We walked for a time in silence, towards the Marble Arch end of Oxford Street, past shops still lit up, but displaying to almost empty pavements. I'd thought I was beginning to get to know her, but her attitude to the vagrant problem made me feel I still had some way to go. I had never heard that small, soft voice so dogmatic, and it seemed odd that it should be about a matter few people gave much thought to at all. I'd only really become aware of vagrants myself when the man I'd tracked down to Huddersfield had hanged himself.

The day I'd first spoken to her she'd been feeding scraps to a lonely goose, and everything I'd learned of her since then seemed to have strengthened that initial impression of her as a woman of generosity and warmth. This new aspect had thrown me. It had given me an almost chilling impression of fascist solutions – of sweeping up the vagrants and quietly putting them down, and then passing on to clear up any other group that might be considered to contribute little to society – the mentally ill, the disabled, the confused elderly.

Perhaps she considered her attitude to *be* compassionate. Perhaps, with what I suspected was a powerful imagination, she couldn't bear the idea of people existing like vegetables in doorways and subways and corners of goods yards. Perhaps she genuinely believed it would be act of mercy to put them down humanely, even though they themselves were keen enough to go on living the way they did.

She rather shyly took my arm, as she had done on our way through Soho, and glanced at me with a smile that may have held a hint of contrition for the harsh line she'd taken about a tattered wretch I'd given small change to. If I were honest with myself I knew I'd become over-sensitive on the question of down-and-outs. She'd only said what so many people privately thought. And she was only human. I was sorry for her and attracted to her. It was probably a headier mixture than simple attraction and made me tend to see her in an idealistic light, perhaps as nicer than she could ever be. She was also older than I was, and I'd found that few people reached their middle years without their own home-grown hang-ups.

I smiled back at her and we continued to the Berkshire, talking in the companionable manner of before. And the incident in Soho Square passed from my mind and would probably have gone for good, had it not been for what happened a month later.

Ten

'Nightcap?'

'I'd love one . . .'

She unlocked her drinks cabinet and made me a gin and tonic and herself a vodka and lime. She was wearing the black dress with the cross-over bodice I'd first seen the night I'd met David Marsh. Perhaps it was a favourite, one of a simple handful of dresses she knew she looked well in.

I said: 'What time am I being taken home tomorrow? Not that I actually *want* to go home . . .'

'Mid-afternoon. We'll be back early evening. All right?'

'Fine – that gives us the morning . . .'

'Perhaps we could walk in the park . . .'

'If we set off from Speakers' Corner we could cross Hyde Park and go down through Kensington Gardens.'

'It should be nice and quiet. It only gets really busy during the summer months.'

It was as if even in London she couldn't exist for long without space and water, the freedom of the open air.

She sipped her drink. 'I've enjoyed it so much today, John, thanks to you. I hadn't realised quite how . . . oppressive things had become until we got on the train. I do love trains. They go so quickly now that your cares and worries seem unable to keep up. Do you find that? I seem to have kept nicely ahead of them all day.'

'But your cares and worries are nearly over now . . .'

'Oh.' She shrugged, her gaze clouding slightly and becoming unfocused. 'There's all the business of selling up, finding another house . . . the removal itself. Moving house is always such a draggy thing . . .'

But soon she'd have sufficient money to pay various experts to make the removal painless; before very long the only thing she'd need to go on doing for herself was clean her teeth. I suspected the real cares and worries were the seemingly endless pain of loss and the complications of dealing with David Marsh.

I was beginning to hope she wasn't his lover, even allowing for the complex lives some people lived, but I accepted she might have offered him secret temporary accommodation. And I wondered if this weekend she'd planned for me, like the multi-layered show we'd just seen, had been made to appear like one thing – an expression of gratitude – but was really another, that instinctive cry for help. Perhaps here, in a neutral place, devoid of associations and without the pressures of time, she had felt she might be able to talk freely with someone she knew she could trust.

'You know I'm more than willing to share the load, Laura. With *all* your problems.'

Our eyes met. 'It's so good of you, John. . . . Can I get you another drink?'

'I think I'll turn in now, if you don't mind. I've had two or three broken nights this week; I'd rather like to catch up, secure in the knowledge the phone's unlikely to ring.'

Nothing could have been further from the truth. I sensed her regret, but it was difficult to tell what she was really thinking, in a woman who had such control of her voice and features. Perhaps with the next drink she'd have been able to bring herself to talk openly about the true situation at the house on Tanglewood; but I felt the better place by far would be the open spaces of the park. I remembered how easily she'd talked about herself when we'd walked on the moors.

She said: 'What time shall we have breakfast?'

'It tends to be academic as far as I'm concerned. If we're making a fairly early start I'll just join you for a strong black coffee.'

She smiled. 'I think we might get you to have *something* to eat. People often do when they're away from home and someone else cooks it. Shall we say eightish?'

She came with me to the door. As I was about to open it we looked at each other, hesitated, then briefly kissed, her lips touching mine lightly and coolly.

'See you in the morning, John. It's been such a nice day . . .'

I let myself into my own room with the security card that was now replacing the old-fashioned key on its great plastic fob. I'd wanted to stay on with her, very badly. But I'd forced myself to come away for the same reason I didn't go back into the house with her when I took her out to dinner. She attracted me too much; but all she really wanted from me, perhaps sometimes despite herself, was help and friendship, and her nearness was too difficult to cope with late at night, in a dimly lit room where one of the beds had had its covers turned back in an inviting triangle and the gin was adding its alcoholic content to the pre-prandials and wine at dinner, and the drinks in the theatre bar. It was the true reason I'd decided the park would be the best place to achieve the objective neutrality I'd need for evaluating the things I hoped to be able to get her to tell me.

I wasn't sleepy; the reverse if anything. I was rarely in bed before one. I changed into pyjamas and a thin dressing-gown, switched on the television – there'd be bound to be some ten-year-old film showing I'd only seen three times already.

I wondered how it would have been if I'd put my arms round her and kissed her as I'd wanted to kiss her. I felt she'd have met me half-way. I felt she was attracted to me. She was a mature woman and perceptive, she'd certainly know I was attracted to her. I wondered if she'd half wanted an approach, she must have known the possibilities that tended to linger in the air when a woman invited a man to her hotel room late at night for drinks. I suspected she'd wanted to go to bed as much as I did.

And I sensed we both knew it could only damage the delicate rapport we'd gradually built up. If we became lovers the relationship would have subtly changed from the one I think we were both instinctively trying to maintain. She was in a difficult limbo-life where it seemed I was the only person she could trust completely. Sex at this stage could only add an additional layer of complication, and for her, almost certainly a sense of guilt.

She might not always want it to be simple friendship, in fact I was almost sure she wouldn't, but friendship was what she really wanted, and needed, until she'd sorted out her life. And tomorrow, in Hyde Park, having hung on to my neutrality by a thread, we might be able to talk through the logical steps needed to find her a sensible solution to the problems at Tanglewood Lane.

There was a tap on the door. I remoted the telly, thinking it would probably be a message Norma had left at the desk; it was impossible to draw a straight edge on PI work.

But it was Laura, in a wine-coloured dressing-gown, her hair hanging loose. She looked slightly downwards, but I could see that her eyes were heavy and moist.

'May I come in, John . . .?'

'Of course . . .'

She moved slowly into the room, then turned back to me and shook her head, almost, it seemed, unable to speak. I put a hand on her arm. She suddenly threw her arms round me and leant her head against my shoulder.

'Let it all hang out,' I said gently. 'Whatever it is . . .'

As if it could be anything else than what it had been since the car crash. I felt her shaking her head, as if still unable to speak. We must have stood there for a full minute, she clinging to me as if some powerful tide was trying to drag her loose. She found her voice at last, but it was barely a whisper.

'May I stay with you?'

'Is that . . . what you want?'

'Will you . . . will you just hold me . . .?'

'If that's what you want . . .'

'Please, John . . . just hold me . . .'

She took her head from my shoulder and looked at me then, her eyes shining with tears. They began to well from under her eyelids and trickle steadily down her face. She made no sound or movement, gave no other indication of the force of her emotions, and it confirmed what I'd always sensed, the endless struggle she'd had to keep her grief to herself and under control.

I took out the handkerchief I kept in my dressing-gown pocket and gently dabbed her streaming cheeks. As I did so, she reached out and pressed the master switch that turned off the lamps still lit.

'Which . . . is the bed you're using?'

'The one nearest the window . . .'

She moved away from me and I heard the rustle of fabric as she took off the dressing-gown, and then, a second or two later, the slight hiss of the night-dress sliding from her body. I took off my own night clothes and tentatively got into bed with her. She drew me to her the moment I was in, and I felt the renewed wetness of her cheek against my arm.

'Oh, John . . .' Her voice, normally so composed, seemed to come from a distance, uneven, tremulous, almost gasping. 'I can't tell you . . . to . . . to . . . be held again . . .'

I kissed her wet, salty mouth, stroked her small breasts and her firm thighs, which would have the clear, white, almost marbled quality that went with her pale looks. Perhaps I'd see that body in the morning, that would seem so strangely unfamiliar beneath a face I'd come to know so well.

We didn't make love. She never spoke again. Her arms never slackened, her cheeks never dried. But I couldn't have believed how intense the pleasure would be of simply holding the naked body of this profoundly private woman who'd fought so long and so doggedly to maintain total self-possession. It seemed to produce in me something of that powerful combination of excitement and innocence, lost in extreme youth, of touching a girl's body for the first time and needing nothing else, because the touching and the trembling and the new sensations flickering across the abdomen seemed more than enough, for the moment, to cope with.

I *could* have made love to her. I knew that whatever move I'd made, however tentative, would have been accepted, probably even welcomed. Once aroused, I sensed she might have reacted with an almost overwhelming passion in what I felt might have been a desperate search for some kind of release, for displacement. But lovemaking wasn't what she'd come for, the real craving had been for male closeness, the mental substitution of my body and arms for those of that man whose memory she found so hard to exorcise.

It was not a role I was unfamiliar with. It went with the casual relationships I sometimes drifted into, with women whose lovers or husbands had taken to the road. I accepted it as one of the penalties of staying loose. With her I knew it wasn't quite the same. It was Simon now, but one day she'd be over him, even if she never entirely overcame the sense of loss. I didn't think, with her ambitions, she'd ever remarry, but I felt the time would come when she'd want a man around now and then, and perhaps she'd see in me the ideal occasional lover. It could be an arrangement that would bring pleasure to both of us.

Eventually she slept, her arms slackening round me, her breathing becoming calm and regular. I held her for another half-hour or so, and then I drifted off too, into one of the deepest sleeps I'd had for some time. When I awoke, a sliver of daylight showed at a point where the curtains hadn't quite met. Laura had gone. I felt very disappointed that I'd not been able to glimpse her alabaster body as she'd disentangled herself from my arms and slid from the bed. But then, we weren't lovers, we were still friends, and had we awoken together, every sense freshened by sleep, I wondered if it would have been possible for us not to kiss again, or embrace, or to stop my body imperceptibly covering hers. It seemed each of us was taking it in turns to be strong for both.

Normally, as soon as I awoke I got up, glad that the boredom of having to sleep at all was over, but today I fell back on my pillow and closed my eyes, as if I could re-enter some incredibly pleasant and vivid dream.

Eleven

She was already waiting at a table in the dining-room.

'I've ordered coffee for two,' she said, 'but breakfast is serve yourself. There's a quite incredible amount of choice at a table round the corner. You will eat something, won't you? If we'll be walking all morning . . . let me get you some bacon and egg . . .'

'Have they got scrambled egg?'

'There are few things you can do with an egg they don't appear to have mastered.'

'All right then – bacon and scrambled egg.'

She went off. She wore the grey pleated skirt and the grey turtle-neck sweater with the diamond pattern, and even these simple clothes seemed to intensify her attraction, because I'd now held the body beneath them.

I'd not been looked after with such tender care since my mother had gone to live on the coast. Most of the women I'd known would have expected me to sort out the buffet, and I'd not have considered that in any way unreasonable. But with Laura, looking after my breakfast seemed to be another aspect of the thought she'd put into my weekend treat. She came back, smiling gravely, with a plate that held not just bacon and scrambled egg, but mushrooms and tomatoes and hash-browns.

'I shall be cross if you don't eat it all up.'

'You'd get on with Mother – she's convinced single men living alone exist on a diet of beans on toast and prawn-flavoured crisps.'

But free of pressure and the bother of having to cook for myself, I ate with good appetite, as she'd said I would. In her usual sparing way, she ate a small piece of grilled fish and a poached egg, but with what also seemed good appetite.

'I bought you a *Sunday Times*,' she said, tapping the bundle of newsprint that lay to one side. 'I went to see what the weather was like and there was such a nice newspaperman just outside the Bond Street tube. I gave him a lot of change and he called me duck and said I must have been raiding my piggy-bank.'

'That was good of you,' I said, and then without thinking, went on: 'I gave my change away last night and so all I could have given him was a ten-pound note. He'd have loved that, I'm sure . . .'

She gave me a brief, impersonal glance, then looked down at her plate again, and I remembered that odd incident of the vagrant and her attitude to down-and-outs in general. But it was over; she had her view and I had mine, and I didn't want her to think that my reference to a shortage of change was any other than casual and inadvertent. And so I said: 'I missed you this morning. For a while I wondered if it had really happened.'

Her grey eyes rested steadily on mine. It was difficult to see this woman, as calm and composed as ever, as the same one who'd wept in my arms with such abandon.

'I imposed on you too much, John. I'll not forget your kindness.'

I wondered if kindness was a euphemism for restraint. 'I think you and I have different definitions of imposition.'

She reached across the table and put a hand over mine. 'Thank you,' she said quietly.

She withdrew the hand and began to pour more coffee into our cups with her usual endearing solicitude. Memories of most of the several other women I'd slept with and made love to tended to be faded and imprecise; it was the memory of the woman I'd slept with and not made love to that would remain clear and sharp-edged.

After breakfast, she settled the bill, and we left our bags in reception ready to collect for our return to King's Cross. Then we set off along Oxford Street towards Marble Arch. It was a crisp day of thin cloud and an enlarged, almost heatless sun, ideal for walking. She wore her trench-style raincoat and a maroon beret drawn sideways over hair that today hung loose. We clipped along the maze of subways at the top of Park Lane and surfaced near Speakers' Corner, where we took the long diagonal path that passed through open grass-land to the Serpentine, calm and glassy in still air that was pungent with the odour of smouldering leaves and moist earth. We walked around the lake and then beneath the bridge to Kensington Gardens, almost deserted at this hour.

Space and solitude seemed to work their usual therapeutic spell on her, and I felt I almost shared her relief at the relax-ation of strain. We walked slowly, hand in hand, she glancing in every direction with the intensity I'd got to know so well, occasionally telling me about the life-style of shoveler ducks and black-headed gulls, and how the grey wagtail could nor-mally only be seen on the Long Water in autumn, before resuming its migratory passage to its winter habitat. I wondered if I'd ever get used to the incredible range of topics she could throw out detailed information on so casually.

We walked for perhaps an hour, beneath the flaring foliage of thinning trees, along pathways so straight and lengthy their destinations were lost to sight in a distant mist. And then I began to feel puzzled. We were away from home, from hotel rooms, from intrusive associations, in open space, with no distractions – I'd been certain she'd want to talk about the difficulties that seemed to be almost corroding her peace of mind. I could scarcely be closer to her now; she'd spent the night in my bed. But we drifted on, and I wondered if she found it difficult to involve me in matters that were obviously deep-rooted in a past that excluded me, to disturb our mood of simple enjoyment in each other's company in the odours, colours and light of an autumn day. If so, perhaps I should take the initiative.

We walked into a clearing, the hub of several paths, where the great statue of horse and rider called Physical Energy towered above us on its plinth. As we stood looking at it, I said: 'Laura, I feel I must talk to you about something . . .'

She gave me a rapid sidelong glance, looked back at the statue. Her lack of response seemed to signal agreement, to indicate that I'd found the opening she'd been searching for herself.

'I know it's none of my business . . .'

She slowly turned back to me and shrugged, her face seeming to flicker from one expression to another, across a range of emotions difficult to evaluate, but each like an aspect almost of despair. She put a hand on my arm. 'This was supposed to be *your* weekend,' she said in a low voice. 'All I seem to have done is bog you down in my dreary hang-ups . . .'

'Look,' I said, 'I've seen you struggling to come to terms with Simon's death, and I know that in the end you'll only be able to get over it in your own way. But there *is* something else, isn't there, something I might be able to help you with.' I hesitated, then said abruptly, 'It *is* David, isn't it?'

178

Again, she glanced at me without s.........g.

'It's the money,' I said flatly. 'He'll probably have a good idea of what you're worth, and he's wanting to borrow some of it, or he's wanting to say how it should be invested. He *is* out of work, isn't he?'

'How do you know?' she said quickly, and then looked at me anxiously, her eyes widening, as if she regretted the admission.

'I can't help knowing. I'm a PI and I can't switch off. People are my business. I've met men like David Marsh before and they've all been bad news . . .'

'Oh, John . . .' she almost whispered, before walking off slowly down one of the paths that ran from the clearing, looking as dejected as a child other children would no longer play with. I half wished I'd left the bright morning as it was, when we'd set out so cheerfully across Hyde Park. I caught her up, took her arm.

'It's quite impossible for you to understand,' she said. 'No one can. The brothers were like Siamese *twins*. David looked after Simon when they were at school. He was two years older. Then again at college; he was in his third year when Simon and I were freshers, but he stayed on to do some postgraduate work. He went everywhere with us – all the parties, the dances. . . . They'd always share their last pound note – it was that sort of relationship . . .'

'I *can* understand, Laura. It's only what I imagined . . .'

She shook her head vehemently. 'You can't begin to. I thought – when we got married – they'd go their own way. David lived with someone; it didn't work out. He got married; that didn't work either. He and Simon – they seemed almost *glad*. I think Simon felt he could begin to pay him back for the incredible amount of advice and support David had put into his education. He began to share our holidays. He'd stay with us almost every weekend. But we all got on together . . . you mustn't think I resented it. He's so much nicer than he seems when you first meet him. But I can scarcely remember what it was like when it wasn't the three of us.'

'Did David ever lend you money? When Simon was setting up in business?'

Her eyes met mine, slid away. 'I . . . don't know. He may have done. They'd have lent each other anything. Simon always felt he owed David a debt he could never repay, for looking after him and helping him with his homework and making sure he wasn't bullied – all that. He felt so much of what he'd achieved was due to David . . .'

'So *you* feel obliged to help David . . .'

'Oh, John . . .' She put a hand to her forehead, as if suffering a splitting headache. 'He wants to borrow so *much*! He keeps saying he'd have done exactly the same for us when he had money, says Simon wouldn't have hesitated had the money been his. He never gives in.'

I put my arm round her trembling shoulders. It was conscience, and I'd been right. I often was right on motivation, but being right this time brought no sense of gratification. Not when it involved Laura. 'Let me speak to him,' I said. 'I'll play honest broker. You could hardly be more emotionally involved, and that's no basis for making decisions.'

'Oh, no,' she said quickly. 'No, John. I must sort it out in my own way. I shouldn't even have *confided* in you . . .'

'You *must*, Laura. If you go on like this you'll have a breakdown.'

'*No*, John!' she said, a faint note of something that seemed almost like panic creeping into her tone. 'He'd be terribly upset if I were to involve you. I *told* you you'd not be able to understand the way it was. He'd think it such a . . . such a betrayal . . .'

We were both now walking distractedly along the pathway, frequently stopping to face each other, almost like one of those couples caught in a public place in an argument so consuming it was as if they'd forgotten they were not in their own living-room.

'It's simply too much for a woman in your state to handle,' I said flatly. 'You must see that. He's caught you at your lowest ebb to make his demands. It's as if you'd been seriously ill – too weak to think, let alone make major decisions. It wouldn't be quite so bad if he'd given you six months to sort yourself out, but to start on you before you've even got the final cheque . . .'

'Please, John, *please* let's leave it. You'd *never* understand, being on the outside . . .'

'I thought I was just a little more than that now . . .'

She seemed not to catch the hurt in my tone, but plunged on again, towards the Round Pond, looking as though she were almost in a state of shock. It was impossible to detect any increase in pallor in a face normally pale, but there was the faintest sheen of moisture over her smooth skin.

'Laura . . .' I took her arm again. She half turned, but would not meet my eyes. 'Just hear me out. If David put money into Simon's business, and the business was a company limited in liability and was more or less going broke, there can be no *legal* comebacks on you. If the business *wasn't* a limited company, and there was a properly documented loan agreement, then David has a *possible* claim against the estate, that is, the insurance money . . .'

'There'd be . . . nothing on paper . . .' she said at last, with extreme reluctance. 'Not between those two . . .'

'Right. Then you may feel you owe him something on an *ex gratia* basis. But you must take advice. An accountant, your solicitor – they can go back in the records and prove what the loan was, *if* there was one. Or, better still, just let me talk to him . . .'

'No . . . no . . . absolutely not, John. Please don't say any more. I must sort it out for myself. I'm the only one who can, you see . . .'

I found it difficult to understand – the moistness of her skin, the inability to meet my eyes, the note of sheer panic in her voice. It was as if the discussion had somehow got away from her and she'd revealed far more than she'd ever intended. Oddly, it was a reaction I saw regularly in the faces of inexperienced young crooks I'd amiably led towards the few unguarded words that were going to put them back in the dole queue. And I'd been confidently expecting relief. Relief that it was finally out in the open, that honest John Goss would be coming up with a solution that Marsh would have to accept.

'Let me just say one more thing,' I said, walking rapidly to keep up with the pace she was now unconsciously setting. 'If you won't let me speak to him will you *please* let me send a completely impartial adviser who can take an overview of your affairs and examine any scheme David's proposing to put your money into.'

She stopped yet again and closed her eyes, seeming almost to sway, to be on the point of fainting. I took hold of her instinctively.

'Please, John,' she whispered, 'no more. I *know* you want to help . . . that you mean well . . . but . . . but . . . you're being too zealous. It's delicate . . . complex . . . I *have* to sort it out on my own.' She forced a rueful smile. 'I was just letting my hair down, making a play for sympathy. Don't you see? You're so *good* on sympathy . . .'

'Come along,' I said, in a gentler tone. 'If we go down from the Round Pond it should bring us to Kensington Road or

Kensington Gore – I'm never too sure where one ends and the other begins. There'll be a pub. We can have a drink and a sandwich.'

I offered my hand to her again, which she accepted, and we began to walk at a more normal pace, in what seemed a companionable silence, like the two ordinary Sunday morning lovers I wished we were.

I didn't see how it could possibly be simply conscience. Her reactions had been too powerful, too near hysteria. I *wanted* it to be, God knows, but it didn't look as if it was going to be as easy as that. I'd almost talked myself into ruling out a sexual angle, but I knew now I had to reconsider it, little as I wanted to. I wondered if the closeness of those three could possibly have led to a ménage. She'd seemed almost to hint at it in her outbursts. But could she still be involved with him if she was here alone with me? I wondered if she was afraid, if she let me try to broke a deal with Marsh, that in all the sordidness of negotiation I might learn too much about the things she didn't want me to know, about the true relationship of the Marsh trio. I wondered if she herself sensed that I tended to see her in a certain way, to idealise a sad and attractive widow, as Dickens had idealised certain of the women in his novels.

She'd be right, of course, my admiration for her had always led me to overlook any shortcomings, even when her views about the vagrant problem had seemed so callous. But apart from her attitude to vagrants, there really did seem to be few flaws in her make-up that I could see as serious faults. She'd always been generous, considerate, fun to be with and able to give my ego a polish like no one I'd ever known.

But whatever the real Laura was like, assuming she could be much different from the Laura I'd been shown, I wondered if that was the real reason she wanted to keep me apart from Marsh – that she *liked* the way I saw her and wanted that image to remain intact. If that was the case, I couldn't blame her for it; it was a trait that affected most of us at one time or another, especially in new relationships. And whatever *had* happened between her and Marsh, if anything, I would always have the satisfaction of knowing it was me she turned to for comfort and friendship, not him.

We stood for a few minutes gazing over the Round Pond, at the handful of children trying not very successfully to coax kites to launch themselves in the almost imperceptible breeze. I doubted I'd ever know the true story of the Marsh brothers, didn't think I wanted to. But I was determined that money would not be transferred to David that came from insurances carefully arranged by Simon for her protection. It wasn't going to be easy.

'The Round Pond simply isn't *round*,' she said, with a return of her old faint smile. 'And it's not really a pond. It's a sort of oblong lake with rounded corners . . .'

'The Danube's not blue either. That came as a dreadful disappointment.'

'It makes you begin to wonder if there's a single yellow stone in Yellowstone Park . . .'

'I shouldn't think the Painted Desert's had a lick of Dulux in fifty years . . .'

She suddenly burst out laughing. Perhaps it was the reaction to strain, but it seemed to be the first really spontaneous laughter I'd seen during all the weeks I'd known her. Perhaps it had done her some kind of good, at least being able to admit to the problem of Marsh, even if there'd been no solution. We walked companionably on, past Kensington Palace and out on to the main road. We crossed over and found a pub called the Goat.

'One-fifteen,' I said. 'We'll get a cab about two. Do you want anything to eat?'

She shook her head. 'I'm not hungry. Would you make mine a *large* vodka. Here, let me pay . . .'

'Laura, for heaven's sake! You've spent far too much on me this weekend.'

I smilingly ignored the proffered tenner, went to the bar. I wasn't hungry either, after the big breakfast, and I also decided to have a double. It was pleasant for once not having to keep my bloodstream clear for the endless daily driving.

I glanced back at her as the drinks were assembled, where she sat in the grey sweater and skirt, her raincoat at her side, but still wearing the maroon beret that gave her the slightly Gallic *jeune fille* look, except that I was probably thinking in film clichés and Frenchwomen no longer wore berets, assuming they ever had. She smiled at me, and I thought of her last night in the dressing-gown, standing at my door, the tears slowly welling in her eyes, of holding the body I'd not seen, her face wet against my shoulder.

In less than an hour we'd be on our way home. I felt I had to give it one more shot. She seemed so helpless, despite all the learning and the braininess. It appeared that Marsh had lost his own money; I couldn't rid myself of the fear that he might lose hers too. I'd never be able to forgive myself, however much she wanted to keep me out of it.

I went back with the glasses and mixers, sat next to her, took her hand. 'I care about you, Laura, very much. I didn't want to interfere, believe me, but it upsets me so much to see you so overwrought . . .'

'I thought I'd made it crystal clear, John, that no one can sort out my affairs but me.'

The cold curtness of her tone startled me. It was the voice receptionists used with people they'd been told to get rid of. It wasn't a tone I could remember hearing before and perhaps, if I'd not been preoccupied with the shortage of time and the pictures I kept seeing of Laura as penniless as Marsh himself, I would have taken more notice of what I realised later was a clear note of warning.

'Let me give you this card,' I said quickly, taking out my wallet. 'Total discretion guaranteed. He'll listen and he'll advise, nothing else. . . . David can't deny you counselling, not with that kind of money. . . .'

'Will you for *Christ's sake* keep your nose *out*!'

Shock seemed to push me back, like a wave of displaced air. Her small voice had suddenly acquired an intense carrying edge. Rage had mottled the clear white skin of her face and distorted her calm features in a way I'd not have thought possible, it was as if they'd been instantly altered by a computer-enhancing technique – they were still recognisably hers but dark and heavy, almost malevolent. Her entire body seemed to shake and I felt an instinctive urge to protect myself, as if she were about to launch a physical attack.

'Laura . . .!'

'Drop it, drop it, *drop* it – how many more bloody times do you have to be *told*!'

For a second, as she stared at me unblinkingly, I had that strange unnerving sensation you sometimes had with people you knew to be mentally ill, that there was a third presence, that some other woman was looking at me through her eyes.

'All right, Laura,' I said, in a low, soothing voice, 'consider it dropped.'

'Don't *ever* bring it up again.'

'I won't . . .'

'Don't *ever* try to tell me how to live my life.'

'You have my word, believe it.'

'Who do you think you *are*, with all your bloody advice . . .?'

'As far as you're concerned, nobody. You've now made your point.'

'Just leave me *alone*, for Christ's sake!'

A heavy man in shirt sleeves looked down at us. 'Everything all right, sir . . . madam?'

Jumping to her feet and picking up her coat, but not putting it on, she almost ran from the bar parlour. Her drink was untouched, but I drained my glass. I needed it. I glanced at the barman and shrugged. He gave me the faint passepartout bar-parlour smile that in this case seemed to translate into the one word: '*Women!*'

She was standing on the pavement, staring at the traffic that flowed along Kensington Road, the raincoat held insecurely over her arm so its hem lay on the pavement. I took it gently from her and guided each arm into its sleeve, then buttoned it up and knotted the tie-belt.

'We'll have to cross over,' I said. 'We need to flag a cab going east . . .'

We found a pedestrian crossing and within seconds of reaching the other side a cruising cab pulled in. She sat as if drawn into herself, like some woodland animal desperately trying to make itself as inconspicuous as possible against lurking predators. She looked wan to the point where her pale skin seemed almost transparent.

'Stay here,' I said to her, as we drew up outside the Berkshire. 'I'll see to the bags.'

She gave no indication she'd even heard, it was as if she was in that state of trauma where it seems barely possible to make even the smallest action or decision.

When I came back, followed by a uniformed attendant carrying the bags, the cab-driver was talking cheerfully, as they often did, requiring little or no response, or even reaction, which was just as well as she continued to exist in some remote world of her own.

As we drove along Euston Road, she slipped a hand slowly

on to my thigh. I covered it with my own. Our train was waiting when we reached the station and was due out in ten minutes. I selected seats in the almost deserted first-class section and swung the bags up on the rack. As I was about to sit down opposite her she said in a low voice: 'Will you sit next to me?'

So we sat side by side, and a few minutes later she slid her arm through mine.

'I'll get you a drink,' I said, when the train was rolling.

I got drinks and the mixings. Not surprisingly, we were both still without appetite. We sipped them slowly as the train flashed rapidly north, not speaking. We both seemed to share the same feeling, that silence was our best option. But I thought a lot.

When she'd finished her drink she drifted into quiet sleep, her head on my shoulder. Sleep, it seemed, as with so many unhappy people, was her refuge.

'If you go on like this,' I'd told her, during that agitated walk in Kensington Gardens, 'you'll have a breakdown.' Prophetic words. There was absolutely no doubt she'd been trembling, as she hurled abuse at me in the Goat, on the edge of her sanity. And it had to be down to Marsh.

I wondered where I went from here. I'd rarely felt so frustrated. I still had zero facts about Marsh's hold over her. It was all conjecture. From Laura I'd had the stark admission that 'He wants to borrow so *much*'. It would be a long time before I could even begin to think of talking to her about it again, if ever – the bitter irony hadn't escaped me that I'd been the one who'd almost pushed her over the edge Marsh had relentlessly driven her towards.

I kicked it around for the entire journey. There were no distractions. She slept steadily, barely moving, and I didn't want to disturb her by fiddling with the three pounds of newsprint she'd bought me from the nice man outside the Bond Street tube.

By the time we'd reached the first of the northern stations I'd made up my mind. I would do what I was best at, follow the man around, get an exact check on his life-style, try to find out what he wanted – or needed – a lot of money for. If she couldn't bring herself to tell me I'd find out for myself.

And when I'd found out it wouldn't be Laura I'd talk to, it would be to Marsh himself. No one knew better than I did how notoriously complex family matters could seem to an outsider, but even allowing for Laura's own possible foolishness in the affair, it was obvious she was being manipulated.

And was still pleading for help, however hysterically she denied it, however frightened she seemed of the consequences.

And so I would get together what I could about Marsh, then tackle him myself. He would tell me it was none of my bloody business and I would use certain manipulative techniques of my own to make him think backing off could be a good idea. It might not work. The Laura Marsh situation might be beyond all outside help. But I'd have done what I could.

Twelve

'Who's our best contact in the Leicester area?'

'Alan Starkey,' she said promptly. 'Fast, accurate – almost in the John Goss class, but nice with it.'

'I . . . need some information about a man called David Marsh. It's . . . Laura's brother-in-law.'

Norma watched me in silence. I said: 'When you had a feeling there was something Laura might be holding back on you were right. I . . . found out Simon's brother is spending time at her house. She didn't want me to know, probably because she didn't want me to think they were living together. I don't think they are, but I can't rule it out. I also can't rule out they might have been lovers for some time. I know for a fact he's wanting to get his hands on a slice of the insurance money.'

I filled her in on the detail. Finally I said: 'Don't say you told me so.'

'You will admit you've got a bit of a blind spot about her . . .'

'If I had I'd find it very hard to *accept* they might have been lovers.'

'Oh, I don't know. You've been a PI for a long time now. I'm sure you can accept that any woman her age might have some kind of a past. What I *can't* get together is why she feels she has to cover it up.'

'I honestly believe she didn't want me to think she was sleeping with David the minute Simon wrote himself off.'

'What's it got to do with you? I'm sorry, John, but I'm on the outside here, and it seems to me that whatever a woman her age does with her private life is nothing to do with a PI, unless it's part of the investigation. Did you tell Zephyr about it?'

'I . . . told them her brother-in-law had visited her,' I said reluctantly. 'It's in the report you typed.'

'But you didn't say he was staying there, if my memory serves me right.'

'What difference would it make? He's out of work, why shouldn't he stay with her now and then? Whether he was giving her one or not makes no difference to the claim.'

'And yet she was anxious that you and the Zephyr didn't find out.'

I sighed. 'Look, Norma, put yourself in her place. I'm positive she's genuinely upset about Simon, but Simon's brother keeps spending the night with her. It might be completely innocent but it looks bad. So she wants to keep it quiet. Surely you can understand her urge to keep the story-line nice and clean. Christ, no one watches as many soaps as you do . . .'

She was silent for some time, riffling absently through the opened mail. 'You may be right,' she said at last. 'And I don't honestly see how the insurance claim can be affected. It's . . . it's the woman herself, drawing you into her affairs like this. Why do you want information on David Marsh?'

'I'd . . . like to try and find out what he needs this money for . . . what he aims to do with it. For her sake . . .'

'I really think you'd be making a big mistake. You'd be getting involved in something you didn't understand and at the end of the day no one's going to thank you for it, families being what they are. Time to walk away, John.'

But I couldn't. Not having seen her so upset, almost at the end of her tether, not when I was certain I was the only one who could help her, if anyone could.

'Indulge me, Norma,' I said. 'Let me just try and find out what the bastard's up to. I'll be able to decide then what to do about it, if anything.'

Her eyes rested ruefully on mine. 'Well, if you're in your dogged mood I suppose you'd better give me the details . . .'

'There aren't many. He's supposed to be working for a firm that processes other firms' payrolls. I shouldn't have thought there were too many of those about. Both he and Simon were at Manchester University at the same time, that might give Starkey some kind of a lead. What I need more than anything is a Leicester address.'

Knowing Simon's date of birth, I could give her the year David Marsh was born, if not the date, and we could also project the year he'd gone to college.

'If those are the only details you've got it's going to cost you.'

She didn't need to tell me. Starkey was good, knew he was good, and charged accordingly – like me. I began to zip up my parka. It was an unseasonably cold day, almost winter-like.

'Before you rush off, young man. I spoke to your chum at Bowling Suites. He said he'd have a look at your down-and-out friend for general labouring *if* he was clean, prepared to work and had an address.'

'Oh . . . right . . .' I said guiltily, the predicament of the man on the bench below the roundabout having been wiped from my mind yet again by my preoccupation with Laura and her affairs. 'I'll speak to him at lunch-time, if he's around.'

'You'd forgotten all about it, hadn't you. I can't *imagine* what you've been up to in London to make you forget your old buddies back in the subway.'

* * *

'Thanks . . . boss . . .'

He looked uneasily at the two pound coins I'd put in his grubby hand, the largesse making him rightly suspicious. He wore a battered camel-hair overcoat and a woollen cap pulled down to his eyebrows, so that his eyes seemed to peer mole-like from beneath undergrowth.

I sat next to him on his bench. An expression of mild alarm crossed his unshaven face at this worrying and unprecedented event.

'You from the council, boss . . .?' Smiling, I shook my head. 'You're not a copper,' he told me. 'That geezer you was wiv wonce, *'e* was . . .'

I supposed they developed a nose for the police as finely turned as a harlot's for the punter or the pusher for the addict. I said: 'How about telling me your name?'

'Who's asking . . .?'

'My name's John Goss. I'm a private investigator.'

The look of alarm returned. He instinctively edged away from me. 'What you investigating?'

'Many things, my friend, none of them to do with you. Why not tell me your name? You've seen me often enough.'

'. . . Tommy,' he said reluctantly. 'Tommy Winthrop . . .'

'Listen, Tommy, I know a man who owns a furniture business. He could do with a strong man like you to help him hump three-piece suites about.'

'A *job*!' The words carried above the muted roar of traffic like a cry of pain. The other vagrants looked on, their apathy suddenly lifted by expressions of hopeful malice.

'Now, come on, Tommy, you must have had a job once.'

He began to grin. 'You don't think 'e'd look at me, boss. I 'aven't got no abode. You 'ave to 'ave an abode, see. They're very particler about you 'aving an abode. I 'aven't got no abode. *And* I've lost me papers somewhere, 'less one of these thieving bastards took 'em. No abode, no papers, boss . . .'

He settled back, having made probably his longest speech in a year, as if the matter was now settled to everyone's total satisfaction.

'You don't need to worry about papers, Tommy. I can sort that out. And I can find you an abode . . .'

'I'm not going in no dormitory. They'll thieve anything – your makings, your bit of money, take the clothes off your back if you let 'em . . . no *thank you* . . .'

'It won't be a dormitory. You'd have a nice warm bed-sit of your own.'

''Ow much would that lot cost?'

'You'd not have to worry about that. You'd have money to pay for it. You'd be able to call in the pub . . .'

He began to rub a hand across his stubble of beard agitatedly, glancing round at the others, who were now taking a pleasurable interest in his discomfort. 'You don't want to go bothering about me, boss. You're not a vicar . . .'

I sighed. I found it difficult enough making complete sense of my motives to myself, let alone to Tommy Winthrop. 'I don't like to see an able-bodied man like you out of work and living hand to mouth. Someone helped that friend of yours, didn't they?'

'Suss . . . you mean Suss?'

'Yes,' I said wearily, 'your friend Suss . . .'

''E were a scaffolder, Suss. Skilled. There's work for scaffolders, see . . .'

He felt in his pocket, took out a half-smoked cigarette and struck a single match with a skilled gesture of a yellowish thumbnail. 'Now if I'd been a scaffolder like Suss we could of both 'ad work . . . no 'ead for 'eights, see.'

'Well, I can get you a nice little labouring job, Tommy,' I said patiently. 'They want a strong bloke to move furniture about in a nice warm warehouse . . .'

"'Ow much . . .?"

'Oh . . . I can't be certain, maybe two hundred sovs a week with overtime. But you'd be back in the system then. We could get you some decent clothes and have the doctors check you out . . .'

'Where would this bed-sit be?'

I tried to conceal my exasperation behind another smile. 'I don't know yet. There'll be men like yourself lodging there – decent working men who've fallen on hard times . . .'

He had the vagrant's knack of smoking a cigarette butt to the point where he seemed simply to be holding a sliver of paper and a shred of tobacco. He reluctantly tossed the minute smouldering fragment to the ground and said: 'Would Suss be there?'

'I can't guarantee that . . .'

'I'd not want to be on me own. I got on wiv Suss, see . . .'

'What's his other name?' I said resignedly. I realised once more how impossibly difficult it was, trying to fit the problem of Tommy into an already crowded schedule.

'Don't know no other name . . .'

'Do you know where he lives?'

"'E's never been back, 'as 'e,' he said, with a trace of bitterness. 'Thought 'e'd of called back, me and 'im being mates, know what I mean . . .'

'So you don't know his real name and you don't know where he lives. It looks as if he's gone for good.'

'I'd 'ave to be in the same kip as 'im, boss. I wouldn't want to be wiv no strangers . . .'

I supposed it was all relative in Tommy's world. Strangers were people who slept in dormitories, friends were people you drank silently with in a garden beneath a roundabout, and close friends were people you knew by a nickname and shared your dog-ends with.

I wondered if I could possibly track down the man. The details I'd had on David Marsh had seemed sparse for passing over to an agent; they were the full monty compared with what I had to go on for finding Tommy's best mate.

'All right,' I said reluctantly, 'if I can find where Suss is living will you think about this job I've got lined up for you?'

His unfocused gaze passed over the raised circular garden. The flowers were long gone, apart from a few discoloured roses, and the deciduous bushes were rapidly shedding their foliage, the only intact vegetation being a few sodden-looking evergreen shrubs. I wondered if he was balancing this atmosphere of raw desolation against the warmth and comfort of a room of his own, a few pounds in his pocket, hot food, nights at the local. I couldn't begin to see the contest, but then so far I'd had no reason to cut myself off from mainstream society, to separate myself from all human problems except the one of surviving the next twenty-four hours.

'Reverend 'Opper wonce got me a job,' he said reflectively. 'Cleaning new cars what came wiv all wax on and that. You know 'im?'

Who didn't? There were few local people with a higher profile in the do-gooding stakes than the Reverend Hopper. 'Give Jesus Christ lessons,' I'd once heard Norma mutter darkly.

'What happened?'

'Missed me friends, boss. I can do anything I like, don't you see. Go anywhere. I went to Scarborough won year. Plenty of caffs there, they'll give you the leavings, no bother. I got as I didn't like being tied.'

'But you'll be old one day, Tommy. You'll not be able to cope, you'll start being ill. If we got you back to work you'd have a proper state pension to look forward to when you retired, you'd be taken care of . . .'

He gave me the blank stare of total incomprehension. I

realised that old age was a concept now well beyond his grasp. There'd been too many of the small triumphs of keeping body and soul together for one day more. For four months of the year he was fighting not just hunger but the climate. There would be times when every atom of his concentration would be focused on the struggle for survival, and I supposed the ability to think long-term, like fit, warm, well-nourished people who could even plan their lives twenty years out, must have atrophied long ago.

'Nah, I'd better stay as I am, boss. I know where I'm at, see. I wouldn't *feel* right, know what I mean. It was like when Reverend 'Opper got me the car job. I didn't 'ave no real company. I'm not one of *them*, see . . .'

I glanced round at the sad, tattered wretches who formed his social milieu, sunk now, as it seemed Tommy was evading the possibility of serious trouble, into their previous apathy. They'd steal his last crust, his last dog-end, if he weren't endlessly vigilant, but they were his own kind, the people he related to, just as other men related to people they worked with or played golf and fished and shot with. And being accepted seemed to mean more than warmth or food or money.

I saw then that he'd had no intention of accepting work from the start, despite the questions that had seemed to indicate a flickering of interest. He'd kept me talking because I was a diversion, it filled a little of that gigantic reservoir of time he had at his disposal. I felt doubly exasperated. It wasn't just the waste of my own time, it was the fact that I wasn't an instinctive do-gooder. I was like the man who develops cancer, then devotes large sums to cancer research. I'd once seen a man in a derelict warehouse in a state of quiet desperation, and next morning he'd been dead. I knew my main reaction to Tommy's obstinacy was profound relief. The accompanying guilt made me give it one more shot.

'Do you want to think about it, Tommy?'

He shook his head. The world was full of people who found it impossible to live a structured life, with spouse, kids, dogs, television jingles, a third of every weekday always forfeited to the provision of a life they found intolerable; but there weren't too many who found the idea of throwing off all the shackles so tempting they'd live as far out of the system as Tommy.

I got up thankfully. I'd done my best. There'd been a job on the table, clothes, food, a bed. But it seemed Tommy had gravitated to his natural setting – like a rat living contentedly inside a rubbish dump – and trying to prise him away from it seemed almost callous. We'd both failed, the Reverend Hopper and I, and I knew I'd not be trying again. I'd laid the ghost.

I put my hands in the pockets of my padded coat, felt an unfamiliar object in one of them. It was a packet of cigarettes – they were to go with the money I'd given him. I tossed them on his lap. He picked them up with a smile of pure pleasure.

''Ow did you know it was me birthday?'

'Goodbye, Tommy. Take care of yourself . . .'

I walked off, reflecting on the absurdity of those last mechanical words.

'Boss!'

I glanced back.

'You're a good bloke. I couldn't talk to Reverend 'Opper like what I done to you. Knew it all, Reverend 'Opper. You're a good bloke. I'll not forget. If I can do you a good turn any time, you just let me know . . .'

'Thanks, Tommy, I'll bear that in mind.'

I moved off, grinning, wondering what he could imagine it was in his power to do for me that could be regarded as a good turn.

* * *

That night, and the following two, I went to Tanglewood Lane, first checking the side-streets to see if the Escort was parked up, then waiting in the one he'd used the night he'd left the study light on, to see if he came later. I waited until eleven each night, but he didn't show. But on the fourth night, arriving about eight, I found the Escort tucked away at the top of the favoured cul-de-sac. I parked my own car in another of the side-streets and walked up towards the reservoirs, on the opposite side of the road to the Marsh house. I wondered if I could get near enough the drawing-room window to be able to overhear anything, pick up some clue as to how much money he wanted, and what he wanted it for. It was a long shot but they occasionally came off.

I didn't attempt to reach the back garden by going directly on to Laura's premises. I knew it was cut off – on one side of the house by the garage, on the other by a tall wooden gate, which she kept locked. I had all the usual devices in the car for forcing simple locks, but I'd be working in the light of a street-lamp and it was too risky.

I passed on, to the entrance to the reservoirs. The iron gates stood open. In theory they should have been closed and locked, but as the nearby wall was barely chest high, and anyone determined to get in at night could do so, there wasn't too much point. The ranger had once told Laura, in all seriousness, that duck-rustling had never been a serious problem. Foxes – now they were a different cup of tea altogether.

I moved across the courtyard of the ranger's house and on to the causeway that ran along the bottom end of the lower reservoir. There was a steep grassy slope that ran from the causeway to join the dense woodland that backed the houses on Laura's side of Tanglewood Lane. I scrambled down this slope, able in the silence to hear water rushing along underground culverts, and made my way steadily and quietly through the undergrowth, counting off the houses until I knew I was at the rear of Laura's. The wall, from the wooded side, was much higher than it seemed from the drawing-room window, and I realised that a good half of it was actually a buttress, holding in the weight of the back garden itself. But there were overhanging trees nearby, and I was able to climb one, swing along a branch and let myself fall so that I could grasp the v-shaped stonework that formed the wall's parapet. I pulled myself over and dropped lightly into the garden.

It was like looking past a proscenium arch. She'd not yet drawn the curtains and the room was dimly lit by the usual sprinkling of silk-shrouded lamps. I approached the long, stone-mullioned window and knelt so I could just see over the sill. They were both standing and I could tell by the way they held themselves they were in an emotional state. For a time they were silent, staring angrily at each other. She wore her usual dark pants and sweater, and he was dressed exactly as I'd last seen him, in the thick Aran sweater and the brown cords. His face seemed slightly different and I realised he wasn't wearing his glasses. Perhaps he alternated them with contacts, like so many people these days, as his eyes didn't have that lack of focus of short-sighted people who'd briefly taken their glasses off.

He began to speak, but the windows had the tight sealing of double-glazed units and none of them was ajar. I could just detect the sound of his voice, but nothing else. His hands were trembling slightly and he seemed just as tense and nervy as before. The moment he finished speaking Laura began, her fists clenched and moving up and down in anger. Marsh suddenly broke in, hands now shaking like someone with palsy, his features twisted in agitation. She cut him off, her own face dark and distorted with a rage I knew only too well.

She suddenly turned from him, so she faced the window. I thought she must see me, but realised it wasn't possible – looking from a lit room into darkness, all she would see would be her own reflection. She closed her eyes, as if suffering a splitting headache, an action I also vividly remembered.

A small table stood before the window, on which several letters lay beneath an ornate glass paperweight. She suddenly seized the paperweight, as if she would hurl it at him or smash it against his head. I sensed my heart speeding up in fear – if she hit him at the wrong point of his temple she could seriously injure him. I knew too much about domestic violence. My knuckles bunched up of their own accord, as if to knock a warning on the window.

But something he said stopped her from doing whatever she might have done. She put the paperweight down almost abstractedly and turned back to him. He shrugged, seemed to sigh, picked up a glass from an occasional table and drained its colourless contents. He spoke again, seeming slightly calmer.

After that, neither of them spoke for some time. Then suddenly she clutched at a handbag that lay on a couch, ripped it open and took out a thick wad of twenty-pound notes, which she flung on to the table where his glass stood. She then came back to the window and tugged at a pulley that drew the curtains. It seemed appropriate.

I made my way back through the wood. I'd learnt nothing that I didn't know already, except that if I didn't do something to sort out Marsh very soon she would be left holding on to her sanity by a thread.

This made twice I'd seen her fly into an almost frightening rage within a few days, and this was a woman who'd seemed more in control of herself, in circumstances of intense strain, than any I'd known.

I decided to go home. I'd debated with myself about continuing to watch his car in case he left, now that he'd got his pocket money, but I'd decided that if he did leave it would be difficult, on quiet roads, to follow it without being clocked. And if he did actually still live in Leicester it seemed unlikely he'd be going there tonight, when there was sleeping accommodation at Laura's, though not, I felt quite certain, in her bed.

If only she could have brought herself to share her problems with me. I knew I tended to idealise her a little, which she probably sensed, but I was a big boy and I'd been around, and there was nothing she could have done in the past, however foolish, or even sleazy, that would ever change my regard for her. 'Poor kid,' I found myself murmuring, about a woman who must have been almost ten years my senior.

But early next morning I returned to Tanglewood Lane and found the Escort still parked in the same place. I waited on the busy highway that Tanglewood connected with, and at about eight saw the Escort nose out into the traffic. I followed it from three cars back. We skirted the city on the ring road, then took the north-west route to the Dales. The road was wide and fast, and I had no difficulty in keeping myself inconspicuous.

But instead of cutting out Skipton on the bypass, he drove towards the market town itself, pulling in to the car-park of a supermarket just outside. I had disguised myself earlier and when he went in I drifted after him. I took a basket and stocked up on several of the items no single man can survive without, like three jars of instant coffee. Marsh himself had a capacious trolley, and was filling it with everything from breakfast items through to dinner. I checked out ahead of him and waited in my own distantly parked car until he emerged and began stacking the carrier loads of goods into the Escort's boot. Was that partly what that great wad of notes was urgently needed for – groceries?

He drove then into the centre of Skipton, where we both inched up the high street in a press of traffic. At the round-about just below the castle, he took the road that led to a string of villages, the first one being Grassington. The route was a narrow country lane, running through farmland criss-crossed by the almost white dry-stone walling of the area, and the cars that had separated me from Marsh had turned off on to other routes at the Skipton roundabout. But there was nothing too suspicious about a single car following his – over-taking wasn't easy, and in any case I'd taken the precaution of wearing a flat cap and an ancient sports jacket and was clen-ching a briar pipe between my teeth, giving a reasonable impression of belonging to that small but ubiquitous band of men who haunt English B-roads, drive steadily just off the centre line and never overtake anything at the best of times, including tractors.

About half-way between Skipton and Grassington, he indi-cated right and swung through an opening, a sort of rustic arch, into what seemed to be the site of a cluster of chalet-type structures. I also caught a glimpse of water and trees.

I passed on to Grassington, where I drove out, and returned to Beckford on a different route. Just in case Marsh was checking to see if a Mondeo doubled back past the chalet village.

Thirteen

Norma said: 'A prelim from Alan Starkey. He faxed it yesterday afternoon.' She handed me the sheets, which I read rapidly.

The Marsh brothers [it ran] were both well known in the computer industry, both very highly regarded. They had similar qualifications and at one time both worked for an international company called Metz Sanders PLC. MS install complex computer systems for companies with extensive networks – they don't look at anything with less than twenty locations. The Marsh brothers got bored with the big picture and wanted more control and more challenge. David was the first to break out on his own – he saw the potential of number-crunching other firms' payrolls and the economies of scale that went with it. He set up with a man called Raymond Sheard in the mid-Eighties. The business rapidly became successful, and still is, but Marsh sold his interest in Ninety-one (for a considerable sum, they say) giving out that he was going to take a sabbatical and decide either to (a) retire, or (b) try something different. He then went on a lengthy travelling holiday, and at that point the trail went cold.

He wasn't apparently very gregarious, but he could

make all the right moves – golf, lavish lunches, Rotary Club – and deliver a mean sales pitch. He was well-liked and admired, but no one seemed to know him particularly well. I was told he'd been very close to his brother, Simon, in the early days (Norma explained you'd been involved in a case to do with the late Simon Marsh's estate, by the way) but according to one of my informants – who still works at MS – they seemed to have some sort of a bust-up and refused to work together. It might have been why they set up in separate businesses – working in harness, he said, they'd have made a dream team.

I know your priority is David Marsh's current address and I'm confident I'll have that in a few days. My best bet is his old co-director, Raymond Sheard, but *he's* away from home too – touring in central France. Will revert soonest. Alan.

I put the report to one side. It hadn't been at all what I'd expected. It posed two big new questions. Why was David Marsh now so broke he couldn't even afford a packet of Rice Krispies, and why had he and Laura pretended the brothers were so close when it had been obvious to their colleagues they'd split up.

I said: 'What do you make of it?'

'I don't know that I want to make anything of it – it would only encourage you . . .'

'Oh, come on, I need your input. According to Starkey, Marsh should be so loaded he doesn't need to work, he could live comfortably for the rest of his life.'

'God, I wish I could. It'll be holidays on a Saga bus when I retire, if I'm lucky. To Eastbourne . . .'

'What would he need to go on living in the style he was

used to, working for an international company?' I said slowly. 'Say fifty grand a year. To be sure of that level of return he'd have to invest at least half a million. Where's it gone?'

'Perhaps he put it into something that bombed . . .'

'But we're talking shrewd business brain here. He'd know everything there is to know about feasibility studies and business plans and cash-flow forecasts. Surely he'd have gone into something new with another business partner? And he'd borrow money from the bank, not use all his nest-egg. The banks will always lend you money once they're absolutely certain you've got a sackful of your own.'

She sipped some of her own excellent coffee from a peculiarly repellent beaker I'd once bought her, after a careful search, which had NORMA stencilled on the side in green lettering that glowed.

'They're often gamblers,' she said. 'He went into the pay-roll firm with this man called Sheard, and I shouldn't be surprised if Sheard was the real entrepreneur, the man who built the business round David's ideas and knowledge of computers. So the business takes off and David can't wait to sell his share and try something new. He'll be full of confidence now, thinking he can't go wrong, telling himself it's a piece of cake. So next time he decides to have a go he doesn't bother with a partner, or faffing about with banks and so forth – he goes it alone. That way he'll not be paying charges and he'll keep all the profit. So he bungs the lot into computer games or sports equipment or the travel business, and inside a year he's blown himself away. How many men have you followed round for creditors who've done exactly that?'

I nodded slowly. 'But he's a computer expert, don't forget. He could go back into the industry, back to Metz Sanders . . .'

'I don't know, John, forty-plus is a dodgy age to be trying to make a comeback in such a high-tech business.'

I nodded again. It was only what Laura had once hinted at. The ferocious pace of change in the computer industry was such that it seemed that if you took your eye off the ball for more than a few seconds you were lucky if you saw the ball again.

'All right,' I said. 'Let's say he's lost the lot. But why do you think Laura feels obliged to lend him money if the brothers weren't on speaking terms? I'd thought perhaps David had lent Simon money to set up *his* business, but it can't be that, can it?'

'No. I think what might have happened is that when Simon hit that rocky patch in the recession he went to David on his knees for a loan. David gave him it, then lost his own money and is now telling Laura that if it hadn't been for him they'd have banked, the term assurance payments would have been abandoned and the policies would have lapsed. Without him, he's probably telling her, she'd not be sitting on a million, she'd be standing in line at the DSS.'

'Nice one,' I said thoughtfully. 'The fact that the brothers split up throws a completely new light on it.' I glanced at my watch; I'd have to go in a few minutes. 'What I can't get together is the hassle he's giving Laura. I know for a fact he wants to get his hands on a substantial chunk of the insurance money. But let's be absolutely realistic – what could he have lent Simon? A hundred grand, two hundred, top whack. So that's all she owes him, and if Simon had a limited company or there was nothing in writing, technically she owes him naff-all.'

'Perhaps . . . it all goes back to that bust-up the brothers had . . . and what the bust-up was about . . .'

She spoke hesitantly, knowing they were words I wasn't keen to hear. I gave her a wry smile. She'd almost certainly put her finger on the real truth. The bust-up had to have been

because David and Laura were having an affair and Simon had found out. It was the old scenario, but with major changes to the plot. The fact that Simon was later to start having affairs with Yorkshire barmaids seemed to be one of life's little ironies, what my chums in the law factories would call a *non sequitur*.

I said: 'It's only what I'd already taken on board. I just had a different spin on it. I thought David and Laura might have had an affair, but Simon had either not known about it or turned a blind eye. What I still can't get together is the leverage David seems to have. Her only real obligation is to repay him the money he lent Simon.'

She shrugged. 'He seems restless, a go-getter, even though he came unstuck. It often goes with charisma. She may dislike him, almost hate him, but . . .'

Domination. The aspect of leverage I'd always shied away from, knowing perfectly well it was the only one that really seemed to provide all the answers.

'But she went to London with me,' I said in a low voice. 'Out to dinner . . .'

'Perhaps it was a relief to be with someone who wasn't forever putting the squeeze on her. He probably never even knew. If he doesn't always stay at her house . . .'

I thought of that silent furious row I'd witnessed through the drawing-room window, the paperweight she'd seized as if she'd smash it against the side of his head. How could that amount of emotion be flowing between people who were just good friends?

'Let it go, John,' she said. 'Please. I know you're taken with her, but . . . but, I've been uneasy about her all along, and now this business with the brothers is beginning to come out . . . I still can't see why she encouraged you, especially when she seems to be more or less living with this man, but if

you're not careful you could get caught in some very nasty cross-fire. There's all that money involved and no one knows better than you that big money always seems to mean big trouble in the end. You've done your job, you've given her a lot of moral support, why not let them sort it out for themselves . . .'

It was good advice and I only wished I could take it. But I knew it wasn't possible now. Even though, had I been standing where Norma and Fenlon were, I'd have handed out exactly the same advice. I was too involved now. I knew she'd been devious about David Marsh and the situation between the brothers, but I'd seen the pain and the unhappiness he'd brought her, to add to the sadness about Simon she couldn't shake off, and I couldn't walk away until I was convinced there really was nothing I could do to help sort it out.

'You're probably right, Norma,' I said, my hand on the door. Her appraising glance told me she didn't give much weight to my words, that she was up against the stubborn streak that had made me the best PI in town, but came with dodgy side-effects.

'Just one more thing before you go, young Goss. Mr Nolan of Bowling Suites is asking about this guy you want him to look at for furniture humping. As it turns out, he's a man down . . .'

'Oh . . . ring him and give him my apologies. Tell him I'll explain the situation later. My subway chum was very much not interested. He'd rather sit staring into space.'

'*Really*,' she said, grinning. 'Well, I can promise you I'll take absolutely *no* pleasure in saying those three little words.'

'What three little words, said he, knowing full well he was walking into it?'

'Told you so!' she said, on a high, trilling note.

That night I went out to the little chalet village on the Grass-

ington Road. I parked my car in a lay-by, then walked about half a mile to the site, kept on walking, climbed over a wall and approached it from the side. The buildings were really log cabins with chalet roofs, designed to appear primitive and rough-hewn, but in fact had been carefully constructed with modern techniques, and their artfully uneven-looking walls would almost certainly enclose modern interiors. There were perhaps thirty of them. A larger cabin stood centrally on a tarmacadam apron – this would be the office and store. It all seemed newish, as if it were the first phase of an ongoing development, and the cabins were well spread, each sited in its own small clearing among trees.

I supposed they were all for rental on leases of varying lengths. There was an end-of-season feel to the site, even in darkness, with only an occasional car at the side of its cabin on a little strip of hard standing. None of them was Marsh's Escort.

I worked my way cautiously and logically from one side of the site to the other, through darkness broken only by squares of light from the occupied cabins. It was windy and the branches of trees creaked. Leaves fell steadily and I gave an involuntary shudder as one touched my face like the stroke of a soft, dry hand. The night was full of muted cracking turbulence when the wind listed, as if sheets were flapping on a clothes-line.

I suddenly kicked over a bucket, outside a chalet with a lighted window. I took cover round the side of the cabin; a second later a door opened and a plump, middle-aged woman in glasses and hairnet stepped out on to the narrow path and peered into the night.

'Must be the wind, Jack,' she called over her shoulder. 'But I'm not happy, not a bit. He gave us to understand they were nearly all taken . . .'

The door banged on her grumbling voice and I continued

my steady progress. The woman and Jack seemed to have been sold the classical pup – 'Well, I wouldn't think it over too long, dear, I can't promise it'll still be here by the weekend . . .'

As I'd thought, it was a new enterprise, struggling to get off the ground, a fact Marsh, who knew all about start-up problems, would have picked up on. This, presumably, had been what he'd been looking for – accommodation he could rent fairly cheaply in a place where there were few people and which was remote from the city, but with good access roads. Somewhere, I supposed, where he could keep out of the way while the insurance claim was being processed, but which was near enough Beckford for him to mount his regular onslaughts on Laura's sensibilities. Perhaps he was mounting one of those onslaughts tonight, as I'd reached the end of the site with no further trace of his car.

But then, as I was turning to go back to the road, I caught the palest gleam of light through swaying branches. I made my way into another area of cleared ground, by a lengthy walk along a path that sloped upwards. This site was larger than the lower one and looked to be the start of the second phase of development – at present it contained a single cabin. Drawing nearer, I could make out Marsh's Escort, standing among trees and parked in such a way as to make it almost invisible at a distance from below.

The cabin stood on a little platform of land slightly above the clearing itself; suddenly its door was opened on a dim oblong of light and Marsh came out. I moved behind a tree.

He was wearing a dressing-gown, but was bare-legged and bare-footed. It was as if he'd been disturbed going to bed or taking a shower, though it was only nine-thirty. But what had disturbed him? – he was now looking around warily, exactly as the woman had looked around at the sound of a kicked

bucket. But I'd kicked no bucket this time, my progress had been soundless against the snapping wind and the creaking trees. Perhaps he'd reacted to some noise that had seemed different from the others. It could only be coincidence that he'd opened the door as I approached.

But why, even allowing for his general nerviness, was he so anxious about his cabin being approached? Anyone could pass this way, people in the occupied cabins taking dogs for walks; surely it would happen all the time.

He waited there for a full minute, then closed the cabin door. About five minutes later, I crept cautiously up to the large main window. The living area seemed lit only by a bulb of low wattage, probably a table lamp. There was nothing to see, as the curtains were drawn, and with this wind there would be nothing to hear, even if the windows were single-glazed. I had at least located the cabin he was living in and could make the decision later about returning one morning to see where he went during the day.

But I pressed an ear against the window and cupped my other ear to baffle off the wind noise. For some time I heard nothing, but then I seemed to detect the low intermittent murmur of voices, then another lengthy period of silence, and then suddenly what seemed to be a small sharp cry in a woman's voice. It could have been of pleasure, but I could be certain of nothing against the endless buffeting of the wind.

I retreated to the encircling trees and stood in thought. Had he really got a woman in there? If so, it gave an interesting slant to the situation. Perhaps he didn't want Laura to know. Perhaps that was why he was anxious to monitor any possible approaches to his cabin after dark. Perhaps, if he was pretending it was Laura he wanted to spend his life with in order to get his hands on a chunk of the money, it was imperative he kept the other woman under wraps.

And if I were to blow the whistle on him it might enable her to walk away at last, like the rich girl I'd told her about who'd finally drawn the line at her husband spending her money on another woman.

I wondered if I should abandon, for the time being, the idea of trying to find out where he spent his days. The shrewder option might be to let him take himself off one morning and then search the cabin for something that might help me identify the woman, if there really was one, and for something that might give me a clue as to what he was aiming to do with the money he was pestering Laura for. I hated sneaking into people's houses, I always had to convince myself that the end fully justified the shabby means. In Laura's case I didn't give it a second thought.

Just as I was about to make my return down the incline, the cabin door suddenly opened again. It was Marsh once more, outlined against the dim light from inside. He went through the earlier process of looking carefully into the night. This time he wore ordinary clothes: I could make out the pale gleam of the Aran sweater.

I heard a voice then. It was high-pitched, female. I could just make out a few words over a brief lull in the wind noise. 'For heaven's sake, darling, get a move . . .'

The rest was lost, unless Marsh had restrained her. They picked their way to the car, almost as stealthily as I'd walked across the site. As they opened the doors the courtesy light came on, with what seemed an almost searchlight glare in the darkness. I caught a single full glimpse of the woman's face as she turned to pull the seat-belt across her body. She had auburn hair, green eyes, full red lips. It was Madge, the barmaid from the Wheatsheaf.

214

Fourteen

'There's Larch House,' he said finally, and with some reluctance, 'but it's beyond Starbotton. I shouldn't have thought you'd want to be *quite* so remote. About an acre, overlooking the river. Two reception, dining-room, kitchen, breakfast room, utility room, study and cloakroom at ground level. Four bedrooms, one *en suite*, two attic bedrooms. Rather large for . . . er . . . one lady . . .'

'Can we see it?'

'Well, it is Saturday, and I'm alone here. I really prefer to show people round personally.' He looked at us carefully. 'I dare say I could let you have a key.'

'Fine.'

'I do rather feel it's too remote and too big . . .'

'I think I can be the judge of that,' Laura said, politely but firmly.

'We have so many very desirable properties in the immediate vicinity. Countrified, yet only two or three miles from Skipton.'

I suspected he'd had trouble trying to sell Larch House in the current stagnant market, that he knew from bitter experience how abruptly people keen for remote isolation could change their minds when they saw a house clinging to a hillside that in winter it was advisable to approach on cater-

pillar tracks. By the time Laura had seen Larch House and given it the thumbs down he'd be closed, and she might return to his agency another day and then again she might not. And he had rapidly picked up the rustle of serious money.

'If you'd like to take an early lunch,' he said, in a wheedling tone, 'I'll be free at twelve-thirty and could personally escort you round three or four of the nicest houses in the area.'

She gave a patient, dogged smile. 'I don't *want* a house in the area, Mr Oxley, I want a house in the Dales.'

'It *is* a most desirable residence,' he said loyally, 'but I do feel it my duty to warn you that shops and services are almost non-existent . . .'

'I've taken that into consideration.'

He grudgingly accepted defeat, torn, as estate agents so often were, between moving the properties that sold themselves and making one more effort to get the turkey off his books. He took some keys from a board on the wall behind him.

'What sort of numbers are we talking?' I said. He seemed conveniently to have forgotten to mention a price and Laura, in her lofty, blue-stocking way, seemed indifferent to knowing it.

'My . . . client has indicated she'd consider a figure *circa* two hundred and fifty K,' he said, keeping his hands out of sight, as advised by the body-language specialists. He'd clearly decided that 'K' sounded a lot less than 'thousand'.

'But she'd accept a sensible offer?'

'I . . . don't believe she regards the figure as negotiable, beyond a token five or ten K . . .'

'In today's market? For a house beyond Starbotton?'

'It's a much-sought-after property,' he said quickly. 'In a superb location. There's already been a great deal of interest, a very great deal . . .'

'But if you're giving us a key it must be vacant possession.'

'Mr Hawkes . . . died quite suddenly. Larch House passed to his daughter – she's my client.'

'How long has it been empty, Mr Oxley?' I said bluntly.

'Hardly any time at all . . .'

'I'm sure the locals will be able to confirm that.'

His hands, as agitated as hungry serpents, had been unable to stop themselves writhing across his desk.

'Three months,' he said defensively, '. . . perhaps six. That's nothing for a house of distinction. They don't turn over like two up and two downs, you know . . .'

I liked it. People who'd been left houses couldn't as a rule wait to unload. There'd be all manner of goodies riding on the sale – winter cruises, ponies, school fees, brand-new Volvo Estates.

'I'm quite sure, if Mrs Marsh expressed an interest, we could reach a figure we were all happy with.'

For a couple of seconds his face had the haggard bonhomie of a comedian who'd sunk to lunch-time quiz shows. The early Nineties had not been a good time for estate agents.

'*If* Mrs Marsh likes what she sees I'm sure we could come up with a sensible offer,' I said flatly. 'Bearing in mind we'll be talking numbers well below a quarter of a million.'

I knew that any realistic offer would be regarded as sensible for a house nobody wanted, and I knew that he knew that I knew. But he was a professional, with tricks of his own up his sleeve.

'Ah, well,' he said smoothly, his hands once more nailed to his chair. 'Mrs Cawthra's in no hurry to sell, you see. Her husband's the Cawthra in Cawthra's Camelot Carpets. I'm sure you've heard of it.'

'They say the carpet people are having a terrible time of

217

it just now, because of the knock-on effect of no one building any new houses . . .'

'Let me get you a coffee,' he said brightly, 'before you set off.'

'We'd sooner not. We'd like to get up there and see as much as possible before the light goes.'

Gracious in tacitly accepted defeat, he explained how we located Larch House, about a mile beyond Starbotton, and how we neutralised the intruder alarm and pressure pads, equipment as essential now in deep country as in the city.

'I've got all that,' I said finally.

'Well, good viewing, Mrs Marsh, Mr Goss.'

'Thanks. We put the keys through the letter-box on our way back . . . yes?'

He nodded. 'If . . . you *do* like Larch House and it would help you to reach a decision, Mrs Cawthra has indicated that she'd consider renting the property furnished for a trial period – say three months – to a person genuinely interested in buying.'

Or, in plain speak, the Cawthras were desperate to get shot.

'That's interesting,' I said.

'At . . . a very nominal rent,' he said enticingly. 'She feels it would help a prospective buyer tremendously to sample the way of life up there before making a final commitment.'

And would also help to keep the house from deterioration during the winter, and warm and welcoming for any other prospective buyers to view. I suspected Mrs Cawthra, no doubt guided by Mr Cawthra of Camelot Carpet fame, was displaying more hard sense and acumen than the estate agent himself. So what was new?

We had a snack lunch at the same high-street pub we'd used

all those weeks ago, when we'd walked on the moors. She was dressed in her usual outdoor clothes, with her sleek hair drawn back, so that the attention was focused on her grey eyes and her down-turned crescent of a mouth and her pale marbled skin.

'I'm so glad you came with me,' she said, in her small, soft voice. 'You're so good with these people. I'd not have had the nerve to do all that tough bargaining. Not when we hadn't even *seen* it.'

'I tend to go for the jugular straight away,' I said. 'It saves a lot of hassle later on. It comes from years of getting it across to people within the first five minutes that investigation work can't be done for five pounds an hour.'

'Poor man – he could see his commission haemorrhaging away by the second.'

'I doubt we'll hear any more nonsense about quarters of a million.'

I could never be entirely sure if her vagueness in money matters was real or apparent. She'd certainly accepted the extreme slowness of the Zephyr payment calmly, despite wanting to get her life sorted out; I supposed that had given me the first impression of her indifference to the detail of financial transactions, despite her sure grasp of money as a concept, as the sixth sense that enabled you to make the most of the other five. I wondered if she would really have been prepared to accept the asking price for Larch House without quibble, assuming she liked it. Or would she have realised that her liquid assets gave her considerable bargaining clout? She could be extremely efficient about detail when she wanted to be. I didn't know. What I did know was that, either way, she had the kind of grace that would always prompt her to let me believe I was leading her by the hand through uncharted territory. It was the nicest trait of many.

At the same time, I knew I'd been putting on a bravura performance in there with Oxley. It had seemed that if talking to her about Marsh's demands was off limits, I had to find other ways of letting her see how tough I could be, how shrewd in money matters, how competent, if she'd only trust me, to sort out Marsh, either by the hardest bargain that could be struck or, failing that, the veiled threat of loosened teeth.

We'd found a good Saturday at last – cold, crisp, completely clear. It was exactly the sort of day we'd once said we'd spend looking for a house for her, when the trees were flaring with their hectic autumn tints; she'd not forgotten. She'd rung me at the office, and I'd been delighted to turn my back on certain supplementary queries on my tax return the Inland Revenue were being sadistic about.

And so we drove up into that land of moors and valleys and dry-stone walls and sheep, past villages so small the car would slide through them in seconds. Our route took us past the site of the chalet village where Marsh was seeing to Madge the barmaid, but it seemed to mean nothing to her. I wondered if she even knew where he stopped when he wasn't staying at the house on Tanglewood. Or cared.

I said: 'Have you been here before?'

'No. Bolton Abbey was the extent of my exploration.'

'I came a lot in my youth. Camping, hiking . . .'

'It's superb country.'

She glanced endlessly from right to left, her eyes seeming almost to consume the shapes and colours of the rolling terrain in the diagonal sunlight, and I remembered how she'd been that day on the moors, like a released bird, briefly free of the stifling sadness and complications of Simon's death.

We didn't speak again. I had a lot to occupy my mind as I negotiated the twists and turns of the narrow road. She

seemed relaxed today, almost happy, if it was always accepted how relative a word happiness was, applied to Laura, how thinly coated it seemed to be over the deeper emotions I had become so familiar with.

I wondered if I also detected a feeling of relief, if she herself had finally struck some kind of deal with Marsh. She was being extremely positive about buying an expensive house, and vague or not about the minutiae of finance, she would know that the life she would be living in a place like Larch House would not be cheap.

I wondered if she had given him, say, a couple of hundred thousand and told him that was that. If she then bought Larch House for around two hundred thousand, it would still leave around six hundred thousand for investment, which would provide a sizeable income.

My mind flicked from the money to the barmaid, as it had done again and again since I'd seen Madge leave the cabin with Marsh. How could it have come about that she'd exchanged Simon in her affections for David? How could she even have got to know David if the brothers were supposed to be at loggerheads?

I wondered if Norma had been spot on in her theory about the brothers and Simon *had* gone on bended knees to David when his business was on the rocks. And what if David, in his wealthy days, had only agreed to a loan if he could examine Simon's books, study his working methods, perhaps even go with him to visit prospective clients? After all, each brother had known the computer business backwards, perhaps David had felt, quite reasonably, that he must have a chance to evaluate Simon's set-up in order to ensure he wasn't throwing good money after bad. And what if, on one of those client visits, the brothers had stopped off at the Wheatsheaf? And what if Madge had found David more attractive than Simon?

Charisma had been the quality Norma had felt he'd almost certainly have.

It could easily be a runner. When I'd been at the Wheat-sheaf I'd asked Madge if she'd been having an affair with Simon, and she'd been so embarrassed and annoyed she'd flushed to her chest. But she'd given no impression of grief. I'd dismissed her as a chancer who'd realised she'd have to make do with the man she'd got. But what if the absence of grief was due to Simon Marsh having been thrown back when David Marsh walked through the door?

And had that been another strand in the web of depression Simon had been caught up in? First his wife and then his girlfriend: it must have seemed there was nothing he could call his own when David was around. I wondered if that had been the downside of the famous closeness the brothers had always known, the kind of closeness where they shared everything, to the point where David even considered their wives and lovers to be in the same category as textbooks and clothes and their last fiver. What a mess it all seemed.

'This must be it,' I said. I got out of the car, swung back two ornate iron gates and we drove through grounds that seemed to be mainly lawn and trees, from what we could see through the thinning beech hedges lining the drive.

The house was stone-built, two-storey, mullion-windowed, ivy-clad. The central front door was pedimented and above the two front bedrooms gables rose, in which were set the small lattice windows of what would probably be the attics.

'It really is very big,' I said, prepared to concede now that Oxley had made a valid point.

But looking back, I believe she'd made up her mind even before we'd stepped inside, as people often did, had seen things about the house that seemed to compare with some precise inner vision.

I turned the key in the door's mortice lock, silenced the activated alarm system in the cloakroom, turned off the pressure pads. She followed slowly, wide-eyed in an almost literal sense, as if to note every detail of the square panelled hall and the sporting prints that hung there. She tentatively pushed open a door, like someone who has awoken in unfamiliar surroundings. It led to one of the reception rooms. It was spacious and had a plaster-moulded ceiling and an Adam fireplace, and looked out over sweeping lawns strewn with bright, dead leaves, through tall windows with stained-glass upper sections. The furniture was sheeted, but would be solid, heavy and timeless. A long-case clock had stopped at twenty-three minutes past four. Chinese rugs lay over unpatterned woollen carpets and curtains of maroon velvet hung, tasselled and anchored by loops of silken cord, beneath swagged pelmets.

She walked slowly around the room, more abstracted than I believe I'd ever seen her, the light catching her preoccupied eyes as she moved out of shadowy corners. Then, almost as if alone, she walked across the hall to the other room, which was similar in size but contained a baby grand piano on a triangular dais in one of the corners.

'This must be the music room,' I said. 'I'm glad of the clue. But what does that make the other one – sitting or drawing? Perhaps even living. My knowledge in this area is decidedly shaky – my mother always called our two front and back . . .'

I doubt she heard a word, as she moved around, drawing back the sheets on ottomans and octagonal tables and bureau bookcases, and running her fingers lovingly over fabrics and surfaces. I felt a slight sinking of the spirits. We'd seemed to share so much since I'd picked her up at Tanglewood Lane, the same pleasure in being together, in the colours of the day, in the anticipation of driving out here. Even our silence in the car had been the silence of people close enough to be able to

dispense with small talk; and for much of the drive her hand had rested lightly on my thigh.

That mood had abruptly ended. She seemed already to be almost obsessed by Larch House. She appeared oblivious to any reaction I might have. It was her money and her choice, of course, but we'd talked so often about the move from Tanglewood, and she'd said so often how much she'd want me to visit her in her new home, that I'd been certain she'd welcome my own input, even if it only served to strengthen her conviction that she'd found exactly what she was looking for. I trailed behind her, like some anonymous servant who carried bags, back into the hall again and towards the rear of the house, where the dining-room and kitchen ran, my slight depression tinged by an uneasiness I couldn't define, as if I were reacting to some vaguely inimical atmosphere by instinct rather than reason.

The rear rooms caught the sun more directly, and the dining-room curtains were drawn to prevent fading in the carpets. It was smaller than the reception rooms, but not much, and narrow bands of sunlight glowed incandescently round the edges of the curtains, to fall across swirling dust-motes. The dining-table was unsheeted and of rosewood, and was extended to its full length, with balloon-backs along the sides and shield-back carvers at each end. There were two four-light candelabra, in the shape of young women in flowing gowns, who held the stems of the candle-holders, which masqueraded as flower heads.

There were sideboards and drinks cabinets standing against walls papered in a dark-green silk-finish paper in a heavy medallion design. I sensed the vague uneasiness deepen; all the room seemed to need now was Miss Havisham, sitting at one end of the table in her faded wedding finery. But the atmosphere had the reverse effect on Laura;

she was almost ecstatic. She drew a pulley-cord that made the curtains glide smoothly apart and the room was flooded in low sunlight. The dining-room looked out over woodland. Between trees we could see flashes of the water of the river.

She stood before the window for a full minute in silence, her slender body turned into a dark outline by the light sharply edging it. 'It's perfect, Simon,' she said at last. 'It's as close to . . .'

She broke off, slowly turned, smiled opaquely, unaware she'd called me by her late husband's name. I tried to be philosophical about it, I hadn't really had an identity I could call my own since entering the house. She was looking towards me but her eyes were unfocused, as if she were already living in the future, when she'd be mistress of a remote old house where the silence ran so deep you could hear your blood move.

'It's as close to . . .' she'd said. As close to what, the house where she'd lost herself in a book and scorched her cardy, where her mother had spent her days doggedly painting those pictures that people found so difficult, where twice a week she'd thrown lavish parties for struggling writers and artists and actors, who had to pay for the hospitality by displaying or reading their work in progress, or by acting a scene or singing a song? She'd called me Simon, but I had a strong impression that if Simon himself had actually been with her he'd have meant as little to her as I did during the time we'd been in Larch House. The images in her mind seemed powerful enough to transcend anything outside it.

'Laura, you can't really want to buy this place. You don't know what snow can be like out here. I've heard of winters so bad they've had to ship supplies in by helicopter.'

She shook her head slightly and looked at me with the brief incomprehension of someone being awoken from a par-

ticularly vivid dream. Then she smiled, her eyes locking
securely on to mine at last, the Laura of the pub and the car.

'That's what it's all about, John,' she said simply. 'Isolation.
I'll be able to work without distraction, all day and all night if
I want to. You can't believe how much I long for the sort of
isolation a really hard winter would bring. As for supplies –
big freezers stuffed to the brim.'

'You could really do with someone to help out in the
house, you know . . .'

'No,' she said firmly. 'I dare say there'll be a woman at
Starbotton or Kettlewell who'll clean for a couple of mornings. I'll cook for myself – except for the times I have a formal
dinner.'

She sat down on the carver at the top of the big table. I
could see her then in the black dress with the cross-over
bodice, her hair loose round her pale face, her eyes glowing
animatedly in the flickering light of the candelabra as she
presided over a table glittering with silver and glass.

'Whom will you entertain?' I said. 'No, let me guess, the
corduroy and suede-shoes brigade . . .'

She smiled again, not put out. 'You're a clever young man
who doesn't forget too much, aren't you, John Goss. Yes, it
will mainly be people who write and paint, apart from you, of
course – I'm sure there'll be an awful lot who want exactly
what I want from living in the Dales.'

It was strange, almost uncanny, but the house seemed
already hers, as if Mrs Cawthra's parents, and the other families who'd lived here, had merely been good caretakers who'd
lovingly looked after it until its natural owner could take
possession. It seemed absurd that a single woman should
want to inhabit all this space, and yet she suddenly seemed
exactly right for it. House and mistress had found their perfect partner.

'I think we should make them an offer for the furniture, John.'

'Antiques?' I said doubtfully. 'Wouldn't they cost more than the house?'

She shook her head. 'They're good but they're simple country pieces that fit in nicely. The only items of real value, apart from the piano, are the candelabra. They're not solid silver, but the design's unusual and gives them rarity value. I think I could suggest a figure for the furniture that would compare favourably with the sale room, and it would cut out transport and commission costs, of course.'

I smiled wryly, marvelling again at her vagueness in some financial matters and her shrewdness in others. Perhaps there were times when she *pretended* not to be shrewd, when it was convenient to let me play the hard man, as with Oxley and the house price. And I knew that her nature was such that she'd want me, in any case, to feel valued. And yet, if that selective vagueness really did conceal a genuinely shrewd mind, it didn't seem to have helped in her dealings with David Marsh, assuming she'd paid him off, which seemed increasingly likely.

Apart from the kitchen and the utility room, the final ground-floor room of any size was the study. It adjoined the dining-room and also looked out over the wood. It had a large oak pedestal desk and a bow-back chair, a wooden filing cabinet and, against the back wall, a half-moon table. Both side walls were shelved and filled with books – reference to the right, novels, often in leather-bound sets, to the left. There was a single landscape painting, of Kilnsey Crag.

She sat down at the desk and looked out over that perfect view of woodland and water, back-lit by diagonal sunlight broken into multi-angled shafts by the hard black trunks of trees.

If it had seemed she'd been barely aware of me in our tour of the other rooms, in here I felt positively excluded, almost as if I were on the other side of a closed door. I wondered if her mind was now filled with the times she'd spend in here, writing her great Gothic novel, that would still be in print when all the others had been forgotten.

I thought of the day we'd been on the moor, the intense nostalgia in her voice when she'd spoken of her youth among the artistic types who'd flocked to her mother's house. She'd not even wanted to go to college because she'd felt she'd miss it all too much. I wondered if those had been the major forces in her life – her love for Simon and her longing for the creative environment of her adolescent years, with its isolation, its solitude and its salons.

If that was the case, I realised how very powerful those forces must have been, if her love for Simon was strong enough to make her relinquish any return to the way of life which had immediately appeared to become her first priority when Simon himself had gone.

'*No one* will come in here,' she said, her words seeming to emphasise my sense of exclusion. 'I couldn't bear a cleaner to disturb a single paper. I'd not be able to tolerate the movement of even one of them half an inch . . .'

She continued to gaze almost broodingly over woodland. There had been something in her tone that took me back to the time she'd run headlong from a bar parlour in Kensington Road. The hysteria and the harshness were missing, of course, but there was the faintest steely echo of the edge her voice had had that day.

'You'll have to make it clear this is a no-go area then,' I said, with a bluntness I couldn't control, 'otherwise your cleaner might start and finish on the same morning.'

My words made as little impression on her as raindrops on

228

waxed cloth, but I doubted if her own words had been meant for me anyway. She crossed to the shelves with the novels and took down a copy of *Vanity Fair*, which she opened at random and began to read. She would almost certainly have read it before, and with her memory would know what each of the characters was doing at the point where she took up the story.

I left the study, quietly closing the door behind me, still faintly depressed, even irritated. She was scarcely relating to me, and yet in the study I felt she almost resented my presence in some obscure way, as you unconsciously resent a stranger reading your paper over your shoulder in a crowded place. I left her to her dreams, if that's what they were, and looked over the kitchen.

Even here, the fittings seemed to have the same timeless charm as the reception rooms, but behind the figured panels in light oak there lurked modern appliances – central heating boilers and microwaves and ceramic hobs. There were also, in a pantry, two massive front-loading freezers, in which she'd be able to store enough food, with her small appetite, to last from Christmas to Easter.

I went upstairs then, looking first at the two attic rooms that lay behind the gables. One of them had been used as a storage room for cases, paintings, odd pieces of furniture, the other as a proper child's bedroom, with a narrow bed still made up, and a little bookcase containing the Ransome novels, the Angela Brazils, the Richmal Cromptons. A collection of toy animals sat on a corner cupboard. I wondered if this had been Mrs Cawthra's room, whether one of *her* children had continued using it on visits until the death of Mr Hawkes. I hung around for a few minutes, riffling through the *William* books, taking a mental trip of my own. I'd had a happy childhood too, surrounded in my own bedroom with similar tokens of parental affection.

'John . . .?'

I retraced my steps down the narrow, creaking staircase that led to the first floor. She stood on the wide landing, smiling the faint smile I knew so well, but which now seemed contrite. There was a moist heaviness about her eyes.

'I'm sorry, John . . .'

'Sorry?'

She shrugged, turning to look through the open door of a bedroom, her face expressionless. It didn't need elaboration – for the past half-hour I'd spent most of the time being either ignored or resented.

'It . . . reminds me so much of her and the life she gave me. I'm what she made me. I loved her so much . . .'

I put my arms round her. She seemed to be leaving the house on Tanglewood Lane because it reminded her too much of Simon, to live in a house in the Dales that reminded her too much of her mother.

'I must have seemed like someone almost possessed,' she said in a voice little more than a whisper.

'If it affects you so much can living here be a very good idea?' I said. 'Why not something smaller, more modern?'

She shook her head against my shoulder. 'It's *because* of the effect. Can you understand? I feel my future in this house. I feel things will happen here. I can feel my destiny.' She gave an apologetic laugh. 'If that doesn't sound too grand a word for what will probably be a rather ordinary life.'

I knew she didn't believe that, and neither did I.

I released her and she put out a hand, almost but not quite touching my face, as if I were behind a pane of glass, with a look I couldn't interpret, it seemed almost of longing, of regret even. She was such a sad, complex woman, still, it seemed, striving to keep her equilibrium in the face of losing the two people who had filled her life, one seeming to take

her over at the precise point the other had let her go.

'Shall we finish our tour?' she said, grasping my hand tightly. 'Before the light goes.'

The old Laura was back in place once more and, as if to convince me I'd not be neglected again, was if anything over-solicitous in asking for my comments on the upper rooms, which were all furnished with the same sure if unremarkable taste as those on the ground floor, each having restful carpets and the sort of large, strong pieces that complemented the dimensions of the lofty rooms.

The main bedroom had a four-poster bed. It was of mahogany, but not heavy or off-putting, with a narrow carved tester and slender pillars. Its curtains were gauzy and light, and gave it an incredibly erotic charge. I could imagine seeing her slender marble body behind those hangings, as if through a diffusing camera lens, and I wondered if I ever would.

'I've never slept in a four-poster,' she said. 'It will be a new experience.'

Our eyes met. I wondered if I imagined the increase in pressure in the hand that still held mine, if it encoded the message that one day, when she'd made the break from life at Tanglewood Lane, there'd be weekends when I'd share not just her house but her bed.

'Do you realise', I said, 'you'll be virtually living in two rooms – the study and this bedroom – and heating about twelve? Blame it on my Yorkshire thrift but it seems an awfully expensive kind of isolation.'

I felt I had to give it one more shot, though I knew she was determined to have it. It was still difficult for me to get my mind round the idea of her living alone in such isolation. However discreet she would be about her wealth, news of it would somehow filter out to the sort of criminals who would be as pleased about her defencelessness as I would be uneasy.

'I must have it,' she said simply, as if propelled by forces beyond her control. 'I didn't want to be able to afford a house like this because of Simon, but . . . but I just feel I can work things out here . . .'

I remembered thinking once that perhaps the novel was going to be a memorial to Simon because his death had provided the means that would enable her to buy the time and the conditions in which to write it. And if it could be written in a house that seemed to contain reminders of her mother's ambience then perhaps that would be a separate tribute, to the woman who'd made her what she was.

'I'm going to rent Larch House, John. I'll take the short lease they're offering. That way I can move in quickly while the solicitors fiddle about with paper. I'll sell Tanglewood as and when; there'll not be much equity anyway once the mortgage is cleared . . .'

We stood at the window looking down over the front garden, where trees cast their lengthy autumn shadows over grass darkening for the winter. I knew there'd be as little point in trying to stop her moving in quickly as attempting to talk her out of buying it at all. Taking the bright view, I supposed that the sooner she bought Larch House the sooner there'd be a fifth of a million less in her bank account for Marsh to try to get his hands on. But I felt impelled to make my token gestures of warning.

'I'd . . . not be too hasty. If you seem so keen to have it you want to move in directly it might encourage them to get tough on price. They are business people after all. Play hard to get and you'll hold the cards. You might easily knock them down to a hundred and ninety.'

'Dear John . . .' She turned to me, the animation fading, her eyes resting on mine for several seconds with the odd earlier look that seemed like longing. 'You're so level-headed, you

232

know so much about commercial matters. You make me feel so naïve at times. It . . . it just seemed to me that once they saw the house inhabited they'd not want to see it standing empty again. Would you not agree? Don't you think it would make them anxious for the deal to go through at any reasonable price?'

It was a good point; it had the edge on mine. There'd be such euphoria in the Cawthra household at Laura moving in on an option to purchase, so many goodies already mentally bought with the dibs, that they'd be unlikely to rock the boat – it might turn out to be the one that would take them cruising in the West Indies. Once again, the acuteness of her thinking – or was it the kind of naïveté that so often provided a clearer view? – came obscured in the lavish praise she wrapped around my own.

'Please give me your blessing,' she said, her eyes shining again with sudden eagerness. 'I could be here inside a fortnight . . .'

It had been a day of mood swings for her. I put my hands on her shoulders. 'Laura, if it's what you really want, go for it. You must know by now I was born playing devil's advocate. It's a lovely house.'

She leaned forward and kissed me fully on the lips. Then she took my hand. 'Come on, let's look at the gardens . . .'

'Don't you want to see the attics? One's being used as a lumber room, the other a kid's bedroom. Rather sweet – woolly rabbits and Monopoly and *The Swish of the Curtain*. Worth a glance just for the *déjà vu*.'

She glanced indifferently towards the attic staircase. 'As long as they're clean and dry I don't think I'll bother. Come on – I *must* see the gardens . . .'

I remembered then she was childless and that her own childhood had been so odd that the aspects of a conventional

one would probably seem as bizarre to her as the rites of a child living in the Amazon jungle.

The front garden was mainly lawn, slightly undulating and dotted here and there with mature trees, two or three being the larches that presumably gave the house its name.

'They'll look superb in the spring,' she said, gazing upwards. 'They seem almost dead in the winter, even though they're a kind of conifer, but in spring and summer they're much prettier than most of the other trees. They're better on mountainsides really, and they like long, cold winters – they develop better. I suppose the Dales are a reasonable compromise.'

'I'm prepared to take your word for it,' I said, smiling, awed as usual by the incredible range of her knowledge.

The garden proper ran between the back of the house and the wood, a formal arrangement of geometrical flower-beds, dwarf shrubs and an ornamental pool. It lay just in front of the dining-room and the study.

'You'll need a little old man to come in at least twice a week.'

'He'd better not bring power tools,' she said sharply. 'He'll have to clip hedges with ordinary shears. I can't *bear* to lose my concentration.'

'What about the grass? Surely you'll not expect him to use a manual mower for that lot . . .'

'Some of the new electrical models are almost silent. I'll get one of those.'

I wondered if she was buying the house for its quality of almost Arctic silence as much as its appearance and atmosphere. She was determined to have such perfect conditions for her writing that I wondered if she'd find it easy to keep any kind of staff if they were scarcely permitted to breathe. But then, with her flawless grasp of wealth as a concept, she'd

know that money would solve most of these problems to her satisfaction. I'd seen signs before of the formidable will that lay behind that quiet disposition.

We walked finally through the small wood, to the river's edge, where the water flowed rapidly following recent rains. A saffron-tinted sun was now setting over terrain that rose beyond the river to a distant purple-edged rim.

'It's only about ten miles to the Pennine Way,' I said. 'Land in England doesn't come much remoter.'

'Really?'

Inside a couple of weeks she'd know more about the area than I'd learnt in a Yorkshire lifetime. We sat on the trunk of a fallen tree, our breath drifting through air that now contained a hint of frost. She was smiling as she glanced round her, at the flaring trees, the racing water, the attractive picture the house presented through woodland, its windows shields of light in the setting sun. It was the same smile I'd seen as when she sat at the end of the dining-table – the smile of possession.

I looked at my watch. 'I suppose we ought to be going if we want to find an hotel. Unless you'd rather we went back home . . .'

We'd brought overnight bags, the intention being to spend the entire weekend looking at properties, a short list of which I had in my pocket. But our search was already complete.

'Let's stay here,' she said.

'Why not. We'd avoid pneumonia if we kept our parkas on. We could perhaps break up a couple of chairs and light a fire, and I've got cheese and biscuits in my iron-ration kit . . .'

'We could turn on the heating,' she said eagerly, as if the irony had bypassed her. 'Perhaps even light a proper fire. I noticed logs at the back of the garage. *Please* let's stay . . .'

It wasn't a joke. I gave her a bemused smile. 'You can't be

serious. It's colder in there than out here . . .'

'Nobody would know. There are still things in one of the freezers. We can get the cooker going. I've got vodka in my bag.'

'Laura . . .'

'*Please*, John, we could have such a lovely time playing house . . .'

I shook my head. I felt dazed. Her voice had the importuning note of a child's who loved her new dress so much she wanted to go to bed in it. 'Laura, you must know we can't do that. The only right we've got is to look the house over. If we lived in it, even for one night, we'd become technically squatters, and you can imagine what alarm bells *that* would ring.'

'Oh, John, who'd find out? Who'd even know?'

'It would only take one local to pass and see a light on . . .'

'We'll use candles. Those in the dining-room. We'll draw the curtains and light the candles . . .'

It was like some dream, where people said the most absurd things in a totally convincing manner.

'Laura,' I said, a rising note of exasperation in my voice, 'I'm *not* staying in a house where I've no right to be. How could I – a professional investigator with a reputation to protect?'

'Oh, for Christ's *sake*, you can be such a bloody *bore* when you start bleating about your reputation!' she cried.

236

Fifteen

We tried three of the smaller hotels; they were all full. Kettlewell was a focal point for ramblers and the settled weather had attracted a lot of people from the city. I drove on to the Fields Hotel, but even they had only one room left. I got back in the car.

'I suppose we could try Grassington.'

'Let's take the room.' She put a hand over mine. 'I feel the need of a drink. And a shower.'

'Are you . . . sure . . .?'

She glanced away, the bright lights of the hotel edging her profile. 'I'm sorry . . .'

'That's the second time today you've said sorry,' I said, with a wry smile.

'You're the only real friend I've got now,' she said in a low voice. 'I don't know what I think gives me the right to have been so rude to you, like some frightful shrew of a wife . . .'

'Look,' I said, 'the three things that really pile on the stress are a bereavement, moving house and losing your job. You've had one of those three and you're on the verge of a second, it's little wonder you're in a nervy state.'

I could have added that David Marsh pestering her for money must also have rung the bell on the stress register.

'I've come to rely on you so much . . .'

'And I'll always be there. You're great to be with, you know, even when you want to do seriously weird things like staying the night in a house that doesn't belong to you.'

'I don't know what got into me . . .'

'Let's check in and have that drink.'

But the earlier uneasiness about her reactions to Larch House had returned and was still not dissipated. She *would* have stayed, there could be no mistake, in a house whose fabric would now be so cold it would need twenty-four hours of heating to bring to a comfortable temperature. And she had been very angry, she had trembled with rage, as I'd doggedly reset the intruder alarm and locked the front door.

I breathed a sigh of relief as we entered the cheerful neutral territory of the hotel. We were led along a warren of dimly lit corridors, up some stairs and down others, until a door on a distant landing was finally opened on a small, chintzy room with a large ornate brass bed.

'The one who gets the last room does the walking.'

'Will we ever find our way back!'

'We could be marooned here until they come to do the bed.'

'Cosy,' she said, with a smile that seemed to return her once more, and for what I hoped was the last time, to the Laura I'd set out with on a crisp autumn morning.

As with so many of the older hotels, the room had lost some of its space because of the sliver that had been cut off to provide the *en-suite* bathroom. We took turns to shower, and when I came out she had a half of vodka and some small tins of tonic arranged on a pedestal table, with the glasses from the hand-basin.

'Is vodka all right? You being a gin man . . .'

'Vodka's fine. I'm told they both have the same base – alcohol.'

She mixed me a large one and it touched the spot perfectly on an empty stomach alerted to those enticing almost imperceptible odours no hotel seems entirely successful in baffling off from a kitchen firing up for the dinner hour. She wore a woollen dress in mid-green, and her freshly washed hair hung loose. We sat on armchairs with our backs to the ornate bed and I deliberately suspended my imagination from what might happen later, because of my growing experience of her shifting moods.

And yet her unpredictability seemed to add to her attraction. The kinds of women normally available to a man my age, who wanted to stay loose, tended to be those who were between major fixtures but not averse to fitting in a friendly. I barely got to know them in the short time I was with them, yet felt I could read most of them easily and with fair accuracy. I'd known Laura going on three months and she'd told me a great deal about herself, but the impression was ineradicable of depths impossible to reach. Perhaps it was her appearance, the pale skin and the dark hair and the eternal stoic smile, perhaps it was simply that she had the looks of the type of actress invariably selected for parts calling for an air of sad mystery, of powerful but repressed emotions, of secrets too painful to reveal. Or perhaps, and more likely, it was the effect of trying to retain her grace under considerable pressure.

She poured more vodka. 'When I'm established at Larch House you must come any weekend you can get away from that punishing schedule of yours. We'll be able to eat out in summer; to go hiking with the wind in our hair, just like you did when you came camping. It might go some way to repaying you for these past weeks.'

I tended not to look either backwards or forwards too often; the past held too much bitterness, the future simply

seemed to be endless weeks of trudging the same flat career path. But Ninety-four looked to be holding out the same illusion of promise as the dawning of a June sun on a clear English morning.

'What if I said stuff the schedule and rolled up every Saturday? It could very easily end up with gritted teeth and: "God, not *him* again . . ."'

Our eyes met and held, and she smiled and almost imperceptibly shook her head.

And it was on that note of promise that we went down to dinner, or tried to. The job I did had sharpened my instinct for direction, but I was defeated by the Fields Hotel that night and we must have wandered for ten minutes without success.

'It's *got* to be here,' I said, for what must have been the third time, before leading us back to the landing outside our own room.

'What do you get for passing Go?' she said and began to giggle, and a middle-aged couple who wandered as bemused as ourselves also started laughing.

We joined forces and finally traced a dining-room so crowded that the harassed head waiter asked us if we'd all share a table, otherwise it would be half an hour before two smaller ones became free. I glanced at Laura, at the man and woman; each nodded.

As we sat down they immediately began to talk, telling us they'd been over Cam Head and had been worried at one stage they might get lost in the fading light. They owned a poultry farm in Lancashire and never took formal holidays because of the demands of the business, but spent twelve long weekends a year either here or in the Lakes.

I told them we'd tackled Great Whernside and, yes, we were only here overnight, and because we lived in Beckford

we too spent a lot of time in the area. As I was in insurance, I added, most of my weekends were free.

We broke off then to give the respective waiters our orders for food and wine, and I realised how very normal we must have seemed, a thirty-something couple having a fun weekend. I wished I could have seen their homely faces if I could casually have thrown out: 'Well, Laura's a widow who's just become a millionaire because of her husband's insurance, and I'm an investigator hired to check her out to make sure there was nothing dodgy about the claim, but we became friends . . .'

When the waiters had gone, Laura began to speak. I knew she'd have sensed that, like doctors and lawyers, I never told anyone my true occupation in chance encounters. She now picked up where I'd left off, in a pleasant, chatty way without a second's hesitation.

'Nicola and Abigail are with John's parents, you see – that's how we could get away. They also pick up the girls from school so that I can go on working – they're a tremendous help, very young in outlook; we try to repay them by taking them on holiday with us, we usually rent a *gîte* in Aix-en-Provence during August . . .

'Yes, I'm the supervisor of a typing pool for a large legal practice. I say typing, but it's actually word-processing . . . one of the girls is complaining about this strange new ailment, RSI – have you heard about it? Repetitive Strain Injury. It's the endless bashing of keys, I suppose, though the partners have warned me to be *very* non-committal about it. They don't have to move a carriage any more, you see, or even bother with paper. Such a lot of changes, even since I began working.'

The other woman seized on the word 'change' and was up and running about the endless stream of legislation affecting

the poultry trade, and as the banal chatter flowed on I smiled and nodded politely as I sipped claret and ate duckling.

It was yet another aspect of Laura I'd not seen before, her ability to sound like a woman who could scarcely have been more removed from the Laura who seemed to know everything, who craved endless solitude, whose mind turned over ideas for a great dark novel.

I couldn't have believed it possible for her to sound so incredibly prosaic. It seemed somehow more than acting. A lot of the people I came up against in my work were acting, and because of my lengthy experience I could always tell. Had I met Laura for the first time in her typing-pool role I could have detected no trace of the woman inside. It was as if she had been obliterated by the one who took the grandies to a *gîte* in Aix. It had seemed not so much acting as *being*.

I wondered if it was yet another form of escape, if I'd lost her once more, just as surely as I had at Larch House, when the house had transformed itself into the setting of her girlhood. I wondered if the pain of being herself since Simon had died would ever completely recede.

'Do have another drink, John, if you like,' she said dejectedly. 'I'll go and change.'

It was as if her performance in the dining-room, which had continued over coffee and liqueurs in the lounge, had exhausted her flow of adrenalin and provoked the depression real actors experience. But I knew it wasn't that. I could remember the night at the Berkshire only too clearly.

I sat next to her on the big brass bed and took her hand in mine. 'I'm sorry,' she said at last. 'It's always around this time . . .'

The end of the sentence was lost, as they so often were when she was in this state. Always around this time, I sup-

posed, when she knew her dreams might soon return her to the days when he'd been alive; but when she awoke there'd be no one breathing there, no warm body she could reach out and touch. Several divorced women I'd known had said the same thing about the break-up – the nights were always the worst, even though, when they'd been together, they'd usually lain there hating the bastard.

'I know,' I said. 'Really I do . . .'

'Oh, John . . . I wish I'd known you when . . .'

I didn't speak and it seemed that this sentence too wouldn't be completed. But after a prolonged silence she said: 'Before Simon. Before I met him. I wish I'd known you then. I sometimes wish I'd *never* met him . . .'

Because of the pain losing him had brought? Because I remained alive while he was dead? I smiled ruefully. 'You'd not have wanted to take up with a man like me, not a bright kid like you must have been. I was going nowhere, even in my twenties. I'd have been too ordinary for a girl like you.'

'Oh, *God*,' she whispered, tears glinting on her lids. 'I *love* ordinary. You can't begin to know how much I love ordinary . . .'

She was sitting on a million, Larch House would soon be hers, she'd be able to spend the rest of her life doing what she'd always longed to do, and she'd have given it all back to have had the life she'd had with him. It was like *The Monkey's Paw* – the wish was granted, to be instantly cancelled by the appalling cost.

We undressed in turn in the bathroom. When I came out the bedroom was in darkness, and when I got into the large bed she was naked.

'Do you want to make love to me?'

'Yes. But I'm not going to.'

I'd been determined not to think ahead to the time when I

got into bed with her, but I'd not been entirely successful, as we'd wandered giggling along the maze of corridors, eaten and drunk in the half-light, pretended to be Mr and Mrs Average – the thought of that pale body I'd touched but not seen had continually forced itself into my mind.

'It's not the right time, Laura. We both know it.'

She sighed gustily; it might have been relief.

'I'll hold you,' I said. 'Like before . . .'

'I . . . feel such a cheat . . . getting you to take this room. It seemed . . . it might be . . .'

Might be that she was getting over him at last, I wondered, as we'd sat in the car in the cheerful glow of hotel lights, like someone recovering from an illness, who has a good morning, only to find the afternoon bringing a return to lassitude and pain.

'Look, Laura, give it time. I'll wait – as long as it takes.'

As before, it seemed almost a privilege simply to be allowed to hold her, to run my hand over her breasts and thighs, along the curve of her waist. I was travelling hopefully towards the time when I'd feel her limbs trembling and her breath catching, and it seemed possible I might never arrive, but I could live with that because she was the woman she was.

She kissed me lengthily; I could feel the inevitable moisture of her cheeks. 'Larch House,' she whispered.

'Larch House?'

'I'll be there in a few weeks, I'll have cut myself off from *everything* to do . . . It'll be different then, I promise . . .'

There was a note of vehemence in her voice. I felt I'd seen her striving towards that new life this afternoon, it must have been that determination that had made her plead with me to stay overnight.

I said: 'Can I sleep in your room? In your lovely four-poster?'

'I'll not let you sleep anywhere else . . .'

She was silent for so long I thought she'd fallen asleep. Then, her voice seeming to come from a distance, she said: 'We'd be good for each other. We'd both have our own work and our own lives. We'd neither of us want to live together, I think. But to meet every week or so . . . keep an eye on each other . . .'

It looked to be the relationship I'd always been searching for and never found. My work had to come first, had to fill my life – it was designed to. It was the never-ending slog that kept the bitterness and the sense of waste almost at arm's length. Like her, I had my own vulnerability, but artfully concealed now due to the length of time I'd had to perfect the covering of the scars. Perhaps she'd always sensed it in me, as men and women could sense in the people they were attracted to a level of sensibility that matched their own. In any case, there was only sufficient time, in a life devoted to blocking out the bulk of the pain, for the sort of relationship she herself instinctively sought.

I said softly, 'I think we'd be *very* good for each other . . .'

Sixteen

'Is that something from Alan Starkey?'

We shared the mail opening; I could see Starkey's discreet logo on an envelope in her pile.

'So it is . . .'

'Gimme . . .'

'You're breaking house rules. First we open everything, and then we go through it in an orderly manner and prioritise. *Your* system, need I add.'

'Rules are for the obedience of fools and the guidance of wise men.'

'Well, thank you very much, sexist pig . . . Here, take your bloody letter – I hope it throws your schedule out for the rest of the day . . .'

Grinning, I slit it open.

Dear John [Starkey had written] Re: DAVID MARSH. In my preliminary report I advised that when Marsh's former partner, Raymond Sheard, returned from holiday I should probably be able to get some idea of Marsh's whereabouts from him. Sheard got back last week and I called at his office. As usual, in this sort of case, he was extremely cagey about telling me anything unless I would tell him why I needed to know. I said

I was working for solicitors trying to trace Marsh in connection with a legacy due to him from a relation's estate. Please bear that in mind if you contact Sheard yourself.

After that, he talked readily enough. He had no firm knowledge of Marsh's movements – said he was always rather self-contained – but he did remember him saying he was interested in some sort of semi-retirement occupation, something to keep him ticking over and bring a few bob in, but nothing too onerous. He talked about buying holiday flats, either for sale or rental, perhaps even one of those sheltered-accommodation complexes for elderly people. He talked a lot about Hunstanton in Norfolk – there's a good deal of development and it's attractive to older people because it's so flat.

Well, the good news is that I contacted Frank Ashdown in King's Lynn to see if he could dig up anything. He came back the same day. Marsh has bought about a dozen flats in a new building on the front and presently occupies one of them himself (address and phone at the bottom of this report). The not-so-good news is that I've not been able to establish that he's actually living there at present. My PA has rung the number several times, but all she gets is his answerphone. She left no message – I assumed you'd not want him to know there was any kind of trace on him if you're after him for unpaid bills or whatever.

However, by providing you with background and an address, I assume the commission is now complete. I thank you for it and enclose my account herewith. Regards, Alan.

Marsh's address was: Flat fifty, Elgin House, Cliff Parade, Hunstanton.

I put the report aside, aware of Norma's attentive look. She disapproved of everything to do with the Marshes, but that didn't mean she was any less curious about what was going on.

I said: 'He's established that Marsh has a base in Norfolk. No one answers calls. That's not surprising if he's never off Laura's doorstep. He's been dabbling in property . . .'

'I knew it.'

'Very dodgy. I wonder if he thought the market had bottomed out and property could only go one way . . .'

'Some hope. They say the days of making big money out of property are just about gone for good.'

'He's supposed to be a shrewd cookie', I said reflectively, 'who'll be able to read the financial pages just like everyone else. Perhaps he bought the flats to rent out during the season, to give him an income, with a view to selling when he can turn a few quid.'

'So why does he need Mrs Marsh's money?'

'He could be over-extended. Found the rentals aren't providing the income he'd hoped for.'

It stretched my credulity to accept that Marsh owned *anything*. I'd stood in Laura's back garden and witnessed an argument that was obviously about money, had seen her almost hurl a bundle of notes at him, which he'd seemed desperately in need of for groceries. I assumed she was still picking up the tab for the Escort.

I said: 'But you're right. Property in the present climate is not for the amateur, however good he was in the computer game. It could be he's caught in the negative-equity trap like so many others. I . . . think I'll go down there and poke around a bit. When will I have a clear day . . .?'

She shook her head resignedly, turned to the desk diary. She knew there was no further point in warning me off, that I

was going to pursue the situation until I'd proved to myself there was nowhere left to go.

'Not for a fortnight,' she said firmly. 'There are too many complex cases I can't farm out. You really could do with someone else in the field.'

'More staff mean more staff problems. I've got as much as I can handle with yours.'

She was making it difficult. If she couldn't dissuade me from wasting my valuable time she could at least put the free day so far ahead that with any luck the Laura situation might have solved itself.

'I'll try and keep a fortnight Tuesday clear,' she said reluctantly.

We turned back to the mail. I'd be going to Norfolk at my own expense, but that was the smallest part of the problem. I'd get it back in spades one day – weekends at Larch House, nights out, presents. I'd never met anyone more generous – when I'd gone to pay the bill at the Fields it was only to find it already settled. She'd not take a penny, not even for the dinner on Saturday night, though I'd become almost heated in my insistence on standing my corner.

'I owe you,' she'd said firmly, 'for being there for me through a bad time . . .'

But her generosity worried me. I wondered how generous she'd been in paying off Marsh. I was certain he'd *been* paid off; she'd been so positive about buying Larch House, about her future in the Dales. I'd seen a dramatic change from the troubled, often uncertain woman of the late summer, forever, I'd felt, preoccupied with the problem of Marsh when she was struggling to come to terms with the death of Simon.

Had she given him too much, to be shot of him? Did that explain those periods of near-euphoria on Saturday, the

swings of mood, the intense anticipation of becoming mistress of Larch House?

There had been times when I'd felt I could reasonably assume Marsh had been sorted out. He'd had what I suspected would be a substantial pay-off, could hand back the hire-car, leave his cabin and return to the Midlands. They'd settled the matter between them, as she'd always seemed to feel they must, and it was in any case none of my business. There'd been, throughout the weekend, the clear impression that she could now get on with the rest of her life, and I'd been very tempted to close the mental file on that difficult man.

But I knew I couldn't. Assuming he *had* been paid off, how long was it going to be before he'd be back for more? Would the money simply go down some black hole in the property business, as the rest of his money seemed to have done? I felt I had to know what he was going to do with it, to try and satisfy myself he'd not be back to disturb her hard-won peace of mind, needed to be forewarned in case he did, so that I'd be in a position to show Laura, however angry she got, that good money had predictably followed bad.

I couldn't get down to Norfolk for two weeks, but I made three flying trips to the little village of cabins near Grassington to see if I could get a fix on his current movements; each time drawing a blank. His cabin was deserted, could even have been vacated. It was difficult to tell, sun-blinds had been drawn across all the windows, their slats turned broadside on.

Coming away from the village one evening, I made a detour to the Wheatsheaf. She might not be able to tell me anything about his whereabouts or his current activities, but it was worth a shot. She was, after all, the person I'd seen him with last.

The bar parlour was as quiet as before. I ordered a gin and gave Madge a warm smile. She gave me back her mechanical barmaid smile. I could tell she felt she'd seen the face before, but then she saw so many faces.

'You probably won't remember me, Madge,' I said quietly. 'I'm the private investigator who was looking into Simon Marsh's death for the insurance . . .'

There was a sudden clatter as she dropped the ice tongs on the bar. Her face began the rapid flush I remembered so well, a flush so strong it could easily be detected beneath the mask of meticulously applied make-up, and which overflowed on to her neck and chest. I believe for a few seconds, as ice cubes slid along the bar like coins on a shove-ha'penny board, it was a physical impossibility for her to speak.

'You . . . didn't tell me you'd begun seeing Simon's brother David, did you, after Simon died. It could have been helpful.'

Swallowing rapidly, like someone reacting to pressure in a descending plane, she finally spoke, in a low, rasping voice. 'I'm sorry, mister, I can't stand around talking – there's only me and Ted on . . .'

She gathered up the scattered cubes of ice and tossed them into the sink below the bar. She was too distracted to remember the ice had been intended for my gin. I righted the vacuum container which had also been a casualty of her agitation and helped myself to what ice remained. I took a sip of the drink and glanced round the bar, at the handful of regulars muttering over full pints. 'You don't look too busy to me, Madge. I'm sure you could spare me a couple of minutes.'

Wide-eyed with shock, she handed me change with a wet hand. 'There's nothing to tell I didn't tell you before . . .'

'I'd really like to decide that for myself . . .'

'Look, mister,' she burst out harshly, 'just piss off, will you, because one word from me to Ted and your feet won't touch

252

the ground when he throws you out.'

I remembered Ted very well too, with his burly frame and the misshapen features that hinted at old fights in rougher pubs. There'd be little trouble at the Wheatsheaf, it wasn't that kind of place, but he stood watching me with a pointed look that seemed to mix anticipation with nostalgia, as if I might provide an interesting exception.

'Very well, Madge,' I said softly, 'you either talk to me or I talk to your husband – the choice is yours.'

The flush deepened as she gave me a look of pure venom. I shivered slightly, as if the emotion were powerful enough to be tangible against the skin.

She suddenly clipped rapidly along the bar to where Ted glowered and spoke softly to him. He replied in a low voice, but it wasn't so low that I couldn't pick up the odd phrase. '... if you're sure ... don't take no humpy ... any bother and ... All right, love, five minutes ...'

Like most pubs these days the Wheatsheaf had been made open-plan, but across the bar parlour and beneath an archway there was a small deserted area that had once probably been known as the Snug. She led me there and sat down at a circular table with an ornate cast-iron pedestal. She was trembling all over now, her hands, her shoulders, her lips. I couldn't understand such a powerful reaction. She was leading a complicated life, but then, in the Nineties, who wasn't?

'Look, Madge,' I said gently, 'I'm really not interested in prying into your private life.'

'You could have bleeding fooled me ...'

'Just tell me how long you knew Simon.'

'... About ... about eighteen months ...' she murmured, seeming almost to force the words past lips that had a twitching life of their own.

'And when did you meet David?'

'. . . About . . . about . . . two or three months later . . .'

'Is that when he was going around with Simon, calling on his customers and so on?'

She gazed at me with her green, frightened eyes in a lengthy silence. I was asking leading questions and waiting too long for answers, but I knew that if I played it any other way I'd learn nothing. She finally nodded, though the movement was difficult to detect, the way her head shook.

'All right,' I said soothingly. 'So you transferred your affections from Simon to David – that's none of my business. All I need to know from you is this: has David gone back to his place in Norfolk or is he still hanging out at the cabin near Grassington?'

Some sort of new shock seemed to quell the shaking briefly, as if I'd told her something she'd not known about. If that was so it could only be the Norfolk flat; she slept with him at the cabin.

'. . . He's . . . still at . . . still at . . . the cabin . . .'

I wondered if I detected a note of uncertainty in the already uncertain delivery.

'You've seen him recently? Like this week?'

Again the trembling nod that was a long time in coming, that seemed to follow frantic conjecture. Suddenly she burst out in a low, hissing voice: 'He's staying there because of me. I'm . . . I'm leaving Jim. He . . . doesn't know yet. . . . Please, for Christ's sake, mister, *please* don't say anything to Jim. He'd . . . he'd . . .'

She couldn't even begin to form the words about what Jim would do, and the flushed skin took on a pallor that gave her make-up the almost garish quality of an actor's seen away from stage lighting. Her terror was all down to Jim, not me and my questions, and I felt my fists clenching in anger, as they always did, at what Jim, and all those brave lads like

him, could do to small, fragile women who weighed seven and a half stone. Whatever the provocation.

'I've got two kids,' she whispered. 'I want them to go with me and David . . . they'll have a better life . . . He loves kids, you can't believe, he has none of his own. I've got to go canny . . .'

It was confession time and it seemed to make her marginally calmer. I put a hand briefly over hers. 'Jim will never hear it from me, Madge,' I told her. 'Believe it . . .'

'He'd kill me,' she said in a flat whisper that held total conviction. 'We're just going to go – me, David, the kids. I'll send the bastard a postcard . . . he'll never find us . . .'

'That's right,' I said softly, 'you just go . . .'

We sat for a few seconds in a silence that was almost companionable. 'Look,' I said finally, 'for reasons I won't go into I need to know if David's all right for money. He's not working at present, is he, he can't be working if he's spending so much time in Yorkshire?'

'He's . . . self-employed . . .'

'I know that, but . . .'

'He doesn't say much. I'd sooner leave it to him. He's been a bit . . . strapped . . . but . . . but . . . he's been working on some deal. Last time I saw him he said it's nearly sorted . . . We're planning to go south, abroad even. He . . . he said this deal would sort everything out . . . there'd be no more money worries . . .'

'You believe him?'

'Yes,' she said simply. 'I *know* him. He wouldn't lie . . . not to me. There'd be no point. It's him who wants me and the kids with him so much . . .'

'All right, Madge. I hope you'll be very happy. I mean that. It must have been hard on Simon when you fell for David, but these things happen . . .'

There was a sudden haunted look on her pale, painted face, and her eyes left mine to travel unfocused into the darkness beyond the uncurtained window. It was as if she'd been over-taken by a different emotion, to do with her relationship with the brothers, which had been pushed to the edge of her mind by fear, by the distraction of my questions. I wondered if it was buried guilt, whether she'd once felt that transferring her affections from Simon to his brother had helped to push him towards depression, alcohol and barbiturates.

'I liked Simon a lot, an awful lot – he was kind, gentle, but . . . but when he introduced me to David . . . you can't believe . . . I knew I couldn't live without him . . .'

Lights had flashed, bells had rung, the earth had trembled. 'I understand,' I said, with a faint, wistful envy, because I didn't understand at all what it must have been like to be D. H. Lawrence and walk into a room and be struck by the thunderbolt that had been Frieda. Perhaps it was the job I did.

'I'm going now,' I said. 'You've told me all I needed to know. I'll not bother you again. Enjoy the rest of your life.'

She slumped against the back of the banquette seating, arms and legs at odd angles with the sudden relief, as if the strings had been released on a puppet.

'You've *finished* . . .?' she whispered.

'For good. All I needed was to know he was in decent financial shape. I doubt you'll see me again. But I'd like you to promise me you'll not mention any of this to David. It won't affect your life together. I . . . gave my word I'd not say anything to Jim.'

An impulse of fear widened her eyes briefly, like the flashing of a car's lamps.

'I . . . promise . . .'

'Goodbye then, Madge, and good luck . . .'

I left her half lying there, the discarded puppet, too weak, it seemed, with relief to follow me to the main bar. Ted, self-consciously polishing glasses, like an extra in *The Bill*, watched me balefully as I crossed to the door. On my way to the car-park in the misty country silence, I could see him through the front window, lumbering protectively towards where Madge lay sprawled.

I got in the car, sat for a couple of minutes with the engine idling. I wondered if that wrapped it up. It all seemed more or less as Norma and I had pieced it together. Simon had asked David for a loan, David had come north to evaluate the business. He'd lent Simon money and then, at some later stage, seemed to have got into money difficulties himself. He'd come back north to retrieve the loan from Laura, she'd finally paid him out and he was using the money to do a runner with Madge, with whom, presumably, he'd always kept in touch. Perhaps he'd also unloaded his Norfolk flats at any price they'd bring.

There were oddnesses. I couldn't really get Marsh's love of kids together too easily, and I'd have thought someone as streetwise as Madge wouldn't have trusted him quite so implicitly; but then, I'd often found the cynicism of the street-wise to be only skin-deep. I was also still fascinated by that double triangle – the brothers and Laura, then the brothers and Madge – with the younger brother, against whom I'd not heard a wrong word from anyone, always somehow getting the shitty end of the stick, to the point where he could take it no longer. No wonder Madge looked haunted and David twitched.

It had to be guilt.

Seventeen

It took some getting used to. She'd said there'd be a few local people to the house-warming, and I'd expected to see a handful of retired businessmen, because it tended to be only the well-heeled elderly who could afford the luxury of such costly isolation. A few grizzled men and their wives sipping glasses of Tio Pepe, eating a buffet supper and going home at ten to watch a tape of *Casualty*.

But as I drove along the metalled drive between the beech hedges, the house was lit up like a public building, and it was difficult to find a space for my car on the square of hard standing in front of the garages to the left of the house. The cars too were nothing special – Fords, Vauxhalls, Nissans, a couple of small Volvos.

As I passed the front windows I could hear the murmur of voices and the faint sound of piano music. I rang the bell of the big front door; a second or so later it was flung open.

'I'm . . . John Goss . . .'

'Of course you are! Welcome, dearest John!'

'Laura . . .?'

I'd thought, silhouetted against the light, it was one of the guests. Her hair was the first shock. It had been teased into one of those deceptively tumbled styles where every strand seems to have definition; it couldn't have been a bigger con-

trast to the sleekly fastened or loosely flowing styles I was so
used to.

Other shocks followed. She wore green eye-shadow
flecked with dots of silver, and blusher, and lipstick so dark a
red it seemed almost purple. Her dress was close-fitting and
sleeveless, in green crushed velvet with a skirt in silvery chif-
fon tiers that ended well above the knee.

She was smiling broadly, itself almost unprecedented. 'Oh,
John, please try not to look *quite* so surprised. I *told* you
things would be different once I was at Larch House. Come
along and meet our new friends . . .'

I let her take me by the hand, almost in shock, into what
we'd called the music room, where a man in a blazer played
light classical pieces with a decent amateur touch.

'Ladies and gentlemen,' she said, in a carrying voice, 'this is
John Goss, a very good friend from Beckford. I won't introduce you individually . . .'

Her guests, all talking volubly, threw brief, abstracted
glances in my direction before turning back to one another.

'Now,' Laura said, 'where's Albert . . .'

She waved, and a grey-haired portly man in bow-tie, white
jacket and black trousers began to navigate his way towards
us through the crowd, as gracefully as a Thames steamer
avoiding smaller craft.

'Would you like something to drink, sir?' he said, offering a
silver tray loaded with glasses of what looked to be
champagne.

Laura and I both took one and with a courteous bow he
backed away.

'Does he work for you?' I said, bemused.

'Good Lord, no,' she said, giggling. 'I've hired a couple to
do the supper and they brought Albert to see to the drinks.
He's a retired butler . . .'

'I'd rather gathered that . . .'

'His father was a butler too. Did you notice how he offered you *something* to drink instead of *a* drink? Shades of Augustus Hare in *The Vagrant Mood* . . .'

Her memory for obscure literary references at least was unimpaired by alcohol – I could tell by the excess of moisture glittering in her grey eyes she'd already had a good deal to drink.

'Oh, John . . .' She put a hand to my cheek. 'It's so *good* to see you.'

I tried to inject the old warmth into my smile, wished I could say similar words to this near-stranger with the painted face and the wild hair and the sort of dress you associated with Karaoke night.

'I'll have to leave you to mingle on your own for a few minutes, darling, and see how things are progressing below stairs.' She went off, giggling again.

'I will have "something to drink", Albert,' I muttered in a preoccupied tone, as I caught him cruising past, my mind almost reeling at the way rooms which, a fortnight ago, had been cold, dust-sheeted and silent were now full of heat and music and people, at the way the Laura I'd known had somehow got lost in the removal.

I was drinking too quickly, but the first glass had done nothing for me, and I felt that if I had half a dozen glasses I'd still not be able to approach the mood she seemed to be in. It wasn't so much the *speed* of the flight to Larch House – I'd known she was determined to take up the lease offer, and money, of course, could smooth every pathway – but how had a woman who lived as solitary a life as I did myself suddenly found friends by the roomful?

I looked at the guests more closely. It was clear that they themselves all knew one another very well. There seemed to

be a fair number of corduroy jackets about, and men wearing those kinds of chess-board beards that would need twice as much careful shaving time as having no beard at all. The women seemed to be the type of women who went with those kinds of men – there was a good deal of primary-coloured make-up and imaginatively piled hair, and their dresses seemed to belong to that flowing peasant style hopefully covered by the word 'ethnic'.

'So you're an old friend of our gracious hostess ... I'm Julien, by the way ...'

He also wore a corduroy jacket, but he was fair-haired and clean-shaven and had an encouragingly ironic smile.

'Depends what you call old,' I said. 'I met Laura about three months ago.'

'That's *really* old.' His smile deepened. 'We just met her last week.'

'*All* of you?'

'We're Demmies ...'

'Demmies?'

'We're all members of the Wharfedale Damien Society. Named for Damien Eugene Holdsworth, now dead and gone. He aimed to bring people together who had a general interest in the arts – literature, theatre, music, art itself. We meet fortnightly and blather on about them. Most of us are in separate clubs – writers' circles, am-drams and so on – but Damien thought a club that had a broader base would get us to cross-fertilise, if that doesn't sound too grand.' His smile strongly hinted that perhaps it did. 'It gets us away from the telly and the kids, if nothing else. We've even got the odd minor celeb or two. That tall, gaunt-looking man with the red hair writes the Tent-peg Books. *Tent-pegs in Cumbria, Tent-pegs in the Auvergne* ... no?'

'Not really my kind of reading ...'

'I believe *Tent-pegs in India* was one bag of tent-pegs too far. That's when he began to look like that. From what I gather, he spent most of the time crouched over a hole in the ground getting rid of his intestines. If you happen to speak to him don't ever bring the words Sholapur and curry into the same sentence . . .'

'And Laura's a member? Of the Demmies?'

'Just. She came to our last meeting and joined on the spot. Then she talked a blue streak about everything that came up. What erudition! Finally, she invited us all here for the house-warming. Most of us had all sorts of other things arranged, with it being so near Christmas, but none of us wanted to miss an evening at Larch House with such a clever, intriguing lady from nowhere, so we all made pathetic excuses and bombed along here instead.'

I remembered the effect this house had had on her from the moment she'd seen it, the times when she'd seemed to live so completely inside some other world, either remembered past or imagined future, that I'd felt excluded, invisible. I also recollected that she'd talked of inviting people to dinner who shared her interests. But I'd thought it would take months for her to break the ice with the arty set. I simply could not see the Laura I'd known, that sad and troubled woman of the solitary walks, the endless grieving and the exhausting secret battle with Marsh, dominating a roomful of people who were almost certainly as clannish as they were voluble. But it was the same woman, the one dressed like someone who danced on tables.

'Are you and Laura what they call an item, or am I being too personal? I usually am . . .'

'No,' I said, 'we're just good friends. I met her in a professional capacity. I'm in insurance.'

He waited expectantly for me to go on, but that was all

he was going to get. Apart from the chronic discretion I'd developed through the job I did, I'd no way of telling what information Laura herself would regard as permissible for release.

'There seems to be an interesting absence of a *Mr* Marsh . . .'

'I . . . assume she's divorced or separated. I didn't ask and I wasn't told . . .'

'She seems to be rather well-banknoted . . .'

'I believe she inherited . . .'

'They say she's renting this place at present but is almost certain to buy. It's on the market for a quarter of a million . . .'

'Really . . .'

His ironic smile was back, and though few people could play a straighter bat than me I could tell he felt I knew more than I was letting on. But my instinct for circumspection appeared to have been in the right place. She seemed to want to be exactly what Julien had called her – the lady from nowhere.

'I do hope she has lots of parties. God, how I love champagne. It's usually château-bottled ferret-piss at our dos. We're none of us in serious money professions, I'm afraid – we teach people things and we run libraries and we have little craft shops, and now and then one of us writes or paints something that earns a few bob.'

It all rather went with the beards and the clothes, the artistic appearance that amateurs so often tended to adopt, with the actorish voices and laughter. My dislike of them was as intense as it was irrational. I felt they'd taken the Laura I knew and cared about and turned her into a giggling, painted tart.

I watched her now, touching the pianist's shoulder, moving from one group to another, where the men looked on in

admiration and the women in warmly smiling envy. I'd thought it would be me and her and a few locals she'd brought in simply to mark the occasion, and that soon we'd be alone together, sitting by the log fire in the half-light, the warm, funny Laura of London and the Fields Hotel, in one of her classic dresses, smiling her faint smile.

A tallish woman joined us. She had lank fair hair and a headband, and wore a beaded shawl over an ankle-length beige dress.

'My wife, Esme . . .' Julien said, without enthusiasm.

'They'll never be the same, the Demmies,' she said, with a bitterness that showed through the bright tone. 'I'm sure she'll take us over, with her lavish parties and her managing ways. They say she's interested in writing – I'm sure she'll write a sensational novel that translates into fifteen languages and makes her even more money than the suitcaseful she already seems to have.'

She looked at me with a polite but accusing smile, as if I were part of a plot to destroy the Demmies' unique identity, and it was clear that the Demmies – the female ones at least – were as deeply uneasy about Laura as I was. I sipped my third glass of champagne and gave Esme a rueful smile, knowing that sooner or later I should have to accept, however reluctantly, that the strange new Laura was nothing to do with the Demmies – it was all her own work.

'Ladies and gentlemen!' Laura cried. 'They're ready to serve supper if you'd like to come through . . .'

'Not before time,' Julien said. 'One more glass of Bolly on an empty stomach and you'd be carrying me in. Thank God it's not my turn to drive . . .'

'You *never* drive, *pig*, except when there's no drink on offer,' Esme said, in a decidedly un-jokey voice, before walking off abruptly.

'Oh dear,' he sighed. 'If only someone as wealthy and

attractive as Laura would develop an overwhelming passion
for me, and rescue me from rude children, smelly dogs and
women who read too many books by people with names like
Naomi Wolf and Katie Roiphe. My papa blames it all on the
Sixties . . .'

He went off chuckling; I drifted behind. I wondered if it
would always be like this now, Larch House regularly
invaded by the kind of people her mother had once filled her
own house with. She'd said that when next summer came
we'd go hiking on the fells, sit in sunny bar rooms, eat our
meals out on the patio; but I could see only umbrella tables
on the front lawn and these same people gathered in chatter-
ing groups as Albert sailed around with his tray.

Perhaps she'd settle down. Perhaps too much had happened too quickly – sudden death, sudden wealth, the sudden
realisation of old dreams. Perhaps there really had been too
many of the climacterics that are said to have such a profound effect on people. And yet, though I'd known a number
of people be changed by sudden dramatic events in their
lives, I'd never known any of them to be changed out of
recognition.

As Laura had.

'Sit here, John . . .'

It was a buffet meal in the dining-room, with people sitting
at small tables or standing, as they preferred. A good third of
the big dining-table was also available for seating, the rest
of it being stacked with party food, and it was here that Laura
seemed to be holding court with what I assumed to be the
brightest and best of the Demmies.

'Can I help you, sir – a mixed selection?' A smiling woman
in a white blouse and black trousers began to arrange a delicate plateful for me from the vast array of freshly cooked

meat, fish and poultry, the salads and quiches, the potatoes in their warmers – julienne, Lyonnaise, sauté, Anna – and from the assortment of sweet-smelling crusty baguettes.

'Something to drink, sir?' enquired dear old Albert. 'I can recommend the Château Lescalle – just nicely peaking now . . .'

Laura patted my hand as I sat down, but went on talking rapidly: '. . . But you must decide what paintings are *for*. Do you want to cover your walls with pretty pictures that are nice to look at but present no challenge, or do you hang paintings that however many times you look at them you seem to see things you've not seen before?'

Julien, sitting to my left, said: 'I suspect that, as paintings on the wall go, you don't see them at all in the end. I'm an unreclaimed Impressionist and I once framed a print of Monet's *Gare de l'Est* – one of my favourites – and within six months it would have been all the same if the National Gallery had given me the original. I'd simply stopped seeing it. Having said that, your mama's paintings seem to satisfy both requirements, Laura, they're pictorially attractive and you certainly want to study them.'

I saw then that the paintings that had been hanging in the dining-room when we'd first seen the house – Dales landscapes mainly – had been replaced by her mother's pictures with their distorted trees, shadows that seemed to angle wrongly, disturbing colours. They reminded me of the day she'd talked about her strange childhood, a childhood that she herself had felt played such a big part in the shaping of her personality; one, I suddenly realised, that I seemed to know less about the longer I knew her.

'I suspect your mother had great technical skill to take the chances she did,' an older man said, glancing intently from one painting to another. They were picked out by oblong

picture lamps, which provided the room's only light, apart from the dimmed glow of the central chandelier, now lowered until it was suspended just above the long table. 'El Greco, for example, knew exactly what he was doing with his elongations, but some of his contemporaries considered him to have defective eyesight . . .'

'Oh, quite, take Turner – he simple rearranged a view to suit himself – he *could* have done a meticulous copy . . .'

'Take Michelangelo . . .'

The talk flowed on, the unwritten rule seeming to be that it must be arts-orientated – politics, commerce and money were only mentioned in passing and usually with contempt. I enjoyed the food and wine, and I listened to the ceaseless chatter with genuine interest, because they all knew so much, but I was largely ignored, as they were not the kind of people to welcome strangers easily, unless of course they were wealthy and open-handed and had the sort of dominating personality Laura seemed to have acquired when she became mistress of Larch House. I glanced along the lengthy table, with its starched cloths, its gleaming silver and glass, its piled salvers and its decanters of nicely peaking wine, surrounded by Demmies who ate and drank as relentlessly as they talked, and I thought how the room had looked on that cold, bright afternoon, when sticks of sunlight had cut through dust-motes, and it had seemed that all it needed was Miss Havisham in her faded wedding gown sitting at the head of the table. But the sight I was actually seeing, of the almost strident, tumble-haired Laura, with her new friends, was scarcely less bizarre than the one I'd imagined.

She sat at my side, talking ceaselessly, meeting erudite opinions with opinions equally erudite, from a memory that seemed bottomless, eating as sparingly as ever, but drinking in regular rapid sips, her eyes shining, her lips moist, her left hand, beneath the table, caressing the inside of my thigh.

As it had done most of the time since I'd sat down.

'And now, ladies and gentlemen, if you'll all settle down again, Roddy and Jane have kindly consented to give us the balcony scene from *Private Lives* which, as I'm certain you'll know, they're helping to present in an amateur production in the new year. Roddy . . . Jane . . .'

Amidst encouraging applause, the pair began to deliver their speeches, while the pianist tinkled 'I'll See You Again' in the background. They performed in a cleared space at the end of the room where the piano stood on its triangular dais, a single light above them, the rest of the room in darkness.

It really wasn't a question of the Demmies singing for their lavish supper – this was obviously the part of the evening they enjoyed most of all. I wondered how often they got such a showcase for their talents; they were queuing up to do their little pieces – the pianist had played a Debussy Arabesque, the ill-looking red-haired man had read a vignette from his current manuscript, *Tent-pegs in Andalusia*, three women had sung a madrigal, one of the beards, holding a piece of A4 with slightly trembling hands, had read his latest poem, another had read from his experimental novel, and now it was the turn of Roddy and Jane, who were surprisingly good, to strut their stuff.

Laura was everywhere, in between giving her graceful introductions; discreetly lining up the next performer, whispering, smiling, nodding, briefly touching arms, ensuring that Albert did the business with the liqueurs. She continued to attract envy and admiration in equal amounts. It was as if those distant skills she'd learnt in her mother's house had never been lost, of motivating and ego-stroking, of mixing the spoken word with music and song, of compèring in an almost professional manner.

The strangeness of it all, which had begun when a woman

I'd barely recognised had opened the door to me, was beginning to recede. It had been like touching down in a foreign country, where not only is the language different, but the buildings and the sounds and the smells, even the gestures of the people. But yesterday's strangeness is today's normality and, though still longing for the old Laura, I was gradually getting used to the new, and the milieu that went with her, though I wasn't certain I'd want to continue a relationship that really belonged to the current Laura's less popular twin.

Even so, the finale to the entertainment provided a new jolt.

'Ladies and gentlemen . . .' A woman with a pageboy hairstyle and a slight squint smiled around at us. 'It's my pleasant duty to thank everyone for their splendid efforts in entertaining us in such an enjoyable manner. I should also, on behalf of us all, like to thank Laura for her lavish hospitality, her organising abilities and her gratifying interest in the WDS . . .'

There was a buzz of appreciation as people glanced round in search of Laura herself.

The woman smiled. 'No, you can't *see* Laura, because she's just outside the door, but she can *hear* us. And she's very kindly consented to round off the evening with a little something of her own. So would you please put your hands together for our gracious hostess – *Laura!*'

As the applause began, the door opened on yet another version of Laura. She walked across the room with complete assurance and took her place beneath the single light. She had changed into dark, mannish clothes – trousers, a jacket, a lilac top, and wore a navy cap pulled over one eye. The piano began to play, and in an amazingly deep and husky voice for one whose normal one seemed so small, she began to sing

'Falling in Love Again', her eyes moving everywhere in the gloom, but seeming always to return to linger affectionately on mine.

Eighteen

She closed the door on the last of the Demmies and turned to me, smiling widely. 'John, I've had no time with you at *all*!'

She suddenly flung her arms round me and kissed me fully on the mouth, the tip of her tongue sliding between my lips. Then she put her cheek against mine and whispered: 'Shall we go up . . .?'

She took my hand and led me to the lofty main bedroom, with the four-poster and its gauzy curtains. A single lamp glowed on a bedside table, beneath a dark-green shade. Her eyes had widened, seeming to gather up and reflect what light there was. We kissed again, lengthily, her hands running up and down my back, and then she began rapidly unzipping and unhooking the tiered dress she'd changed back into for what had been left of the evening. Within seconds she stood before me naked, her white body in the dim light seeming almost to be a marble sculpture of itself.

'Come along, John,' she whispered, unfastening my tie, then pressing her lips on mine again. She lifted the curtain and slid into bed. But the room was still very warm with the heating that had only recently turned itself off, and she lay on her side half-covered. I saw her body then as I'd fantasised about seeing it when I'd first looked the room over – diffused, glowing, almost classically exotic behind the curtains.

And it was a disappointment, because in my imagination her hair had been loose against the pillow, her face pale and clean, and she had been smiling shyly.

This Laura had had no time to remove the vivid make-up or comb out the tumbled and lacquered hair. She had simply taken off her clothes and waited for me to join her with an undisguised anticipation. In most of the other women I'd known it would have given me a similar excitement, but in her it left me saddened, almost reluctant, and now very uneasy.

I undressed, switched off the lamp, and got slowly into bed with her.

'Laura . . . I . . .'

'Don't,' she whispered, putting a finger to my lips. 'Don't speak. Words spoil things. Just make love to me . . . just make love to me . . .'

I just made love to her. Though it seemed the other way round. She had a hunger I'd rarely known. I thought at first it was down to the length of time she'd been without a man, but it was more than that. I felt submerged by the intensity of an almost voracious passion. Her lips seemed literally to consume as they covered my mouth, wide and moist, like the petals of a predatory tropical plant, her teeth sinking softly into my own lips. She clasped my body so tightly I could hardly breathe. Somehow I found myself on my back with Laura laid over me, pressing and rotating her small breasts against my chest, guiding my hand between her thighs and manipulating it with the urgent pressure of her own. When she finally slid off me and drew me over her raised and trembling legs, my head held to hers as if caught in a brace, her body began to shudder with its first, almost self-induced orgasm.

'Oh, John,' she whispered hoarsely. 'Oh, John, John, darling John . . .'

Later, we lay in a silent embrace until she drifted into sleep. I lay awake for a further half-hour, filled with a powerful longing for those other nights when she'd undressed in modest privacy and got into bed in darkness, and I had simply held her and stroked her to sleep, as if to comfort and protect her from the things that had made her so unhappy.

I awoke in darkness, knowing I'd not sleep again. I showered, using the main bathroom instead of the *en suite*, so as not to disturb her.

I went downstairs. It was cold and I overrode the seven-thirty start-up on the central heating boiler. I made a cup of instant and sipped it, moving about rooms that had now regained that profound original silence. I felt clearer in mind this morning. I was a night's sleep away from music and chatter, from a Laura who'd been voluble, vivid and demanding. I realised now the extent and depth of my confusion last night. There had been too many shocks, too much to cope with. I had swung like a weather-vane through bitterness, resentment, distaste, had had an urge to walk away and leave her to get on with her new friends and her new life. She'd got what she wanted, a recreation of her girlhood, however pale or inaccurate, and there had seemed no place for me, either now or in the future. Last night, when she'd finally slept, I'd decided that if I could get up without disturbing her I'd quietly take my leave, because there would seem to be nothing to say to a woman I appeared neither to know nor particularly care for.

I returned to the main bedroom to see if she was awake. I drew the flowered curtains back a little. Pale sunlight was now beginning to filter through a white mist against which trees seemed as insubstantial as smoke. The lawns were stiff with frost. She lay on her side behind the gauzy curtain, still sleeping, still in the mask of make-up, now smeared like a

much-used palette. But at some point in the night she'd wept, the tears had tracked eye-liner diagonally across each painted cheek.

I went back downstairs, took a parka from the car boot, walked through the little wood to the river, my breath hanging round me in the freezing air, and stood looking down at the fast-moving water.

I couldn't walk out on her, however disappointed I'd been. She needed me more than ever, more than during the lowest days of her bereavement. Because what had happened last night – the chatter, the food and wine, the Demmies working through their card – hadn't been a means of recapturing her youth, it had been a desperate attempt to join up two parts of her life so seamlessly, the old and the new, that the near past had been almost surgically removed. I couldn't understand what impelled her to do it, and perhaps never would; I just knew that such a forcible attempt at removal couldn't be healthy, that trying to avoid the effects of trauma by alcohol, people, a new image, sensation, could only mean she was bottling up emotions that would begin to gather such power that one day, if they could not force the stopper, would destroy the container itself.

She was teetering on the brink. I'd seen clear signs of it already – the Goat in Kensington, the night she'd argued with Marsh so vehemently, her anger when I'd refused to spend the night in a cold, dust-sheeted house that wasn't hers. I couldn't walk away. I'd have to keep in touch, calm her down, try and steer her clear of the Demmies, to get her one day to cope positively with the years with the Marsh brothers that seemed to have brought such an unbearable pain.

Try to get her to be the person she really was – the Laura who'd promised quiet weekends of walking and sitting out and making affectionate love in the four-poster bed. The

ordinary things that an ordinary man like me could give her, that she'd once said she wanted so much.

I heard a faint crunch of footsteps over frozen leaves. I watched her come into view out of the mist, in her outdoor gear of pants and parka, her hair drawn back into a slide, her pale face clear of make-up.

'I thought you must be here . . .'

Our eyes met, then she glanced away to the faded trees across the river. 'Do you want some breakfast?'

I shook my head. 'I've had coffee. It's all I wanted.'

We looked at each other again. Her eyes had a guarded yet faintly defiant look. She seemed somehow to be neither the Laura of the lights and music nor the Laura of the reservoir walks, but something in between, as if the full transformation to the painted woman who could do excellent impressions of dead German cabaret artistes could only be achieved by alcohol and the party atmosphere.

'What would you like to do?' I said. 'Go for a walk? Pub lunch?'

She turned away and glanced up at a sycamore, touched its bark. Her tree. Everything around here would be hers when the lawyers had swapped their bits of paper.

'Jacintha rang a few minutes ago . . . to remind me she's having a lunch party. Gargrave. It rather got lost last night among all the other invitations. Will you . . . come with me . . .?'

'I think . . . if you don't mind . . . I'll get back home. I tend to use Sundays for paperwork . . .'

There was nothing I could do for her reclamation while the Demmies were around, discussing the powerfully erotic impact on Picasso's artistic development of Marie Thérèse. It was time to cut losses. I'd come back and do what I could to help her, but only when it was one to one.

277

'Please go with me, John,' she said with sudden urgency, her eyes meeting mine in what seemed to be near-desperation.

'No. I must get back,' I said gently but firmly. 'To be honest, I find a little of the Demmies goes a long way . . .'

I wished I'd not let that second sentence get past. She turned away, as sharply as if I'd slapped her face. We stood in silence for a full minute, as the white, freezing mist drifted round us, so still that I could hear the scuttering of woodland animals among the piles of brittle leaves.

'*Please* go with me, John,' she said again. 'I'm sorry . . . I just need them . . . I know they're a bit overwhelming . . . it's hard to explain. Please come this once. Another weekend we'll . . . we'll . . . it'll just be . . .'

I'd never seen her so confused, so unable to express herself coherently. It was as if she too somehow accepted that these divergent aspects of her personality that seemed to pull her in separate directions would one day have to be reconciled, whatever the cost.

'*Please* come. You needn't stay. Stay an hour – we'll take both motors . . .'

'All right,' I said at last, with reluctance. 'I'll stay an hour . . .'

Her shoulders sagged slightly. She turned and began to walk slowly back towards the house, her drooping figure giving somehow a sense of dejection and self-reproach. I started to follow her. She didn't want to take my hand or link my arm as she usually did now when we were alone. I couldn't help measuring the weekend I'd had against the one I'd wanted. This morning I'd seen myself cooking her a light breakfast and taking it to her bedroom, where she'd be lying with her marbled pallor smiling up at me through the gauzy curtains.

'If you don't mind I'll leave you and have a bath,' she said, almost formally, when we were in the house. 'The water was only warm earlier and I like it very hot. Help yourself to more coffee, or whatever . . .'

She left me in the drawing-room that overlooked the lawns. The sun, slowly cutting through the mist, was beginning to melt the white coating of frost and the grass was gradually turning green, as if colour were being added to a black-and-white sketch. I wondered if it would be a bath plus the elaborate make-up and hair-style and the clothes that seemed appropriate for meeting Demmies. It could take some time and my mind seemed to crave a break, a suspension of thought from the endless turning over of her situation. At home I'd have had the papers, but none seemed to have been delivered here.

I remembered the little study with its book-lined shelves. There'd be something there I could read, some peaceful tale of nineteenth-century life that might help to shake off a persistent depression.

I opened the study door and went in. An elaborate word-processor stood on the large desk, its small screen lit and gleaming against the milky light and the desk's dark surface. I should have ignored the twenty or so lines of text in dark blue that covered the screen's surface; it was private, none of my business. But the instinct of curiosity, developed to its full extent by the work I did, was too powerful to overcome. Apart from which, I felt certain she'd not really mind my looking at work in progress. The Demmies wouldn't, they probably left their work about *hoping* people would take a peak.

. . . Oliver strode towards her across the heath. 'Maria!' he cried, his voice faint against the howling wind. 'Maria – you can't leave me now!'

A furious moon raged through ragged clouds. Her heart pounded in her breast as the wind tore at her hair and dashed away the tears she could not restrain. How *could* she leave him now, this man who meant so much to her, even though they accused him of dark, terrible deeds, of leading women astray and discarding them, of wanting only her inheritance to squander on gambling and drink?

'How *dare* you!'

I swung round. Laura stood at the open door in a towelling robe, her face dark and contorted with an anger so powerful her entire body quivered as if being shaken by an external force.

'Laura,' I said, pretending a calmness I didn't feel, 'I only wanted something to read. Your machine was on ... I couldn't resist ...'

'How *dare* you come in here! No one comes in here – no one, no one, *no one*!'

She suddenly picked up a paper-knife from a side-table. It was small, insubstantial, but dagger-shaped, and she brought it above her head as if to plunge it into my chest. I felt real fear then, not because of the little knife, but because of her astounding reaction, her face distorted almost beyond recognition.

I grasped the hand that held the knife and firmly turned it so that the knife fell to the floor. It wasn't easy. For a moment it was like grappling with a man my equal in strength. I was astounded at the effort it took to make her release it. But I couldn't risk her using it – small as it was it could easily damage an eye or puncture a lung, with the strength she seemed able to find. I'd known worse damage inflicted by smaller objects.

'*Get out!*' she screamed. 'Get out of my study! Don't ever, ever, *ever* come in here again or I'll kill you! I'll *kill* you!'

Nineteen

I took the A1 route and got there in about two hours. I drove past small villages at the side of the Wash, a grey, sluggish sheet of water that seemed to creep almost slyly across lengthy strands, towards cliffs so small they seemed like models. I was used to the great battered cliffs and the ferocious tides of North Yorkshire.

As Alan Starkey had reported, there had been much development in the area. Sea-front blocks of flats, enclaves of sheltered accommodation, new estates of executive housing. I wondered if this had been the carry-over from that ebullient Eighties period when London office workers had begun to commute as far as Norfolk because the relative cheapness of the housing made it an attractive proposition despite the distance involved. Was that what David Marsh had bought into, at the tail end of a booming property market, only to find himself with bricks and mortar nobody wanted?

I was determined to find out today, one way or the other. The chalet house near Grassington remained deserted, and I'd also checked on the house at Tanglewood Lane, just in case. It had had FOR SALE signs up and seemed equally unoccupied. So it appeared he'd either gone off with Madge or he'd returned to Hunstanton. I'd had a distinct impression from Madge that she'd not known about his Hunstanton base

and it worried me. It could mean he'd been feeding her a line, ready to drop her when he'd got the money from Laura; and was now back down here throwing the money at his financial crisis.

I had to know. I was certain Laura's condition was some-how down to Marsh. If I could satisfy myself he really had begun a new life with Madge it would give me an easier mind. If not, if he was back in Hunstanton, I was going to have it out with him. I didn't know yet what I would say or do. I was going to leave it until I was facing him and let the experience of years guide me, but when I'd finished with him I had to be sure he'd be out of her life for good. The way she'd been this weekend *had* to be some kind of reaction to paying him off. I didn't like to think what might happen if he staged a comeback.

I pulled in outside Elgin House, a white six-storey building, rather narrow, which would mean all the flats would be sea facing. I climbed to flat fifty on the top floor and rang the bell, but it went unanswered. I returned downstairs, where there was an attractive and quite spacious hall, with paintings and well-tended planters. There was a door at the back with a sign saying PRIVATE. I tapped on it. A heavy, middle-aged woman with dyed-looking black hair and elaborate glasses opened it on the voice of Terry Wogan and a littered desk.

'Can I help you?' she said reluctantly.

'I'm looking for Mr David Marsh . . .'

'Perhaps I can help . . .'

'I do need to see him personally . . .'

'If it's about the lettings we've stopped booking before the February adverts – it gets too complicated.'

'No, it's not about lettings.'

'I look after the office for Mr Marsh. Were you . . . interested in *buying* a flat?' Her manner became appreciably

warmer. 'Or we also do time share. Perhaps you'd like to see
our show flat?'

It was the sort of ball investigators tended to run with.
'Does Mr Marsh own all the flats?'

'The whole building now – so if there were any particular
flat or position you were interested in I'm sure we could
help . . .'

The whole building now. Since when, I wondered. Since
two or three weeks ago? 'The trouble is,' I said carefully, 'I
seem unable to contact Mr Marsh by phone. I assume he's
away a lot . . .'

She looked puzzled. 'He's not been away since April.
That's when he takes his own holiday, before the season
begins.'

It was my turn to be puzzled. 'The phone – it's always in
answer mode . . .'

'Oh, he'll never pick it up when he's working. He hates to
be distracted. He sets aside an hour each day to reply
to messages. Did you not leave a number?'

'I'm afraid not,' I said slowly. 'I move around quite a bit.
But would it be possible . . . to see him today?'

'I don't see why not. He'll not be long now. You mustn't
mind if I seem protective. He likes to delegate as much detail
as he can to me. But of course if you're interested in the flats
he'll be delighted to show you around.'

I couldn't get any of this together. She didn't look like a
woman working for love, the building was well cared for.
None of it fitted with a man driving a hired Escort and needing money for boiled ham. I wondered if she'd know if he was
away nights, if, say, he were to drive north after work and
return mid-morning the day after. She seemed the type who'd
know the boss's movements very well. Perhaps if he was only
gone overnight she didn't regard that as being away.

'Ah!' she said, glancing through the glass entrance doors, 'Here's Mr Marsh now . . .'

A dark-green Jaguar glided to a halt behind my car, just beyond the neat apron of lawn in front of Elgin House. A man got out, glanced at the Mondeo for a second or two, turned towards us.

'That's . . . Mr Marsh?' I said. 'Mr *David* Marsh?'

'That's him,' she said cheerfully, not picking up on the note of incredulity in my voice. The man pushed open one of the glass doors with a ready smile.

'Morning, Mr Marsh. This gentleman has just been expressing an interest in looking at the flats. I thought perhaps you'd like to show him round yourself . . .'

'Of course, of course. How do you do, Mr . . .?' He shook me warmly by the hand.

'Goss. John Goss . . .'

'I'd be delighted to show you round, Mr Goss. You couldn't have chosen a better time to buy. Values can only increase from now on. We've had such a lot of interest in Elgin House. It's the situation, you see, the views. Do come this way. Thank you, Stella, I'll catch you later . . .'

It was not the David Marsh I'd met at the house on Tanglewood Lane, not the one I'd watched from Laura's back garden having money flung at him, whom I'd come to know and loathe.

'This way, Mr Goss . . . may I call you John? There are still one or two available on each floor. Shall we start at the top and work down?'

We went up in the lift, he still giving out his confident patter. As the door slid open at the top floor, I said: 'I'm sorry, Mr Marsh, but I'm not here to buy flats. It's a private matter which I didn't think you'd want me to discuss in front of Stella.'

He watched me suspiciously, his manner instantly switching from bonhomie to caution.

'You *are* David Marsh? Brother of Simon Marsh?'

He went on watching me. He was medium-sized, lean and greying, casually dressed but wearing a well-cut sports jacket and trousers of cavalry twill, leather brogues, a cotton shirt, wool tie. He had the indefinable sleekness that went with prosperity, good health, a comfortable life-style. He couldn't have been a bigger contrast to the burly, twitching man at Laura's who'd *called* himself David Marsh.

'What has . . . Simon been up to . . .?' he said guardedly, at last.

I stared at him and all the training of years couldn't help me to conceal the signs of a mind reeling almost out of control.

'Mr Marsh . . .' I said, my mouth suddenly as dry as if it contained the dental device that removes saliva, 'did you not know? Simon's dead . . .'

He didn't know. And he wasn't acting he didn't know. Changes of skin colour could not be acted, they were controlled directly by the emotions, and David Marsh's face had suddenly mottled in shock.

'Dear God!' he whispered. 'Dear *God*. When did this happen? How? This weekend . . .?'

He suddenly wrapped both arms around his chest and hunched over, his eyes closed and his lips twisted in pain. He seemed almost on the verge of a seizure. Alarmed, I took hold of his shoulders. 'Can you make it to your flat?' I said. 'It's on this floor, isn't it. Do you have heart trouble? Do you need medication . . . a doctor?'

He managed to get a key-ring from his jacket pocket and I half carried him to his flat door. I opened it, helped him across a small hallway and into a comfortable sitting-room. He pointed silently to a drinks cabinet. I set him down,

opened the cabinet, poured brandy into a glass, put it in his hand.

'Do you want me to get Stella . . . David?'

He took a mouthful of the brandy, swallowed it down and breathed deeply, sucking in air like a man who'd been underwater. 'No,' he said at last, 'I'm all right now. It was the shock. Jesus . . . it was like a kick in the guts . . .'

'I'm very sorry to bring you this news,' I said gently. 'He died in a car accident near Harrogate in Yorkshire.'

'This . . . weekend . . .?'

'In . . . July.'

He stared at me in consternation. '*July?*'

I nodded.

'*July!*' he suddenly shouted. 'Why didn't she *tell* me? Why didn't the bitch *tell* me? *July* . . . and I find out from a *stranger* . . . in *December*!'

'Take it easy, David,' I said, the words coming mechanically from a mind trying to cope with a shock not much different from his own. 'Drink some more of the brandy . . .'

He obeyed me, the hand that held the glass trembling so badly that I steadied it. Eyes unfocused, he gazed into space for fully ten seconds. Then he said in a low voice: 'Who *are* you?'

'I'm . . . engaged by solicitors who are sorting things out. They had a bit of a problem tracing you . . .'

'There was no problem,' he said flatly. 'She knew where I lived. Christ, we did at least send Christmas cards. I can't believe this, even of her . . .'

He looked ravaged with grief. It had been like seeing a film actor's face change before the eyes, by skilful photography, from prime of life to haggard old age. His eyes glistened moistly in the flat grey light that filtered in from a flat grey sea. It seemed the last time I'd seen such sadness had been in

Laura, before the inexplicable strains of her life had made her the stranger I'd known at Larch House. Simon Marsh had clearly been a man who'd aroused powerful emotions. Except in Madge Horton.

He sat in silence for some time, steadily sipping the rest of his brandy. No other situation in my life had ever produced such total confusion. It was like the sort of dream where people keep changing into other people who are not even in context with the tenuous narrative of the dream itself. The only concrete facts I seemed to have left were that Simon was dead, that this man was the real David Marsh, and that there was an imposter flitting around Yorkshire who had some kind of hold on Laura that now barely bore thinking about.

'You'll have to forgive me . . . John,' he said in a voice now under control, almost brisk. 'He was my only brother, he was younger, and he was very dear to me. Tell me what happened.'

'He'd . . . been to a farm co-operative in Yorkshire, to sell them a computer package. Coming home, on the way to Harrogate, he . . . just went off the road and crashed into a valley.'

'Not . . . drinking . . .?'

'The equivalent of about three shorts. But he'd also taken barbiturates . . .'

'Not . . . not . . .?' His voice broke; he couldn't speak the final word.

'Not suicide,' I said. 'The drink and the tablets were obviously a contributory factor, but the coroner's view was that there wasn't enough of either for a suicide verdict to be returned. The feeling was that he'd underestimated the potency of the tablets.'

'Poor boy . . . poor boy. It was *so* unlike him to do anything like that. I always impressed on him that people like us . . . lose our licence, we lose our livelihood.'

'I . . . gather he was under considerable pressure. Business-wise . . .'

'I knew he would be,' the other said almost curtly. 'It's no business for a one-man band. You need technical service, someone up-front sorting the wheat from the chaff. No wonder he was under pressure . . .' He broke off, then added in a softer tone, 'Poor boy – if only he'd come to me. I had the money . . . and the time . . .'

I nodded sympathetically. If he was ready to talk I was more than ready to listen, till dusk if need be.

'It must have . . . been a great shock to Laura,' he said, giving an impression of a reluctance he was struggling to overcome.

'It was a dreadful shock,' I said simply. That I knew to be the complete truth, if nothing else.

'You . . . know her?'

'Only . . . through my work . . .' I said warily.

He looked at me steadily, as if reminded of the pain of being told of his brother's death by a total stranger.

'And you're a . . . did you say you worked for a solicitor . . .?'

'Not directly. I'm a private investigator, working on an assignment. We run a lot of errands for the legal profession.'

'How . . . is she placed? Does that come into your remit?'

'I believe Mr Marsh was suitably insured and I imagine Mrs Marsh will be the principal beneficiary. There . . . were, I understand, one or two additional bequests . . .'

'But surely not important enough for you to come all the way here from Yorkshire to seek me out?'

Grieving or not, he'd lost none of his shrewdness. He had the businessman's brain, trained to probe, examine, question.

'No,' I said. 'I got your address through a local agent. I'm on my way to Norwich on a separate matter. I just thought I'd

take a chance on catching you in at the address I was given.'

'You could have rung . . .'

'I . . . prefer the personal touch where possible. To be honest, you're not the only one to learn from me first about the death of a close relative. I'd not have wanted you to hear about Simon over the phone.'

He nodded dejectedly, convinced at last of my bona fides, which wouldn't really have borne much more scrutiny by a mind as sharp as his.

'Well,' he said, 'I'm glad she'll be looked after. I never . . .'

Tantalisingly, he broke off and glanced at his watch.

'What are you doing about lunch?'

'I've nothing planned . . .'

'Care for a bar snack?'

'Thank you – I'd like that.'

He looked at his empty glass. 'I'd better not drive – could we go in yours?'

'Of course.'

'There's a decent place in what they call Old Hunstanton. It's in your direction, you'll be able to push on to Norwich from there. Stella will pick me up in mine . . .'

It was a small hotel that fronted directly on to the main road. I parked the car beneath trees just beyond a side garden. It was this garden, in its bare and melancholy December state, we could see from window seats in the bar parlour.

He bought me beer and a sandwich, but had nothing to eat himself. He sipped brandy again – it looked to be a triple.

'I've no appetite, John,' he said heavily.

He glanced across the lawn, its grass tufty and dull, its edging of evergreens dripping in a fine mizzle of rain. 'He wasn't just a brother, you see, John; for a long time he was my closest friend. There were only two years between us – I

suppose I guided him. We both had the same brain for the sciences, took similar degrees, knew computers would be where it was at, liked the same sports even.' He smiled in rueful misery. 'With a brother like that you don't really need best friends. I dare say we were a bit clannish . . .'

He took a mouthful of the brandy. 'Well, that all finished when he met Laura Wilder, didn't it – she very quickly put the kibosh on the special relationship.'

His voice had become harsh and bitter, with a tone I'd sometimes heard in the voices of women whose partners had deserted them. He caught my neutral eye on him, looked a little sheepish, shrugged. 'Perhaps we *were* too close,' he admitted reluctantly. 'Our father was an export director, away weeks at a time. I suppose I stood *in loco parentis* – guiding, listening, playing games with him. We'd work on summer jobs together, hitch-hike through France, share a joint in Ankara . . .

'Laura . . . didn't like it. She wanted him to herself. I went on holiday with them once or twice – I was unmarried, you see – but it didn't work . . . she made it perfectly obvious three was a cottage-full, perfectly obvious. Oh, well . . .'

I nodded encouragingly as I ate my salt-beef sandwich. I'd spent years perfecting a technique of appearing to listen to people talking under stress like a sympathetic therapist, devoid of normal curiosity. With David Marsh I faced one of my hardest tests. It seemed utterly monstrous that Laura had never told him of his own brother's death, but on the other hand I wondered how many women could be expected to put up for very long with the unconcealed jealous hostility I suspected she'd received from David because she'd dared to fall in love with the brother who happened to be his best friend.

'They met at university perhaps?' I said with bland detachment.

He emptied his glass. 'She was doing English Lit,' he said scornfully. 'I ask you. You might as well do bee-keeping. She was very arty, she could talk a streak about Trollope and Conrad and that lot; if she saw a painting on a wall she could tell you everything else the bugger had done. All very fine and large, but what damn good for earning a living in the real world? Only it didn't matter about that because she'd latched on to Simon, hadn't she, and he was going to make enough money for her to spend her life dabbling about at writing . . .'

However hard he tried he couldn't prevent the bitterness filtering into his tone. It began to get easier to see why Laura had been driven to the point of breaking off communications completely.

One of the barmen stood above us. 'Can I get you anything else, Mr Marsh?' he said, very respectfully.

'Another brandy, Justin, same measure. John?'

'No more, thanks. It tends to make me drowsy on the road . . .'

He relapsed again into haunted silence. I wondered if he was reliving the old college days, the weeks of summer waitering, the carefree jaunts on the Continent.

'So Mrs Marsh did a bit of writing?' I said quietly, the analyst encouraging a full mental clear-out.

'They let her edit the college magazine. No one else wanted to do it anyway. I think she wrote most of it herself. I don't think she ever really twigged that people only took it for news of the gigs and who needed a mate to climb a mountain with.' He picked up his refilled glass. 'She was too arty by half, was Laura Wilder – that would be down to the mad aunt, I suppose, though living with the mad aunt must have been a hundred times better than living at home . . .'

I put down my glass, because my hand shook slightly. 'Mad . . . aunt?' I said, completely unable for a second or two to sustain the note of polite neutrality. But he'd had so much

brandy, and was so enclosed in the past, that it went unnoticed.

'Her mother's sister. She was an artist. Well known in the Leicester area. Strange as a chocolate teapot. Weird landscapes – nothing the colour it should be, everything seeming to stand the wrong way; not my taste I can tell you. But she was highly regarded, and I was reading only the other day that her value's increasing quite rapidly now she's safely dead. End up like Van Gogh, I shouldn't wonder . . .'

The words: 'But that was her *mother*, not her aunt!' were almost past my lips before I realised that, apart from acting out of character for my counselling role, I couldn't have known those kinds of details. 'Perhaps', I said, when I'd collected myself, 'the artistic leanings came from her aunt . . .'

He finished his brandy once more and held up a finger to the bar; it rather looked as if he were going to tie one on. He laughed sarcastically. 'Well, they couldn't have come from her real home, could they. The *Wilders*! Anyway, I did my research, didn't I. If Simon was hell-bent on marrying her I thought I had a positive duty to let him know what he'd be marrying into.'

'A . . . difficult family?' It was getting to be hard to impossible to force my lips back to the smile of polite uninvolvement.

'*A difficult family!* Harry Wilder was a *villain*! Do you know the term "draughtsman"? Well, that's what he was. He set things up, did the planning, got a few hard cases together, provided finance. His end would be a third of the take, even a half. And no one could ever touch him because he was never the one holding a blowtorch. But everyone knew . . .'

I sat in a daze, for a time my mind almost blank. It was as if my brain had reached overload with the complexities of Laura's background, the new things I was learning about her,

like a CPU given more detail than its discs had storage for.

'The mother was no better,' he said, his voice seeming to come from a distance. 'Heavy drinking, sleeping around. Not so much a whore, they said she liked it so much that when she'd had a few she'd do it for free drinks. And then there was the brother . . .'

I shook my head, like a boxer who'd taken a near-critical blow to the jaw. 'Harry's brother?'

'No, no, no – Laura's. Errol. A real chip off the old block, except that he went in at the sharp end to keep a tally on what they nicked. Now he *did* do porridge – more than once. As I say, I made certain Simon knew what a wonderful family he was marrying into . . .'

Even then, with my brain in head-crash mode, I wondered if he had never been able to see that digging up that kind of dirt had almost certainly helped to bring Simon and Laura even closer together.

'Oh dear,' I said, striving once more for the tone of polite friendliness. 'But I thought you said the lady who did the paintings was Laura's mother's sister . . .'

'She was a very different cup of tea. All she wanted was her art. She kept well clear of Tina and the Wilders. She taught art and did her own stuff at the weekend. Well, the principal of the art college where she taught realised what a talent she had, and he married her to give her the chance to paint full-time, from what I could make out. He came of a wealthy family and had private money. Widower, much older than her – he died a few years later and she copped for the lot, as they say.'

'And . . . Laura stayed with her?'

'She had this big place near a river. She was fond of Laura, took her in, more or less brought her up, put her through college. I don't think they even noticed she'd gone, *chez*

Wilder. She wasn't christened Laura, by the way, they hadn't got that kind of imagination. Would you believe – *Lana*?'

'She . . . didn't *seem* a Lana, I must admit . . .'

'Her aunt called her Laura. Did a lot for her, despite being half crackers. It was all a bit spartan and catch as catch can, what with the old lass never being away from the easel, but she did a fair amount of entertaining – arty types, as you can imagine. That was the atmosphere Laura grew up in – a bunch of bad lots on one side, one of arty farties on the other. I told Simon it had to end in tears with a background like that, but he'd not have it . . .'

His gaze moved unfocused over the sodden garden and he fell silent again. I could understand only too well why Simon wouldn't listen. With a woman like Laura I'd not have listened either. I watched him, my mind seeming to begin once more the apparently impossible task of trying to get some kind of final fix on that woman I cared so much about.

'Did you . . . not consider going into business together – you and Simon – with you both being so good with computers?'

His face suddenly flushed. 'Don't you think that's what I always wanted? I couldn't wait to start a business with him, we were both sure we'd get a better income and job satisfaction from designing dedicated systems. But she put the kibosh on that too, didn't she . . .'

'She . . . preferred the safety of him being in a large company?'

'It wasn't that. She was all for us starting up together if it was on her terms. And they were that we'd set up a limited company with a nominal share capital and she'd have a twenty-per-cent holding and we'd have forty each. The deal was that she'd do the admin and double as company secretary. Need I spell it out? If the company was very successful

and we ever sold it she and Simon would walk away with
sixty per cent of its final worth and I'd get forty. And I'm
certain that was her game-plan – selling out a flourishing
business and having the time and money to write the world-
beating novel.' He finished on a note of bitter sarcasm.

'It does seem a little . . . disproportionate,' I said, with
reluctance.

'I told Simon to keep her nose out of it,' he said bluntly.
'We'd have *two* directors – me and him. He'd concentrate on
designing systems, I on selling. We could both do anything,
but he was quicker at putting packages together and I had
more experience of shaking hands. I know damn fine what
she thought – I'd be playing golf and sipping gin and Simon
would be doing the real work. Well, it doesn't work like that –
someone has to be out there on the links and patting backs at
the Rotary Club. Play a round with a man you know to be
looking to update and you can come home with an order
worth thirty thousand.'

He signalled to the bar for yet another triple. I'd observed
before that people in shock seemed able to drink almost
endlessly without noticeable effect. He neither slurred his
words nor talked nonsense. He simply talked, wanted to talk
as urgently as I wanted to listen.

'In the end,' he said harshly, 'I said if she was in I was out.
And that was the end of that. We went our separate ways.
And I'll admit I did pretty well, I made enough to live in
semi-retirement and run the flats and one or two other bits
and bobs. But between us we could *both* have done well and
enjoyed what we did. But the poor devil went off on his own,
trying to do everything himself, and look where he is now,
God rest him . . .'

'I . . . had the impression he was doing quite well at one
stage . . .'

'In the Eighties?' he said almost belligerently. 'The office cat could make money in the late Eighties. But when you get a recession that's when you need to be a team – brain-storming, analysing, considering different approaches. That's where I'd have come in because I keep an ear to the ground. God knows, I'd have come in anyway . . . any time . . . I could have helped him, John. But with that bitch round his neck . . .'

Again flushed, he fell silent once more. That incredibly adaptable instrument the human brain was, in my case, beginning to adjust at last to the new shocks and revelations about Laura. She certainly seemed, on the face of it, to have had a very cold and calculating side when it came to the question of the brothers setting up together. But a picture was also slowly emerging of Simon Marsh. He seemed to have been a nice man with lovable qualities, but I wondered if he'd been under the influence of a dominant and protective brother for so long that his own ability to make decisions had begun to wither. And whether Laura had felt, rightly or wrongly, that if the brothers had set up together Simon really would have had the lion's share of the work. I'd often met computer technicians at the various firms I'd worked for – some of the hours they'd put in could make even mine seem like part-time. Sitting all night to track down a bug in a system was commonplace. Is that what she'd foreseen, Simon working round the clock while David stroked egos? I felt I could see both sides.

It might have been why she'd felt that she and Simon should have had sixty per cent of the holding. That, to her, must have seemed fair, measured against Simon's long days, the exhaustion, the cancelled evenings out. Perhaps she'd felt she had to be tough on behalf of a husband who seemed to have lost the ability to do anything but follow.

It was all very human and sad. I liked this man, now sip-

ping his umpteenth brandy, but it was clear he'd been obsessively protective and, worse, incapable of dissembling. In the end he'd seemed to be his own worst enemy, and Simon's as well. Perhaps there was more than a tremor of guilt behind his anger towards Laura, maybe he sensed, however remotely, that if his approach to his brother's wife had been less abrasive Simon would now be alive and prospering.

'Was he buried?' he said suddenly.

'I . . . understand – cremation . . .'

'Pity.' He sighed heavily. 'I'd like to have visited the grave. Paid my respects. I'd better go up. We can't behave like savages, even if she couldn't bring herself to tell me he'd gone. There are a few bits and pieces I gave him over the years – cuff-links, books, a couple of paintings. I'd like something of his back to remember him by . . .'

Emotion choked off the words; he reached for his glass.

'She's . . . away at present,' I said. 'She was advised to get away from things for a few weeks – I don't believe she's due back till the new year.'

Some instinct warned me to keep him away from the north until I could sort things out with the man pretending to be him. David Marsh flailing about in Yorkshire in his present state would be one straw too many for a Laura who seemed close to complete nervous collapse.

'Perhaps I could give you a ring when she's back?'

'You're a good sort,' he said at last. 'You've got honest broker written all over you. I've said far too much, I know that . . . I'm pretty well pissed . . . I just needed to talk . . . I must have bored you rigid with our silly squabbles . . . forgive me.' He smiled unhappily and tapped me on the knee. 'I'll not go up there with all guns blazing, you know. I couldn't stand her and she couldn't stand me, but we always managed to be polite to each other, for his . . .'

He broke off, again unable to finish the sentence.

'It often helps to be able to talk freely,' I said. 'Rest assured it'll go no further – mine's a very discreet occupation.'

I'd heard a lot of confessions, listened to many pouring everything out under stress, but I'd never learnt so much in so short a time about a group of people. I wondered if the picture of Laura was now at last almost complete, if some clue to the identity of that shadowy man who flitted in and out of her life was buried in what I'd just heard, which would become clearer when I could get away from David Marsh and do some uninterrupted thinking.

'I can't begin to tell you how much I miss him,' he said in a low voice. 'I'd not seen him for such a long time. And now I'll never see him again . . .'

Justin the barman stood at our table once more to ask if he wanted another drink, but I put a finger to my lips and shook my head. After about a minute I said quietly: 'I'll have to be going now, David. Can I run you back to the flats?'

'No . . . no . . .' he said, giving his head a little shake, as I'd done earlier. 'It's the wrong way for Norwich, old son. Stella will pick me up, she loves driving the Jag. I'll give her a ring presently.'

We both got up – he gave me his hand, put his other over the top of mine.

I said: 'I'm sorry to have brought you this news . . .'

'Yes . . . well . . . you've been very kind. Perhaps it was for the best I heard it from you. Had it been Laura I doubt I could have controlled myself. If only she'd *told* me they were having a bad time . . .'

I left him in the circular lounge, still standing at the table we'd occupied, gazing vacantly out across the dank, dripping garden, his normally erect figure so stooped that from the back he could have been taken for a man of eighty.

Twenty

'Write to Alan Starkey again, would you, Norma. Ask him for some background on a man called Errol Wilder in the Leicester area. His father's called Harry, his mother Tina, and he has a sister called Lana.'

'The parents sound as if they once went to the pictures a lot. I don't suppose this has anything to do with the Marshes, by any chance . . .?'

The phone rang; she picked it up. I went on scanning the opened mail. It had only taken a few miles on the A1 returning north. My feeling had been right. I'd had so many shocks from Marsh's words that I'd not been able to see then what later, after a little time on my own, quickly became obvious.

The pretend David Marsh was Errol Wilder. Nothing else now fitted. I'd decided a long time ago that the only person who could exert any kind of leverage on the newly wealthy Laura would have had to be close. Family close. And David Marsh had been her brother-in-law and I'd thought he'd once lent Simon money. Only the bearded man in glasses hadn't been Simon's brother, and Simon's real brother hadn't even known he was dead. But she'd given part of her fortune to someone, I was certain of that, and who else did you do things like that for, however unwillingly, except family?

Not Simon's family, but a much closer family in ties of blood – her own.

Norma put down the phone. 'Shoot . . .'

I told her everything I'd learnt. Her pensive features gave an impression that uneasiness and curiosity were almost evenly balanced.

'And you think it's Errol . . .'

'Got to be. A crook just like his dad and keen to put the squeeze on a sister who's done well.'

'But why pretend to be Simon's brother?'

'That was for my benefit. Remember, as far as Laura was concerned I was investigating the circumstances of Simon's death. And she knew I was doing a proper job, even though I'd more or less admitted the investigation was simply a device for the Zephyr to slow down payment. Now Simon's death was open and shut – I found it straightforward and so did the police and the coroner. But what if Laura thought that if she said her visitor was Errol Wilder I might routinely look into *his* background – and find he was a criminal with previous. She might think that would be enough to make me suspicious and start digging deeper, perhaps drawing it out for months.'

'Well, wouldn't you?'

'Probably, to be on the safe side, but that's about it. Look, you know as much about professional small-time crooks as I do; they hardly ever get involved in anything bigger – armed robbery, protection, killing people for the insurance – right? The Wilders follow a pattern that goes back to the growth of the cities – the elders setting up and fencing, the young males easing doors off their hinges, the women on the game. In criminal circles they're regarded as the equivalent of respectable working class . . . yes . . .?'

'But Laura wouldn't have realised how well you under-

302

stood those kinds of people,' she said slowly.

'Exactly. And all she wanted was to be paid off in a reasonable time so she could get away from everything that reminded her of Simon. And she could see brother Errol hanging around as seriously bad news, especially if I clocked him, so to save time and trouble she said he was David Marsh.'

'Could you not tell what he was from his manner the night you met him? His accent?'

'He didn't say too much and he was careful about what he did say. But it's a skill many crooks have, isn't it, finding the right voice for the occasion.'

'But what hold *had* he got?'

I shrugged. 'What hold has any family got? If your Gerry called tonight and said he was down to his last tenner, and you knew it was his own stupid fault, you'd still take him in, wouldn't you? Perhaps the Wilders had hit hard times, or he was just out of stir and trying to make a new start.'

'But the real David Marsh told you she hardly knew them . . .'

'That might have been part of it. He was her natural brother and he was the one left in the inner city while she lived in the big house by the river. The conscience of the rich, what else? She does nicely, he nicks gear and keeps going inside.'

'Are you seriously telling me she'd wear an ex-con living in her house, hire him a car, give him a slice of the insurance money?'

I sighed. 'I know you find it difficult to accept, but I've got to know her quite well, and she comes across as a basically good-hearted woman who tends to be generous to a fault. I don't think there's any doubt the sod's played on it and nearly driven her over the edge with his demands, but I'm

prepared to bet it's because she couldn't help measuring his upbringing against her own.'

'But . . . hold on . . . how could *he* have got involved with the woman Simon was seeing – the barmaid – and why did *she* think he was Simon's brother?'

I smiled. 'You're only asking me all the questions I asked myself, between King's Lynn and the M62. And that threw me as well. I doubt we'll ever know the true story, but I think Errol came into Simon's and Laura's life before Simon died. Simon was doing badly towards the end, but to Errol they must have *seemed* well off – nice house, car each, the usual trimmings. I think she let him stay with them now and then out of pity, and I think Simon probably took Errol out on his business calls with him to give Laura a break. And on one of those trips he must have taken him for a drink at the Wheatsheaf, and Madge and Errol just clicked. I'm not being snobbish, but Simon was respectable middle class and Errol . . . well, he'll have been around bar rooms since he was sixteen, and from what I've seen of Madge I dare say he'd have been more on her wavelength than Simon.'

'That doesn't explain why she pretended he was Simon's brother . . .'

'Because Errol told her to. Don't forget, I was sniffing around the Wheatsheaf from day one. I think Madge would have told Errol, and as Errol would know shortly after that that Laura intended to pass him off to me as David Marsh she told Madge to say the same if I ever went back. She more or less admitted the two men had been driving around Simon's territory together some time ago.'

It would explain Madge's almost catatonic shock when I *had* gone back, her release from tension when I'd said I'd not need to see her again. She too must have realised what muddy waters I could stir up if I were to find out who her new

boyfriend really was. She could see it all coming out in public, the violent husband reacting with total predictability.

'I think Laura's given him a substantial sum to go off with Madge and get lost,' I said.

I thought again of how Laura had been that last weekend. Her release from tension had been as great as Madge's, it had simply had a more bizarre outlet, that was all.

Norma watched me, the uneasiness that had been held in check by her curiosity to hear yet another instalment of that complex story now gathering strength. 'Please don't go on, John. Not if shady characters like Errol Wilder are involved. This whole Laura Marsh thing – it just seems to get weirder and weirder, and an outsider's never going to get it together. Please draw the line . . .'

'I don't honestly think I can, Norma,' I said. 'I need Starkey's input on Wilder, but I'm sure I'm right. And the trouble is that Laura's probably thinking she's honourably settled an old debt, and you and I both know that crooks don't know what honour is. He might be back for another slice.'

But there was more to it than that, and it was something I couldn't discuss with her, not now she was just about over the shock of being broken into and attacked. Because Norma's break-in was very much in my mind again. The potential grudge bearers had all been checked out and eliminated, but what if the intruder had been Errol Wilder? Few men would have the edge on him for making it look as if a house had been turned over, and he would have had a lot of incentive for wanting to keep me out of Laura's way – it wouldn't be simply a question of her money, it would be the possibility I might turn up his record and start making waves about the pay-out. I'd told Norma that crooks like Wilder rarely deviated from a certain, usually non-violent, crime pattern, but what if there was really big money involved, a chance to

make a new life with an attractive, green-eyed woman? Wouldn't that be worth risking a little GBH?

If Wilder were to make a come-back I had a score of my own to settle.

I was very busy that day and the following, catching up on all the work Norma had put on hold for me while I went to Norfolk, but Laura was rarely out of my thoughts for long. I wondered sadly if this might be the point where the relationship began to drift. I couldn't bring myself to ring her, after the way we'd parted, felt somehow that the first call should come from her, with some tacit understanding that we had to get back to where we'd once been.

She'd come into the bedroom, later on that Sunday morning when I'd had to wrestle the paper-knife out of her hand. I was packing my bits and pieces into a travel bag.

'I'm dreadfully sorry, John, I don't know what to say . . .'

She wore a sleek suit, plum-coloured and collarless, with two gilt buttons on the jacket, her hair was drawn back, and her make-up, though vibrant, was muted. She looked nothing like the wild-haired Laura of the previous night, but also somehow nothing like the Laura of the London elegance that had seemed exactly right for her.

I shrugged. 'I shouldn't have pried. I'm sure I'd feel the same way myself about private things.'

Our eyes met. We both knew I'd never react to the point of uncontrollable fury.

'It's just that . . . I can't *bear* to have anyone look at work in progress. I'm sorry . . . it was unforgivable. Mother was the same – I suppose I get it from her. She felt that if someone looked at a half-finished painting some thread was broken. She felt she sensed judgement when she herself didn't know how it was going to turn out. It affected her terribly. I've seen

her destroy a canvas because someone had gone into her workroom and seen it half finished . . .'

'I shouldn't have gone into your study. I know how you feel about it . . .'

'When it's completely finished you'll be the first to read it . . . if you'd like to, of course . . .'

'I'd like to very much.'

'I didn't mean to fly off the handle. Not with you, John. I don't know what came . . .'

I took her by the shoulders with a wry smile. 'Look, Laura, it's me . . . John Goss. *Nobody* knows better than I do the strain you've been under.'

Her face slowly lost expression in the milky light, as if she felt numbed again by the recent weight of those mysterious obligations she found impossible to discuss, and I was filled with the old urge to protect her, however erratic her behaviour, protect her now, it seemed, almost from herself.

That urge had sent me down to Norfolk, but I'd not known then that the man she'd pretended was David Marsh was really Errol Wilder, and that only she, as she'd once said, could sort it out, because only she could relate to the complex demands of her own flesh and blood, however undeserving or irrational.

We got in our separate cars and drove to the village of Gargrave, where we went to a house off the green which had once been two cottages. It was now crammed with Demmies, talking so volubly about the same topics they'd dismembered last night it was as if they'd not gone home at all but driven directly there from Larch House. Laura had seemed to gather an instant radiance as she went through the front door, like the sort of lamp that is activated by the presence of moving bodies. The Demmies sucked her effortlessly to their centre, but discarded me on the periphery, as if I were too

much of a mouthful of a substance they found in any case not to their taste. And Julien, my only real link between me and them, was absent, no doubt coping, with a heavy heart and a hangover, with his rude children, his smelly dog and his aggressively liberated wife.

After an hour of being vaguely smiled at and generally ignored, I quietly took my leave. Laura was nowhere to be seen and I wasn't all that sure I wanted to search for her too carefully when she was in Demmy mode.

Shortly after my trip to Norfolk I fitted in a last flying visit to the chalet village near Grassington. All the reasons that had sent me to Norfolk applied. I couldn't stop playing the protector. I wanted to ensure Errol Wilder really had gone off with Madge. If he hadn't, I had a good deal more confidence in my ability to handle it. Small-time crooks were very much my line of country, and I had exactly the weapons in my armoury to scare him shitless.

It was cold and wet, the dampness seeming to make the chill air cling to the body. The site of the cabins, beyond the central complex, was heavy with mud, and dead, sodden leaves shone yellow in the dull light. At first glance I thought the entire site was finally deserted, but then I saw a couple of lamps burning through the gloom.

I picked my way towards the distant clearing which housed the single cabin. A door suddenly opened, and the stout, bespectacled, rather moon-faced woman I'd once disturbed by kicking over a bucket peered out.

'Looking for anyone in particular, dear?'

'The . . . last cabin – the one in the next clearing – I wondered if I could catch him in.'

'Been gone a good week, dear, easily . . .'

'I don't suppose you'd know where he went?'

She shook her head reluctantly. I sensed she was the type who waited and watched, her skills honed to their sharpest pitch in an environment with so little to wait and watch for.

'It's funny you should ask, dear. I was just taking Pippy for his walk the other day when I saw the gentleman putting a bag in his boot, so just to be neighbourly I asked him if he'd be away long. He said he didn't know. Just that: "I don't know" and nothing else, not even a smile. He's never been very friendly, to tell you the truth. Stand-offish . . . do you know what I mean. So I asked him would he like to leave an address with me or a phone number, just in case anyone wanted to get in touch with him, you know, if there was a break-in or anything, but he didn't hang on, said he wasn't sure where he'd be. I ask you. As if you'd go off and not know where you're going. Jack and I always leave an address when we go to Brid. And now look, here you are and I've no address for you. Jack says he doesn't know why I bother, but I tell him we have to be neighbourly. Would you like a cup of coffee, dear, the kettle's just boiled, what a shame you've had a wasted trip . . .'

It was too tempting to turn down. Warmth, coffee, a woman who was a born surveillance unit. She took me into a surprisingly spacious living-room. It was carpeted in a green floral pattern and had one of those peculiarly inflated-looking modern suites and a gas-log fire that burned warmly in a stone fireplace, presumably fed by concealed cylinders. Soft, indirect light fell from wall lamps, and I had a sudden fleeting desire to sit quietly in this cosy room, with its views of wet trees and misty fields, and read some completely absorbing but untaxing novel.

'Jack's gone for the pensions,' she said. 'He always goes for them on a Thursday. That's when they pay them – Thursday. Milk and sugar?'

'No milk, one sugar, please.'

She bustled off into the kitchen and was gone too long for her assurance that the kettle had just boiled to be true. I took off my parka, glanced at the titles of the books in a wooden stand on the sideboard – they seemed to be exclusively of the revelatory type about actors and members of the royal family – and smiled when I saw the folding binoculars that lay almost furtively just behind the stand. They'd be a great help when people began taking bags out to cars.

She returned, with coffee in Tetley Tea-men beakers, and pressed me to have a chocolate wafer from a Tetley Tea-men biscuit tin.

'Is it about the rent?' she said, submerging herself heavily and happily into one of the floppy armchairs. 'That other gentleman, from the estate agent, had a lot of trouble catching him in too. I thought it was sorted out, and in any case I understand the lease finishes at the end of December. Is that what you were given to understand?'

I could see there'd have to be a trade-off, anxious as she was for a good gossip; knew she sensed, as the shrewder gossips did, that the information she possessed might have bartering value.

'Oh, I'm just here to talk to him about life insurance,' I told her. 'I met him in a pub and he seemed interested, so I thought I'd call by on the off-chance. I don't believe he's on the phone . . .'

'It's not worth it for a short lease. We've not had one put in ourselves yet and we own this. We paid with Jack's lump sum. There's a public one down at the office – we use that for the time being, not that we do much phoning . . .'

'And you think he'll be leaving at the end of the year . . . Mr Marsh?'

'Is that his name, dear, Mr Marsh. I didn't know, it just

shows how secretive he is. I must admit I like people you can have a nice chat to. Well, the gentleman from the estate agent did say he was only booked in till the end of December, unless he's renewed. There'll be no one left if it goes on. Jack and I thought it was going to be a proper little community all the year round, not just the summer months. Jack's always loved it around here, but I don't know . . . I'm glad we didn't let the semi go, but we can't go back at present because we've leased that, you see, to a young couple . . . I hope Jack's not letting them slip with the rent, they had good references. *They'll* not be gone till next June, they're having one built at Horsforth – well, between you and me, *I* think *her* father's paying for it. Anyway, I told Jack straight, we'll have to think of going back to the semi, it's just too quiet here, too cut off . . .'

I listened patiently, working through the repertoire of nods and smiles and little exclamations I'd developed over a decade.

'They gave us to understand there'd be lots of older couples wanting to settle here, but there aren't, you know. Apart from Jack and I and Mr and Mrs Coupland and the two Smythe sisters and little Norman with the wooden leg, there's no one. I mean your Mr Marsh doesn't really count because we hardly see him, and he comes and goes such a lot.'

'You'd think he'd *want* to be part of the community,' I said encouragingly. 'His cabin seems very isolated . . .'

'Just *exactly* what I said to Jack!' she cried triumphantly. 'Whatever's a young man like him doing in a place like this, I said, and not wanting to mix in? We had a little fire on Plot Night and a singsong. I did gingerbread men and little Norman did such a nice cake – he used to be a baker, you know, till he fell off that gantry, and he wouldn't even come

to *that*, your Mr Marsh. Anyway, I thought he'd want to live somewhere nearer his work, whatever that is. Did he mention what he did for a living?'

I shook my head. 'I believe he may be a salesman of some sort, what with him moving about. Of course, I'd *have* to know what he did if he decided to take out a policy . . . Has he been here long?'

'Now then, it was after us, and we moved in in May. It runs in my mind he moved in July time. I remember remarking to Jack, why ever take that cabin over yonder when there were still some left down here, with nice friendly people about. Jack doesn't know why I bother, but I tell him we should take an interest, to be neighbourly. Of course, he wasn't on his own then – the other man came and went too.'

'Oh, he has a friend, has he? That's interesting. I might be able to advise them both about a policy . . .'

'Well, like I say, it was only early on when I noticed the other chap. Mind you,' she said, with a wistful smile, 'there was such a lot going on down here, wasn't there. I like to keep an eye on things for people, you know, just in case . . . I thought at first they might be . . . sort of . . . you know . . .'

She held an arm at right angles to her body and let it dangle from the elbow in an obscure gesture.

'*Oh* . . . you mean Mr Marsh and his friend . . . you thought they might be . . . a bit sort of . . .'

'That's right, dear,' she said, with a demure sidelong glance. 'A bit *that* way . . . what our Jack calls *sugar-plum fairies* . . .'

Her voice became a sibilant whisper on the last words, in exactly the arch, confiding manner of certain northern comedians imitating exactly this kind of Pennine woman.

'I *see* . . .'

'And *he* didn't mix either. He'd either stay in or go off on his own. Then I thought one time they might be brothers –

they were quite similar in build. Anyway, the other man left and Jack and I must have been wrong about them being . . . you know . . . because recently Mr Marsh seems to have befriended a young lady, but he's keeping *that* very quiet too. Though Jack did wonder if he might be . . . you know . . .' her voice dropped again, '*bi-annual* . . . but *I* think they're committing adultery. There's such a lot of it about these days. You may find this hard to believe but when Jack was at the store he came home one day and he said: "Gladys, we're not going to stock twenty-fifth anniversary cards any more because there aren't enough couples staying married that long." Isn't that sad? It's a different world, dear, you can't imagine how it was in the Fifties. But when the Sixties came in, and all that wazzy-wazzy music and men with their hair like big daft lasses with yellow socks on . . .'

'So Mr Marsh has a lady friend,' I said, in a musing tone. 'That's interesting. They can often talk their boyfriends into taking out decent insurance. And that's only since the other man left?'

'Oh, yes, she was never there when the men were together. That's what led Jack and I to think they were, you know . . .'

'Sugar-plum fairies . . .' I whispered delicately, in the approved manner.

'That's right, dear,' she said, with a coy flash of her glasses. 'I've often wondered since if Mr Marsh didn't want her coming to the cabin in case the other man tried to entice her away. There's such a lot of that carry-on now too, isn't there?'

'Just what my mother says, all the old standards seem to have disappeared . . .'

I suspected Gladys might have scored a direct hit with that carefully considered surmise, except that Madge wouldn't have been allowed there by the *other* man, because the other

man would have been Simon Marsh, and Madge must have been *his* lover then. And perhaps he'd already begun to sense the attraction that had sprung up between Errol and Madge, and wouldn't have wanted them to meet in the romantic setting of the chalet village.

'That was excellent coffee,' I said warmly. 'Thank you so much. It's been nice talking to you, but I really must go. I'll just pop up to to Mr Marsh's cabin and put my card through his letter-box, and then I'll be on my way.'

'Oh, do you *have* to . . . I made a big pot. It's been so nice talking to someone who takes such an interest in things . . .'

'If only duty didn't call, Mrs . . .'

'Call me Gladys, dear.'

'I'm Brian. Brian Hobbs. I'll probably be back, Gladys. I would like to catch him before he goes for good. He seemed very interested in our products.'

'Oh, you *must* call in. Any time . . .'

I could have stayed for lunch and afternoon tea had I wanted; we'd not even scratched the surface on the private lives of the Couplands and the Smythe sisters and little Norman with the wooden leg. I had a lot of time for the Gladyses of life, and it wasn't simply that they were such prime sources of information for people like me. She was a nosy-parker, but it was the unquenchable curiosity of a woman who loved life, who had an endless and, on the whole, benign fascination with what other people did with their own lives. When Jack, easily satisfied with the pale imitation of life on his television screen, was long gone, Gladys would still be by a window somewhere, watching, wondering, hijacking milkmen and window-cleaners and men who read the meter.

I walked along the muddy track that led up to the clearing where the last cabin stood. It was still locked, lightless, deserted, the sun-blinds again broadside on.

314

I turned to go back. Among the trees something seemed to move. My eyes had caught the movement peripherally, it could have been a squirrel or a fox. Any sound would have been baffled by the carpet of sodden leaves. Motionless, I stared into woodland for several seconds, but saw nothing else. But I was certain something *had* moved. I did a good deal of watching around premises at night; it developed powerful instincts for an additional presence. But I doubted it could be human, not with Gladys's evidence that Wilder had gone and the cabin so shuttered looking.

I set off back to my car, waving to Gladys as I saw her curtain flutter, and drove rapidly to Beckford on the bypass road. I'd spent more time here than I'd allowed for and I had a lot of catching up to do. The Laura Marsh case seemed as multi-faceted as a well-cut diamond. Errol Wilder had had the cabin *before* Simon's death. Why? Had Simon and Laura had enough of him hanging out at the Tanglewood Lane house and rented him the cabin? After all, she'd later provided him with a hired motor, given him grocery money. But why somewhere so remote? Why not rent him a room in the city suburbs and on a bus route? That way he'd not have needed a car. And the cabin wouldn't have been cheap, especially mid-season. Also, at that time, Simon and Laura would have been struggling financially. On the other hand, demand for the cabins hadn't been brisk, and Simon was a businessman – perhaps he'd had the chance of getting it at a knockdown rate and had considered it worth the sacrifice to get Errol off their hands. Perhaps Errol had just finished another stretch and Laura had wanted him to have some kind of rehab in healthy surroundings. It was the sort of thing she'd do.

And when Gladys had seen both men there, that must have been Simon helping him to settle in, sharing an occasional

meal with him. I doubted he'd ever spent the night, not with Errol, whom ten to one he couldn't really stand and only involved himself with for Laura's sake.

There was, of course, the possibility that the two men had struck a deal for Simon to use the cabin now and then as a *pied-à–terre* to spend time with Madge. Gladys had been certain Madge had not been at the cabin when both men had been around, but anything to do with shipping Madge in, with the sort of husband she had, would be bound to have been managed as discreetly as possible.

I'd once thought Simon's real brother had taken Madge from him. But brother or brother-in-law, I supposed the pain would have been exactly the same.

Twenty-One

I touched base with Norma at five, knowing there was a report she wanted me to check before she faxed it. As I came through the door she said: 'You have a visitor. I put her in the private office.'

'Her? *Not* a leg-over case. Assure me it's not a leg-over. Not in December. Christ, they're supposed to have a truce in December. He might *want* to give the PA one but he needs the time to buy Sonic the sodding Hedgehog . . .'

'It's . . . Mrs Marsh.'

'Oh . . .'

'I've put her in the private office.'

'She . . . didn't say she was coming . . .'

'She hoped she might catch you in.'

She shrugged, gave a faint smile. It was almost as if she'd reached a stage of guarded acceptance of Laura. She'd been suspicious of her from the start and her instincts had been sound enough, because Laura had swept a great deal under the carpet. But we knew the truth now, and perhaps Norma could accept the reasons for the secrecy and take a slightly less abrasive attitude to that troubled woman. We were, after all, in the run-up to Christmas, the season of goodwill.

The private office was rather a grand name we gave to a small room where we stored the reference books and boxes

of old invoices and accounting records. It had a circular table on which lay a few *Sunday Times* magazines, a couple of hardback chairs, and a picture on the wall of the Wool Exchange in the days when merchants were still actually selling one another bales of wool. We never let visitors sit in my office unattended, there was too much confidential paper in there, but it seemed churlish to sit someone as close to me as Laura in the lumber room.

'Hello, Laura . . .'

'Hello, John.' She smiled the old, faint smile. 'I had to see the legal people again and I thought I'd call in on the off-chance.'

'I'm . . . very pleased you did. I've . . . missed you.'

It seemed an odd thing to say when I'd seen her so recently, but I wasn't thinking in terms of time.

'I wish you'd told me you were going', she said, 'when you left the lunch party. At Gargrave . . .'

There was no criticism in her soft tone, just the faintest hint of reproach.

'You seemed . . . so tied up with your friends . . .'

Our eyes met. I wondered if she sensed from my lack of apology that I wasn't prepared to share with the Demmies any other times I spent with her – from now on they'd have to have their nights and I mine.

'Could you give me another five minutes or so,' I said. 'There's something I need to sort out with the spider woman. Let me put you in my office – it's much more comfortable.'

'No,' she said, smiling again. 'Your office is private territory, I understand that, John. I'll wait here and read about this month's brilliant new actress . . .'

It was difficult to be certain if there was an implied rebuke, if she was laying down her own ground rules – that there were certain areas of our lives that we had to regard as off

limits to each other, as well as offices and studies. I wondered if my urge to protect her had begun to seem, in her eyes, dangerously like possessiveness. I had to remind myself that she was almost ten years older than me, though she always seemed younger.

'Would you like to go for a drink? There's a place I use – the George. It's the oldest boozer in the city centre. It's a kind of Beckford *Cheers*, if you've ever watched it.'

'Sounds fun . . .'

But I doubted she ever had. Watched *Cheers*.

But she liked the George, with its high, plaster-moulded ceiling and lancet windows and great stone fireplace in which now, inevitably, glowed a gas-log fire. She sat at a table in the body of the bar parlour and, while Kev poured the drinks, I watched her intense bird-like scrutiny pass over the room as she evaluated its age and its style, sensed her listen to the banter at the bar as she'd once seemed to listen to the sounds of Soho streets, a detached student of esoteric manners on a field trip. She wore a camel-coloured woollen coat with a shawl collar, open on a white turtle-neck and a heather-mixture skirt. Her hair was taken back and her make-up was as understated as it had once always been.

'How are you making out up there?' I said, as I put the drinks down.

'I love it,' she said simply. 'I work and walk and work again. I've found a cleaning lady to come in three times a week. She comes on the days when various men drive round with grocery vans, so she can do the shopping too. She's even sorted out a supplier of ready-cut logs for the drawing-room fire.'

Just as long as she didn't risk flicking a duster around the study and getting a paper-knife through the back of her hand. It was an ignoble thought which I thrust away. She seemed to

have reverted to the Laura I knew and cared for, and perhaps the peace and quiet of country life would gradually ensure she stayed this way. The strange, tousle-haired creature of the party and the four-poster bed was someone from a dream that had bordered on a nightmare.

'Anything else planned . . . with the Demmies?'

She shrugged. 'They're all rather locked into Christmas things now . . . and family. I dare say it'll be the new year before they get together again.'

I wondered if I could begin to hope that we might, during the Christmas period, be able to rerun that weekend as I'd so much wanted it to be. I said: 'Would you like to go for a meal?'

'I'd love to. Perhaps we could go somewhere mid-way and then neither of us drives too far afterwards.'

'Why not stay in the area? You could stop over at my place. Compared to Larch House it'll be like staying at the lodge instead of the castle, but . . .'

'I'd rather go home, John,' she said, gently but firmly. 'I start work very early in the morning and I don't want to break the routine I'm in for the time being.'

'I understand,' I said, trying to conceal my disappointment. I'd wanted her to stay because I'd then have suggested we ate at my house too. The restaurants would be heaving even if we could get a table; party time, in this neck of the woods, started on December the first.

I wanted her to myself. We could drink at my place and not have to worry about driving, then have a simple, leisurely meal. We'd be able to talk for hours, it would be like it had been in London and at the Fields Hotel. I'd missed her sad eyes and her little smiles, her jokes and the intelligent talk that came out of that well-stocked brain.

'I'll give the Four Keys a ring,' I said. 'They might be able to fit us in.'

They could, but not before nine. On my way back from the phone I bought two more drinks, dodging the numerous requests from Kev and Co. to provide information on my new girlfriend with a skill honed over many years. It seemed the entire Happy Hour brigade was anxious to see me settling down, let alone Norma and my mother and Mrs Firth. Bruce Fenlon had once summed it up in his usual supportive way: 'You see, Goss, *we're* all married and we don't like to see a jammy bastard like you getting off scot-free.'

'We'll have to drink these very slowly,' I said. 'Dinner's a long way off.'

She put a hand over mine. She had her back turned a little to the bar and I tried to ignore the encouraging thumbs-up signs that Kev and Irene and Dee Dee were giving me.

'I wondered if you'd like to come to Larch House for Christmas,' she said. 'I'm sure even investigators as successful as you have two days off. And as it falls at the weekend you'll not even have to break into the working week, unless you decide to give yourself time off in lieu.'

The shock of surprised pleasure was almost instantly neutralised by wariness, and I gave her a non-committal smile, as if running through a mental diary. Did it mean Demmies, wolfing her food and giving me the elbow and flipping her back into being the dishevelled woman who'd seemed to think that sensation and alcohol would provide a quick fix for the natural pain of loss?

As if sensing my ambivalence, she added: 'Just the two of us – a couple of quiet days. I've got a goose in the freezer.' She gave me her faint smile. 'There never was such a goose . . .'

'I'd like that very much, Laura. Very much indeed.'

'Lovely! Then that's settled. You'll come on Friday night? Why not stay the four days? Let's give ourselves a proper break . . .'

Larch House, Demmy free. I could see again the lawns stiff with frost, the low sun angling through the trees in the little wood and just the two of us, sitting at the log fire in the silent drawing-room, or pottering around the kitchen sipping wine. Sleeping in the four-poster, taking those walks along icy country lanes we'd not had on that other disastrous weekend.

It would be the sort of Christmas I'd not known since my father had died and my mother had gone to live on the coast. Laura had been wrong in saying even investigators must have Christmas off. I didn't. I invariably spent the period working on the accounts of the business in order to minimise the cost of the professional audit. Like recently divorced couples with children, Christmas was the time of year I found hardest to handle. I wouldn't play Radio Two because it only needed a few bars of 'White Christmas' to give me that shiver, that tremor across the stomach, and I'd be back to the Christmasses of my youth and early manhood, when my father had been alive, and we sat down to dinner with half a dozen friends and relations, and we all wore paper hats and pulled crackers, and the entire house seemed to smell of turkey and rum sauce. Bing Crosby singing 'White Christmas' had been one of my father's favourite records – it seemed to spin, at seventy-eight revolutions a minute, a dozen times a day.

I had an open invitation to Bruce Fenlon's for Christmas dinner; I'd gone only once. The memories of the close, happy family life that had ended abruptly with my father's heart attack, had been too overwhelming.

With Laura it would be different. Together, we had no shared past and so there could be no inadvertent reminders of people we'd loved and lost; we'd simply have ourselves and the newness of our friendship in Laura's new home.

'I'm counting the days, John,' she said softly, as if she'd also been thinking how it would be.

'Me too . . .'

We set off then, my arm through hers, and I suppose my pleasure must have been obvious because, as I turned to call good-night to the bar-flies, Kev's hands were now clasped in a gesture of triumph – this time that jammy bastard, Goss, had got three cherries in a row, not only was she pretty but, according to the rumours that would almost certainly be circulating, she had enough money to settle the public sector borrowing requirement. It would be the equivalent, in Kev's murky brain, of getting off with a nymphomaniac who owned a pub in Blackpool.

We retrieved our cars and she followed mine the twenty or so miles to the Four Keys. As I drove I thought of the picture the real David Marsh had drawn of a Laura who'd not even told him his brother had died. It was as if we'd known two different women – his, cold, calculating and unforgiving; mine, warm, good-hearted, generous.

I knew I couldn't overcome that tendency to idealise her a little. I was aware that she had flaws, exactly like every other human being I'd ever met. I'd seen examples of an almost uncontrollable temper, which couldn't really be excused even though I was certain it was untypical. But I felt David Marsh had given me a very one-sided version of the split between him and Simon. He was a tough, successful, domineering man who'd imagined Laura could be managed as readily as Simon himself, had never sensed that strong wills didn't invariably come in the same packaging as his own, or grasped that if he'd bothered to use on Laura the same negotiating skills he employed in business the break would never have come about. As it was, I suspected he couldn't possibly have selected a more frightful weapon to undermine her with Simon than the fact of her criminal background. The desperate unfairness of it must have been the real reason she'd been

unable to forgive him, either then or ever.

We got out of our cars in the restaurant park and walked slowly towards each other. I put my arms round her and kissed her.

'Oh, John, we'll have such a lovely time . . .'

Right then it seemed the only real problem I had left about looking after Laura was in trying to decide what you bought a woman for Christmas who'd just been able to give herself a present as nice as Larch House.

Twenty-Two

The euphoria lasted until just after nine the following morning. The fax-machine began to hum as we were putting the diary together; Norma went over to ensure it was receiving legibly. A couple of minutes later I glanced up to see her looking down at me with an uneasy expression.

'Trouble . . .?' I said, with a sigh.

'I'm afraid you were wrong, John, about the Wilders. You'd better read it . . .'

Dear John [the fax ran] Re: THE WILDER FAMILY. I thought I'd better fax this with the Christmas pressure on post. As you hinted in your request, the Wilders are one of the oldest, most respected sets of crooks in the area. I will give you a brief run-down on Harry and Tina Wilder and sister Lana further down, but you asked me to concentrate on Errol's activities over the past six months. That was the easiest assignment this year. Errol's been taking a much-welcomed (by the police, anyway!) vacation in Armley prison for the period you're covering, and has a further three months to go before his normal good behaviour earns him his normal remission. He's pencilled in to have the police back in business next March. He's been badly missed at the Fox and Ferret!

I stared at Norma in alarm. It was like a kick in the belly.

'Get him on the phone, Norma. There's *got* to be some mistake.'

Without a word, she glanced at the fax heading and then keyed out the number, handing the phone to me when Starkey was actually on the line.

'Alan – it's John Goss. Hello there. Look, Alan, I'll come straight to the point – I've just got your fax on the Wilder family. Look, there *must* be something wrong with your information about Errol being inside. Do you think he could have been given early release or something? He *can't* be inside . . .'

There was a silence at the other end that, had I not been so agitated, I'd have realised was shock that one total professional could doubt the word of another.

'John,' he said at last, his voice raised in surprise, 'if the Home Secretary himself were to tell me he had Errol Wilder banged up I'd still check it out with the prison in question. I don't even go by the official release details. I actually *spoke* to my contact, who is a screw at Armley, yesterday morning, and he assured me Errol had been there since last July, and had barely moved, even to go to the hospital. He wished there were more like him. He knows bloody well he's plotting a nice break-in for when he's released, but that's another story . . .'

'Look, Alan, it couldn't possibly be the father – Harry?'

'John,' he said incredulously, 'I can't believe you're asking me these things. Harry Wilder hasn't done porridge for twenty years. He's a draughtsman now, pure and simple . . .'

'I'm sorry, Alan,' I said distractedly. 'Forget I spoke. I know perfectly well you don't get your facts wrong.'

After a second or two, he said: 'I'm sorry too, John; I can only assume this case has a personal angle . . .'

'You'd be right. Very personal . . .'

I handed the phone to Norma, too confused to lay it on the rest myself. She put a hand on my shoulder. She rarely saw me looking any other than calm and collected, knew how grave the situation had to be if I couldn't, after all these years, even pretend to be in control.

'There's probably a simple explanation, John,' she said. 'Let's talk it through before we finish off the diary.'

'There's nowhere else to go,' I said. 'Don't you see? Had it been David Marsh or Errol Wilder I could have seen an end to her problems. But it's neither, and I couldn't see her going through that kind of stress again and I'm afraid she might have to . . .'

'She seemed fine last evening.'

'I know, but . . .'

'Why not look on the bright side then. He's got what he wanted, whoever he is, and he'll disappear with Madge.'

'He'll be back, Norma,' I said in a low voice. 'Don't ask me how I know because I can't tell you. Call it instinct. Whatever his leverage is he'll not want to stop using it. Once this dollop of loot's gone he'll be back. Christ, if only she'd trust me. I just don't care what mess she might have got into once, I can cope, I can sort it out. You and me, we *know* about people, it's written in all these bloody files . . .'

'Calm down, love, and let's think about it. I don't suppose it could be anything to do with the father – Harry?'

I shook my head. 'He'll be at least sixty. The man I saw wouldn't be much older than Laura herself.'

'Perhaps it was someone acting for the Wilders – a go-between . . .'

I shook my head again. 'The Wilders are too crooked to trust anyone outside the family. He might do a runner with the money himself, which is exactly what *they'd* do in his position.'

'And there's no one else in the family – the Marshes or the Wilders – who could be putting pressure on her?'

'Not that I can see.' I sighed, threw myself back in my chair, glanced at my watch; time had me in its usual strait-jacket. 'I simply can't get it together, can't see how anyone outside the family can come on so strong. She hasn't even *got* a past, apart from being born a Wilder. She lived with her aunt, she went to college, she met Simon and married him. All that's borne out by what Simon's real brother said . . .' I pulled the diary towards me, feeling that wave of fatigue that always seemed to affect me when I had a problem that defied solution however much head-banging I did. 'Maybe I should call it a day. She knows whom she can trust if the shit ever hits the fan again, God knows . . .'

Norma sighed. 'I shan't say any more, John. I know it's not going to make a button of difference. I just hate to see you getting yourself so upset about something you'll probably never understand. I only wish you *would* call it a day, but I know you won't . . .'

I barely took in the sense, it was like listening to words on a car radio when you were making a complicated manoeuvre. I got up, walked to the window, looked down at wet cobbles, cars parked inches apart. 'Well,' I said at last in a low voice, 'there's only one person now who has the handle on who this guy is. Apart from Laura herself.'

After a couple of seconds, she said: 'Of *course* – the barmaid at the Wheatsheaf.'

The fact that it was party month seemed not to have filtered through to the Wheatsheaf. A large, heavy woman with short, bleached hair and an unhealthy complexion stood behind the bar, talking to a handful of regulars in a low, secretive voice. She talked on for a good half-minute before moving reluc-

tantly to serve me. She didn't smile and there was resignation in each feature of her puffy alcoholic's face.

I ordered a gin and tonic, and as I paid her said casually: 'Is Madge not in tonight?'

On the point of handing me my change, she suddenly became very still. 'Haven't you heard?'

'Heard . . .?'

'She's gone missing. Didn't you see it in the *Herald*? They've got the police out now . . .'

'When was this?'

'Monday . . .'

'I'd no idea. I'm only in this area now and again.'

The rather shiny pinkness of her face faded then, as if I'd said something significant. She abruptly thrust the change into my hand, then went off rapidly through a door behind the bar. Seconds later, the landlord, presumably her husband, appeared in the doorway. He gave me a long, hard stare, then came over.

'You were here not long ago,' he said aggressively. 'You went over there with Madge and when you'd gone she looked ready to pass out.'

I stared back at him steadily and without speaking for about ten seconds. 'Yes,' I said evenly, 'I was in recently and I did speak to her.'

'Well, what did you say that upset her so badly she's gone missing?'

I took my time again. 'What I said to her was between me and Madge, and it had nothing to do with her going missing.'

'I'll be the judge of that.'

'You'll be the judge of sod all.'

He flushed, made a sudden movement, then restrained himself with an obvious effort. Throwing trouble-makers out was one thing, laying hands on a respectable customer

because an argument was going the wrong way could lose him his licence.

'That lass is like a daughter to me. There's a husband, kids – they're off their heads with worry. If I find any of this down to you, matey . . .'

'You don't know me, you know nothing about me, so just mind your own business and back off . . . matey.'

I went on watching him steadily as his face grew so red that if they'd taken his blood pressure they'd have got a reading that would have made medical history. His wife stood anxiously at the door to the bar, shaking her head slightly. Nipping his short fuse had probably been the story of her dismal life. The regulars looked on in silent anticipation.

Leaving the gin untouched, I went over to the main door and out to the car-park. As I drove past the front of the pub and on to the road, he was standing in the entrance, his heavy frame back-lit by the glow from the bar parlour.

I drove towards Skipton, my hands trembling slightly. Not because of him – I was used to anger, raised voices, the threat of fists, and I knew how to look after myself.

I didn't like this. Even though I knew she'd intended to leave her husband. She'd stressed that it was to be her and the kids, not just her. And I'd believed her, because in my experience few women could walk away from the kids. And she'd not have been gone all this time without letting the husband know, even though she'd have made sure they were separated by several hundred miles. People were my business and in Madge I'd sensed a basic decency.

But vanishing without the kids, and no message to the husband, had meant police involvement. And because they'd not have had time yet to uncover the secret affair they'd be taking it very seriously.

I couldn't calm my hands. I drove over deserted country

roads and there was a throbbing in my temples that seemed like a soft, sinister drumbeat. The first dreadful suspicion began to form on that drive, at the far edge of my perception, like a dark shape in deeper darkness that you sense but cannot define.

Suddenly, there was a police car at the edge of my headlamps' reach, a uniformed officer standing at the side, making a flagging-down gesture. What was this? A random breath test? A routine check because of some major break-in?

I drew in to the left. The police car was on the opposite side of the road; the uniform came across.

'Yes, officer . . .?'

'Would you be the gentleman who left the Wheatsheaf public house about ten minutes ago, sir?'

'Yes.'

'We're making enquiries about a missing person, sir, a Mrs Madge Horton, and we believe you may possibly have some information that might help.'

It would have been the landlord. He'd have taken my number and rung the local nick, almost certainly adding his own twopennyworth to the effect my talk with Madge had had on her.

'I doubt it,' I said. 'I'm a private investigator. I spoke to Mrs Horton recently on a matter I'd been looking into, but apart from that I know nothing about her. I'd no idea she was missing until the landlady told me.'

'Could I ask for some identification,' he said politely.

I handed him the little wallet with my photograph and particulars. He read the details carefully by torchlight and compared the photograph with my face.

'I believe you wanted to see Mrs Horton tonight, Mr Goss,' he said, handing back the wallet. 'Would you mind telling me what that was about?'

'It's . . . confidential, officer. I have to give that promise to be able to get information.'

'I understand that, but this is a very serious matter of a local woman's disappearance and we shall have to insist. It would be very helpful if you'd follow me to the station, where we can talk more fully. We'll try not to take up too much of your time.'

It was like interview rooms in police stations everywhere – basic decor, basic furniture and ashtrays that looked as if they were never properly cleaned. A tall, dark-haired man in a charcoal-grey suit joined me there. He looked hard and tired, as they always did.

'Detective Sergeant Croller,' he told me, holding out his hand briefly. 'I'm told you're a private man. Know anyone in the Beckford Force?'

It was a little test. If I hadn't I wouldn't have been a PI worth spit, and therefore, in his eyes, less to be trusted. I gave him four names, starting with Bruce Fenlon.

'I know Bruce well,' he said more warmly. 'A good man. Look . . . John . . . it would be a great help if you'd tell me what you were into Madge Horton about.' He smiled faintly. 'Confidentially . . .'

'I was hired by Zephyr Insurance to check out the details of a big claim. A man called Simon Marsh had been killed in a car accident. There was nothing dodgy about it and they've since paid up. Madge's name only came into it because she'd been having an affair with Marsh.'

'Oh, shit!' he groaned, his shoulders sagging. 'And we've been giving it everything we've got. I've got people on *overtime* . . .'

'But he's dead,' I said. 'He's out of the picture.'

'So what, if she's an amateur tom she'll have pissed off with some other boyfriend . . .'

And amateur toms who disappeared, like youngsters over sixteen and middle-aged married men, didn't just go on the back burner, they were lucky if they hit the cooker at all.

'She wouldn't leave the kids,' I said urgently. 'Men do, yes, but not a barmaid who's had a single affair. And she'd not leave the husband in the dark as long as this, either . . .'

'There *are* exceptions . . .'

'Not Madge Horton. I talked to her. Believe me, I know garbage when I trip over it and that description doesn't fit.'

Our eyes met. He'd picked up on my intensity and was wondering what the disappearance meant to a professional who should have been disinterested. And I had to risk his suspicion because I suddenly knew I couldn't let him pull off the dogs. All she'd really wanted was to get away with her kids from a violent husband and make a new life with someone who seemed to care. And she had to be in some kind of trouble.

'Okay,' he said reluctantly. 'I believe you. But look, the landlord said you were up there not long ago and you told her something that sent her into shock.'

'That was just a courtesy call – to say the investigation was complete and she'd not be hearing from me again.'

'Why was she in shock then?'

'That was relief. She has a jealous, possibly violent husband – she was terrified he'd find out about the affair.'

'So why were you up there tonight then, asking for her again?'

'I wasn't asking. I had a job in the area and I just called in. My actual words were: "Is Madge not in tonight?" Ask the landlady. It was her husband who wrote the additional dialogue.'

He sighed. 'Yes, well, we all know about big Ted, don't we. Thinking doesn't come easy to him. Were you ever at the house – Madge Horton's house?'

'I don't even know where she lives.'

He didn't find it necessary to explain this and I wondered what the significance was. He gave me a dispirited look. 'So that's it? Nothing more you can add?'

There was more, a lot more, but I'd had time to think on my way down to the station, and I'd decided to tell only what I'd picked up on my routine investigation for Zephyr. Beyond that I was in any case as much in the dark as the police. I didn't know who the man at the cabin was and he wasn't anyway at the cabin any more. The police had the resources and as long as they gave it priority, sooner or later they'd find her. Nothing else I could tell them would be of any help, but it could stir up a lot of new trouble for Laura. And she'd had enough. Whatever had happened to Madge could have nothing to do with her.

DS Croller let me go and I drove home. I poured a large brandy and stood in the kitchen. I should have eaten, I'd had nothing since lunch-time, but I couldn't face food any more than I could face the dark shadows that struggled to gain substance at the edge of my mind.

Almost in desperation, I reviewed every aspect of the Marsh case. Who'd actually known them in Beckford? Hardly anyone. Tanglewood was a road where the occupants respected privacy. Why had the real David Marsh not been told of his brother's death, despite the break-up? Why term assurance – cheap, plentiful, but scarcely good business sense? In the past, I'd often tried to push away awkward facts because they'd not fit into some neat theory I'd thought out; now, I tried to push them away because they made the theory even neater.

With the second brandy I began to take a grip on myself, to feel easier in my mind. I suddenly realised that it was now *too* neat. Life was never like that, even with the smart operators,

and I'd looked into the efforts of a good many. Life was messy, full of loose ends, of incidents that couldn't be foreseen however clever you were. And the clincher had to be the police. They handled those kinds of matters very thoroughly. British systems were among the best in the world. I didn't know who the guy was, but I'd find out. One day I'd know.

I found the appetite to eat then, and after that I turned on the television and let my brain slip thankfully into neutral as I watched an old film in which Paul Newman gave several of his distinguished portrayals of a man being beaten senseless.

I also managed to sleep, but I awoke at four, and I knew then that I'd been right first time, before I'd started on the brandy. What I had was something that was like the algebraic problems of boyhood in which, if you were given the values of certain letters, you could prove the values of others, if you thought it through according to precise, if complex, rules.

I lay awake until the radio came on automatically with the *Today* programme at six-thirty. It was my normal time for getting up, once I'd caught the headlines, but today I lay on, listening to the sound-bites and the interviews and the city prices. And then I was suddenly in a heavy sleep that lasted about twenty minutes. When I awoke the value of the last letter in the equation lay unbidden, and certainly unwanted, on the surface of my mind.

Twenty-three

I tracked him down to a large, gloomy basement beneath a battered inner-city Anglican church. It was lit by grey daylight filtering in through small, high windows just above ground level, and several unshaded electric bulbs. A young vicar, rather shabbily dressed, but cheerful, enthusiastic and fresh-faced, ladled quite a good thick stew on to chipped soup-plates. A woman, thin, lank-haired and equally cheerful, carved doorstep slices from fresh loaves.

'I'm afraid this isn't really for anybody,' the vicar said politely, glancing at my clothes. 'We used to serve anyone who came in at one time, but I'm afraid people began to take advantage. We feel we must limit our efforts to those genuinely in need.'

'I'm not here for the food, Reverend,' I said. 'I'm looking for Tommy Winthrop.'

'Oh dear,' he said, 'I hope he's not in trouble again. He's over by the wall there.'

'No trouble that I know of. Thanks, Reverend.' I handed him a ten-pound note. 'Perhaps this will help with tomorrow's stew.'

'Thank you, friend, and God bless you.'

There was no change in Tommy: stubbly, grimy, bundled in his creased and dirty good-quality coat, which must have cost

its original owner enough to keep Tommy ticking over for a year. I stood above him. He didn't look up. His first rule of survival seemed to be to avoid eye contact wherever possible. I put two packets of cigarettes at his side and a bottle of cheap red wine. He studied the offering warily for several seconds, his fogged brain searching for the catch, before finally, with extreme reluctance, looking up at me.

'Oh, it's *you*, boss,' he said in relief. 'I thought I'd 'ad me birthday . . .'

'What are you doing here, Tommy?' I said, smiling to put him at his ease. 'I thought you didn't get on with Reverend Hopper.'

'I get on wiv 'is stew and bread,' he said, breaking into his almost soundless laughter. 'I get on wiv 'is stew and bread a treat.'

I sat down beside him, realising for the first time how much better he smelt in the open air. 'Where've you been, Tommy? I couldn't find you down the subway.'

'Keep moving, boss. Too cold to sit about this time of year. Catch me death . . .'

'Where do you sleep?'

'Here and there,' he said warily, glancing round at the ragged men and occasional woman who noisily ate. He'd have his secret hidy-holes – warm-air vents above boiler rooms, corners of office car-parks, cottages scheduled for demolition – and he would keep them to himself, because too many vagrants would attract unwelcome attention.

'Now look, Tommy, the last time I saw you you said I had to let you know if you could ever do me a good turn . . . Yes . . .?'

As soon as the words were out, I realised it was like asking a victim of Alzheimer's what he'd had for lunch. He watched me uneasily through blue, red-tinged eyes.

'I don't want no 'assle, boss. I don't want to get no one in

no bovver . . .' He pushed the wine and cigarettes away from him with an agitated gesture at the possibility they might be Judas money.

'Look, Tommy,' I said patiently, 'I'm not trying to give anyone grief.' I pushed the gifts back until they touched the hem of his coat. 'I just want to know if you ever found out where your pal, Suss, got to?'

He turned away, passed a bleak glance over the shadowy, cavernous room, where the Reverend Hopper continued to greet shuffling down-and-outs with the grace and charm of a courtier welcoming guests at a royal garden party. 'Don't talk to me about Suss,' he muttered bitterly. 'He *swore* 'e'd keep in touch. We was mates, me and 'im. I shared me biddy *and* me makings wiv 'im, many a time. 'E said 'e'd come back and see me, diden 'e, but wonce 'e'd got work and a proper kip it was no thank you . . .' He sank back, as if briefly exhausted by this, for him, lengthy speech.

'Tommy . . . someone came to the subway and offered him a job scaffolding. What did the man look like?'

His blank eyes locked slowly on mine. I sighed. There was no point in this. His life was lived in hermetically sealed capsules of twenty-four hours – every atom of his being was concentrated on surviving for that length of time. The concepts of past and future were as meaningless to him as they were to a dog. He remembered me because I gave him things, Suss because they'd been friends. The rest was shadowland.

'Don't ask me, boss,' he said superfluously.

'Was he fair, Tommy? Dark? How tall was he? Was he my height, for instance.'

He put down his soup-plate, so carefully cleaned of every trace of nutrition it could have been in a dishwasher. He took out part of a cigarette but didn't do his thumb-nail and match trick.

'Reverend 'Opper won't 'ave no smoking in 'ere,' he

explained. 'Says it 'elps shorten us lives.' He began his soundless laughter; he retained vestiges at least of a sense of irony.

'Can you remember *anything* about him, Tommy?' I persisted. 'It's very important.'

'Sorry, boss – I see that many people . . .'

'What did Suss look like then, Tommy,' I said, trying to conceal a near-desperation I knew would only unsettle him.

'Suss . . .?' He began visibly straining a memory in which even the features of his closest friend were now fading like the values of a colour photograph left in sunlight. Inevitably, he shrugged.

'Oh, come *on*, Tommy, he was your *friend*. Was he dark?'

He thought for a few seconds. 'No . . .'

'Then he must have been fair. Was he very fair?'

More time passed and then: ''Is 'air was a bit the colour of Reverend 'Opper's 'air.'

It was like drawing teeth, but it was a start. The Reverend Hopper's hair was somewhere between fair and light brown.

'Was he as tall as Reverend Hopper?'

'Might 'ave been about 'is 'eight. Trouble is, 'e was nearly always sitting down.'

'But when the man came, who offered him the scaffolding job, he must have stood up then.'

'S'pose so . . .'

'Now think very carefully, Tommy. Did they look a bit like each other? In build . . .'

His thinking was the lengthiest yet. He stared at his wine and cigarettes as if suspecting the gifts might have to slide back my way once more if he didn't come up with something. Suddenly, as if a shaft of sunlight had shone for the first time in a dusty loft, he grinned on yellow and decaying teeth. 'Funny you should say that, boss, when they was stood

together there *was* a bit of a likeness. 'Cept the other geezer 'ad a beard, of course . . .'

They said that everything you'd ever seen was in there somewhere if you could just find the right key, even if half your brain cells had fused like fairy lights. My hands were trembling and I felt physically sick. 'And did he', I said, dragging the words out reluctantly, 'wear heavy glasses?'

'That's *right*, boss!' he said in admiration. ''Ow did you know that?'

As he'd done earlier, I slumped back on the bench seat. I just wanted to go. I wanted to drive up on to the moor road and then run, as if I could leave it behind me, run until I was so exhausted my brain would shut down in protest.

Tommy watched me incuriously. I suspected shock must have given me an unhealthy pallor, but the people he hung out with had them permanently.

'You've been very helpful, Tommy,' I said at last. 'Have you no idea what Suss's name was?'

He didn't need to think about that, at least. He shook his head decisively. 'Never called 'im nothing but Suss . . .'

'That was a nickname,' I said. 'Like Nobby or Paddy or Gazzer. Why did you call him Suss?'

The vagrant next to him, who had seemed sunk in the normal apathy, suddenly spoke. ''Cause of 'is suspenders, innit . . .'

'That's *right*!' Tommy said, as if memory had been forcibly yanked into life, like the engine of an outboard motor. ''E wore them fancy suspender things, diden 'e. 'E'd 'ardly got no socks at all, boss, they was all in 'oles round 'is legs, but 'e kep' 'em up wiv these posh suspenders.'

'They was red,' the other announced importantly. 'Them suspenders. Red . . .'

'*That's* why we called 'im Suss!' Tommy cried triumphantly. ''Cause of 'is suspenders . . .'

'Well, I just said that, diden I!' There was a note of grievance in the other's tone, that he should be robbed even of his tiny growl of thunder, let alone his makings and his crusts.

I sat staring into space, the voices and the scraping of spoons seeming to recede into silence. I felt numb to the bone, sick almost to the point of nausea, the thick, savoury smell of the stew now making me want to vomit. I must have sat there for ten minutes, frozen into immobility, my brain for long seconds seeming almost disabled.

I couldn't, wouldn't believe it, could scarcely think about it at all. I could only take it in in snatches, obliquely, because it was too much, too incredibly painful, like trying to look at the sun with the naked eye. But I knew I'd found the answer. And proof would be no problem, none at all, despite the man called Suss having disappeared.

Suspenders. Suss had been short for suspenders. And when I'd been looking around the area where Simon Marsh's car had left the road and crashed into the valley, I'd picked up something from the grass verge. *A single red suspender.*

It only confirmed what I'd already known. It added the QED flourish to the equation I'd solved this morning, when the final letter had yielded its value, when I'd suddenly seen how very unlikely it would be that an employer would walk around subways offering scaffolding jobs to vagrants. It was only men like the Reverend Hopper who did those kinds of things. Or guilt freaks like me.

'Are you all right, sir?'

It was the woman who worked with the Reverend Hopper, probably his wife, a look of professional concern on her scrubbed-looking face. I glanced vaguely around. Tommy had disappeared, taking his wine and cigarettes with him, as

silently and inconspicuously as if he'd been sucked into a parallel universe. So had the vagrant who'd proved so devastatingly knowledgeable about suspenders and their colour.

I looked at her for some time in silence. I must have made an odd contrast to the rest, in my good suit and raincoat. 'I'm just going, ma'am,' I said in a low voice. 'I only came to see Tommy. I give him the odd pound coin . . .'

'Not to mention cigarettes and alcohol,' she said briskly. 'We *do* ask people to give them food and clothing, you know, rather than wine and cigarettes, or even money . . .'

The words of the first lesson rolled over my mind, scarcely rippling its surface. After a while she sat down at my side.

'You're very disturbed . . .'

I glanced at her. She was a professional sympathy-monger, trained to listen, to make the right noises, to advise and counsel, but for a couple of seconds I wanted to feel her arm round my shoulder, to tell it all to that calmly attentive face.

Perhaps she sensed the profound shock I'd had from adding the last few pieces to the jigsaw, a shock that left me dazed, almost speechless. Her face seemed to take on genuine concern then, to fill with the sort of emotion she'd been warned always to be on guard against, because she'd need to save the real stuff for those close to her, otherwise she'd wear herself out.

'Would you like to come to the vicarage?' she said gently. 'Paul and I, I'm sure we could help you . . .'

'Thank you,' I said, 'but it's one of those things where no one can help.'

'Has . . . someone left you? Someone died?'

'Both,' I said, 'in a way.'

My work had to go on, and it helped me to pull myself together. I was shadowing a man who worked for a construc-

tion company, whose boss suspected he was passing vital tender information to rival firms. The man himself, obviously wired in to the paranoia that seemed to affect the entire industry, took care of his back with such skill that keeping him in my sights was a genuine challenge.

But there were the usual periods of waiting, and it was then that I tried to decide what practical steps I should take. Madge, at least, was no longer a worry. My mind had been full of shapeless forms when I'd talked to Croller at the police station; it had been impossible to decide if she'd really been in trouble and who the trouble would come from. It could have been her husband, it could have been the man at the cabin. It had seemed even then more likely to be her husband, and if Croller had examined his notes he'd be reminded that I'd touched on the husband's violent tendencies.

But I knew who the man at the cabin was now, and I was certain Madge was safe from him. In fact I was certain she was *with* the man from the cabin. She'd not taken the children and she'd not told her husband, but I realised now what a very complicated disappearing act had to take place. She'd get the children later, perhaps by the old favourite method of quietly picking them up from school and then driving off rapidly. After that she'd send the husband a letter with no address, informing him of a *fait accompli*.

So what to do about the police? I knew I could prove everything, but only if the man was caught. Would they ever catch him now, a man of such incredible skill? He'd have changed his appearance, would have a name now known only to him and Madge. The vagrant called Suss I could forget about – he'd come from nowhere and even his best friend had never known his real name.

The man I was presently shadowing came out into the car-

park of the British Queen. I was parked to the rear, my head just below the dashboard. He looked around carefully for some time, then got quietly into a Bentley. It belonged, as I knew, to the MD of a rival building firm. The case was now a wrap. I seemed to be involved these days in an endless number of cases of middle-class fraud. It appeared to be a trend that went with the times.

I tried to make some decision on Laura. My mind seemed to bounce away from any direct thought about her like microwaves off metal. I was tempted to pull out, very strongly tempted just to leave it to the police and their routine investigations. Nothing, in any case, would hang together without him and I doubted anyone would ever find him now. And everything I'd learnt had been unofficial, I could simply have worked through the case and taken everything at face value. I'd been encouraged to do just that often enough by everyone concerned, God knows. Why not walk away from the whole sorry mess, and from Laura too? If I couldn't prove it without the man there was no point in wasting my or the police's time, assuming the police would give it house-room. From where they stood it would be in the Lord Lucan class, it would have no-win running through it like letters in a stick of rock.

Eyes just over the dashboard, I watched my target leave the Bentley, his overcoat pocket almost certainly stuffed with fifty-pound notes, and when he was in his own car I discreetly followed him home. It marked the end of a long, emotionally draining day. I went on to my own house and poured myself a drink. I knew I couldn't leave it. I was a policeman's son, I'd hoped to be a policeman myself. A man was dead here, insurance companies had paid out more than a million. I doubt I could have walked away had my own mother been involved.

* * *

Early next morning I drove out once more to the chalet village near Grassington. I parked in a lay-by a good half-mile away and approached the cabins as unobtrusively as possible on foot, bypassing the lower clearing completely, to home in at length on that single, isolated cabin on the higher ground. It was, as usual, locked and shuttered-looking, but the door lock was a standard one and I had my bunch of keys in one of the big pockets of my parka. I was inside in three minutes. It was the last place I'd known him to be at and I simply hoped to find something, anything, there that would give me a clue to his current whereabouts. It was barely worth a try, but I tried just the same, because otherwise it would have to be Laura in the firing line, and even now I couldn't rid myself of the urge to protect, to limit the damage as much as possible. Because the man I sought would have been the driving force.

I moved into the main room that gave directly from the outside door. The uneasiness was instant. There was a pair of mud-caked trainers beneath a dining chair, a cagoule hung behind the door itself. There was a pile of paperbacks on the dining-table, a half-full bottle of vodka on a narrow side-board, together with glasses, some clean, some dirty. There were newspapers, a portable radio, a portable television.

I was astounded. Why had all this stuff been left behind? Didn't a shrewd operator like him understand about finger-prints? Or had he assumed, possibly rightly, that fingerprints wouldn't help anyone? Had he gone in a hurry, taking only essentials? Had he not yet gone at all?

I moved softly right into the area that housed the kitchen, bathroom, bedrooms. I went into the larger of the two bedrooms. The double bed was unmade. A pair of slippers poked out beneath it, a dirty T-shirt hung over a chair. Not knowing if he'd really gone or was just temporarily absent, I prudently

opened the bedroom window in case I heard a key in the outer door and had to make a quick exit.

I opened the door of a built-in wardrobe. There were clothes hanging there, all male, all casual – several pairs of slacks, a parka, two sports jackets. He couldn't have gone for good, couldn't possibly want to risk leaving all this gear around. All I'd ever expected to find, admittedly the slenderest of hopes, was a scrap of paper in a waste-bin with perhaps part of an address on, an envelope in the back of a drawer, some rough notes hidden in the fridge's freezing compartment, a favourite place, and forgotten in the rush. The rest should have been bare rooms.

I wondered if I was in with a chance. If he'd not left the area yet perhaps he'd return at nightfall with Madge. Maybe they were not leaving for good until they'd got Madge's children. Perhaps I could return at nightfall too and watch out for them. If they came back I could alert Croller on the car phone, tell him I'd found Madge. Not confuse him with the rest till I'd had a chance to contact Laura and tell her what was going to happen, to prepare herself.

I gave the hanging clothes a final riffle, checked the pockets of jackets and trousers. And then I saw it. In the darkness of the rear of the wardrobe stood a document case. Perhaps I'd not need to come back at nightfall. The case might contain positive proof of the man's identity and I could simply hand it to the police and let them arrange the stake-out. As I reached for it, I only heard the slightest sound of movement behind me before I felt the blow.

Twenty-Four

I surfaced to the sick headache of a lifetime. I found out later that the blow had triggered a migraine, something I'd never had before, and so I wasn't just contending with nausea and pain, but with a frightening arc of lights that flickered in bright colours, badly impairing my vision. But I could see enough, could see the man standing above me, with the brown beard and hair, and the thick glasses over tinted contact lenses, the padded body.

I groaned, closed my eyes on what seemed like a flashing disco without music. I wondered if my skull had been seriously damaged, tried to put a hand up to find out, realised my wrists were tied behind my back with cord.

'You didn't really think you'd get away with it, did you . . . Simon?' I muttered.

'Bastard!' he shouted. '*Bastard!* I knew you were trouble. I *told* her you were trouble. Why couldn't you keep your bloody nose out!'

I'd rarely seen a man more agitated, and I'd seen plenty. The sawn-off fencing post he'd hit me with lay on the dining-table, and I realised then I'd been dragged through from the bedroom to the living-room. He wasn't without wiry strength behind the padding. He suddenly picked up the fencing post and I instinctively flinched. But then he threw it down again

and walked distractedly about the room, his head jerking like someone with a nervous tic.

'I'd give yourself up,' I said. 'They'll track you down, wherever you go. Not just the police, the insurers. It'll be worth offering five per cent of a million as a reward to get the other ninety-five per cent back. I'd give yourself up and save yourself any more stress. You obviously can't handle it.'

The effort of thinking, let alone talking, made my head feel as if it were being clubbed, in time with my heart beat, by the blunt end of a hatchet. He shook his head again and again as he moved restlessly up and down the room. 'Not now,' he said harshly. 'Not after all this. No chance . . .'

'They're on their way now, Simon, the police . . .'

'If the police were coming they'd be here. They'd not be letting you sniff around on your own. You're trying to do it your way because of that bitch at Larch House. That's why you've talked Madge into clearing off, because you knew I'd not go without her.'

I began to tremble. It was cold in the cabin, but it wasn't that. He was raving. He was going off his head because it had all been too much, as it nearly always was with people who committed a single serious crime. But it wasn't that either, it was the sudden realisation that *neither* of us knew where Madge was.

'I've got nothing to do with her whereabouts,' I said. 'I'd thought she must be with you . . .'

'Liar! Where did she go? Her sister's? The friend in Coventry? You knew bloody well I couldn't ask that swine of a husband . . .'

'I don't *know*! I was convinced she was with *you* . . .'

I closed my eyes on lights and pain. I'd have to remember not to raise my voice.

'You're not leaving here till I know where she is. You'd better believe it . . .' His trembling hand rested on the fencing post again.

Except that even if I could tell him, I'd still not be leaving here. He'd killed once, once more would make little difference, the state he was in. Be calm, they stressed, or give an appearance of it, when you're talking to someone who's holding a hostage or threatening to jump off a roof, because if you show agitation it transmits itself to the other and increases theirs.

'Simon,' I said evenly, 'if I knew where she was I'd tell you.'

He suddenly grasped the fencing post and shouted: 'Perhaps this'll improve your memory.'

'Simon,' I said, 'if you hit me with that once more there's a good chance you'll kill me. That's how it works in real life. And if you kill me too you'll never see daylight again.'

He held the post uncertainly. An experienced hard case would have known to strike me on the elbow or the side of the knee, in order to produce pain without loss of consciousness. His eyes took on a vagueness, as if he'd lost the thread of what he was trying to do. I wondered how much sleep he'd missed since he'd spiked the drinks of the man called Suss, driven him to the road above the valley, pulled him into the driver's seat and released the handbrake at the top of the incline, so that the car had gathered enough momentum at the bottom to go straight through the fence, where the road swung right, and crash into the valley itself. I suspected that since then sleep had been a scarce commodity, and it was a fact worth knowing.

'I can't see why you think I'd have anything to do with Madge going into hiding,' I said calmly. It was a front I was finding almost impossible to keep up. I felt ill with pain and I was seriously worried about the damage to my head; I didn't know about migraine headaches and I thought I might have a detached retina.

'Because you *knew* I'd not go without her,' he said again.

But I heard him put down the post. From what I could

make out of him through the flickering lights I could see the faint similarity to his brother, David. He spoke with something of the same accent too, but he had nothing of David's dominating presence, as I'd once surmised. Beneath the heavy beard there was an impression of boyish charm, when his face was relaxed, that seemed bizarre in the circumstances, but there was also a weakness about the mouth that was emphasised by lips that still twitched. I was always very wary of weak-looking men; frustration with themselves could drive them to do considerable damage. They often found their bottle too abruptly and the sensation was so heady they lost control.

'I *know* you talked her into going into hiding,' he said doggedly. 'She told me you'd gone to the pub, that you'd said she'd not be seeing you again. I didn't believe it. I *knew* you'd be back. I *warned* her.'

I made no reply, hoping he'd go on talking. That's what they advised, let them talk, try and build up a rapport. The least it could do was let me play for time, until the pain eased enough for me to think straight.

Finally I said in a comforting voice: 'Do you know what I think, Simon? I think Madge had had enough of the lot of us – the husband, you, me – and went somewhere on her own to think things through. Who could blame her?'

I was simply playing with words, but I wondered if I might have hit on the truth. I remembered her collapsing on the banquette at the Wheatsheaf. She must have known Simon had committed some sort of crime, to be hiding out. She might not have known all the details, but she had to have known some. And she, like Simon, would be new to crime and would probably have the same inability to cope. Looking back over the past weeks, didn't I know the signs.

He rubbed a quivering hand against the beard. It would be

a real beard now, and tinted; fake in the days when he needed to remove it and the wig and the contacts, and revert to being nice, fair-haired, clean-shaven Simon with the blue eyes.

'She wouldn't leave me,' he whispered, almost in desperation. 'Not Madge. Not without telling me . . . I *know* Madge, I've never known anyone as well as I know her . . .'

It was a strange admission from a man who'd spent so many years with Laura. He was really talking about infatuation, blind passion, but a passion that had ruined both his life and Laura's. At the same time I remembered how Madge's green eyes had shone when she'd told me she couldn't live without this man.

'She'll be back when it's all over,' I said soothingly. 'Let's get it sorted with the police now. You can't go through life with this on your conscience. I'll help you. I can get you one of the best defence lawyers in town . . .'

'What about *her*?' he suddenly cried. 'That bitch at Larch House. Do you think she doesn't need a defence lawyer . . .?'

'Well, of course . . .' I wished I could bring a hand to my throbbing head, it felt as if it needed holding to my body. 'She's obviously deeply implicated. But . . . let's face it, you're the one who'll need the best boy. It was you who promised Suss a job and brought him here to clean him up and feed him, you who got him into one of your outfits, with your wallet and papers in the pockets, you who sat him at the wheel . . .'

'It was *her* idea!' he screamed, smashing a fist on the table. '*She* worked it all out. Do you think *I* could have come up with a scheme like that!'

'Of course not,' I said hurriedly; the pain was making me handle it badly. 'Laura worked it all out and you just did the humping . . .'

'I haven't got that kind of *brain*, for Christ's sake!'

'It was Laura,' I said firmly. 'It's obvious now you point it out.'

But he would, of course, say it was all down to her. However close they'd been, he was now in love with Madge, and people found it easy to load all the blame on to the partner they'd discarded. I'd seen it a dozen times in domestic cases.

Laura had a clever mind, but Simon's was the analytical one. He designed computer systems and had applied the same nit-picking technique to a murder as near perfect as made no difference. Term assurance – relatively cheap because there was no endowment element, but paying out in spades in the unlikely event of death. The move to Beckford, where no one knew them. Suss, the vagrant, new to living rough and in good physical shape. I supposed Simon had kept Suss's papers so that he could use his identity for easing himself back into state systems. Because Suss was still theoretically alive, even though it was his body that had ended up in the mortuary, more or less in one piece. I saw then the brilliance of the fine detail: that almost empty petrol tank so the car wouldn't burst into flames. Simon had *wanted* the body intact, wearing his clothes, complete with his papers, didn't want a body that couldn't be easily identified so that the forensics had to start doing tedious things with dental charts. Which would have proved the body *wasn't* Simon's.

'Who identified the body, Simon? You, posing as your brother, or Laura?'

It was an unwise question, the train of thought and the disabling pain had carried me unthinkingly into asking it.

'Not her!' he cried. '*She* had to be the devastated widow, hadn't she, too upset even to look at it. So they let me identify myself while she wept. *What* a performance! She even had the bloody WPC crying. You're right, she sat back, I took the shit. I always did. But I'm not taking it for this lot.'

'Look,' I said quietly, 'I agree. She's just as much to blame as you. She's an accessory. The law will be completely even-handed, take my word. You'll not have to carry the entire can . . .'

But I'd guessed he'd have made the identification, because I was certain she'd been coerced into all this. I had to accept the part she'd played in it, but I knew it had been an unwilling one. She'd been coerced, and when she'd wept at the mortuary she'd wept from a wretchedness and guilt that had never really left her, all that late summer and autumn. It explained why she'd not been able to break our friendship. I felt now that at some unconscious level she'd almost *wanted* me to discover the truth. She'd never wanted any part of this mess, but she'd never really stopped loving this weak man who'd suddenly found a terrible decisiveness, and she'd been unable to expose him. It explained so much. The outbursts, the need to have me in her bed as she wept, the periods of what, in hindsight, had obviously been remorse, the wildness at Larch House as she'd tried to lose herself in alcohol, sensation and the golden days of her girlhood.

Simon now sat staring vacantly through the window, eyes glinting in the low December sunlight. He seemed to be having another of those patches of mental blankness that went with a prolonged lack of sleep. I suspected he'd have given ten thousand of his stolen money for a good night's oblivion.

'Let me sort it,' I said, with gentle persistence. 'For both of you.'

He ignored me, took out a plastic container, shook two or three capsules into his cupped hand, swallowed them. Tranquillisers, downers, and he was clearly building up a tolerance. But they might bring a valuable period of calm.

'I'd had enough,' he said, almost as if to himself. 'And when

I met Madge . . . she's a sweet kid . . . all she wanted was a decent life, someone who'd take care of her and the children. We both needed what the other had. She knew I'd take care of her, I knew she'd just be herself. She'd not change . . . she'd always be the same, always the same woman I met at the Wheatsheaf.'

I'd seen it all before. The mid-life crisis, the job that was going wrong, the stress of trying to go on providing a partner with the accustomed life-style. It seemed such a tempting way out, the attractive thirty-year-old who had her own problems and saw an escape hatch, and wouldn't ask too many questions about how it would be achieved. But so far I'd only seen it drive men to dip a hand in the till, not kill people.

The flickering lights that disturbed my sight were diminishing, but the pain was losing none of its intensity and was being enhanced by a peculiar spaced-out sensation. It was all I needed, as I lay hunched up against the wall, my hands bound, trying to reason with a killer at the edge of his sanity.

I said: 'Madge is very pretty. A stunner. I can understand any man wanting to make a new life with her.'

He watched me for a few seconds in silence, as if he'd just realised I was still there. 'You don't see it, do you,' he said at last. 'It wasn't her looks. It was *her*. It was because she'd never change into anyone else.'

I thought I did see it then. It was the Lauras of life who evolved, because of their complex minds and their ambitions. Madge at forty would be little different from Madge at thirty. And something in him seemed to yearn for the comforting contrast she provided to the two strong, focused people he'd spent his life with, first David, then Laura. It was incredible the appalling things he'd been prepared to do for the love of a woman so unremarkable.

He fell into another silence, his eyes half closed. I thought

he was dozing and began to move my hands to see if there was any way I could free them before the circulation became too impaired, but the movement alerted him and he looked down at me sombrely.

'*Do* you know where Madge is?' he said at last, with a note in his voice that sounded like fatalism.

'No. I swear it. I feel she must have gone off to have time to herself. It can't have been easy for her, you know.'

'You could be right,' he said, with a heavy sigh. 'That bastard at home and an outlaw in a cabin. It did get to her at times, even good-hearted little Madge . . .' He gave a faint smile, the first I'd ever seen. It lent his face a peculiarly engaging charm, that still had something of the trust and openness of youth. Looks could be fatally deceptive, as I knew to my cost, but I thought I could see now the urge people had had to look after him.

'Do you think you could undo my hands?' I said casually. 'And then we could make a proper start on sorting out your life.'

He smiled again, but shook his head. 'Sorry. You're taller than me and obviously stronger. I'm afraid that's why I had to hit you so hard. When I heard you open the window I could tell you knew all about being in tight corners.'

'None as tight as the one you're in.'

He shrugged. 'Would you care for a drink?'

'Would you care to tell me how I'd drink it?'

'We'll sort something out. Do you want a pain-killer? I can see you're suffering. I'm sorry. I've no argument with you, except you very nearly cocked up everything. She had to say I was David Marsh, you see, because she knew that sooner or later you'd spot me going to the house.'

'I'd worked that out.'

'You're a pretty sharp investigator, aren't you?'

'The best in town.'

He smiled a third time. 'You remind me of my brother. He's good too and not burdened with false modesty.'

I could have told him I'd left his brother a wreck of a man, but he was so much calmer now that I didn't want to say anything that would turn him back into the distraught, twitching creature of a few minutes ago. I wanted to build on this period of synthetic tranquillity.

He went off, in the chunky Aran sweater I knew so well. It seemed he'd rarely let the disguise slip – the dyed hair and beard were permanent now, of course, but a less careful man would have left out the brown-tinted contact lenses now and then, removed the padding and the glasses. I had only seen him once without glasses, as I'd crouched outside Laura's window and watched them furiously argue. But then, as I had been told by a man in a garage right at the start, Simon Marsh was a detail freak.

He returned, with the document case in one hand and a packet of straws and a strip of Anadin in the other. He poured vodka from the bottle on the sideboard into two glasses and put my glass on a low occasional table, which he drew in front of me. Then he put two straws in the glass and helped me to hunch into a position to get my lips to them. Before that, he put two of the Anadin on my tongue. The knowledge that the pain in my head would begin to ease a little brought a surge of relief, and I sipped the vodka gratefully.

'I'm going soon,' he said. 'I *was* going to clear my things, but as you know it's me anyway I don't think I'll bother.' He tapped the document case. 'This is all I really need.'

'I can imagine,' I said, giving him what I hoped was a disarming smile. I could guess the form. Several bankers' drafts from Laura, separate accounts opened in different

banks, the balances to be filtered finally into an account in the correct name of the vagrant called Suss, which only Simon would know. There was a lot to sort out but he was the expert.

'I thought you'd not leave without Madge,' I said, like a man making small talk in a bar parlour.

'I'm going to find her,' he said, 'and then we'll clear off. I've got a few ideas.'

'I could give you the name of a good investigator. He does little else but missing persons . . .'

He smiled in faint contempt, didn't bother to reply. It was a fairly obvious trap, but with the lesser brains I was forever trying to paint into corners the obvious sometimes worked. He'd select his own, if necessary, pay him over the odds, no questions asked. I'd not do that kind of work but I knew a man who would.

The pain was finally beginning to ease. It was the sensation of the year. I'd sipped all the vodka; he poured more. He seemed very relaxed now and I sensed it was more than the capsules. It was the sort of relaxation that came with a decision arrived at, by a man who found decisions hard work. Even so, I knew *I* couldn't relax, not for a second. He was a killer, who'd badly injured me. When the effect of the capsules wore off he could easily decide I was too much of a risk and beat my head to a pulp. The thoughtfulness with the vodka and the Anadin meant nothing. Bruce Fenlon had once been involved in the capture of an armed and violent criminal, who'd held the wife of a bank manager hostage in her own house. He'd fed the dog and made her tea and told her about his place in Spain. The woman had been sorry when the siege was over and she'd had to go back to making do with the pin-stripe, even though there'd been every chance she could have been maimed for life.

He sat above me at the dining-table. He glanced at his

watch, but without urgency. It was as if he was making the most of the peaceful glow that followed the capsules and the vodka, before his haunted life reclaimed him. 'You still don't believe she masterminded it,' he said finally.

'I . . . doubt it much matters now, Simon,' I said carefully.

'She's got the memory, you see. She forgets nothing, not the smallest thing. And she can think things through. For hours . . . days . . .'

'She does have a very good memory,' I admitted.

'It's not just her memory. It's the way she can take things apart. Tell her what you do for a living and half an hour later you're still telling her, and none of it's ever lost.'

I was forced to admit to myself, however reluctantly, that that at least I knew to be the exact truth; I could remember the microscope she'd held to my own occupation on the moors that day. I shrugged, smiled. 'She wants to be a writer. I suppose writers, by definition, have a particular interest in the detail of other people's lives.'

He finished his own vodka with a small sigh of satisfaction, poured a little more. It had been the only trifling flaw in the way he'd set up Suss. The inquest report had referred to stomach contents containing *whisky* and barbiturates, but Simon seemed only to have drunk vodka, like Laura. I supposed Suss hadn't liked it, would only drink scotch.

'Ah!' he said. 'The great novelist. I feel certain you were seriously impressed by that quiet determination to write the towering novel – the one the tide's going to leave behind, di-dah, di-dah . . . Yes, well, we've all been waiting with bated breath for a long time for that masterpiece, haven't we, and we're just beginning to ask ourselves why, if she has this monumental talent, she's reached forty without getting it together.'

'Oh, an awful lot of people reach forty without making it,' I

said mildly. 'Mary Wesley reached seventy and her books are best-sellers now. And Laura did have an awful lot of office work to cope with for your business . . .'

'She didn't fool the aunt, did she?'

'The . . . aunt . . .?' I said warily, wondering if it might be wise not to appear *too* knowledgeable about Laura's background.

He smiled, but thinly now. 'I suppose she told you those pictures that make your eyes ache were her mother's. Her *mother's*, for Christ's sake!' He gave a short, almost hysterical laugh. 'Well, that's another story and I won't bore you with it. Laura spent most of her girlhood with her aunt. Batty old bitch; when I married Laura she couldn't even remember my name, kept calling me Selwyn – funny how things like that stick in the mind, isn't it? If you weren't painting or acting or writing she didn't want to know. And if you were in *commerce*! Well, she lived in this big, isolated house and did nothing but paint, and I couldn't stand her pictures, but I knew they were the real McCoy, don't ask me how.

'And the old lass was loaded; but you know what – she left nothing to Laura. And do you know why – because she didn't think Laura had any talent worth a pound coin. And she wouldn't subsidise people without talent, regarded it as money thrown away. Have you *seen* any of Laura's work?'

'Well . . .'

'No, of course not. She once showed me some and I said she'd make more money addressing envelopes, and she's never shown anyone anything since. She's just concentrated on putting a top spin on the legend . . .'

It called up an instant memory of her catching me reading what was on her word-processor screen, of snatching up the paper-knife, of flying into an ungovernable rage. His words, calmly spoken, brought with them my first real doubts, a

sudden shiver, as if my neck had been touched by a cold hand.

Earlier, he'd adjusted the sun-blinds to an angle where, though it was still difficult for anyone to see in, he could see out, and his gaze passed unfocused into the woodland beyond the clearing. All he really seemed to be looking at was what spooled past his inner eye. I felt he talked because it relieved him to talk; it was a trait common to all amateur criminals; but I sensed it was more than that, that it was an urge to prove to me, someone who found a sympathetic affection for Laura almost impossible to conceal, that it was *all* down to her, that even the killing of a vagrant was the smallest part of that frightful labyrinthine plot.

Sweet Laura, with her faint smile and her sad eyes and an air of vulnerability that had seemed almost permanent. I'd had few shocks to equal that of realising she *had* to have been involved in this ghastly business, but even then I'd felt certain I could explain her involvement. She'd been forced into it, and that was the reason for the unhappiness and the swings of mood, even the bizarre behaviour at Larch House. But as he spoke, almost without emotion, so much seemed capable now of a different interpretation.

'She couldn't get it out of her mind, you see, life with that mad old bitch. Isolation, her only real company people striving to write or act or paint. *What* an artistic temperament she developed – it was just too bad she never had the talent to go with it. *Christ!*' he said, with sudden bitterness. 'What *I* needed was someone like Madge. A nice wife, nice kids, while me and Davey . . .'

He broke off, and for a second I seemed to catch a glimpse of the bleak anguish that went with knowing what might have been.

'Why . . . marry Laura then?' I said warily.

'Why marry her?' His eyes came back to mine almost wonderingly, as if he'd pondered the question himself many times. 'I think it must have been because she was playing at being the girl next door so well in those days. She'd teach for a few years and I'd design systems. We'd do up a little cottage out of town and we'd have children. She played it *very* well, because she'd rubbed shoulders with a lot of actors, only she doesn't actually play parts, and that's what fools everyone. While she's doing different people she actually *is* them. It's nothing to do with technique. In fact it's not really acting at all.'

His words sparked yet another image in my battered skull – the night at the Fields Hotel when we'd invented a background for ourselves, and Laura had given her character such a wealth of telling detail there'd been moments when I'd almost believed in Nicola and Abigail and the grandies we took on holidays with us to a *gîte* in Aix-en-Provence.

'But she soon phased the little woman out,' he said, turning back to the window. 'The cottage proved to be something grander, something I couldn't really afford. In fact *every* house we had was more than I could afford. And then, when I wasn't making money fast enough for her to stay at home pretending to write, she pushed the idea of starting my own business. I wanted to go in with Davey, but she talked me out of it. Worst mistake I ever made, next to marrying her. She thought I'd be able to make enough money to afford to buy somewhere like Larch House, and she could do her own thing. The children had got lost in the woodwork by now, of course; she didn't want anything to come between her and herself. Anyway, I didn't make enough money and she was furious because she had to do office work. And then, when the recession came . . .'

My sluggish brain swung ponderously from Simon to

Laura and back, like some heavy pendulum. He was insisting it was all Laura and yet, weak and manipulated as he'd so often seemed to be, he'd had free will, a mind of his own. That complex scheme for robbing insurers could only have been achieved by two people working together, and all he'd ever had to do was say No. If it *had* all been Laura.

'And then I met Madge.' His voice suddenly softened. 'You can't believe . . . Madge . . . she was fish and chips and *Coronation Street* and pot ducks on the living-room wall and holidays in Morecambe. You can't believe, you can't begin to understand, after living in that mausoleum on Tanglewood and the great sodding novel . . .'

'Look, Simon,' I said in a warm, friendly voice designed not to disturb his mood, 'why didn't you simply go off with Madge and live in a cheap terrace somewhere? She'd not have minded as long as she had you.'

'What with?' he demanded. 'Laura would have used my money to get herself the best lawyer in town, who'd think she was wonderful, and they'd both batter me down till she'd got everything – the house, the possessions, what money there was, ongoing maintenance . . . because *she'd* not re-marry . . .'

His face became suddenly screwed up, almost like a child's on the verge of wailing tears, and it was as if he were laying out his fatal flaws for inspection – the lovable, trusting little boy whom everyone had looked after and protected at a critical stage of his development, so that he then found it almost impossible to take decent care of himself.

'Even so,' I said cautiously, as anxious now to get a proper fix on the truth as I was to continue building the rapport, 'you'd have been out of it. And Madge would still have wanted to live with you, however simple the life-style.'

'She found out about Madge the minute I said I wanted a separation,' he said in a low, bitter voice. 'She's good at ferreting out information, you see. She found out about that

homicidal maniac Madge lived with. She threatened to tell him what was going on before I could make proper arrangements to get Madge out of it. She knew he'd knock her about so much for even daring to *want* to leave him she might as well be dead. I . . . couldn't do that . . . not to Madge . . .'

Only to anonymous, uninvolved and inoffensive vagrants. The irony of it all seemed to bypass him. But people were like that, and I supposed that Donne had written about the bell because he'd realised sadly that on the whole people couldn't give a sod for whom it tolled, unless it was someone they knew and cared about.

'She worked on me,' he almost whispered. 'My business was on the rocks, she could see her dream house going down the tubes . . . she knew about tramps around subways, she passed them on the way to the reference library. She'd set up the policies a long time before, all I'd done was sign them. I left all the routine paperwork to her, I was working flat out on systems . . . She'd planned it for ages. We . . . me and her . . . were so obviously respectable middle class, she knew the police wouldn't waste five minutes on it – my car had crashed, there was a dead man inside it with my clothes and papers. I'd pretend to be David, who'd rushed north, and go along with her to identify the body as me . . .'

'What if he'd not died?'

'It was a chance we had to take. But I'd given him about half a fatal dose of barbiturates and it was unlikely anyone would find the wreckage for the best part of a day.'

And had it been decided at the inquest that it was suicide the policies had been running long enough for it not to matter.

'Anyway,' he said, still in an almost whispering voice, 'he was very dead. She'd . . . had to find a lever to make me do it, and the lever was Madge.'

I began to tremble again, uncontrollably. I'd been follow-

ing the details of that appalling plot so closely that the sheer horror of it hadn't made its full impact. It did now. I'd been like a cameraman at a war front, so engrossed in getting the best pictures, in the minutiae of angle and focus and position, that there'd been little attention to spare for the actual atrocity I was filming.

I gazed bleakly into space, the growing numbness in my hands, the discomfort of my position, the echoing chamber inside my head, forgotten. He was saying he'd been given a stark choice – kill a tramp or see the woman he loved half killed.

When I'd first pieced it all together, during that period when my mind had seemed almost to close down because of the dreadful facts it kept gagging on, I'd clung to one certainty like a drowning man clinging to the wreckage of what had once seemed a sound and graceful craft – that though two people had gained, one of them must have been driven by the other, because that's how I'd always found it to be in my work. And the driver *had* to be Simon.

'She said it was only a tramp,' he went on, as if sharing my own sense of mental turmoil and nausea. 'Someone better off dead. We'd be doing him a favour, giving him hope for a while, nice things to eat and drink before . . .

'She never gave in. Day after day she'd say: "I've got her number; all I need to do is pick up the phone and talk to her husband. I can pretend to be just as jealous as him and say I want *my* spouse back too. He'll not need any more convincing, he'll start on her the minute she's back from her barmaiding . . ."

'And then she'd take the other tack: "Half the money each, then we can live our own lives. You get Madge and I get independence and a tramp gets put out of his misery. And nobody really loses on the insurance – it might make frac-

tional differences to future insurance rates, but that's all . . .'"
His face etched a faint, sour smile. 'If that reminds you of
something Alec Guinness once said in an old film called *The
Ladykillers*, that's where she probably heard it too – nothing
she saw or read was ever lost . . .'

I felt as if the breath was being squeezed out of my lungs
by the gathering weight of the evidence against her. I'd been
able to react at first, to cope with the detail, to interpret it
favourably, but in the end there seemed to be such a volume
of it that it was like being suffocated beneath densely falling
leaves, a ton of which would do just as much damage as a
single concrete slab that weighed a ton.

'Of course, once she had the money she tried to talk me
out of my full share.' He laughed as before, that single, near-
hysterical laugh. 'She said I'd only done the straightforward
stuff, all the meticulous planning had been hers. She wanted
to pay me off with a *quarter*! We had some spectacular rows
about *that* . . .'

I'd seen one, from her back garden. But I couldn't stop
myself speaking out then, unwisely or not, it was a blind
reaction, the defence counsel losing control with a hostile
witness who seemed to be running away with the case against
a client he couldn't stop believing in.

'For Christ's sake, Simon! I've never seen a woman as
unhappy as Laura's been these past weeks. I've seen her
break down, weeping uncontrollably because she was so
upset. I just *can't* believe she wanted to do this thing, that she
was acting it all . . .'

He watched me for some time with brown-tinted, brooding
eyes. 'She doesn't act,' he said evenly at last. 'I told you
before. She becomes what she wants to be.' It was suddenly
as if the roles were reversed, as if he was the calm one trying
to soothe the seriously disturbed. 'What you won't know is

that she had a crook for a father and a hooker for a mother, and she was rescued by a woman who was brilliant but crackers. Laura began to live in a fantasy world very early on. The big house, make-believe night twice a week, this dream of being a great novelist, batty Auntie Lily as a role model . . .'

He looked away and silence fell again in the cabin's big living-room, with its impersonal landlord's furniture. 'Did you ever see some film,' he said then, 'where you really envied the characters for the life they lived or the things they did? A film that really got you where you felt it? Look at all the women who got hooked on *Shirley Valentine* – they say it's even one of the Queen's favourites. And it's all fantasy . . .'

He was hunched over on his dining chair now, and leaned even further, so that his face was closer to mine, his eyes for once intensely focused. 'Well . . . everything about Laura's the other way round. She *lives* in a fantasy world. And sometimes she sees things in the real world she envies, longs for. And I've seen her cry too, because the real world's beyond her grasp now, just like women in the real world wept because they couldn't have Shirley Valentine's fantasy world, where she leaves that scumbag of a husband and goes to Greece and the man on the boat . . .'

His penetrating stare left my eyes, to drift again over woodland, and he was silent for a good half-minute. When he spoke again his voice seemed to have thickened with what appeared to be genuine sadness. 'Do you know why she got upset when she was with you, why she seemed so unhappy? Did you have no idea? It was *because* of you. She couldn't get you off her mind. Don't I know it. You were strong, dependable, sympathetic. You were a real man from the real world, and she wanted you just like the housewives wanted Shirley Valentine's boatman. That's why she couldn't let you

go when the insurers paid up. You do realise she only took up with you to keep an eye on what you were doing? Well, it must be obvious now. Believe me, Goss, what she began to feel for you is probably going to cost her her share of the money . . .'

He fell silent yet again, a silence that this time lasted so long the sounds of the day began to gather in intensity – a spattering of sudden rain against the window, a light wind that gusted, the monotonous ticking of a battery-clock. There was nothing more to say and I could not think coherently. I seemed to lie in the centre of a strip of no-man's land, between fronts that had no good side, where each fought from equally despicable motives.

'It wouldn't have lasted,' he said suddenly. 'You and her. She's not really been into human beings since Aunt Lily died. Now she's back in a big house, writing the novel of the century, what she had for you would have withered on the vine. No contest. Sorry.'

It was like a blow falling on a part of the body already numb with the pain of other blows; I barely felt it. I was in any case preoccupied now with what was going to happen next. I wondered how much more time he'd let pass, what else I could do to stop him from leaving me like this. He might even bind my ankles and gag me, so that I couldn't attract attention. I could starve to death. The calming effect of the vodka and the capsules would soon wear off and he'd realise he'd said too much to a man forced by his job to operate on the right side of the law. He might not think it safe even to leave me bound and gagged.

I still wonder what he might have done. The silence this time lasted for minutes. As it stretched slowly out he began to look at me with different eyes, eyes that no longer showed any signs of conflicting emotions but seemed now to be som-

brely calculating. Perhaps he was wondering whether to bind and gag me and then let the police know anonymously. He'd killed once, but he was not a killer; it was still as much an anathema to him as to any other average citizen. And he must have known about the man-hunt the police would mount if he killed me. If he left me alive there would still be a man-hunt, but the police would have a bird in the hand with Laura and would concentrate their attention on her. I hoped to God his mind was working on those kinds of lines.

There was suddenly a bleeping noise. I thought at first it was the battery-clock, its alarm set to a deadline, but he leapt to his feet, deactivated some instrument that lay on top of the television, and snatched up his document case. I guessed then that he must have some device attached to a tree or bush somewhere at the side of the track that led to the upper clearing, a beam or scan that when crossed would trigger the bleep-alarm. That was how he'd known there was someone about the night I'd caught him with Madge. It hadn't alerted him to me this morning because I'd not used the track; but my various attempts to unlock his cabin door had given him just as much time to conceal himself.

'Give yourself up, Simon,' I said. 'You're not the type who'll ever be able to live with what you've done.'

'Shut it,' he said curtly. He was thinking, hard. He had perhaps just over a minute before whoever had passed that sensor was in full sight of the cabin. If he was going to kill me he'd still be at it when whoever it was reached it. For all he knew it really could be the police. I didn't believe it was possible but he didn't look as if he wanted to find out.

'Do *not* come after me,' he said, 'and *don't* tell them anything about me and Madge. If you do I'll find you and I'll kill you. I mean that, Goss. I'll always know where you are, but you'll never be sure where I am . . .'

He suddenly kicked me with all his force in the thigh, as if to underline the threat. And then he was gone. He'd have a map of the woods in his mind by now, would know every path, each short cut, that would take him rapidly to where he'd hidden his car.

I began to lever myself up, groaning and gasping, as one pain merged seamlessly with another to give an impression my entire body was throbbing steadily. It took some time to reach a standing position, and when I finally did so it was to see the upper half of a bulky figure, in plastic rain-hat and glasses, slowly pass the window.

'Gladys!' I shouted, at the top of my lungs. 'Gladys, *help* me!'

Nothing happened for such long, worrying seconds that I thought she'd not heard. She'd not bothered peering in through the window because her experienced eye would have told her that with the sun-blinds set in the position they were she could forget it. The wind and rain-hat might also be baffling off her hearing.

But then the door was hesitantly pushed open. In his headlong rush he must have thought it not worth locking. 'Hello ... Did someone call? Hello ... I was just taking Pippy for a walk ...'

She came in slowly, her spectacled moon-face diffident but intensely curious beneath the capacious rain-hat. When she saw me, dishevelled, leaning against the opposite wall, my hands seeming for some reason to be fastened behind my back, her gaze was an exact mixture of genuine concern and deeply pleasurable anticipation.

'Why ... it's *Brian*!' she said, with delighted anxiety. 'Brian Hobbs. *Whatever's* the matter, dear?'

'Gladys,' I said fervently, 'I love you!'

Twenty-Five

The moment I'd eased myself gingerly behind the wheel the phone rang.

'Yes, Norma . . .'

There was a silence. 'It's . . . Laura, John . . . I've been trying to contact you all morning . . .'

'I know everything, Laura,' I said brusquely. 'About David being Simon . . . the insurance money . . .'

'I . . . know, John,' she said, in a voice that was subdued but calm. 'I think I always knew you'd find out. Will you . . . will you help me?'

'Not to get away with it. There's a dead man involved . . .'

'Nothing . . . you can say will make me feel any worse than I do. It'll be on my conscience till the day I die. I *know* I have to be punished. I accept it. Will you . . . help me to accept it?'

'Your best plan is simply to go to the police. I'm afraid they'll be at Larch House soon enough anyway . . .'

'Will you . . . speak to them? Please. Please, John. But just spend a little time with me first.'

'You're at Larch House now?'

'Yes.'

'I'll be there in about half an hour.'

'Thank you . . .' The words were almost lost in a half-sob. 'Thank you, John . . .'

I broke the connection, dialled out. 'It's me, Norma . . .'

'I do wish you'd get your arse down to this bloody office. Where've you been? I've got all this mail and all these calls and I *just can't cope*!'

'Nonsense,' I said, with a bluff jollity I only just managed to make sound realistic, 'you always cope. Look I'll be back mid-afternoon. Something's come up. Recycle all appointments for tomorrow, farm out anything that won't wait. In about half an hour I'll be at Larch House . . . Laura's place . . .'

'Oh . . . does this mean . . .?'

'It's . . . all sorted. I'll be back around four, full story then. If you have an emergency you'll find the number of Larch House under Marsh in my phone pad . . .'

'You're not expecting trouble?' she said anxiously, as if sensing the real reason I'd advised her about the Larch House number.

'Not now,' I said reassuringly. 'I hit one or two problems this morning but it was nothing I couldn't handle.'

How very sound her instincts had been, right from the start, and how close I'd been to serious injury because I'd never been able to achieve a similar objectivity in my dealings with a woman who'd conspired to murder for money. I still found it difficult to believe I could have been taken in so completely, especially with the Rainger case and Fernande Dumont only a year or so away. But I'd known Fernande acted a lot, professional acting had been her aim in life. And Simon had said that what Laura Marsh did was nothing to do with acting, that in the frightening world she inhabited she simply became what she needed to become. I began to shiver again.

'Come in, John . . .'

She wore the sort of clothes I knew so well from the early days – dark pants, a turtle-neck sweater. The skin beneath her eyes seemed almost bruised, and her hair hung loose but untidy, as if she'd simply drawn a brush indifferently through it once or twice, According to Simon she was a monster, but I still couldn't stop myself momentarily wanting to touch her.

She took me through to the room we'd called the drawing-room. A log fire smouldered in the dog basket. In a week or so it would be Christmas and I remembered how keenly I'd been looking forward to spending those few days out here with her. But that had been Laura the sad widow, not Laura the calculating murderess.

'Coffee . . .?'

'Oh, forget that rubbish!' I flicked a hand impatiently. 'The reason you couldn't contact me is that I was at that cabin he's been living in. He surprised me searching it and hit me across the head very hard with a fencing post. And the reason I'm walking with a slight limp is because he kicked me in the leg, also very hard . . .'

She watched me with an odd, wounded look, like a child who'd been unfairly scolded. 'I'm . . . very sorry, John,' she said at last. 'Can I bathe it, your head . . . I've got dressings . . .'

'No,' I said, in a more reasonable tone, gently touching the broken skin. 'A woman at the chalet site did some running repairs. It's not as bad as it might have been and the swelling's coming out, which I take as a good sign. I'll call at Casualty on the way back . . .'

She nodded, heavy-eyed, as if she too had lost sleep lately. She looked even paler, something that seemed barely possible in a woman who already had one of the palest, most flawless skins I'd ever seen.

'Simon's . . . very sick, John . . .'

'I'm not surprised, after what you've done to him.'

She nodded again, wanly. 'I know how it must seem. I can't blame you for it. But, you see . . . he's always been unstable . . . almost from the start . . .'

'Laura,' I said in a firm, patient voice, 'don't try to load it all on him. When I came round from being almost disabled for life he told me everything. He couldn't stop himself, and one day he's going to give himself up, because he can't handle it . . .'

'Have you *any* idea where he'll be now?' she said anxiously, as if she'd barely taken in a word I'd said. 'He'll not be at the cabin, of course . . .' The question threw me. I shook my head mechanically. 'I can't *bear* to think of him wandering around in the state he's in . . .'

'Laura,' I said, patience beginning to shade into irritation, 'will you stop treating me like the village idiot . . .'

'You just don't understand, John, if he runs out of medication . . .'

'Don't you mean tranquillisers? He seemed to have plenty of those. To give himself a few minutes' peace from his obvious and ongoing remorse . . .'

'He has a history of mental trouble,' she said, with a sort of weary indifference to my sarcasm. 'I doubt he told you that, John.'

'It must have slipped his mind . . .'

She ran a hand through her tousled hair, sighed, briefly closed her eyes. She seemed almost submerged in apathy and it hadn't been quite what I'd expected. I'd thought I'd find her as I knew her best – sad, pensive, vulnerable. It was an appearance she seemed to have developed to perfection, and which had always made me want to do everything I could to help her. And it was an aspect I'd felt I had to be most on guard against, because we wouldn't be talking damage

limitation now, this time it would be simply a cool outlining of her single option.

But this was a Laura in whom every emotion seemed to have been extinguished except pity, pity about Simon; and I couldn't get it together.

'I'm sorry for bringing you out here,' she said at last, in the same low, exhausted voice. 'I just wanted to see you for a little while, probably the last time . . . on our own. You've been so very kind. I know there's really nothing you can do for me now, and that I don't deserve it. I just . . . wanted to see you again. I know you'll never be able to forgive me. I'll ring the police in a few minutes . . . I just need to collect myself . . .' She forced a travesty of a smile. 'Do I go to them, do you suppose, or will they come for me, with flashing lights and a siren?'

I also tried for a smile and didn't make it. I knew all these dreadful things about her now and yet the words that seemed to have made the greatest impact on me had been those about a woman locked in a fantasy world desperately reaching out for someone in the real one.

'It might be best if we went down to the station together. They're going to need my input anyway . . .'

'No.' She shook her head decisively. 'You're a busy man; you've already lost half a day's work. They'll send for you when they need you.'

I was wary of being disarmed by a thoughtfulness that seemed ineradicable, but she had a valid point. I could be hanging about for hours to no good purpose.

'I don't know what to say to you, Laura,' I said, after the pendulum of the long-case clock had whittled away the best part of a minute. 'I just can't get my mind round the things I've been told . . .'

She moved to the long, mullioned window. It had stopped

raining, but a strong Pennine wind was scouring the sodden fields and shaking the branches of the leafless trees. Heavy, bruised-looking clouds moved rapidly across a turquoise sky. It was a backdrop that seemed to reflect her life, as if Thomas Hardy were symbolising human darkness and frailty in a description of weather and terrain.

'Why did you come here, John . . .?'

I didn't answer; I was unable to understand the question.

'Would you have come', she said, 'if you'd *really* believed I was the creature he'll have made me out to be? Would you, John? You're the only other person who *knows*. You'd have thought I'd try to kill you too . . .'

She was right, of course. I'd not have come. Once through the great front door anything could have happened; according to Simon she'd have the twisted ingenuity to come up with a suitable plan. Even so, I was back with the old confusion, staring once more at the *trompe-l'oeil* painting where one scene merged into another before my eyes, until it seemed I'd never pin down the true image.

She sighed, turned back to me. 'I knew you'd find out. I just hoped that when you did I'd be able to tell you it as it was. I know now it's quite impossible for you to decide whom to believe.' She shrugged. 'It . . . doesn't really matter too much . . . I'll just give the police the plain facts. What . . . I really wanted to tell you, John, was that without you I'd never have held on to my own sanity.' She gave a forced and wretched smile. 'From where you're standing it must seem that perhaps I never did . . .'

The hard winter light silhouetted the slender body I'd once held protectively when she'd cried herself to sleep. It's not really acting, Simon had said, while she's doing it she *is* that person. But Simon had had to gulp down coloured capsules – which may or may not have been tranquillisers – to stop his

body twitching. Simon, she'd said, had mental problems.

'You're a very clever investigator, John, but I wish you'd got it together sooner. It would have spared me three months of living hell . . .'

'You . . . could have gone to the police. At any time . . .'

She nodded. 'That's what I should have done.'

Just that. She looked drained to the point of collapse. I didn't see how that kind of apathy could be feigned. You could sense apathy, you could almost feel it, it seemed to draw the spirit out of others as coolant drew warmth from a freezer.

'Laura . . . God knows, I'm too close to be able to judge any of this properly. It's probably best if I say nothing at all. There've been times when I felt I was in catatonic shock. But . . . are you seriously trying to tell me everything he said was lies? Because . . . well, I felt that what I'd seen myself seemed to make sense of a lot of it.'

She smiled then in an almost kindly way. 'It would,' she agreed. 'He lies with all the cunning that goes with his form of paranoia.'

'Well, *tell* me, for Christ's sake!' I couldn't stop myself suddenly shouting. 'You *owe* me that. I tried to help you because I felt so sorry for you and your own husband tells me you're one of the most evil women I'm ever going to know.'

'I can't *do* that, John,' she said, the apathy almost giving way to exasperation. 'Don't you see? You'll think I'm loading it all on to Simon. You said it yourself. Oh, *God*, just leave me now to go to the police, and try to believe that whatever I am, whatever I've done, I did care about you . . . so much . . . so very much . . .'

She suddenly began to flick her head almost angrily, as if trying to shake away the tears I could see glinting on her lids.

'Oh, Laura,' I muttered, 'what a bloody mess . . .'

I put my arms round her. I couldn't stop myself, even though I remembered every word he'd said about her, about that cold, long-term plan, passing vagrants in the subway, the threats to engineer a beating for Madge.

'I loved him so much, John,' she said, her voice coming in wavering gasps. 'And he's so very sick . . .'

I led her to a couch, made her sit. There were decanters on a sideboard, I poured brandy into two tumblers, joined her on the couch, wincing slightly.

'I'm sorry he hurt you,' she whispered. 'A blow like that . . . he could have killed you . . . I'm so sorry . . .'

I shrugged. I wasn't playing at being indestructible, but now my sight had cleared up the endless pounding in my head was the least of my worries.

She sipped some of the brandy, shuddered, wiped one of her cheeks with the back of a hand.

'Did he . . . force you to go along with it, Laura?'

She shook her head, a single movement. 'It . . . wasn't like that . . .'

'He . . . couldn't have done it without your help.' I breathed deeply, forced myself to go on. 'He . . . said you did the planning, he did the practicals . . .'

'I know . . .' Her voice was still low, but more controlled now. She patted my hand. 'I know him. I know pretty well what he must have said. But, you see, it doesn't really matter very much, John, because I'm going to tell them I planned it anyway. They'll find him soon – he can't cope for very long without the people who understand him. It used to be David, then it was me. I'll say I did it all and that'll make it easier for him. He'll get proper treatment in a secure unit . . . perhaps one day they'll let David look after him again. I'm . . . afraid his barmaid friend would never really understand how very much care he needs . . .'

Too much had happened today. And I'd tried to handle it with a brain badly impaired by a heavy blow to the head. I'd never really had a chance to rationalise any of it. I'd known he was weak. It was obvious he was unstable. I'd thought she was inventing a mental condition for him, to clear herself. It had been like reading a complex article where you missed the main thrust by getting lost in the detail. It was possibly the first time in my career that I'd overlooked the obvious – that he really was strait-jacket mad, with that special form of madness that lends unique authority to every spoken word.

'Laura,' I said in a voice I could barely control, 'you *can't*! You can't take it all on yourself. Not if you were dragged into it. However sick he is . . .'

She shrugged, breathed in so laboriously it was as if the air in the room was as thick as water and too heavy for her lungs. 'I shouldn't have married him, John. His brother was so much against it . . . he tried to hint . . . perhaps he was right. It took me a long time to understand . . . and by then I loved him too much. He . . . can be a very lovable man.'

'Look, Laura, you can't go to the police in this mood. One more day makes no difference. I can get you a proper defence. Just tell him exactly what you've told me . . .'

'No, John,' she said, softly but firmly. 'I shall tell *everyone* I planned it. Because . . . the moment . . . it happened . . . I should have gone straight to the police. I shouldn't have tried to bury my own guilt in this lovely house . . .'

Her hand, trembling, lay over mine. When she spoke again it was in the earlier, barely audible whisper. 'I'll only tell *you* the truth, if you still want to hear it, but no one else. Don't try to make me . . . please . . .'

I looked at her, at the moist, dark-circled eyes, the untidy hair, the hunched shoulders. And I knew whom I finally believed. Because I'd heard some very damning evidence

from Simon this morning, evidence that had seemed almost unshakeable. What I'd *not* heard, if she did, as he'd insisted, inhabit a fantasy world, was a single word of pity, or compassion, for the woman he'd spent so much of his life with. All his sympathy had been for himself.

'Just tell *me* then,' I said gently, prepared to let the question of a good defence ride for the moment, but determined to return to it later.

She looked away from me, out over the trees and fields she loved so much, her small kingdom. Finally she began to speak. reluctantly, almost as if dragging the words out. 'He . . . just . . . did it. He came home one day with the dyed hair and the false beard and the glasses . . . it was done. I thought it was a sick joke . . . he had . . . he had a line in sick jokes when he was in his depressive phase . . . When the police came he pretended to be his brother . . . who'd come to be with me . . . when he'd gone missing . . .'

She closed her eyes, as if coping with a splitting headache. 'I was in total turmoil. I either exposed him or I went along with it – there was no time to think. I . . . I couldn't bring myself to expose him . . .'

She took a large sip of the brandy, brought her eyes slowly to mine. 'He'll . . . he'll have told you I took out the insurance . . .'

It was a statement, not a question. I nodded.

'I'd *never* have let him spend that kind of money on term assurance. He said it was for a flexible pension plan. It seemed a lot, but . . . he said he could reduce payments if the business didn't pick up. He . . . kept all the paperwork. He kept saying he'd dig it all out for the file. I trusted him . . .

'He . . . worked a lot in North Yorkshire. That's where he met Madge . . .' She smiled unhappily. 'Poor Simon – he needs such endless direction . . . support . . . motivation . . . I

suppose we must always have seemed like strict but loving parents, David and I. I . . . I think he saw Madge as a favourite auntie . . . undemanding, indulgent, only seeing his good side . . .'

'He said . . . you were rather difficult about a separation . . .'

'And a lot more, John, didn't he?' Her heavy grey eyes rested steadily on mine. 'He told you I'd tell Madge's husband about the affair – it's . . . it's an aspect of his paranoia. I tried to talk him out of a separation, of course I did, I loved him . . . I still love him. He wouldn't listen. When I saw it was useless I said I wanted an equal share of the assets. He went . . . well, he went berserk . . . said I'd have to make do with a quarter because he'd have Madge and her children to provide for. He kept shouting: "You'll tell *him*, won't you, if you can't get your own way, you'll tell *him*!" ' She shook her head, her eyes widening slightly, with what seemed an old bewilderment. 'He dreamed it up and then he *believed* it!' She shook her head again. 'Well . . . can you *see* me ringing Madge's husband . . .?'

I couldn't; I shook my head with a faint, wry smile.

'Poor John . . .' She smiled at me differently, as if briefly released from preoccupation with the dark history of the past months. 'You look so formal sitting there in your jacket. You must be uncomfortable . . .'

I was. The central heating was on and the log fire burned. I was sweating beneath the jacket. I supposed I'd kept it on because I'd not wanted the meeting to seem anything other than formal. I took it off and laid it over an arm of the couch.

'Just like it used to be,' she said, her eyes clouding once more. 'Oh, God, John, if only . . . they must be the saddest words in the language . . .'

She was silent again, gazing forward into the dark recesses

of the big fireplace, dried tears leaving tracks on her pale cheeks. I remembered how I'd once seriously considered, when I'd first pieced it together, simply walking away, leaving the scam uncovered and her to live out the life she'd chosen. Even now I found it difficult to ward off a strange yet powerful sense of guilt that I'd be responsible for taking all this from her, this house, these grounds, that I'd once felt had seemed to be waiting for a mistress exactly like her. But discovery was what she herself had wanted from the start. She turned back to me, and when she spoke it was as if, as so often in the past, she sensed my thoughts.

'You can't begin to understand the relief I feel. To know that you at least know the truth. I know he'll have said I lied and pretended all the time. He never stopped accusing me of it. Well . . . I *did* lie about one thing – to everyone. I said my aunt was my mother. I'm sure he told you my true origins . . .' After a short time, I nodded. 'He never let me forget it. And because I lied about that . . . in his mind he began to project it into this woman who couldn't tell the truth about *anything* . . . who *lived* in fantasies . . .

'Oh, John . . . he'd invent these things about me and then he'd get morally indignant about the things he'd invented . . . it's a frightful syndrome . . . it could make our life so difficult. I asked him so many times would *he* like to admit to a father and brother who stole things for a living and a mother who was little better than a whore . . .'

'Nobody would,' I said. 'And had it been me it would just have made me realise how lucky I was to have had parents I respected.'

'I loved Aunt Lilian.' A single tear ran down the side of her nose. 'She was everything to me, everything. I didn't want to know about my real parents. I *did* fantasise, I fantasised *she* was my mother because I loved her so much. *Another* stroke against me . . .'

She patted my hand again, got up and crossed to the door, where she switched on wall lamps. The light was already falling, we were not far from the solstice. It all seemed so incredibly secure and cosy, with the old pieces of polished furniture and the lamplight and the logs that stirred in the basket-grate. Such a charming environment in which to discuss raging paranoia, and murder, and a million-pound fraud. It was like those times you walked a city street, filled with the ordinariness of cars and paper-sellers and people sleep-walking to work, and you glanced at the sky and suddenly realised once again that you were on a revolving planet, itself slowly orbiting an inferior star, in some microscopic corner of an incomprehensible and indifferent universe.

'He was bitterly upset when Aunt Lilian left me nothing.' She came back slowly, as if wading against a flow tide, but didn't sit. 'Poor Simon, he became *so* frustrated if things didn't go exactly as he wanted them to. I *knew* she'd not leave me anything, she'd already told me she wouldn't. She felt the money was a sort of sacred trust . . . her husband had left it to her so she'd always have freedom to paint. She in turn felt she must leave it to encourage talent in others; it was all used to set up various bursaries and awards . . .'

She sighed heavily. 'I explained it to him patiently again and again. She'd already *rescued* me, given me love, a home, a college education. Her investment in me had been more than money could buy. He wouldn't have it. He began some new invention – that she'd left me nothing because I had no talent . . .'

My eyes fell uneasily from hers, because of all the things he'd said his attitude to the gap between her aspirations and her ability had been identical to mine.

'We had our worst scenes about my writing,' she said in a low voice. 'I think he almost saw it as a threat. People like Simon, they always have so much attention when they're

young they can't live without it. It was almost impossible to find the time or a corner to write in when he was around. I had to hide my work in the end. But . . . he knew I'd not stopped and he'd go looking for it. If he found it he'd ask me what I was still writing rubbish for. It was always rubbish to Simon.' She shrugged. 'He was right, of course. It *was* rubbish. A lot of writing is until you know where you're going or what you're trying to do. I'm *still* writing rubbish. I *know* it's rubbish. I'm still searching, you see, for the style and the story. The only difference is that I could work in peace here. I had all the time in the world to experiment. And, of course, when I was working I could shut out, for a little while . . .'

Her resigned candour provoked an instinct of defensiveness in me, as if I too had accused her of writing rubbish.

'Laura . . . I don't know anything about the writing process . . . I couldn't begin to judge . . .'

She smiled, briefly and ruefully. 'Oh, John . . . I'm touched, but please don't pretend. That morning in the study . . . I *knew* you were surprised by what you read. Can you begin to understand – I'd had so much of Simon never giving me a *chance* to see if I'd got any talent, forever ferreting out what bits I'd done and calling it rubbish and getting so angry because the spotlight had been off him. I *tried* to keep calm, I knew about his hang-ups by then, but he'd always go on and on until I was driven to anger myself. I'm afraid . . . it rather spilled over on to you . . . that day . . .'

'I'm not surprised. I don't know how you managed to put up with it for so long.'

'It must seem odd . . .' Her eyes left mine and she gazed out over her doomed lawns, where the falling light gave the garden the muddy darkness, in contrast to the acid slivers of colour from a reddening sky, of an over-exposed photograph. 'It must seem odd,' she repeated, 'but if you'd known him as

he could be, so kind and trusting and funny . . .' She shrugged. 'All you're getting is the downside.'

But I understood something of what she was saying. I'd seen him give an occasional smile that had been open and friendly, almost endearing, the little petted boy who'd never really made the breakthrough to manhood. I'd seen the twisted features too of a thwarted child about to burst into tears of anger and frustration.

She turned back to me. 'Oh, John . . . how odd *I* must have seemed too, at times. The way I was when I came here, like a *mad-woman*.'

'I thought it was . . . reaction. To getting away from it all . . . Tanglewood, the accident, all the reminders . . .'

She nodded. 'You were right, in a way. I'd tried so hard to get him to give himself up . . . and I'd sort it out . . . but he wouldn't listen. I . . . gave in, gave him his share. I suppose I went crazy when I got here, because of the sleepless nights, the sheer guilt. You probably guessed what I was trying to do – make it as much like when I was a girl as I could. Arty people . . . silly clothes . . . silly hair. Pouring alcohol down. Acting the fool . . .

'It was done. He wouldn't agree to give himself up. . . . I couldn't bring myself to expose him. He'd killed some poor down-and-out and we looked such respectable professional people the police simply let us walk away. Even the insurance investigation was really only to slow down the payment. I . . . just decided in the end to go along with it . . . try and close a door on the dreadful things he'd done. Bury myself here, try to write. It didn't work. Even when I was drunk. *Especially* when I was drunk . . . and behaving with you like . . . like a harlot's daughter . . .'

'Oh, Laura . . .'

'We were . . . in Soho that night . . . and you gave your

change to a poor tattered man in a doorway. I was *so* nasty
about it. I must have seemed so callous. For callousness, read
guilt. For crazy outbursts read guilt. For every strange thing
I've ever done since I first met you read guilt, read guilt, *read
guilt*!'

The last words were almost a shriek. I got up, put my
arms round her again. Her entire body throbbed; it was like
touching some small, terrified field animal.

'Come along,' I said quietly. 'Come with me. Put some
things in a bag and we'll go to my place. It'll be somewhere
neutral where we can talk it all through. You must see a good
lawyer. Don't you see, if he knows the truth he'll be able to
arrange the sort of defence that could mean only a nominal
sentence, perhaps even a suspended one. The fact that you're
giving yourself up freely and never wanted anything to do
with it in the first place will make an enormous difference.'

She shook her head, again and again. 'I can't *do* that. I've
got to say it was me. They'll look after him then. I should
have *seen* the state he was sliding into. It's all my fault. I
should have been more understanding about Madge, given
him what he wanted. He was under such terrible stress with
the business, working round the clock. . . . I should have got
him help. And now there's a dead man!'

'All right, all right . . .' I said, forcing a soothing tone into
my voice with an effort. 'But you really couldn't have done
any more for him, you know. You protected him all his life.
How could you possibly know he was deranged enough to be
planning all this? Look . . . Laura . . . they'll run tests on him,
they'll get reports . . . whatever the verdict is he'll be looked
after . . .'

'You don't see . . .' I could hardly make out the words, her
lips were trembling so badly. 'I've *got* to pay. I *know* I have.
I'll never feel clean otherwise . . . you must see . . . you *must*

see . . . I don't *want* clever lawyers . . .'

'Look, Laura . . .' I held her away from me, my hands on her quivering shoulders, 'you *must* try to calm yourself. The money can go back to Zephyr – you'll only have spent a fraction of it. They'll be anxious to keep it as low-profile as possible, believe me. And to be brutally frank, it comes down to the death of a middle-aged vagrant with nowhere to go. No one knew him, there's going to be no one in his corner. You were forced into it by Simon, and Simon is obviously so sick that careful handling of his case could mean . . .'

'That *nobody* pays!' she cried. 'And *someone* has to. You can't just *kill* someone and *forget* it!' Her high-pitched voice seemed to leave an echo in the lofty room. It was the voice I'd heard in the Goat, in the garden when I'd refused to let her stay overnight in a house that wasn't hers, in the study when I'd been caught reading words on a screen; the voice of a woman with a cigarette paper between her and total breakdown. 'Oh, *God*, John, I can't *stand* it, I can't live with it now, whatever happens . . .'

She suddenly tore herself away and ran from the room. Fear gave me a sensation like iced water trickling across the stomach, fear of how far the fall would be from the edge she was clinging to by her fingertips. I ran after her into the hall, my aching leg forgotten. She was nowhere to be seen, but the door to the kitchen was sliding to on a pneumatic closer. I rushed in. She was standing at the far side of the room, a kitchen knife held in both hands, its blade gleaming in the glow of a concealed lamp above a work surface, its tip touching her breast.

Twenty-Six

'*No, Laura, NO!*'

I ran across the room, slipping and almost falling in my haste. 'For God's sake, *Laura*!'

When I was within a yard of her she swung round, raised the knife and brought it arcing towards my chest. Only blind instinct saved me, the instinct that must have been programmed when she'd once stabbed at me with a paper-knife. I swung to the right, felt the knife hit the side of my rib cage with astonishing force and break the skin in a long, tearing graze.

She drew it back for another blow; I caught her wrist in my right hand. I didn't know where her strength came from.

'*Shit!*' she said, in a clipped tone that bore no relation to the hysterical voice of a minute ago. I began to twist the hand that held the knife almost in desperation. Suddenly another hand took it from hers.

'Let her go, Goss . . .'

It was Simon. I'd forgotten how silently he'd learnt to move around, not that I'd had much attention to spare for detecting additional sounds and movement.

'You took your bloody time,' she snapped. 'You were supposed to be waiting behind the door.'

I let her go, backed away so we stood in a triangular forma-

tion with me at the apex. 'Christ,' I muttered, the words seeming to come from shock of their own volition, 'you're *both* crazy . . .!'

'No,' he said, in a harsh, agitated voice, the knife held firmly in his hand. 'I'm just someone who's going that way with the nervous strain. Unstable maybe, but not *quite* crackers, not yet. Now if you want a *real* nutter, your actual twisted genius, one of those who can do the lot because they're born without a conscience as well, you need to come to the lady wife here . . .'

'Shut up, Simon,' she said, without emotion. 'You did enough talking this morning. It's taken me an hour and a half to sort out *that* particular mess.'

It was a Laura I'd never known, nor sensed, nor caught even a glimpse of. She spoke with the clipped assertiveness of the sorts of women who rose to be politicians or barristers or company directors. She brushed her tousled hair from her eyes, combed it carefully with her fingers, as if it was important to give it something of its normal sleekness. The dark smudges beneath her eyes would be the kind of theatrical make-up that would withstand the tears she could produce at will. The rest would be Laura Marsh not acting but *being* whatever she needed to seem.

I absorbed the detail in nano-seconds with a fraction of my mind; the rest was focused on survival. I could feel blood trickling down my left side, see it peripherally flowering on my white shirt, that she'd arranged would be uncovered by a jacket of strong worsted cloth.

I could have taken either one of them. I knew how to fight, to disable. But he had a knife and could move. Behind her, on the wall, hung more knives. They both seemed to have the strength that went with manic energy. I waited, bleeding, poised, vigilant, looking at this unknown woman, who was

now so calm she might have been handling a small crisis with the cleaning lady, and at the man she controlled, who twitched and shook like someone with a tropical disease, and whose face was as white as bone and glistened with sweat.

'Simon,' she said, with what seemed like carefully restrained impatience. 'Get it over. He'll have told his PA he came here and we need all the time we've got.'

Fear seemed to become distilled, as if vapour were liquifying into the drops of sweat that trickled down my spine. Because I'd seen, also peripherally, what covered the kitchen floor, what it was I'd slipped on and almost fallen in my headlong rush across the room. The entire floor was covered in heavy-duty plastic sheeting. It was there to catch my body and then to wrap it up, so there'd be no mess, no bloodstains, they could simply drag the bundle out to Simon's car and drive it somewhere remote, in this remote area, and bury it. When Norma started to worry and rang, the story would be that I'd never arrived. I was standing on my own winding sheet.

I glanced from her to him. They were equidistant from me at the base of the triangle, perhaps by a yard. I wondered if I could strike her some disabling blow and in the same movement make a leap for Simon. There seemed no other way. But even as I made tentative calculations, she casually produced a small can from her pants pocket and without any change of expression levelled the nozzle at me. I knew exactly what it was – an aerosol spray that if released would temporarily blind me. The police used them in riot situations: women who drove alone were encouraged to keep one in the glove compartment. If I moved an inch towards her she would blind me and Simon would have no trouble stabbing a man who couldn't tell which direction the attack was coming from. She was almost certainly going to use it anyway. Like

everything else, she'd thought it through very carefully.

'Get it *over*, Simon . . .'

I glanced towards him in desperation. There'd been times, in the cabin, when I'd thought he might have been open to reason, loose cannon though he was, when he'd seemed unable to stomach another killing. I decided to go for that, to ask him how he could bring himself to kill another innocent man when he'd never got over the death of Suss.

But he wasn't looking at me. 'I thought we were sharing,' he said to her in that harsh, shaking voice. 'And you always did like the lion's share . . .'

She hesitated briefly, as if herself slightly puzzled, but her eyes never left mine. 'Don't *argue*, Simon, just *do* it. You know perfectly well it's *always* best if you do exactly as I tell you. Now get on with it, there's no need to be afraid, he knows what's in this . . .'

She gave me an impersonal, almost apologetic smile, as if she were a receptionist sorting out some trivial delay. The smile's frightful banality seemed to freeze my muscles, giving me the impression I could hardly move even if I wanted to.

'No . . .' he said, a quivering lip jutting like that of an obstinate child. '*You* have another go, you seem to be getting a taste for it. There are plenty of knives on the rack . . .'

Her eyes rested steadily on mine, but I sensed an almost imperceptible confusion. 'Simon,' she said, with the skilled calm of a newsreader receiving urgent instructions through an ear-piece, 'I'm having difficulty getting this together. You've got your money and I've got mine and there's only the detective standing between you and your new life with Madge.'

Blood oozed steadily from my side. I knew it wasn't a serious wound, but also that if I bled too much I would begin to weaken.

'But where *is* Madge?' he said, his lips wet and shining in the dim light.

'*Don't* start that again, Simon. How should *I* bloody know. She's your mistress, you must understand barmaid behaviour patterns better than me.'

Behind the assured delivery I thought I detected a faint note of contempt, and I remembered how ruthlessly, in Simon's version of events, Madge had been used as a pawn in the killing game.

'I went to Skipton before I came here,' he suddenly blurted. 'I should have gone sooner . . .'

'We can talk *later*. We have no *time* . . .'

'I looked up the report on Madge's disappearance in the *Herald* . . .'

'*Simon* . . .' There was suddenly the smallest lack of control in her voice, which she strove to conceal, because she, more than anyone, would know how unpredictably this unstable man could react to the least sign of uncertainty in others. I searched frantically, in these seconds of breathing space, for any possible chink in their defences.

'Someone called for Madge,' he said doggedly. 'A slimly built man with a deep voice. Madge asked a neighbour to look after the kids, she was needed at the pub. The neighbour watched her go off with this man. He wore a cloth cap and drove a Peugeot. She didn't get the number – why should she?'

'Simon,' she said, in a voice I now felt was too collected. 'I'm really not *interested* in where your woman is. If she went off with someone else you'll just have to accept it. That's what barmaids *do*.'

'Not this one.' The words came out almost as a gasp. He wiped his dripping forehead with the back of the hand that grasped the knife. 'You see, *you've* got a Peugeot. I've just

been looking at it. I had to force the lock, but I found a man's cap and a man's raincoat in the boot. And you can do a deep voice a treat, can't you, when you need to . . .'

I had a split-second image of the night of the party, when she'd cross-dressed to do an impression of Marlene Dietrich in a voice of amazing depth and timbre. And in another fraction of that same second I knew that Norma's attacker during the apparent break-in had also been Laura. In that first meeting between them, she'd picked up only too acutely on Norma's suspicions of her, had been frightened they'd be transmitted to me, that I'd really start taking the case apart. She'd know all about body-padding to make her look stocky and male; also that though Simon had done one piece of dirty work he was no longer in a fit state to be forced into doing another.

'I suppose you told Madge you were from the cabins and I'd had an accident or something. *She'd* know you weren't a man, she'd just think you were one of the cabin weirdos, but the neighbour would *think* it was a man. She obviously did . . .'

The hand that held the aerosol can began to take on the infinitesimal tremor of an insect's wing. Even so, the steely, almost inhuman composure stayed in place. 'I was worried about what she knew,' she said. 'The detective had been hanging round her – you told me yourself. I told her who I really was in the car, to go right away till we could sort things out . . .'

'She'd not have gone anywhere without telling me,' he said, echoing the same conviction he'd hung on to doggedly at the cabin, which I'd never really shaken. His voice was more controlled now, but contained a note of sadness I was uncertain how to interpret.

'I told her just to go,' Laura repeated. 'Immediately. I

drove around till I'd convinced her it was the right thing to do. Said the detective had made a lot of waves. Told her not even to contact you for at least a fortnight. I gave her money, took her to Leeds station.'

He shook his head. 'She'd not go without telling me or making proper arrangements for the children. You'd not be able to get your mind round that, a woman's love for her kids, for . . . her man. It's beyond you . . .'

He spoke almost impassively now, as if to himself, like someone who'd finally accepted an unpalatable, long-fought-off fact.

Laura said: 'I told her we were all in a very dangerous situation, but we'd sort it out. She *was* worried about the children, of course, but I said you'd make sure she got them back later.'

She'd lost nothing of her confidence, but spoke very slightly faster now. She could think on her feet with incredible speed, but even in my distracted state, searching for some point where I could act, I could see the gaps in the story.

'You killed her,' he said simply, in that weary, almost indifferent voice. 'You told her I had to see her and then you took her somewhere and you killed her somehow; and then you covered it up in your usual meticulous way . . .'

For the first time I seemed to glimpse that sliver of light, that first fragile chance of survival. I sensed her quandary: she had to settle this crisis with Simon before disposing of me, because disposing of me had to be a joint effort – I wasn't the lightweight Madge had been.

'Don't be absurd,' she said. 'I know how much she meant to you. Why should I want to harm her? I just knew how dangerous it was with the detective around.'

The eyes that never left mine had the slightest lack of

focus, which indicated the concentration she was giving to solving this new problem.

'She was the only other person who knew I was still alive,' he said. 'And you knew that with her gone Goss could prove nothing if he couldn't find me.'

'You've got it wrong, Simon. I simply wanted her off the scene for a little while . . .'

'She'd have told you where she was going – so you could tell me.'

'She was *agitated*. Obviously. She hadn't decided. She said she'd ring me . . .'

'Well, she won't be ringing now, will she. There won't be any phones where you've sent her.'

'Simon, I did *not* do anything to Madge except leave her at the station.'

He looked calm now, as dangerously calm as he'd looked up at the cabin, when he'd swallowed coloured capsules and drunk vodka. And Laura was becoming more obviously rattled, though it would have been a grave mistake to believe she wasn't still in total control.

'You never liked her,' he said evenly. It wasn't an accusation, more a simple statement.

'I . . . never knew her,' she said, on a note of faint wariness.

'You never liked the idea of her. You could never stand the *idea* of me wanting someone else.'

'You're . . . not making any sense. We *couldn't* have stayed together anyway . . . afterwards . . .'

But, for the first time, she sent a single glance in his direction, and I wondered if he'd hit a nerve. It *would* have been almost impossible for her to go on living with a man supposed to be dead, but she'd be losing the man she'd had total domination over since she'd wrested him from the domination of David Marsh, and the loss of that complex relation-

ship must have been profounder than she could have foreseen. It was as if powerful men and women had to live with submissive ones to keep in practice. I moved my right foot slightly behind my left and brought my weight forward to the balls of both.

'You couldn't really believe *anyone* could take your place, could you, but being replaced by a *barmaid*, just a nice kid who only read tabloids and had never heard of Widor and wouldn't know a Seurat from something painted on a tea-tray, that got your pride where it really did the damage.'

'Rubbish!' Even with her iron control she couldn't keep the harshness from her voice. 'If you wanted to run off with an air-head that was up to you. But she knew too much and she'd crack too easily.'

Abruptly she broke off, herself instantly aware of the construction that could be put on those last words.

'So you *had* to kill her,' Simon went steadily on, as I balanced my weight carefully, 'and the fact that you despise air-heads was conveniently incidental.'

'Simon, I *did not* . . .'

'Produce her then. Show me the only woman I ever loved, alive and well . . .' He looked at her in a silence that must have lasted ten seconds and then he suddenly shrieked: '*You filthy, murdering bitch!*'

'She *had* to go!' she cried. 'She *had* to go, she *had* to go . . .'

She was looking fully at him now, trembling as obviously as he was. I felt I knew *this* woman very well, the one who seemed to be occupied by another presence; and I sensed my time was near.

'Can't you *see*,' she seemed almost to implore him, 'she'd have put us *both* inside. I did it for *us*. We can have our old life back now, only it'll be so much *better*. This place is only rented . . . we can disappear and live anywhere with your new

identity. We can even go abroad. You can get your business going again and there'll be no money problems. It'll all be as it was, you building your business and me writing my novel. I'll have time and money too, and I'll be able to create a classic, a book that'll never die. That's what it's all been about, a means to an end, and the end will justify *everything*, you'll see . . .'

Her voice had become impassioned and yet tender, and it was an incantation that seemed to hold something of the ecstasy that went with idealism and lovemaking and youth. She'd all but lost sight of me in this new vision, and I leapt forward and sliced at the hand that held the aerosol with all my force. I meant to give her the same hand across the side of the neck and swing towards him, but he was almost upon me, as if he'd begun to move at the exact moment I did. His hand was already raised, and I saw the blade flash in the half-light, but it all happened too quickly for me to stop him.

The knife plunged into her left breast, almost at the point where she'd held it herself earlier, when she'd put on the suicide act.

She fell heavily to the floor and lay on her back, her eyes wide and incredulous. She lived on for perhaps half a minute. I dropped to my knees at her side. 'John . . .' she whispered, her eyes seeming to plead with me, as if a strong, dependable man like me could solve even this, a mortal wound, as I'd helped her to sort out so many other things. 'John . . .' she whispered once more. It was me she was gazing at when her eyes became fixed and empty. Not him.

He stood above me, muttering, like a man talking in his sleep. '. . . she'd never have paid, you see . . . she never paid for anything . . . they'd never have found poor Madge . . . she was too clever for that . . . so I *had* to make sure she paid for it somehow . . .'

I touched her smooth white cheek, felt for what I knew would be a non-existent pulse. It never occurred to me to disable Simon – I knew he'd killed all he was ever going to.

'Come on, Simon,' I said as calmly as I could through dry, quivering lips. 'I'll get the police and we'll sort it all out.'

'I want Davey . . .' he said with a half-sob. 'Get my brother . . . I want *Davey*!'

His mouth began to pucker and to make those soft, irregular clicking sounds a baby makes just before it bursts into wailing tears.

Twenty-Seven

'John!' he cried, racing across reception, reaching up for my hand and pumping it vigorously. 'Come this way, old son . . .'

He ushered me down the big open-plan general office and into his own, too excited to throw out his stream of unnecessary instructions to underlings.

'Sit yourself down, John. You'll have some coffee?' A flask bubbled fragrantly on his very own sideboard machine. He poured from it, brought the cup over to me. 'There you go, John, can I offer you a King Edward?'

'I . . . don't smoke, Mr Snee, thanks . . .'

'Marcus, John, *please*,' he said, scrambling lithely on to his lofty chair. 'I feel we're old friends now after all we've accomplished. I *knew* there was something iffy there. I just *knew*. My nose and your painstaking work, eh! I said to DS Fenlon, "Bruce," I said, "give me the name of the best private man in town, I've got a claim upcoming that has an iffy feel to it. Don't ask *why* it feels iffy because it *seems* as right as ninepence." So Bruce says: "Don't hesitate to get John Goss in – he starts where the others leave off." Was he *right*! Was . . . he . . . *right*!'

'I'm glad I could be of help . . .'

'Oh, come *on*, John, it was a *triumph*! And taking the

403

hint the way you did, well, that was the mark of the true professional.'

'The . . . hint . . .?'

'I *knew*, you see, John, even when we were under pressure from her solicitor to fork out. I knew *you* weren't happy about being taken off the case, so I dropped you the hint . . . yes? I couldn't keep you on *officially*, but if you kept at it under your own steam I'd see you right in the end, one way or the other.'

I didn't bother searching my memory for a hint I knew had never been dropped. If he wanted to rewrite history he had many distinguished role models. I tried to look pleased, modestly proud, so as not to spoil his fun – he paid well, I had an agency to run, work always had to go on. I just wished he'd get it over because of the pain it was bringing back.

'The company's *delighted*! I saw our legal man this morning. He's had his ear to the ground – you know how they can get information together when they all know one another.' He laid a finger against the side of his nose. 'Well, off the record, we'll be getting the bulk of it back, plus accrued interest. It'll take time, there'll be all the red tape and mumbo-jumbo to get through, but the husband doesn't seem to have touched his share and she'd not spent much of hers – thank Christ she'd not *bought* that bloody great house and was only renting; smart move of yours that, John, getting her to rent.'

I nodded, trying to keep the smile intact over the bleakness. He was right, she'd not spent much, her only extravagance had been a lavish party at Larch House and a weekend treat in London for John Goss.

'You got to know her really well, didn't you? Taking her to dinner, staying at the house. That shows real dedication. I can relate to that, John, that's the kind of effort I put into my job.

Tell me,' he said, his eyes glistening slightly, 'did it ever get as far as . . . you know . . .' he flicked his head sideways several times, '. . . you know . . . getting her kit off?'

'It never really came to that. I just pretended I was helping a grieving widow. Anything else might have jeopardised my position.'

'Oh, quite so,' he said righteously. 'We pros have to know where to draw the line, eh, John. She really was the widow woman from hell, wasn't she . . .'

'Well, she wasn't really a widow . . .'

'Of *course*! I keep forgetting. It was some poor bloody derelict who wound up in the morgue. And that husband . . . well, he must have been *really* under the thumb. But we had her sussed, eh, John, from day one.'

'I have to admit, Marcus,' I said mildly, 'that I wasn't anything like as quick off the mark as you.'

He threw himself back in his merry-go-round chair and smiled generously through the wreaths of blue cigar smoke. 'That's why I gave you such a strong *hint*, John. I could tell she'd even taken *you* in a bit. She was one of the clever ones, admittedly. There was nothing I could actually put my finger on, I was going by the pure instinct of an old Claims man. The nose. Did I tell you, by any chance, about a client of ours, a titled man from an old landed family, who put in a claim for the theft of a very valuable painting?'

'I believe you did refer to it in passing, the first time we met.'

'I *knew* there was something iffy about that too, John, but my colleagues wouldn't have it. This was the pitch . . .'

He began to relate the big one to me again. I smiled, nodded, widened my eyes in admiration at appropriate high points, and it was as if I were in a time loop and just beginning on the Laura Marsh case. I'd recently seen a film in

which a man relived the same day over and over again, and
kept trying to improve on previous versions of it. I'd sat in the
cinema, sunk in melancholy, wishing I could start that dreadful case once more and somehow get that right too, make that
sad-looking woman, who'd drifted around sheets of water
and talked to an adoring goose, exactly what she'd seemed.

'Well,' Snee said, five minutes later, 'you don't want to hear
an old Claims man rabbiting on. You want to know why I
asked you to drop by, don't you?'

'I assumed you'd have another half-million pound claim
for me to investigate, from an attractive-looking widow,' I
said, striving for the flippancy he seemed to feel went with a
case involving three murders and a broken man.

Shaking with laughter, he flung himself backwards again so
that he seemed to lie almost flat. 'We showed them, John, eh,
we showed the buggers. I won't conceal from you that certain
people in this office suite thought we'd be throwing good
money down the drain hiring John Goss to check out something that *they* all considered open and shut.' He swung back
so that he loomed over me, where I crouched in the low chair
on which he liked to sit men taller then himself – it must have
been most of the men he knew. 'Well, I've got something to
show *you* now . . .'

He handed me a cheque. It was for twelve thousand
pounds, equal to almost half the drawings I paid myself annu-
ally. I wished I could feel *anything* of the delighted pleasure I
feigned.

'Two grand to cover the extra work you put in at your own
expense, ten grand as a bonus from a very grateful company.'

'Marcus . . . I don't know what to say . . .'

'Worth every penny, John, for what you've saved us. And
there's more,' he said, leaping gazelle-like from the heights of
his chair and darting to a corner, from where he returned
with a carton.

'A dozen Moët,' he said, 'from me personally. And from now on, regard yourself as Zephyr's sole investigator for all non-technical cases.'

I pushed my way through the crowd. The air smelt of cigars and scotch and hot water. The amateur drinkers, as Fenlon called the people who only patronised the George in December, were out in force. Over the cheerful talk and laughter the voice of Judy Garland could thinly be heard, singing 'Have Yourself a Merry Little Christmas'.

'There you go, John!' Kev shouted, automatically placing a gin and tonic on the counter, loyally putting a regular ahead of people who'd been waving glasses at him for minutes. I picked it up, moved to where I could see Fenlon in a corner by one of the lancet windows. He looked as depressed as I felt.

'Bad day?'

He said: 'Jack Carter's going to walk.'

'I don't *believe* it . . .'

'They've given our main witness a doing over. God, you should have seen him. All he'd say was that he fell down a flight of steps at the flats, apart from saying there'd be no way he'd be testifying. Naturally the other two are scared shitless they might lose *their* footing . . .'

'Oh, Bruce . . . how many years have you been waiting to nail the bastard . . .?'

'If you had a rotten tooth,' he said, 'you'd have it taken out so it wouldn't poison your body. Well, that swine's the rottenest tooth this city's got – armed robbery, GBH, extortion, loan-sharking, drugs, toms . . . you name it; and we just stand around and watch him doing it. Christ, if society were right in its bloody head it'd let us take him round a corner and put him down.'

He lit a cigarette with a quivering hand, a habit he'd tried

again and again to conquer. 'Oh, sod it, let's talk about something else, it's nearly Christmas, for God's sake. I must say *you* don't look in any mood to go carol singing . . .'

'I went to see that close personal friend of yours this morning – Marcus Snee. He's certain they'll get the bulk of the Laura Marsh Claim money back. He gave me a cheque for twelve thousand and a case of champagne. Said the other insurers would almost certainly be slipping me a few notes as well.'

'So *that's* why you looked so pissed off! And I thought *I* had grief.'

'I could replace my motor,' I said flatly. 'I could update the computer. I could go to Paris for New Year. I could build an extension. It's all decisions and I can't handle it.'

He finished his beer, signalled to Kev over the heads of the outsiders for another drink, turned back to me. 'She must have been some woman,' he said. 'There aren't too many you can't take or leave.'

'Did you know that Barden Towers used to belong to a guy they called the Shepherd Lord?' I said harshly. 'And that there are people in Madeira who've never seen the capital, even though the island's only thirty-five miles by thirteen? No, I didn't know either. And then there's the shoveler duck – the things I could tell you about the shoveler . . .' He made no reply, his eyes on mine through his cigarette smoke. 'Did I tell you about the weekend in London? She'd got seats in advance for a show she knew I'd want to see. She paid for everything – we even had a Mercedes to take us to the theatre. She went out first thing in the morning and got me a *Sunday Times*, found out what I wanted for breakfast and fetched it. Christ, Bruce, she was such marvellous *company*. I've never known anyone like her . . . the things she knew . . . the way she listened . . . she could make you feel so good

about yourself . . . you know? We were going to have a no-ties relationship – I'd go up to Larch House at weekends; it's all either of us wanted. She was a damn near perfect companion for a man like me. Apart from murdering people, of course . . .'

After a while, he said: 'That Gothic novel she was supposed to be writing . . . it seems as if she was living one . . .'

They said it all, those few throw-away words, seemed to sum up the eeriness of the past months – the darkness, the riddles within riddles, a woman who sat in a dimly lit drawing-room, her distorted, glittering mind endlessly planning those dreadful, perfect killings. It was almost as if, to satisfy that flawed and desperate creative impulse, she'd had to carry out in real life the actions of those convoluted plots she'd been unable to commit to paper.

I gazed absently round the heaving bar parlour, as if through the wrong end of field-glasses, my gin untouched, the noise seeming to fade, numbed by a depression that had recently begun to seem almost clinical. 'I don't suppose you've heard of an artist called Lilian Rushworth?' I said finally. 'A Japanese has just bought one of her early paintings at a Christie auction for a hundred and fifty thousand. She's suddenly become very hot. One of their people reckons that'll seem a very modest figure in a year or so.'

Puzzled, he shook his head. 'Never heard of her . . .'

'She was Laura's aunt. Laura's house was stuffed with early Rushworths. . . . She must have known the market was turning – she knew everything else.'

'*Bloody* hell . . . so she only needed to sell a few of those and she'd have had a million anyway . . .'

I nodded. 'But you see she'd *never* have sold any of Aunt Lilian's paintings . . .'

He watched me blankly. He didn't understand. Who could?

I stared into my gin for another couple of minutes, then he touched me softly on the arm. 'How much champagne did you say the poison dwarf gave you?'

'A dozen Moët . . .'

'Feel like going to your place and getting pissed?'

'Yes,' I said, 'let's go and get pissed.'